Enchantment

"I beg your pardon, sir," Augusta said.

Noah couldn't help himself. And before she could react, he had pulled her firmly against the full length of him, lowering his mouth over hers.

He felt her stiffen instantly and struggle to free herself, but she was slight and he had her well and good. Her lips were warm and soft. He took the opportunity to pull her closer by cupping his hand beneath her bottom, a gesture that only caused her to struggle more. Finally she did manage to free her mouth. It would prove her worst mistake, for as she prepared to condemn his actions, she also afforded Noah the opportunity to deepen the kiss. And this he did, covering her mouth again and sliding his tongue against hers.

She tasted of sweet wine. The scent of her was exotic, spicy, floral. But instead of the loathing he'd expected to feel for her, Noah's body was responding with a passion he hadn't felt in months. Hot. Wild.

Stunned by his own reaction, Noah released her, setting her back on unsteady feet. He took a deep breath. "It would appear it is I who must beg your pardon now, madam."

White Magic

by

Jaclyn Reding

A TOPAZ BOOK

TOPAZ
Published by the Penguin Group
Penguin Putnam Inc., 375 Hudson Street,
New York, New York 10014, U.S.A.
Penguin Books Ltd, 27 Wrights Lane,
London W8 5TZ, England
Penguin Books Australia Ltd,
Ringwood, Victoria, Australia
Penguin Books Canada Ltd, 10 Alcorn Avenue,
Toronto, Ontario, Canada M4V 3B2
Penguin Books (N.Z.) Ltd, 182-190 Wairau Road,
Auckland 10, New Zealand

Penguin Books Ltd, Registered Offices:
Harmondsworth, Middlesex, England

First published by Topaz, an imprint of Dutton NAL,
a member of Penguin Putnam Inc.

First Printing, August, 1998
10 9 8 7 6 5 4 3 2

For Olga,
my grandmother and fellow Aries,
who nurtured my love of reading
and filled my imagination with stories to tell

Chapter One

Lord Noah Edenhall didn't stir an inch from his relaxed position in the comfortable caffoy-covered wing chair set before the blazing hearth. His booted feet stayed stretched out at full length before him. His chin remained as it was, resting placidly upon his fist. The cuff of his navy cutaway still barely brushed his knuckles as he regarded his friend, his closest friend in life, over their respective brandy glasses.

A moment passed, then two. Still he simply stared. And then finally, incredulously, he said past the scowl crossing his mouth, "Surely you have gone even madder than the old king this time, Tony."

Anthony Prescott, Viscount Keighley, was unaffected by his friend's less-than-enthusiastic response. As likely as not he had expected it, thus he persisted in smiling that absurd fool's grin, the same lopsided sort of expression a puppy would wear when begging for a table scrap. It was a look which had been pasted upon Tony's face from the moment the two men had met earlier that evening. It had continued throughout their supper at White's, the subsequent gaming rounds, and all along the walk here to Tony's town house on King Street, just the other side of the square from Noah's own house on Charles Street. Only bathed as it was now in the wavering glow from the fire, the only light in the room, the grin appeared even more inane.

"Madness?" Tony said, taking up his glass with a short shrug of a laugh. He continued on a sip, "Perhaps it is madness, and if that be the case then it is the sweetest of any madness I've felt before, an affliction to last a lifetime."

Noah stared at the stranger before him and wondered what he'd done with the Tony he'd known, the Tony he'd grown up with over the past two decades. His frown deepened. He should have seen this coming. Tony had always been reckless, living by a sort of devil-may-care code that contrasted with his blond, some might even say, angelic looks. But those who knew him best knew there had always been something more, something in his eyes, light blue and filled with adventure, that hinted at his true impetuous nature. It was, in fact, this very quality about Tony which had first drawn the two men together as boys.

"Perhaps a dip in a cold bath would do better to cure you of this affliction, this *madness*, and restore you to your proper senses," Noah said. "I am gone from town to Scotland but four months to visit my brother and his family, and on the very day I return, hours after my arrival actually, I am greeted with the sorry news that my closest friend in life has become a candidate for Bedlam."

Tony chuckled, quite oblivious of how serious Noah truly was. "You may say whatever you wish, my unfortunately jaded friend. Color me a lunatic if you will, but I assure you I am in complete control of my faculties."

Tony stood then, stretched with cat-like tranquility, and made for the drinks table to refresh their brandies. All the while Noah watched him, his brow deeply furrowed.

He had seen this sort of idiocy before, he himself having been the one exhibiting it not too many months ago. And he could recall having given the same foolish disregard to his brother Robert's well-meaning words of warning when it had been he, Noah, who had been the eager puppy wearing the lopsided grin. But that grin had gotten him nothing except the worst sort of betrayal, and because of it, because Noah loved the man before him now as close as he would a brother, he knew he must do whatever he could to keep Tony from falling victim to the same mistakes he'd so recently made.

"Well, then," Noah said, taking the glass Tony offered him, "if you are not mad, at least tell me I was mistaken in what I believed you just said. Tell me you did not just proclaim you are running off this very night to wed a woman you barely know."

Tony took a contented sip from his glass as he leaned back in his chair, a match to the one Noah occupied, grinning all the while. "Ah! She may be a stranger to you, my friend, but she is certainly no stranger to me. Faith, I feel as if I have known her all my life."

Good God, Noah thought to himself, realizing he had voiced a very similar version of those words to Robert. What was it about women that turned a man's common sense to jelly? "And how long have you known her, Tony—really?"

"*Her* is too vague a term for this vision, this paragon among all others of the female persuasion." Tony waxed on with bad poetic prose, "She is a goddess among mortals. A veritable angel sent from the heavens above us—"

Noah had to battle hard against the words he wanted to speak, words which among other things would have labeled his friend a consummate ass. "How long, Tony?"

Tony glanced at him, seemingly reluctant to answer before finally, he admitted, "A month past."

Noah managed to swallow his groan under another sip of brandy. A month of fluttering eyelashes and stolen moments and he was ready to spend the rest of his life with her? What the devil was Tony thinking? Unless . . . "Tell me she is not already with child."

Tony shook his head. "She is a lady, Noah, chaste as the day she was born. I would not dishonor her by behaving otherwise."

Ah, so that was it. She had entrapped him by the oldest design there was, the allure of taking her innocence—and a strong temptation it was for a man to venture first where no other had gone before him. Throughout history men had continually fallen victim to this singular feminine artifice. The promise it offered was bliss, but the end result of it was most often ruination and despair. And because of it, Noah knew he must find a way to stop Tony now—before it was too late.

"A month? That is all you've known her? Good God, Tony, she is as much a stranger to you as she is to me. Do you not see this? Did you learn nothing from my own folly?"

But Tony was oblivious, still grinning that puppy's grin, twirling his goblet between his thumb and forefinger with ease. Recognizing that his words were having little if any effect at all, Noah attempted another course. "Does this paragon have a name? Or hadn't you gotten around to asking her that yet?"

Tony ignored Noah's sarcasm. "Yes, of course she has a name and though I doubt you would chance to recognize it, she will unfortunately have to remain a stranger to you, my friend, but only as long as it takes me to make her my wife."

Noah stared at Tony, dumbfounded. He was refusing to even tell him her name? He, his closest friend, the one who had covered his gaming losses countless times, who had even followed him to the Peninsula, leaving only when injury had made it necessary? The two friends had never kept anything from each other—until now, and that made this situation far worse than Noah had first thought. "Are you saying you do not trust me with the lady's identity?"

Tony's expression sobered. "Of course I am not. I trust you with my life, Noah. You know that. But this is different. I must take every precaution. And I made a vow to my lady that I would not reveal her name to anyone until I could do so as my wife. I mean to stand by that vow. I cannot break her trust in me now, at the very beginning of our lives together, even for you, my friend. But know that once we are wed, you will be among the first to know her and I will cheerfully proclaim the identity of my lady love from the very rooftops if you would like."

Noah accepted then that he would make no further progress. In fact, this meeting was only succeeding in bringing forth a familiar sour taste to his mouth which he quickly doused with a very generous swallow of his friend's excellent brandy, a fine liquid that swirled rich amber in the equally fine cut-crystal goblet which held it. It had always been thus for Tony; only the best for him, in brandy, in clothing, and certainly now in a wife.

A thought struck Noah then. Tony was forever overextending himself with his creditors to keep himself turned out in a style he deemed suitable for a viscount. But even the suit of clothes Tony wore now was both new and a degree richer than was his usual selection. And earlier that evening at White's, Tony had wagered more recklessly than he did normally. The lady must therefore be heavily dowered.

"An heiress?" Noah asked, voicing these same thoughts.

"Very much so," Tony said, grinning proudly. "And the greatest part of it all is that her father is presently abroad, and thus will be unable to return before I have his daughter well on her way to our first child, the future heir to the

House of Keighley. That should serve to stem any objection he might have to our match."

"And Lady Paragon has no objection to any of this?"

Tony shook his head before taking another sip of his brandy. "In fact it was she who encouraged me on this very point. Seems her mother exercises far too heavy a governing hand over her. She seeks her freedom, an escape, and being the chivalric gentleman that I am, I am more than willing to provide it."

"She secures her freedom from a domineering mama in exchange for bestowing you with her father's sovereigns, as well as the prize of her virtue. Ah, a veritable match made in heaven this is."

Tony looked at Noah, his voice subdued. "Regardless of what you may think, I do love her, Noah. And she loves me. I fail to understand the reason for your continued objection to her. She is unsullied, her reputation as a lady unquestioned. She is of the quality and thus will make me an ideal viscountess. I know you find this difficult to believe, but not all women are to be classed with Lady Julia Grey."

At the mention of *that* name, Noah fixed a stare upon Tony that silently warned he'd begun treading in territory he should quickly abandon. And Tony wisely did, pursuing another defense instead. "Besides, what of your brother?"

"What of Robert?"

"He has made a successful marriage and he adores his wife unreservedly."

"Yes, but Catriona is different. She was not raised among society where the first lesson learned is how best to assess a man by the prestige of his title or the size of his purse, shopping by comparison until settling upon the most profitable or the most advantageous of the bunch. Catriona loved Robert even when everyone else thought the very worst of him."

"Nor is it any different with my lady. Trust me when I tell you that with her father's position, she could do far better than a viscount prone to heavy spending."

And so why hasn't she? Noah thought, but he decided to keep that notion to himself, finally giving up to failure his attempts to darken this lady's character. It would do him no good. He saw that now. If anything it would only make Tony more determined to wed her for he was quite obviously and thoroughly bewitched by the girl.

Still Noah wasn't giving up the effort entirely. "And what of Sarah? What has she to say to all this?"

At that, Tony looked immediately away, focusing on the fire. Finally he muttered, "I have not yet told her."

This brought Noah forward. "Tony, she is your sister, your only relation in life. Would you not think to at least warn her there will be a new mistress arriving to replace her at the home she has been mistress and manager to since your parents died?"

The puppy's grin had definitely gone, replaced now with a guilt-cast frown. "You are right, of course," he admitted. "I should tell Sarah. I know I should, and I will. I promise you, once I am wed, I will send her a letter giving her ample time to prepare herself and Keighley Cross for our arrival."

Noah shook his head in disappointment. "She deserves a more personal notification, Tony. From you directly."

"And I would like nothing better, but there simply isn't the time. We leave tonight for Scotland. My coach stands ready as we speak. I but await the message from my love telling me when I may come for her at the arranged meeting place and then we are off to Gretna Green before anyone is the wiser. I know the suddenness of it is unfair to Sarah, but it really is the only way. And once Sarah sees my bride, meets her, loves her as I do, she will understand. Sarah always understands."

That was one point on which Noah could not argue. Sarah Prescott was the most accommodating woman Noah had ever known; she'd had plenty of practice at it for this wasn't the first time Tony had fallen prey to his own impetuousness. Not by far. No matter what it might have been, Sarah always managed to bear adversity with tolerance and acceptance. Even when Tony had suddenly and without warning purchased his captain's commission in the Lancers, abandoning his responsibilities to both his sister and his title, determined that he alone would fell that devil Napoleon. Sarah had responded with an admirable poise. She never showed her fear, her very real fear that her brother and only living relative had placed his life and the future of his birthright, the Keighley title, in such voluntary danger, a fear she'd shared with Noah.

Noah would never forget her expression of relief when she'd learned that he had managed, through his father's influence, to join Tony on the Continent. *Take care of him,* she'd said. *He's all I have left.* And Noah had assumed that task in earnest, standing beside Tony through Talavera, Albuera, and Badajoz. In the midst of it all, though, it had been Noah who had been injured, a clean shot, but one which had seen him sent home to England while his friend had remained to face the bloodiest of the battles alone. Noah would never forget Tony's face on the day of his departure from Spain, nor the words his friend had spoken to him.

Promise me you'll take care of Sarah should anything happen to me over here. You are all she has if I am gone.

It had been one of the only times in their relationship when Tony had spoken with a true seriousness, showing Noah for the first time that Tony was indeed capable of fear, and Noah had given his solemn word to fulfill his friend's wish.

In the end, thankfully, Tony returned from Waterloo, injured, yes, but alive, and his wounds from that experience had healed in time to where one might never know the death and destruction he had witnessed firsthand. But this? Elopement with someone he barely knew? Noah found himself wondering if this exercise might prove far more fatal than if Tony had faced Napoleon's armies on the battlefield alone.

"But I do agree you are right," Tony said then, cutting into Noah's thoughts. "A letter is far too impersonal. Someone should tell Sarah." Already he was eyeing Noah. "And I think you are certainly the man equal to the task."

Noah looked at him, already growing wary. "Tony—"

"You are the only one who can do it, Noah. You know Sarah has always held a special affection for you and you are a far better orator than I will ever be. Who always managed to talk the two of us out of whatever trouble we'd gotten ourselves into? You, and thus you will know just the way to best phrase the words for Sarah to understand."

"I will not—"

"I daresay you would accomplish the task with more aplomb than even I could muster."

"I mean it, Tony. I won't—"

Tony cleared his throat. "Besides, I believe it was I who took the blame—and I might add the punishment—when you set that sow loose in Mr. Blickley's chambers at Eton?"

Noah glared at him. "That was nearly twenty years ago, Tony. We were boys, but twelve years old."

"Then it would appear I am well overdue your requital."

Noah stared at him, his argument faltering already. Their friendship had indeed been struck that first day when, on a dare issued by an older student, Noah had heedlessly gotten himself on the wrong side of the headmaster's birch rod. It had been Tony who had distracted the vicious Mr. Blickley from one of his famously savage beatings with a slight deviation from the archery target—to the target of Blickley's hindquarters—earning him a beating far more severe than the one Noah would have received.

Noah did owe Tony, for their days at Eton, yes, but for far more than that, for from that day forward, Tony's loyalty to Noah had never faltered. It had been Tony who had helped Noah to come to terms with the loss of most every member of his family to the horrific fire two years earlier, Tony who had acted as Noah's second in that foolish duel just the year before, a senseless affair that should never have taken place, and which had forever changed the course of Noah's life.

And recognizing this, Noah could not refuse his friend now—even if he felt Tony was making a mistake that would plague him through the rest of his life.

"I knew I could rely upon you," Tony said, realizing his victory even before Noah had given voice to it. "By the time you reach Sarah at Keighley Cross, I will be well on my way to becoming a wedded man." He lifted his brandy glass high. "A toast then, to my future wife and to my good fortune at finding her . . ."

Noah took up his glass and touched it to Tony's, uncertain as to what he wanted to do more, congratulate his friend or offer his deepest sympathy. Instead he eyed the crystal decanter now standing between them on the table, wondering if perhaps a good knocking on the head would serve to clear his friend's wits and end his unfortunate madness.

It was a knocking on the door which came instead.

"Ah," Tony said, that puppy's grin immediately returning to his eyes, "my lady finally beckons."

Tony's butler, Westman, entered the room. Even at this late hour, he was impeccably turned out in tailcoat, pristine white waistcoat, and breeches, his powdered wig pulled back in an old-fashioned queue. His expression was at its usual composed, the silver salver he held in his white-gloved hand indeed bearing the letter Tony had been expecting.

"This has just arrived, my lord," Westman said reservedly. "Delivered by footman. He indicated no response was required."

Tony crossed the room, taking up the letter with all the eagerness of that same grinning puppy when finally rewarded with the longed-for ort. *Had he a tail,* Noah thought to himself as he watched him, *he'd surely now be wagging it.*

"Thank you, Westman." Tony turned back toward Noah. "I hope you won't mind my leaving you for a few moments while I set my plans in order . . ."

Noah simply waved his hand in a dismissive gesture, turning his attentions to the fire and what remained of his brandy.

Well, that had it, he thought as Tony hastened off. There would be no hope for changing his mind now. Tony was determined and once decided, no one could dissuade his friend the viscount from his aim, regardless of what the outcome would be. So, instead, Noah concentrated his efforts on the unpleasant task he faced come the morrow, that of breaking the news to Sarah.

Miss Sarah Prescott was eighteen, more than ten years Tony's junior, and pretty, with wispy blond locks the exact shade of her brother's, framing a delicate and pleasing face. She was Tony's only living relative save an uncle who would have nothing to do with them, and Tony completely adored her. In fact when Tony had first asked Noah to join him at White's for supper this evening, telling him he had news of some import to share with him, Noah's first thought had been that perhaps Sarah had been offered for. He'd even expected Tony to make a last-ditch effort to convince Noah he should finally press his suit, for Tony had decided long ago his friend would be the only man worthy of his beloved sibling. He'd spent the past eighteen years since her birth trying to convince Noah to it as well.

But after the events of the previous Season, marriage was the last thing on Noah's mind. In fact, he was determined that he would pass the remainder of his days a bachelor. Four months in the company of his brother Robert, his wife, Catriona, and their infant son, James, hadn't managed to soften his resolve. And now, with the image of Tony before him this evening, the memory of his own foolishness had been renewed, leaving Noah as committed to his bachelorhood as ever. He would just have to make certain when he saw Sarah and told her the news that he could somehow push his own misgivings to the side and assure her that Tony was indeed happy and thus they all should be for him.

In other words, he would lie.

The minutes ticked by slowly while Tony was away preparing for his grand adventure. Finishing his brandy, Noah yawned, his eyelids growing heavy. His journey back from Scotland had taken more of a toll on him than he had realized, and the thought of a ride to Hampshire and Sarah on the morrow held very little appeal. But he had little choice in the matter, so he would need to get some sleep. He glanced at the sofa nestled invitingly in the shadowed corner, weighing its promised comfort against the walk back to his house on Charles Street, one likely dampened by rain for were those not raindrops he heard tapping at the window? Perhaps, instead, he would just remain here in this overstuffed armchair near the fire, but then he would need to set some things in order, as well as a clean change of clothing and a shave before he could depart for Keighley Cross and Sarah on the morrow. No, he'd best just get to his own bed and secure a good night's sleep.

Noah sat up from the chair, rubbing his eyes as he stood and stretched, blinking hard to ward away his weariness. He looked to the ormolu clock on the mantelpiece. What the devil was keeping Tony? He'd been gone nearly a half hour. Had the besotted fool gone off to Gretna Green already without first saying farewell?

In the shadowed hall outside the study, Noah found a single candlestick burning on the small side table set near the foot of the stairs. Thinking he would just bid Tony farewell and be on his way, he took up the candle and started up the steps. He turned down the third-floor corridor when he noticed the sliver of candlelight burning beneath Tony's bedchamber door. Coming to it, he raised his hand, taking the handle to enter as he said, "That must be some letter—"

A sudden and unexpected report of a pistol silenced Noah's next words.

Chapter Two

"Tony!"

Noah tore the door to Tony's chamber open. There came no response from the figure of his friend slumped awkwardly over the table across the room. No sound. No movement. Only a terrible, deadly silence.

"Oh, God, no!" Noah rushed for him. In the quivering of the candlelight burning there, he could see blood spilling over the polished edge of the mahogany writing table, puddling on the thick Axminster carpet at his feet. Noah took Tony up to him, keening at the sight of the damaged flesh and bone which was all that remained of his friend's face. Behind him, the Chinese silk wallpaper, the rich brocade drapery, the overmantel mirror, everything had been sprayed with blood and gore. On the desktop was a polished wooden case. Discarded on the floor lay the pistol Tony had turned upon himself.

A cadence of footsteps sounded from the hall behind him. A maid and then Westman the butler were the first to enter the chamber. The maid screamed at the gruesome scene. Westman merely froze.

"Send for a physician," Noah said sharply to the sobbing maid, even as he knew it a hopeless and unnecessary gesture. Still he felt compelled to do something, anything other than stand there, clutching this lifeless body against himself, faced with the sickening reality that his closest friend, his most trusted intimate had just taken his own life.

The maid was wide-eyed. "But, milord, wouldn't a—"

"Damnation, woman—go!"

She bolted, spinning off in haste to see to his command.

Noah closed his eyes, fighting back his horror as he gently cradled his friend against him. *Oh, God, Tony, why? Why would you have done this to yourself?*

"My lord?"

Noah looked to see Westman still standing at the door, his face having turned as ashen white as his periwig. He knew the butler awaited some sort of instruction from him, an employment he might perform, but Noah could offer nothing in response. He could scarcely find the ability to breathe.

Finally Westman spoke. "Perhaps it would be better if we were to move Lord Keighley to the floor, my lord."

Westman was right, Noah knew, and somehow his suggestion managed to break Noah out of the torpor which had seized him. He nodded and with the butler's help, he slowly lowered himself, and with him Tony's body, to the floor. Tony's weight fell heavily against the carpet, his limbs lax as they positioned him carefully on the floor. All the while, Noah struggled not to look at the evidence of his mortal wound. He wanted, needed to remember the Tony who had always been there for him, the laughing, carefree Tony of his youth, not this final tragic figure who bore no resemblance at all to the man he had been.

Westman quickly, thankfully shielded the body with a heavy linen coverpane from the bed while Noah slowly rose to his feet, staring vacantly at the makeshift shroud. His shirtfront, his hands, every inch of him it seemed, were stained indelibly crimson with blood. *Tony's blood.*

And then the realization struck him. Tony had committed

suicide. Suicide was a crime, prohibited by law, with a burial forbidden in hallowed ground. Tony would instead be
buried at a crossroads, his grave unmarked, and with the
further humiliation of a stake driven through the heart in an
archaic and thoroughly inane effort to keep the deceased
person's soul from wandering. The Keighley line would be
permanently marked, Tony's name forever held responsible. And Sarah, sweet, innocent Sarah, would be left with
nothing, no family, no funds to keep her, and certainly no
property, for by law, everything Tony owned would be
confiscated due to the criminal nature of his demise.

Noah knew he could never allow that to happen.

"Westman," he said, his voice low and oddly lucid,
"clear the room and then return. I will need you here to act
as a witness."

"Yes, my lord," Westman said, his years of service keeping at bay any questions he might have regarding Noah's
unusual request.

As Westman went off to see to his task, Noah walked
slowly around Tony's body to the writing table. There
awaited the pistol case and Noah promptly opened it to retrieve the tools from inside. He placed them at intervals
across the desktop, taking up the powder horn to let some
of the black gunpowder scatter. His heart pounded furiously, his hands trembling as he arranged everything in an
effort to disguise what had really taken place.

It was as Noah stepped back to give one last glimpse to
the scene that his body began to shake. His arms, his legs,
every part of him quivered as if he were standing in the
midst of the harshest winter night wearing naught but his
own skin. He could think of but one thing. Tony was gone.
Tony had taken his own life. And Noah hadn't been there
to prevent him from it. They had been so much a part of
each other's lives for so long, it felt as if some vital part of

himself had suddenly vanished forever and Noah knew nothing in life would ever be the same again.

Noah glanced to the floor. He noticed something white against the dark carpeting, nearly hidden beneath the desk's kneehole, a sheet of paper, partially folded. He took it and quickly scanned its few short lines.

My Lord Viscount Keighley,

I am writing to inform you that I will not be meeting you as planned this evening. Nor will I at any other time in the future. I have decided that our association no longer holds my interest; I am therefore severing it. Any attempt by you to reach me, either by writing or through a personal meeting would be an exercise in futility and would only serve to bring shame and dishonor upon your name and that of your family. Know that I am absolutely decided in this, thus I ask that you accept this letter as notice of my immediate disassociation with you. No response to this message is desired.

She hadn't signed her name to the letter, only an initial—*A*—but there could be no doubt who had written it.

The angel.

The paragon.

The bitch.

Noah took in a slow and even breath in an attempt to calm the incredible rage that pressed in on him as he reread the hateful words so thoughtlessly scribbled before him. *An exercise in futility. Shame. Dishonor.* Sharp, distinct, her meaning could not have been any clearer. She had toyed with Tony, used him, and now she was finished with him. He had been nothing more than a temporary amusement.

Swallowing back his revulsion, Noah folded the letter, tucking it calmly into his coat pocket.

As he stared down at the shrouded form of his friend's lifeless body, Noah pictured Tony clearly in his mind's eye, how he'd risen from the desk after reading the letter, the page dropping heedlessly from his fingers as he walked calmly to the cabinet where he kept his pistol case. He saw Tony loading and priming the weapon and then taking the time afterward to return the powder and tools to their proper places. He saw Tony lifting the pistol upward, turning the barrel against his temple, and—

If he had only gone upstairs a few minutes earlier, he might have prevented it from happening. Noah's gut twisted until he felt he might vomit.

He turned, pushing the dreadful images of Tony from his mind and instead faced a window that gave onto nothing except the empty darkness of the night. Otherwise he would have surely wept.

He pressed his fist against the window sill. Why? Why would Tony have done such an unthinkable thing? Surely not for her, this witch, for no woman could ever be worth more than one's own life, and especially not a woman who had so obvious disregard for others. What could be so different about her to make death preferable to the loss of her? She was flesh and bone like any other, with but one exception; she had no hint of a heart.

And that made her the most dangerous sort of woman possible.

Noah didn't know how much time had passed before the physician finally arrived. Westman had come in, announcing the man, but Noah forgot the name the moment the butler had spoken it. Noah nodded stiffly, wordlessly toward Tony's body stretched out upon the floor, watching on as the physician moved to him, drawing in a startled breath himself despite his vocation as he lifted the coverpane to reveal what lay underneath.

The man stood and turned to Noah, his mouth set in a grim frown. "I assume you called for me to pronounce death?"

When Noah didn't readily respond, he added, prefacing it with a deep breath, "The coroner would have been more appropriate. Of course the authorities will have to be notified, and a coroner's inquest pursued . . ."

Noah stared at him. Despite his attempts to hide the truth, this man had immediately seen through to the fact that Tony's death had been a suicide. Still Noah held to his design, struggling to keep a sense of calm to his voice.

"I would hope, sir, you are not suggesting that Lord Keighley might have taken his own life."

"My lord, surely even you can see—I mean to say, from all appearance self-murder would seem the likeliest cause of death."

"Be careful not to be too hasty in your judgment, sir. Surely you can see from the evidence upon the desk that Lord Keighley was in the process of cleaning his pistol when a terrible accident took place."

A moment passed in silence. The two men stared at one another before Noah looked to Westman, who stood silently apart from them, observing the exchange. "Is that not the case, Westman?"

The butler's expression didn't waver a moment. "Yes, my lord. Lord Keighley was indeed in the process of cleaning his pistol. He had just asked me to fetch a polishing cloth for him. I heard the discharge when I was at the stairs."

"So you were the first to find him?" the doctor asked.

Westman glanced at Noah. "I—"

"No," Noah cut in. "I was first in the room. Lord Keighley

and I had been in the study downstairs taking brandy. We were discussing firearms and the viscount had offered to show me the pistol left to him by his father. He came from the study here to retrieve it and when he didn't come back down after a spell, I decided to come up to see what was keeping him. I was in the hall, nearly at the door when the pistol discharged. Westman came in immediately afterward."

The physician stared at him, quite obviously caught with indecision. He looked to the door where the maid who had summoned him remained, her thoughts hidden behind saucer-wide eyes as she took in the conversation. The physician glanced back to Tony's body before meeting Noah's stare once again. Noah simply remained where he stood, awaiting the physician's response. Silently the two men came to an understanding.

"It is my estimation," the physician said, "after further investigation, that given the appearance of the room and the placement of the open pistol case, his lordship suffered a mortal injury while in the process of cleaning his pistol. The authorities will be thusly informed.

Noah nodded coolly. "My thanks to you, sir."

The physician looked at him with an expression that clearly conveyed his thoughts—and his suspicions. He still believed Tony's death a suicide, but without any concordance from the witnesses at hand, his case would be a difficult one to prove and one that would likely leave him embarrassed. "Good evening, my lord. I am glad to have been of assistance. I shall request the coroner come directly to see to the removal of the body. My condolences to you on your loss."

And with that the physician tipped his hat before turning from the room.

Chapter Three

The sun was halfway to rising when Noah's horse came to a halt just above the rise overlooking Keighley Cross. Nestled amid the slumbering green Hampshire hills, the century-old, weathered brick house lay shrouded by stately elms and the swirling morning mists below him. Peaceful, quiet, from its recumbent, grassy pastures to its tranquil pond, it was a place to offer warmth and comfort even in the harshest winter. But no amount of warmth or comfort would make the events of the previous evening any easier to confront.

Noah paused atop the hill a moment, taking in a deep breath of the chill dawn air. Only now did he allow himself to think of all that had taken place since the jarring report of the pistol had shattered the night before. He had left London as soon as was possible, having made the arrangements for Tony's removal from the town house and the closing up of the house. From there he'd gone home to clean himself and make arrangements in preparation for his journey. By the time he'd left the city, it had been well past three in the morning. He had ridden through what remained of the night under a dismal rain which hadn't slowed until but an hour ago. But the wet, even the cold night air, nothing seemed able to penetrate the numbness Noah felt, no more than the several washtub scrubbings had been able to drive away the image of the stain of Tony's blood on his hands.

And the most difficult task was yet to be faced, that of telling Sarah that her brother, the only person she had left to her in life, had killed himself.

Sarah Prescott had not had a childhood of ease and frivolity like that enjoyed by so many of her contemporaries. She had barely reached eleven years when their parents had died unexpectedly in a carriage accident, leaving their two children alone without any other family to comfort them. Tony, at twenty-two, had assumed his father's place as viscount easily, having been groomed for the responsibilities of the role since birth. But Sarah had been left at a time when she had needed her mother's guiding hand most. When she should have been playing at dolls or learning to dance, she had instead been made to take over her mother's role as lady at the Keighley seat. From the looks of it as he stood overlooking the well-kept grounds of the estate, it was evident to anyone she had weathered even that challenge well.

Noah started his horse slowly down the hillside, drawing nearer to the back of the house with its twin terraces and carefully laid out parterre. He took in the close-clipped hedges, the flower beds already blooming with new spring blossoms. It was a pretty scene and evidence of Sarah's hand was everywhere. On the western side, workmen were atop the roof making repairs to a patch of loosened slates. Noah spotted Sarah then standing below on the lawn, keeping watch on the progress overhead.

She turned, having been alerted to his approach by one of the workmen. Shielding her eyes against the morning sun, she watched his figure curiously—until she recognized him and then she began waving enthusiastically, taking up her skirts and cutting across the west lawn to meet him.

Her face was as light as the spring morning, her eyes

bright with her pleasure at seeing him as he drew his mount to a halt before her.

She patted the horse's neck. "Noah, my goodness, but this is unexpected. You should have written you were coming."

A groom scuttled forward behind her to take the reins of his horse. The poor beast looked ready to drop from exhaustion and likely he himself looked no better, still Sarah smiled on him a warm welcome, taking his arm after he had dismounted and drawing him toward the nearest terrace.

"I'm afraid there wasn't time for a letter," Noah began, already struggling over his words.

But she didn't notice his faltering. "Come, I was just going to sit for tea. You look soaked through. Why don't you go up to Tony's suite and change into something of his, then come join me for a cup and Mrs. Willickers' biscuits? I know how very fond you are of them."

Noah would have loved nothing more than to do exactly as she had bidden him—except that the thought of wearing Tony's clothing filled him with a chill far icier than his ride through the wet night ever could have. He needed to tell Sarah what he'd come to say, for the longer he waited, the more difficult the task would become. Still he could think of no other way then to just have it out. "Sarah, there is something I must tell you." His voice broke then. "Something has happened."

His anguished tone immediately captured her attention. Sarah backed wordlessly toward the table, lowering slowly into the chair as she stared at him through eyes that no longer smiled, no longer shone, but that were instead now filled with dreadful unknowing. Noah could read her thoughts clearly for they had been his own not so long ago when he had learned of the fire which had claimed the lives of his own family. And he knew all too well the shock she would feel, and what she would think later.

So many things he'd wanted to say, to tell his father and his eldest brother, Jameson, but had never given voice to, always thinking there would be time enough later. Seeing Sarah now, the fear, the unimaginable grief that would soon darken those innocent blue eyes, Noah could have been staring at a mirror image of himself not two years earlier.

He pulled the other chair close to hers and took her hand, her skin so white against the dark wet leather of his glove. "Sarah, it is Tony."

But she had already known that. What other reason could Noah have for coming?

"He's done it, hasn't he?" she whispered.

Noah lost the words he'd been preparing to say. "He has done what, Sarah?"

"He's married her, hasn't he? And now he has sent you here to tell me, the coward."

Noah was trying to follow her words, but his insides were twisting into a dreadful knot. She had already known of Tony's plans to elope? "He told you?"

Sarah shook her head, a small smile turning her lips. "Oh, no. He did not tell me at all. I only learned of it by chance. A jeweler's note was delivered here instead of to his address in London. It was for the resetting of a brooch, one of the Keighley estate pieces. It had belonged to my mother and was very valuable. Since my birthday had just passed, for which he had given me a pair of gloves and a shawl, I knew the brooch couldn't have been meant for me. Besides Tony would never have given something so costly to me, even if it had been our mother's. It is not that he didn't love me, it just wasn't Tony's way. That is why I knew it must have been intended for someone else, someone who has captured him rather thoroughly it would seem."

Noah was uncertain what he should say. Instead he simply stared.

"Who is she?" Sarah asked. "Is she pretty? Does she come from good family? Are they madly in love? When are they to wed? I do hope he will at least allow me to meet her first before—"

"Sarah, I wasn't aware that Tony had had any attachment."

She silenced, and Noah wondered if it was at the heaviness she must have heard in his voice or that she realized he'd just referred to his friend, her brother, using the past tense.

Noah looked at Sarah, swallowing back his grief, his horrible dread at telling her what he would have to say. Eyes so blue and so trusting stared back at him to where he had to look away. He could not bear watching the pain that would soon fill them. Instead he stared at her hand, still clasped in his own. "Tony has—"

Noah hesitated, realizing then he could not possibly tell her the truth, not with everything else she'd had to face thus far in her short life. To lose Tony would be terrible enough, but to lose the only comfort she might find in his memory as well would be far too much for her to have to bear. At least, if he kept the truth from her, she would still have the memory of the man Tony had been, the soldier, the joking brother who had adored her, not the pitiful figure he'd ended.

Noah took both of her hands, looking down at them. "Sarah, there has been an accident, a tragic accident." He closed his eyes. "Tony has died."

They were probably the last words Sarah would have expected him to say. The shock did not register for some time, instead she was silent, still. Too still. Noah looked up at her and her eyes were clouded, first by unshed tears and then by an emotion he immediately recognized as fear. Still she made no sound and her only movement was the rapid and uneven rise and fall of her chest as she struggled against the emotions that were no doubt ripping through her heart. Finally she managed a single word, her voice cracking as she breathed it out.

"How?"

"We were at his house. It was late last night. We had just returned from a supper at White's."

She looked confused. "You were with him?"

Noah shook his head. "He had gone upstairs to . . ." He looked into her eyes now. "He wanted to show me a pistol. He was in the process of cleaning it when it discharged."

Sarah stared at him, almost as if she didn't understand what he had just told her. And how could she understand? Tony had been an expert with firearms, his father having schooled both him and his sister to be a crack shot. The honors Tony had earned during the Peninsular War were only further proof of his excellent skill. A death, an accidental death such as the one Noah had just described would be difficult for anyone who knew Tony well to believe. For his sister, who knew him better than anyone else, it might be impossible. What would he do if Sarah realized that it was a lie?

Noah wasn't left to trouble over it for long as Sarah then began to weep, lowering her face into her hands, her slight body rocking with her grief. Feeling what little control he still had over his own emotions slipping, Noah drew her forward against his shoulder, giving her the one thing he could offer her amid the chaos that surrounded them. His friendship.

As he listened to Sarah's soft sobs, Noah's thoughts

turned to the letter and the feminine strokes of the pen upon it which had prompted the end of his friend's life. He envisioned the initial that had been written at the bottom of the page—*A*. Who was this woman? He would not call her lady. Only a witch with a heart of black stone could be so thoughtless and cruel. He tried to picture her then, what she must look like, a willowy, elegant figure draped in silk and poised at her writing table as she wrote those hateful words, giving less thought to them than she would a dress pattern.

A.

Tony had been naught but a dalliance to her, no doubt merely a means for securing herself a better prospect.

A.

She had made him believe she cared for him, loved him, accepting his gift, a family heirloom, all the while knowing she had no intention of seeing through the plans she had made with him to marry.

A.

Even though he had no notion of who she truly was, still Noah could see her, all light and innocence, dressed in elegant silk gowns, peering coyly through her lashes at the men who surrounded her, worshipping her, eager for the gift of just one of her smiles.

But this nameless creature was no stranger to Noah, not at all, for she was very like another who had wrought the same havoc on his own life. A creature very like Lady Julia Grey.

And while this person, this *A*, hadn't had the conscience to sign her name to her cutting letter, she had left behind a single clue to her identity: the red wax seal still clinging to the letter's edge.

Chapter Four

"Augusta, you must wake up!"

Blinding shafts of sunlight accompanied the unexpected overture, pouring through draperies that were suddenly and unmercifully shoved open. Stunned by the noisy intrusion, Lady Augusta Brierley endeavored to lift her head from the warmth and softness of her flock-filled pillow as she winced against the harsh daylight that now filled her bed-chamber.

What in God's name was the matter? Had war been declared in England overnight?

Taking up her wire-rimmed spectacles from the bedside table, she fumbled, slipping them on and peered sleepily toward the figure of her stepmother, Charlotte, the second and current Marchioness Trecastle. She presented a slender silhouette against the open window across the room. Her arms, however, were crossed at an impatient angle over her bosom and the frown on her face, visible even at this distance, told Augusta there was no true disaster pending after all. No, instead, the source of Charlotte's displeasure was more likely than not something Augusta had done.

In other words, a day like any other.

Augusta rubbed her eyes beneath her lenses. Her plain linen nightdress was worn and wrinkled from the fitful few hours of sleep she'd had, her black hair rioting loose from its nighttime plait as it hung carelessly over one shoulder.

Charlotte, on the other hand, had no doubt risen with the dawn and was already dressed in a delicate lace-trimmed daygown made up of her favorite color, pale lemon yellow. Not a coppery blond hair fell out of place beneath the small white lawn cap she wore; truly a pretty yellow canary bird to the magpie that was Augusta.

"Do you have any idea what hour it is?" Charlotte crowed, shattering the songbird image as she turned to snap yet another drapery back on yet another window, allowing in yet more of the wretched daylight.

Augusta shrank back behind the cover of the heavy brocade bed drapery. "I was just going to ask . . ."

"It is nearly one o'clock, Augusta. One o'clock in the afternoon."

"One?" Augusta flopped back onto her pillow, pulling its mate from the other side of the bed over her face to shield it. "Why in heaven would you barge in here and wake me at so early an hour?"

"Early?" She heard Charlotte come to stand at the side of the bed. Even with her face buried beneath her pillow, Augusta knew Charlotte would have both hands at her hips and her mouth would be puckered in its seemingly eternal, yet curiously attractive pout.

"Early?" the marchioness echoed. "Perhaps if you wouldn't keep such ungodly hours, you might exist on a schedule befitting a gently bred young lady."

Augusta frowned beneath her pillow covering, wondering for what must surely have been the hundredth time why Charlotte insisted on terming her such a thing as "young lady." At eight-and-twenty, Augusta was considered by most to be well beyond it; this coupled with the fact that even though Charlotte was wedded to Augusta's father, but a handful of years actually separated the two women in age, making her use of the term even more inappropriate.

Charlotte really took her role as stepmother too far.

Augusta raised the pillow slightly to where it now rested on her forehead, barely covering her eyes. "Charlotte, I am eight-and-twenty now. My habits, however terrible they are, have been long ingrained."

"Yes, well, it isn't your fault, you know," the marchioness replied. "I must blame your father more for the sorry situation you find yourself in. He allowed you too much freedom as a child, Augusta, far too much, taking you along with him on all those sea voyages after your mother died. On board a different ship all the time, in a different port, among all those different sorts of people—savages, many of them—it is no place for a lady of quality."

"Travel abroad is one of my father's duties as an ambassador to the Crown," Augusta said. "You knew that when you agreed to marry him."

Charlotte wouldn't hear it. "You've had nothing except coarse and unruly men for company nearly your entire life! Regardless whether you are eight-and-twenty, or eight-and-eighty, you are still a lady of quality, Augusta, whether you like it or not."

Coarse? Unruly? Ha! It was unlikely any of the various crews they'd sailed with through the years would have barged into her cabin to wake her at so early an hour unless, of course, the ship had been sinking or perhaps under attack by Moorish pirates. "I am of the opinion that my upbringing, however unconventional, gave me great advantage in allowing me to experience sights I might never have otherwise seen."

"Poppycock!" Charlotte exclaimed. "You should have been raised here in England at a finishing school like Lettie has been, learning the proper deportment of a lady born to your station."

"Ah, yes, 'deportment,'" Augusta said sourly. "This

some Frenchwoman's interpretation of spending hours with a board strapped to one's back and hooked around one's elbows, books balanced upon the head, and a bodkin shoved down the bodice for the all-important purpose of teaching through torture how to hold oneself at an angle far straighter than nature had ever intended. And they said France released all her English prisoners-of-war after Napoleon was defeated."

Charlotte was not amused. "Madame Tessier is an émigré, a respected noblewoman who held a position of great distinction at the court of Marie Antoinette. Her apothegm is emulated throughout England . . ."

Augusta groaned inwardly at knowing the litany that was to follow. Silently she mouthed the words along with Charlotte as she cited, " 'A young lady is known by her manners and carriage. She must be ladylike in all that she does. If she does this, she may not be praised, but she will certainly be condemned if she does not.' "

"It is unfortunate that my father wed you too late for me to gain the full benefit of your tutelage."

Her sarcasm was completely lost on Charlotte. "Yes, that is true, but surely your father has family somewhere who could have seen to your upbringing. In the absence of anyone else, he certainly could have charged Hortense with the task."

An immediate shudder passed over Augusta as the image of her father's eccentric elder sister flashed through her mind. Even Madame Tessier's Finishing School would have been preferable to Aunt Hortense, she thought, wondering fleetingly if her aunt still believed in the curative properties of a bog water bath.

"Your father has indulged your every whim since you were but a child. Need I remind you that you were wearing breeches the first time I saw you? Breeches! You scarcely even knew what skirts were and fell flat on your face the first time you tried walking in them. He even allowed you to choose this house for us to live in, positively hidden away from all good society."

Bryanstone Square could hardly be considered hidden away, situated as it was on the northern perimeter of Mayfair. Still it was set outside of the more fashionable areas of Grosvenor and Berkley; for Augusta, that had been the very thing which had decided her for it. That and the wonderful belvedere that graced the roof, giving an open view to all sides through its tall bow windows. It was the ideal place for her to pursue her work.

"But you see," the marchioness went on, interrupting Augusta's thoughts, "your behavior is only secondary to the true obstacle in your path to a successful marriage." She paused, heaving an audible sigh and no doubt shaking her head dolefully as she whispered those two hated words:

"Your age."

Charlotte spoke them as if they tasted of sour milk on her lips and certainly, at eight-and-twenty, Augusta was well nigh as high as one could climb on the shelf of the unwedded. Still Charlotte had made it her life's goal these past ten months to wed her stepdaughter off through any means at her disposal—cajoling, arranging, and manipulating whatever situation she could toward that very aim. The fact that Augusta rebuffed her every effort only seemed to make Charlotte that much more determined, so that of late, her manipulations had become so blatant they had begun interfering in Augusta's work.

And that just could not be allowed to continue.

Augusta's one hope for relief lay in the knowledge that the marchioness would soon turn her sights on the unwedded state of her own daughter from her first marriage, Augusta's sixteen-year-old stepsister, Lettie. But Lettie was yet one Season from coming out, which left Augusta to tolerate Charlotte's meddling at least through the remainder of the present Season, meddling that would surely be all the more apparent now that Lettie had gone off on a country visit.

"Think on it, Augusta. By the time I was your age, Lettie was past ten years old. Still I have not given up hope entirely. I will continue to look out for your future interests, even though you refuse to see that I am doing my best for you. I did, after all, arrange for you to meet that nice viscount at Hatchard's."

Augusta finally sat up. "Oh, yes, Charlotte, you surely did arrange that, he a man whose interests lay strictly with the purse I would bring him. Thank you, but I'd rather not be valued strictly for the size of my dowry. Besides, the man could not even pronounce a proper *R*. When he first came upon me, he asked if I were Lady Augusta B*wiew*ley."

The marchioness settled a stare on her. "Augusta, really. He comes from a very prominent family."

"Then have Lettie marry him."

Charlotte seemed to pale at the mere suggestion, her hand coming up reflexively to rest at her bosom. "I'll thank you to leave my daughter out of this."

"And I'll thank you not to use my visits to Hatchard's as the arena for your matchmaking games again. When I wish for a man's company, I am quite capable of finding it on my own."

"Yes, but must it always be with a man who is older then your own father? At least that nice viscount still could lay claim to his own teeth. How old was that last one you took to associating with? You know, the infirm one with the bad hip?"

Augusta frowned. "His name is Lord Everton and he is

not infirm by any means. He and I share an interest in common topics of discussion. I should think you would be grateful for any male companionship I would attempt to cultivate."

Recognizing that there was little possibility of Charlotte allowing her another hour or so of sleep, Augusta rose from her bed, only to find her path to the corner washbasin barred by her stepmother. She remained standing at the side of her bed, unable to do anything other than endure yet more of Charlotte's tirade.

"Really, Augusta, no good can come of these pursuits. You are off alone through all hours of the night, surfacing only when the sun is just rising. You sleep through the day, and you care nothing for the rules of society. Young women do not initiate conversations with men, no matter their age. You should spend your days visiting or riding in the park, and your nights dancing like every other young society lady. Instead you pursue indelicate activities at night like some sort of—of phantom, locking yourself away in that horrid little chamber that no one save yourself has ever seen the inside of. And those spectacles." She curled her lip in distaste. "Ladies do not wear spectacles with any regularity, Augusta."

"And thus they end up colliding with walls and conversing with plant boxes," she retorted. "I should think you would prefer me able to see clearly."

"It isn't seemly. I read of it in *La Belle Assemblée* just this past week that 'The use of spectacles should never be admitted publicly, only in private and only sparingly.' Do you want to further ruin your poor eyesight, perhaps even permanently? Myopia is a sign of learnedness in ladies and that, my dear Augusta, is never a good thing. Men do not seek out women whom they think might be more learned than they are. You must, after all, allow a man his due superiority."

Augusta felt her stomach lurch at that bit of advice.

"You know, Augusta, it would do you a world of good to utilize your time reading *La Belle Assemblée* instead of all those ancient tomes you are constantly bringing home from Hatchard's. The dust alone from them will be the ruination of your complexion, and that, my dear, is your only saving grace since you rarely see a spark of daylight. You might even learn a thing or two about the current fashion from Mr. Bell. You certainly do your dressmaker no honor by parading around as you do."

Augusta eyed the gown her maid had thoughtfully set out for her to wear. Draped over the back of her dressing table chair, the simple gray bore no adornment save the row of tiny buttons that stretched from navel to the neck. The sleeves were equally as strict, reaching to the wrist, the skirts straight and very plain. But the garment was serviceable and it suited Augusta well, for it was free from the unnecessary frills and bows that only managed to get in the way of her work.

She looked from the gown to Charlotte, critically assessing the numerous rows of lace which trimmed the hem of the pale frock she wore.

"Augusta, I am only doing what I can to look out for you. You will become the talk of Town you know, especially if you persist in behavior such as that last episode. How we survived it I will never know."

Augusta couldn't help but feel a small bit of triumph at the mention of the first, and last, social event Charlotte had cajoled her into attending. It had been a small dinner party hosted by the sister of Charlotte's first husband, a man who by all accounts had lived a creditable existence before he had been dispatched to the hereafter on the Peninsula.

Charlotte had wanted to introduce her new stepdaughter, although Augusta suspected her reasons for bringing her along were more to prove she had indeed wed the Marquess of Trecastle than for any social nicety. Soon after their wedding, Augusta's father had been called away on another assignment. He hadn't returned as yet.

Whatever Charlotte's reasoning for the outing, though, from the onset of that ill-fated evening, things had only progressed from bad to worse when one of the other guests made the grave error of trying to color Augusta a half-wit.

"That pompous ninny tried to make me out to look a fool and then sought to escape before I could publicly contradict him," Augusta said in her own defense, even as she knew it would do her no good.

"Ladies do not argue publicly with men, regardless of the circumstances, and especially not with men whom they have followed into a gentlemen's parlor at a dinner hosted by a prominent hostess. Men go there to—to relieve themselves!"

Augusta gave a small smile. "So it would seem."

"Augusta!"

"Would it ease your mind to know I was far too occupied with pressing my point upon the man to see anything of any consequence?" She hesitated. "If he had anything of consequence, that is."

Charlotte drew an astonished breath. "Do you know what they begin to call you?" She didn't even pause long enough for Augusta to frame a response. "A bluestocking! Good God they might as well have labeled you a pariah. Augusta, please, if you will not think of yourself, then think of your father. He is a public figure—a marquess. It is he who faces the ridicule over your antics."

Now Augusta frowned. "Papa has never indicated to me that he has been held to ridicule at my expense."

"Well, allow me to enlighten you, for he has. Depend upon it. His colleagues snicker at him. Fortunately he is far away and thus does not learn of their scorn firsthand. And even if he were here to know of it, he would be too kind-natured to admonish you for it."

Augusta furrowed her brow. Whatever label society chose to bestow upon her mattered very little to her, but her father—she would hate to see him ridiculed because of her eccentricities. Still, Charlotte could have fabricated the entire thing, thinking it might bring her around. Hadn't she resorted to much the same chicanery in telling her Hatchard's had sent a note that the book she'd requested had arrived, only to have that *w*idiculous viscount lying in wait for her outside the door?

And since she knew she couldn't trust what Charlotte was saying, Augusta decided she would simply wait until her father returned from the Continent. If he indicated he was concerned over what others thought of her, then she would take the matter under further consideration. Until then, she saw no reason not to continue on as she always had, but perhaps a bit tempered.

Augusta forced the marchioness back as she moved for her dressing table. "I would assume you had some purpose for coming here to awaken me?"

"What?" In all the talk of what Augusta should or shouldn't be doing, Charlotte had momentarily forgotten herself. "Oh, yes, of course." She paused a moment in preparation. "I have come to give you notice that I shall require your company on Tuesday evening next."

Augusta sat before the dressing glass and began working the plaits from her hair, letting it fall in loose ebony ripples over her shoulders. She hated the thought of fussing over her hair and generally wore it as simply as possible. "What is to take place Tuesday evening?"

She could see Charlotte roll her eyes in the reflection as if Augusta were the most oblivious being that had ever walked the planet. "There is a ball, Augusta. The Lumley ball, only one of the largest and most prestigious events of the Season. You will attend the ball with me."

"You know I do not attend balls," Augusta replied negligently, pulling the brush none-too-gently through her hair. "And most especially not on a new moon night, which Tuesday will certainly be."

She glanced again to Charlotte's reflection, a reflection that had gone very sour indeed. The marchioness's voice, however, was surprisingly calm as she said, "Well, you will make an exception this time and attend this ball with me. With Lettie gone to the country now, I have no one else to accompany me in your father's stead. Already they call me 'The Widowed Marchioness Trecastle' because I never have a proper escort when I am out. If not for your presence in this household, some would doubt my marriage to your father even existed."

Augusta tugged the weight of her hair over one shoulder. "I was not aware Lettie would be away so long."

"My mother has taken ill. Since I will be unable to go to her until after the close of the Season, I had no choice but to send Lettie in my stead. She will remain and see to my mother's care until we can join her."

Augusta remained silent as she replaited her hair.

Charlotte persisted, "Augusta, please, think of Lettie."

Augusta looked at Charlotte in the mirror, wondering how she hadn't seen this coming. First she had played on her relationship with her father, and now Lettie, whom she knew very well Augusta was truly fond of.

Charlotte must have sensed the hint of a weakening and grasped at it. "As you know, Lettie is to be presented at court next Season, thus I must begin making preliminary inroads now for potential matches for her. And even though she stands at my side whenever we are out in public and speaks to no one, I have already begun to notice interest brewing in her from several prominent families. Therefore, I must cultivate a closer association with them now, before her coming out, so that she will stand a better chance for the best of marriages come the spring. Otherwise she will be doomed to spinsterhood."

Like her elder stepsister, Augusta knew Charlotte was thinking. "I still fail to see how any of this concerns me," she said as she coiled the thick braid into its customary knot, fixing it firmly at her nape with pins.

"If you will recall, Augusta, your father did ask that you see to his affairs while he is away. Were he here, he would be the one to accompany me, thus it is your duty as his daughter to take his place."

Augusta checked her appearance in the glass, pushing her spectacles more firmly on her nose. The resulting effect was just as she wanted it, no paint, no curls, just herself, as plain and as severe as she possibly could be. She found her appearance thus offered obscurity, and with obscurity she could more easily move unnoticed among society.

Having finished with her toilette, Augusta pivoted in her seat toward the marchioness. "I believe when my father asked me to see to his affairs, Charlotte, he was speaking more about his accounts and correspondence than in making an appearance at a ball."

Charlotte pouted. "I will not miss this event, Augusta. Several of the connections I consider most advantageous for Lettie's future are certain to be in attendance."

Augusta regarded the marchioness. There was a seriousness about her this time that was not customary. This event was very important to her, more so than most. Since having been thrown together by Charlotte's marriage to the marquess ten months earlier, the two women had thus far managed to live a somewhat peaceful existence sparked only now and again by disagreement. Even though lately Charlotte's efforts to marry Augusta off had grown from mere inconvenience to distraction, they had avoided any significant discord between them. Somehow, though, Augusta suspected, if she refused her this time, Charlotte would increase in her marriage-making efforts enough to make Augusta's life downright miserable. Still, she couldn't acquiesce too easily, else Charlotte might attempt something more troublesome the next time. Such as a visit to her mantua-maker, Heaven forbid.

Augusta patted back her hair, pausing a moment longer before she stood to face her stepmother.

"I will consider it."

And with that she turned from her room, leaving Charlotte little choice but to stare behind.

Chapter Five

Two days later, Augusta was working on the Trecastle accounts in her father's study when she heard a knocking on the door. She looked across the room to see the advancing figure of the Brierley butler hovering just above the rim of her spectacles. She pushed her spectacles up to better see, taking into account as she did the time. She'd woken earlier than usual that day—just before midday—for she'd had some household paperwork long in need of attending to. It was now past five in the afternoon. She wondered where the day had gone to. "Yes, Tiswell, what is it?"

As lean as he was tall, the butler favored fashions from the previous century and one might think these characteristics would make the man appear undignified. Instead he had the appearance and bearing of someone who had served royalty, which indeed he had, having once been employed in the household of the king, the third of the Georges, that is, before he had run mad.

His last employer, however, an upstart earl, had dismissed Tiswell from his service without any notice, hiring in his stead a younger, more fashionable variety of butler, this a fact the man had admitted proudly to Augusta when she had written him for a reference. Augusta had promptly offered Tiswell the position in the Trecastle household the following day.

"I have your tea, Lady Augusta," the butler said, coming

forward with a tray. "And I thought you might like to know the letters have just arrived."

Augusta was fond of Tiswell, and when he brought her the tea, always at half past five o'clock, he generally stayed on with her to share a cup and a bit of conversation. Were Charlotte to know of this, she would undoubtedly be horrified for in her eyes fraternization between servant and master was out of the question.

But then, what Charlotte didn't know certainly wouldn't hurt her.

Augusta completed her notation in the ledger book, setting the quill in its stand before wiping her ink-spotted fingers with a cloth. "Thank you, Tiswell. I will join you directly. You may set the letters there on the side table and I will see to them later."

The butler did as she bid and began preparing them both a cup of tea as he said, "My lady, I thought you might be interested to know . . ."

"Yes, Tiswell?" She quickly scanned her entries to confirm the tally at the bottom of the page.

"There is a letter from your father."

Augusta immediately put down the ledger and stood, making for the side table. "From Papa?" She drew up the stack, thumbing through invitations and calling cards—all addressed to Charlotte—until she came to the one bearing her father's distinctive script. She noticed immediately it was addressed to her, and not to Charlotte as was usual. Setting the other letters aside, she looked up at Tiswell. "He is writing to me?"

"Yes, my lady. That is why I thought you might wish to know of its arrival."

Augusta had already slipped her letter knife beneath the seal to open the letter which had come to her from his most recent post in France. It was a lengthy discourse, covering the page and then crossing half, not like her father at all, for his letters were always short and concise, rather like himself in that respect.

Taking her seat at the tea table, Augusta began to read.

My Dearest Augusta,

   I know you will immediately find it strange that I am writing this letter to you, and not to Charlotte, my wife. But it is on this day, of all days, that my thoughts are with you, my daughter, and with your mother, my sweet Marianne.

   She would be so very proud of you, my dear Augusta Elizabeth, as am I. You are everything she would have wanted you to be, strong, independent, and I need have no fear for you other than my one wish which is that you might one day find a love like the one which I shared with her, a love so much in my mind this day of all days.

Augusta stopped reading, looking immediately to the date scratched at the top of the page. April 28, 1818, exactly twenty years from the day when her mother had died. A sobriety, cold and unpleasant, came over her for it had been nearly a month since her father had written this letter. In all that time, through several weeks, she'd never even realized it. How could she have forgotten the significance of that day?

She had been but eight years old when her mother had died. The preceding two years, Marianne had been too ill to do anything more than watch her young daughter as she played outside her bedchamber window. It was on the second night after she'd died that Augusta's father had taken his daughter with him to the rooftop of their home in the country. Holding her tight against him, he'd pointed outward at the many stars scattered throughout the night sky.

"There, Augusta Elizabeth," he'd said to her, "there your mother watches you now from that star, instead of at the window. Whenever you have need of her, you can look up to her star and she will be there for you."

And at that moment, one star in particular had seemed to shine brighter than the others around it, glittering as if to give credence to her father's words. On the nights following her mother's death, whenever Augusta had been unable to sleep for the nightmares, she had gone to her window to peer out at that same star and to find comfort in knowing her mother was still close by, watching her as her father had said.

Within six weeks of Marianne's death, the marquess had accepted the ambassadorship and had gone from England, taking his young daughter with him. On the open sea, the sadness of her passing seemed somehow easier to face. Still no matter where they found themselves every year afterward, on the twenty-eighth day of April, Augusta and her father would go together to look at their special "Marianne" star, to remember her, to be with her, to feel her gentle spirit.

Augusta stood from the table and moved across the room to where her mother's portrait hung, no longer above the hearth, but relegated to a darkened corner since Charlotte's arrival.

Augusta carefully tied the drapery back from the window to see better. Soft eyes, the same deep dusky green as her own, peered softly down at her from the canvas above. Marianne's hair had been a rich chestnut brown beneath the powder worn in the portrait, softly curled, hanging to the middle of her back when her maid would brush it. The gown she wore, with its wide hooped skirts and narrow waist, covered across the stomacher with delicate bow knots, was in her favorite colors, green and violet. In her hand she held a small book of poetry with a red ribbon. It was a book she had often read from to her daughter as a child.

"Forgive me, Mother," Augusta whispered as she closed her eyes against her tears.

It was several moments later when Augusta finally turned back to the tea table. She did not take up the letter to finish reading it, but folded it and set it aside to return to later. She looked up to see that Tiswell was watching her and his eyes were filled with sympathetic understanding. Still, thoughtfully he said nothing, realizing her need for privacy. Instead he simply presented her with a teacup.

Several moments passed. Augusta said, "Where has Lady Trecastle gone off to?"

Tiswell placed a small dish with several cakes and confections upon it between them on the table. "I believe her ladyship indicated she was off to her shoemaker's to retrieve the new slippers she had ordered for the Lumley ball."

Augusta frowned over a bite of strawberry tart. "Yes, the singular event of the Season. She tried just the other morning to badger me into attending with her."

Tiswell took a small sip of tea. "You know it might not be all that adverse a notion, my lady."

Augusta stared at the butler, wondering if he'd perhaps slipped a splash of spirits into his tea for he never agreed with any of Charlotte's whims. *Ever.* "Tiswell?"

The butler shook his head, a balding one that did not wear a wig like so many of his contemporaries, and which only added to his appearance of distinction. "Consider this, my lady. What if you were to strike a bargain of sorts with the marchioness?"

"A bargain? With Charlotte?" It was an interesting concept.

"Have there not been occasions of late in which she sought to arrange certain introductions for you with young men? Eligible young men?"

Augusta watched him as he added a spot of cream to his tea. "Go on."

"Well, I was thinking, what if you were to agree to attend not only the Lumley ball, but perhaps a set number of engagements with her ladyship each week, two or three perhaps, in exchange for her agreement to cease arranging any further such introductions. It might also provide a way for you to secure her agreement that she would leave you to those personal pursuits which she is constantly voicing her objection to . . ."

. . . such as Augusta's work.

It was, indeed, a brilliant notion. A plan that would serve to satisfy Charlotte, as well as guarantee Augusta she would meddle no more in her private affairs. Two nights each week in the company of Charlotte amid London society would be difficult yes, but manageable, especially considering it would leave her the other five nights of the week to pursue her interests without the constant interruption, as well as the fear of discovery she had been faced with before.

Augusta looked at the butler with a smile. "Mr. Tiswell, have I told you lately how truly indispensable you have become to this household?"

Tiswell simply smiled in response, and took a sip of his tea.

Chapter Six

Noah was shown into the cheery back parlor with the usual informality, the butler, Finch, welcoming him through the front door and merely nodding his head in the proper direction before retreating toward his pantry at the back of the house.

The parlor was decidedly feminine in decor, shades of pale yellow and green splashed upon the walls, over the windows, and across the delicate satinwood furnishings, brightened all the more by the sunlight that seemed ever beaming through tall casement windows whose sills were littered with curios and tiny china figurines. This same elegant femininity was displayed throughout every room in the modest red-brick Georgian house, and well it should be since for as long as Noah could remember, no man other than Finch had ever dwelt there.

It was a place in whose halls Noah had played as a child, sliding with his brothers down the polished walnut banister or hiding in the dumbwaiter and scaring poor Finch out of his skin when he'd chanced upon him. It was the sort of place that instantly made one feel welcome, where Noah had found a sense of warmth and security as a child—the same warmth and security he needed now, and would find at Number 17 Savile Row, the home of his spinster aunt, Amelia Edenhall.

Noah paused just inside the chamber's doorway, watching two women across the room seated opposite each other at the Pembroke table. A number of cards were spread out before them, a tea tray beside, looking untouched for the cups were still neatly stacked as well as the small plate of confections undisturbed atop it.

The women were so engrossed in their cards, they didn't notice him standing there.

"You see, Betsy," chattered the older of the two, her be-capped head bent over the cards, "you must pay close attention. Piquet is not so difficult once you know the way of it. Now, dear, you are the elder and I am the younger, but only for purposes of the game, of course, since we both know very well that I am the elder of us both in truth. But as elder of the game, you are entitled to discard a number of cards and re-place them from the talon. Hmm? What, dear? Oh, the talon. It is that little pile of cards there. Yes, dear, I know it is a curious name, but that is what it is called, I assure you."

Noah couldn't resist a smile. "Haven't you learned your lesson yet, Aunt? It can be no wonder that you cannot keep anyone in service to you for long. You teach them all your tricks at cards and they soon learn they can earn more at card play than they can working for you."

Amelia Edenhall turned in her chair to regard her youngest nephew. "Ah, Noah, dear," she said, completely ignoring his remarks, "your timing is perfect. Come, you can make a third hand and better help me explain to Betsy how to play. She is new to the household just this week, but she knows very little of cards." She turned back to the maid then. "Betsy, dear, this is my youngest nephew, Lord Noah Edenhall. He is devilishly handsome, don't you think? But don't allow that to fool you, dear. He is quite sharp at his cards."

Noah chuckled. "If I am, it is only due to your expert tutelage, Aunt."

Amelia beamed under the compliment.

According to most in London society, Lady Amelia Edenhall was the truest example of an eccentric, a woman who spent her inheritance employing "fallen" women (prostitutes and pickpockets among them), and who measured a person's importance not by wealth, not by family connection, but by their skill at the cards. She was a small woman, no more than four feet and ten, with hazel-colored eyes that mirrored his own and an easy, welcoming smile. She seemed never to age, her true years indeed a mystery, for when asked she would simply reply that their number fell somewhere between nineteen and ninety. Today, as every day, she wore her usual garb, a gown lace-edged with a fichu neckline which matched the cap on her head, her silver-peppered hair peeking out from underneath.

She motioned for Noah to join them, but even before he could seat himself down, Finch appeared at the door, his height completely filling it. He stood well above six feet.

As children, Noah and his brothers had invented a fascinating and scarlet past for the butler which had included everything from piracy to highway robbery among his other prior occupations. In truth Finch had once been a pugilist-for-hire in one of London's darkest boxing rings before coming into Amelia's employ; just how the two had ever crossed paths in the first place was a fact which puzzled Noah to this day. One thing was for certain, though, Finch presented quite a remarkable figure when he would first meet a visitor at the door; coupled with his great size were numerous scars marking his face and most noticeably the unnatural and broken-looking slope to his nose. As a result, he frightened off more than he admitted, which was likely part of his appeal—Amelia simply hated to be disturbed from her cards for frivolous visitors.

Somehow, though, Amelia failed to notice his bulk

standing there at the door, so after a moment, Finch cleared his throat politely.

"Yes, Finch, what is it?" Amelia asked without looking up from her hand of cards.

"Excuse me, madam, but it seems Cook is in immediate need of Betsy's assistance in the kitchen. Something about a pudding and some mislaid parsnips."

"Parsnips?"

Finch didn't bat an eye. "Yes, my lady, she was most disconcerted. She said only Betsy could help her to remedy the predicament."

Amelia frowned, setting her cards facedown on the table-top. "Well, then, you had better go see what you can do for her, Betsy. We shall just have to continue our card lesson a bit later."

The maid stood, shot the butler a quiet look that told of her gratitude for his timely rescue, and bobbed a quick curtsy before hastening off. Noah found himself wondering just how long before his arrival his aunt had held the maid prisoner at the cards. Amelia never could quite understand how there could be anyone who didn't share her enthusi-asm for play.

Amelia stared thoughtfully at the vacant doorway. "I am beginning to wonder if I shouldn't hire another assistant for Cook. She seems constantly in need of Betsy's assistance, and always when we have just begun to play at cards. I shall never be able to teach her at this rate."

Her brow furrowed beneath her lace cap as she added, "Parsnips . . . hmm." And then she immediately perked upon noticing Noah still standing there. "But you are here now, so you can fill her place."

"Actually, Aunt. I had wanted to . . ."

Three hands later, Noah finally managed to secure her attention.

"Noah, dear, that is the third rubber you have lost to me now, and I even tried to give you that last hand. You are never so careless when you play. What is it that is troubling you, my dear?"

Noah looked at her soberly. "Actually, Aunt, I'm surprised you have not already heard since I'm sure half of Town is abuzz with it by now."

She shook her head, waiting.

"It is Tony." He hesitated. "He died on Thursday last."

Amelia's mouth fell open and she immediately reached out to cover Noah's hand with her own. "Oh, good heavens, no. I had no idea. I have been at home the past several days nursing a sore throat and haven't been out. Oh, Noah, Tony? No, it cannot be. How can this have happened?"

His eyes held hers as he said, "Aunt Amelia, there is something more, something which I have told no one else, not even Sarah. It wasn't an accident. Tony died by his own hand."

Amelia just stared at Noah, speechless. Tears of regret began to well in her eyes and she took up her handkerchief, dabbing them away.

Noah had decided to tell his aunt the truth about Tony's suicide because he knew he could trust her, yes, but also because he'd needed to finally tell someone what had actually taken place that night. After breaking the news to Sarah that morning, he had stayed on at an inn near Keighley Cross, to offer what comfort he could until all the arrangements for Tony's swift and private burial had been made and all the necessary notifications written. By the time he'd left, Sarah had so visibly declined that she had become but a shadow of her former self, making the necessary motions, but nothing more. He hadn't seen her eat more than a bite or two each day, and once Noah had even found her standing in the portrait gallery, staring at Tony's likeness as if she thought by doing so she might somehow bring him back. To see her suffer thusly at Tony's loss, Noah knew he had made the right decision in keeping the truth of the suicide from her. If she had known, her devastation would have been doubly harsh.

"Aunt, this is something only I, Tony's butler Westman, and now you know the truth of."

"But how will no one else learn of it? Surely there will be questions . . ."

"Anyone else will learn only that there was an accident while Tony was in the process of cleaning his pistol." He hesitated before adding, "I concealed the evidence of what truly happened."

"But you could—"

"I know, Aunt, but I am willing to face whatever repercussions there might be. It was a chance I had to take; there was nothing else I could do. Sarah is alone now. Had the truth come to light, by the law, Tony's property could have been confiscated. She would have been left with nothing. As it stands even now, she is not on solid financial footing. I have spoken with the Keighley solicitor. Somehow Tony amassed quite a bit of debt shortly before he died, far more than anyone ever realized. And there is no way of knowing how much more might even be yet outstanding."

Amelia shook her head. "And you believe that is why he took his life?"

"I suspect as much, but I cannot be certain it is the sole reason for his actions. There is something more."

Noah removed the letter Tony had received that night from his coat pocket. He handed it to her. Amelia took it and quickly read it. She asked, "What does this mean?"

"When I met with Tony that night, he revealed to me that he was about to elope, but he would not reveal to me the lady's identity, only that she was an heiress. Apparently, they had been carrying on a secret liaison over the past month in effort to hide from her disapproving family. It was immediately after receiving this letter that Tony ended his life. Given the evidence now of his financial troubles, my conclusion would be that he had staked everything on wedding her and gaining her dowry."

"And since there is no indication of its authorship, you will never know who the lady was," Amelia said, shaking her head sadly as she laid the letter on the table between them. "It is a sad, sorry situation."

"So you might think," Noah added, "except that the seal remains intact."

Amelia took up the letter again, peering at the letter's wax seal.

Noah said as she studied it, "It appears to be a crest of sorts. It even bears the author's initials, *B* and *R*, and then beneath it *L* and *Y*, and a design. You see the castle there in the background set beneath a crown."

Amelia narrowed her eyes. "And there appears to be some sort of plant in the foreground."

Noah nodded. "I plan to pay a visit to several goldsmiths to see if they might help to determine its origin."

"What will you do if you find the lady?"

Noah shrugged. "I do not know for certain. Most likely nothing. If anything I may just confront her."

"But Tony is already gone. What will confronting her serve?"

Noah frowned deeply. "Sarah told me that she'd received a note from a jeweler indicating Tony had given this lady an heirloom Keighley brooch. At the very least I'm going to request that she return it, for she really has no right in keeping it, especially now. It should, of course, go to Sarah."

Amelia nodded in agreement and took the letter up again,

this time peering at the seal more closely. "Let us hope a jeweler can assist . . ." She paused in midsentence then and stood quickly from her chair, crossing the room to a standing corner cabinet. She fished for something inside and returned to Noah a moment later, this time peering at the seal through a small quizzing glass.

"I think I may just be able to save you the trouble of going to the goldsmith, my dear."

"You are familiar with the crest?"

"No, I am not, and I do not think it is a crest. I think instead it is a rebus of sorts, and if that is so, then all we need do is figure its meaning between us." She quickly fetched a sheet of foolscap and a quill and ink from her writing desk. "Now, let us see if we might reason this out. The crown above the castle is actually a marquess's coronet." She jotted down the word *marquess* on her sheet. "We have the initials *B* and *R*." She scribbled more. "Then the plant. It looks as if it could be wheat. I suppose with the *L* and the *Y* that might mean Wheatley, but I know of no Marquess of Wheatley. There was a Wheate and he was a baronet, which could signify the *B* and the *R*, but he passed on several years back. Also, his name was William, his wife Heloise, and they had but one son, which certainly wouldn't explain the *A* at the bottom of the letter or the possibility of an heiress."

They continued on, scribbling other possibilities onto the sheet for over half an hour, but to no success. Finally Noah conceded, "Well, it appears I will be making a round to the goldsmiths after all."

Amelia still stared at the seal, puzzled. "Just another moment . . ." She paused, scribbling. "What if the plant were not wheat, but instead something which looks very similar?"

"Such as?"

"Perhaps rye. Thus we would have *B*-rye-*R* and *L-Y*."

Noah worked it together in his head. "Brierley?"

Amelia grinned, sitting back in her chair and pointing the handle of her quizzing glass at him. "Precisely!"

"Brierley," Noah repeated. "I am not familiar with the family."

"Nor should you be. Although you may recognize his title."

Noah looked at her, raising an anticipatory brow. "A marquess?"

"Indeed, my dear, the Marquess of Trecastle to be exact." She pointed toward the seal again. "You see the rye? It shows three stalks in the fore of the castle's image."

"Trecastle." Noah thought on the name, which he had heard, but couldn't quite place. "An ambassador of sorts, isn't he?"

"Yes, dear. Left England many years back at the death of his first wife. Returned to wed again less than a year past, although I can't fathom why since he is away more than he is in residence. In fact he is presently away on the Continent I believe. I haven't yet become acquainted with his second wife. Charlotte, I believe, is her name. I have heard she was a widow before he wed her and has a young daughter. I would assume the marquess returned from his journeys only long enough to find someone to assume his own role as parent, not that he ever played the role too seriously."

"He has children of his own, then? From his first marriage?"

Amelia nodded. "One. A daughter." She paused. "Augusta."

Noah stared at her. The *A* at the bottom of the letter. *Augusta.* "Is she married?"

"Oh, Augusta has never wed. But I highly doubt she

would have written the letter, Noah. Augusta isn't the sort of girl to involve herself in the sort of intrigue you have described Tony as having."

"Nor have I said I thought she had written the letter, Aunt. I would simply like to speak with her, to see if she might have the brooch. Surely there is no harm in that."

Amelia was no fool. "Well, even if you are only seeking an introduction, you might find it a bit difficult."

"Difficult? Surely I can accomplish something as simple as an introduction to her. The Lumley ball would be an ideal opportunity, although I was hoping I wouldn't have to wait so long as next week to begin looking into this."

Amelia took up the teapot and began pouring them each a cup. "It really won't matter, dear. I rather doubt Augusta will be at the ball."

Noah shot her a doubtful look. "Really, Aunt, everyone in Town attends the Lumley ball. It is all but as obligatory as a court presentation."

Amelia gave a slight smile as if he'd just said something humorous. "Yes, dear, but you do not know Lady Augusta Brierley. From what I understand, Augusta is a lady with a mind of her own. You might say she is somewhat an enigma, a lady who follows her own course, so to speak. In fact, few have ever seen her for she rarely moves about in public and she cares little for the dictates of society."

"So, you are saying . . . ?"

"I am saying that obligatory or not, whether Lady Augusta goes to the Lumley ball or not will depend entirely upon her."

A mind of her own. Follows her own course. Noah's mental image of the lady was rapidly developing. "No one in London is totally inaccessible, Aunt. And especially a woman. All I need do is put in an appearance at the linen draper's and wait. She will turn up eventually."

"If you'd like my advice, you might do better to try Hatchard's instead. Augusta is rather well-read and from what I understand, she pays a visit there at least once a week."

Noah wondered for a moment how his aunt came by all her information, for she seemed to know just about everything about everybody, but then that was just one of her many interesting qualities. But no gossip was she, for although she knew much, she rarely deigned to share her knowledge with anyone else, unless it was for a good purpose.

Noah stood, bending to press a kiss to Amelia's cheek before leaving. "Thank you, Aunt. As usual, you have been most helpful. I shall indeed try Hatchard's."

"Yes, dear. Do let me know how things go."

Amelia watched Noah turn then to leave, taking up her cup of the tea which was now unfortunately cold, but still quite tasty.

As she sipped, she reflected somberly on her nephew. How she missed the careless, carefree man he had been, a man who had been passionate about everything in life, a man who still believed in the goodness of others. Noah had changed, and the circumstances of Tony's death would see him change even more.

The past several years had been most difficult for him. He'd lost his father and eldest brother to a fire that had been set by the greed of human hands, had seen his remaining brother accused of the crime of it. Somehow he'd managed to fall in love, in the proverbial heels-over-head fashion, with a young lady whose character most everyone praised. Everyone, that is, except Amelia. When she'd first heard the news of their betrothal, Amelia had had her own personal misgivings, and unfortunately for Noah, her misgivings had proved correct. The lady's betrayal had

wounded her nephew far deeper than most would have
thought, leaving him cynical, doubtful, and hard of heart to
all but those who had proven their loyalty to him. And now
to have lost Tony . . .

Amelia could only hope this tragedy wouldn't see him
changed forevermore.

Chapter Seven

Noah grabbed for the door handle to Hatchard's just as another patron was pushing it outward to leave. He stepped back, tipping his beaver hat as a slender lady, accompanied by a footman, her face hidden from view beneath the black veil of her poke bonnet, emerged from within. He then proceeded inside.

Hatchard's was situated on the south side of Piccadilly Street, across from the great stone gateway to Burlington House and the adjacent former York House, recently renovated and now known as The Albany, with its newly designed bachelors' chambers. Benches lined the footpath at the shop's front, providing a place where servants could sit and await their masters while they made their selections inside. As was the custom this time of day the shop was bustling, for Hatchard's was not only a bookshop, but also a place for people to meet and discuss the news of the day provided by the many newspapers littering the tables set before the fireplace.

Noah stood surveying the area a moment until he spotted a clerk, his arms brimming with books, trying desperately to make his way around the other patrons without losing hold of his precarious load.

"Excuse me—"

"A moment, sir . . ." the man said, passing him swiftly.

It was actually a quarter of an hour later when the clerk finally returned to see him.

"My apologies, sir. I'm afraid we're a bit overrun today. Is there a particular title I might assist you with?"

"Actually, I wasn't looking for a book. I was instead wondering if you might be familiar with some of your more regular patrons?"

The clerk nodded. "Yes, indeed, sir. Mr. Hatchard calls for all of us in his employ to know his best patrons and their particular interests. 'It's what keeps them coming back,' he always says."

Noah nodded. "I am attempting to locate a lady whom I am told visits your establishment regularly."

The clerk stared at him, waiting for Noah to continue.

"Her name is Lady Augusta Brierley."

The man nodded enthusiastically. "Oh, yes. Lady Augusta comes here quite frequently. An avid reader, she is. Indeed she is one of Mr. Hatchard's best patrons."

"And so you would know if she has been in the store recently?"

"Yes, sir. She has. In fact, she is here now."

Noah felt an odd sensation pass through him, a disquieting sort of swell rushing through his insides. "Lady Augusta Brierley is here, you say? Right now? Then might you point her out to me?"

The clerk surveyed the milling patrons. "Hmm, I cannot seem to find her here"—still he looked—"but perhaps she has retired abovestairs. Lady Augusta prefers the older volumes and likes to take herself off to a far corner when she finds a particularly interesting title. You might try looking there and I'll see if I can't locate her down here."

The clerk started to turn away to see to his task, but Noah quickly stopped him. "I am not actually acquainted with Lady Augusta. I wonder if you might give me a description?"

The clerk seemed to hesitate in his response. "She's, ah,

how would you say, um, Lady Augusta is different. She doesn't dress herself like the other ladies."

Again that word: *Different*. Just as Amelia and Tony both had described her. What was it about this lady that merited such a distinction? She had arms, legs, a head—didn't she? "I was meaning more for a physical description of her, such as her hair color or perhaps the shape of her face."

Now the clerk did hesitate. In fact he was silent for a good ten seconds. "I'm afraid I wouldn't be able to tell you that, sir."

"I beg your pardon? Did you not say you are acquainted with Lady Augusta?"

"Yes, sir."

"But you cannot tell me what she looks like?"

"No, sir."

"May I ask why?"

"Because I have never actually seen her, sir."

Noah was fast growing impatient. "Well then, perhaps you might direct me to another clerk who might tell me what she looks like."

The clerk swallowed nervously at Noah's seemingly irritated tone. "I'm afraid I cannot do that either, sir. You see, none of the other clerks have seen Lady Augusta, actually seen her, I mean. I could describe her voice for you, though."

Noah blinked, then stared at the man. "You mean to say you have spoken with the lady, stood before her, but you have never seen her face?"

"Yes, sir"—the clerk floundered—"I mean no, sir. I mean I have spoken with her, yes. We all of us have, but none of us have ever seen her since she always wears her bonnet when she comes in."

"Her bonnet?"

"Yes, sir, you know, the sort that has a wide brim, only hers has a black veil over it that covers her face."

A black veil . . .

Noah looked reflexively to the door. The woman he'd stepped back to allow out of the shop at his arrival, could it . . . ? He shook his head.

"Even Mr. Hatchard has never seen her," the clerk went on, pulling Noah's attentions back. "But I'll go and ask him if he knows where she might be."

As the clerk hastened off, Noah was reminded again of his aunt's comments earlier that same day. *Somewhat an enigma. A lady who follows her own course.* And then he thought of Tony's words that last night when he had been speaking of the lady he had fallen in love with, the lady whom he thought returned that love. *Quite an original. Not at all what you might expect. An angel.*

An angel who wore a black veil.

Suddenly, it all seemed to fit. Why else would this lady seek never to be seen or recognized? Why else would she have forbidden Tony to tell anyone her name? She was a jade who occupied herself with leading vulnerable and foolish men on a merry dance of deception. Everything he had learned thus far about Lady Augusta Brierley only convinced him all the more that she was indeed the one he was looking for, the one who had promised to wed his friend, and then had abandoned him at the very last minute. And veiled or not, Noah was determined now he would find her.

The clerk's words when he returned a few moments later, however, made Noah realize that finding Lady Augusta Brierley might prove far more challenging than he'd at first thought.

"I'm afraid Lady Augusta has already gone, sir. She must have departed when I was engaged with another patron. If you'd like, I could give her your message when next she returns."

Noah looked at the clerk. "That won't be necessary. Thank you for your assistance."

Noah made to depart. As he pushed the door to the shop outward to leave, he nearly collided again with another patron, this one coming in. His irritation with the situation was fast turning to anger.

"Pardon me, sir," a soft voice said. And then, immediately afterward, "Noah, I hadn't expected to see you here."

"Sarah," Noah said, more than just a little startled at finding her standing there when he had just left her days before at Keighley Cross. "I wasn't aware you had come to Town."

She was dressed in a black crepe mourning gown that reached to her chin, her blond hair pulled back severely beneath a black silk bonnet. It wasn't a color particularly suited to her, making her appear even more pale and drawn than she had the last time he'd seen her, standing, looking lost and alone on the terrace at Keighley Cross as he'd ridden away.

"I could not remain at Keighley Cross, Noah, not with all the memories, not with Tony's portrait waiting there in the hall outside my bedchamber every morning."

Already her eyes were filling with tears. Noah quickly steered her away from the shop doorway where other patrons were coming and going. He led her to an empty bench seat outside the shop and gave her his handkerchief.

Sarah sniffed, wiping her eyes. She made to hand it back to him, but he shook his head and motioned for her to keep it. Her black gloved fingers clutched to the bit of fabric as if it were a lifeline.

"Had I thought of it, Sarah, had I known you would have

wanted to come here, I would have seen you to the city myself."

Sarah started to weep, her frail shoulders rocking. "Oh, Noah, everything is so different. I cannot bear to even think about living at Keighley Cross knowing Tony will never be there again."

Noah reached for her hand and she looked up at him, her blue eyes red, the skin around them swollen from many such bouts of crying. She hiccuped. "I thought, even though it wouldn't be proper for me to take part in this year's Season, perhaps the diversion of the city would keep me better occupied. Do you think it was improper for me to come?"

"Not at all. I only wish I would have thought of it myself. You are staying at the town house, then?"

"No." She took a deep and steadying breath. "Since it is not entailed, I have asked my brother's solicitor to put the house up for sale. I cannot go there, Noah, not after what happened there. I don't even want to lease it to someone else. I felt a need to remove it from my life and the solicitor thought selling might help to settle some of Tony's debts."

Noah nodded. "I think it is a wise decision. It is a fashionable address, so you should be able to bring in an ample sum. But if not there, then where are you staying?"

"Eleanor Wycliffe sent a letter offering for me to stay with her and her family at Knighton House. You know her mother and my own were very close friends. It was because of her letter I decided to come to the city. It seems she, her mother, and her brother, Christian, have come to Town for the Season. Her letter arrived the day after you had gone. I decided to accept her invitation to come and traveled with my maid, Lizzy, on the Lambton post coach." She motioned toward Lizzy, who stood waiting a space away.

"Eleanor will be good company for you, I'm sure."

Sarah didn't respond, just nodded as she forced a smile

instead. There followed several moments of an awkward and uncomfortable silence.

Finally Noah said, "Well, it is good to see you." He squeezed her hand reassuringly before releasing it. "If you have need of anything while you are in Town, Sarah, anything, you know you need only call on me."

Sarah nodded, her eyes still rimmed with tears. "Thank you, Noah. You have done so much for me already. I don't know how I shall ever repay you."

"Your smile is more than enough reward."

Noah stood and watched her go to Lizzy then, waiting until after they had entered the shop before he hailed the nearest hackney coach he could find, barking to the coachman his destination.

"Bryanstone Square, and be quick about it."

Tiswell, the Brierley butler, frowned when he heard the sound of a knocking at the front door. And then he sighed. Could he never have a moment's peace? He had just managed to find enough time to sit for a cup of tea and one of the cook's fresh lemon tarts, having spent the entire morning since waking at half past four inventorying the wine cellar. Even now, he still felt the niggling sense of a sneeze coming on from the dust that seemed to cover every inch of that dank cellar closet. He really must have one of the maids see to the task of cleaning it.

But now was the ideal time for him to take his ease. Lady Trecastle was on her way out for her late-morning round of visits, or as Tiswell liked to refer to them—her "tittle parties." Lady Augusta was yet abed and would likely remain so for at least another hour, perhaps two. If the timing worked out the way he hoped, he would have a half hour or more to himself. He planned to use that time to respond to the latest letter from his sister in Wiltshire, send-

ing along his recipe for the mead as she had asked of him.
Afterward, he would then have silver to polish, and a dis-
pute between the cook and one of the scullery maids to settle, something about a loaf of bread and an alleged
impertinence.

All in all, it would be a very full day.

The knocking at the door sounded again. Tiswell waited
a moment to see if Tom, the usual footman on duty at the
door, might yet be at his post instead of awaiting the marchioness in the carriage on the mews outside. At the sound
of a third knocking, however, the butler gave it up, pushing
his tart and teacup aside as he made unhappily for the front
door.

"Yes?"

The young man he found waiting on the other side had
the look of an aristocrat, if somewhat dandified in his dark
blue coat, buff-colored breeches, and admirable polish to
his betasseled Hessians. It was not so much his attire, but
rather his appearance which struck Tiswell as peculiar, for
in the ten months he'd been in service to this household,
there had rarely been any visitors at all. Few of Lady Trecastle's acquaintances would actually venture north of Port-
man Square, and Lady Augusta simply had no
acquaintances to speak of. It was one of the true advantages
of his position in the Brierley household.

"Good day, my good man," the gentleman said then,
doffing his tall beaver hat. "I wonder, can you tell me is
this the home of the Marquess of Trecastle?"

Tiswell furrowed his brow, frowning. The man was obviously a stranger, otherwise he would have already known
that the marquess was not—in fact had never really been—
in residence. "Yes, sir, it is indeed, however, the marquess
is abroad at present. You may leave your card, should you
prefer."

"But I—"

"Tiswell," sounded a familiar shrill voice from behind him then, a voice which placed all emphasis on the second syllable of his name, even speaking it an octave or two higher on the vocal scale. Hearing it thusly, Tiswell found he truly hated the sound of his own name. He likely would have groaned, if not for the man still standing before him at the doorway.

"Excuse me, sir," Tiswell said before disappearing behind the front door, which he only closed partway.

Lady Trecastle approached with all the bluster of a brewing storm, the pale blue-gray of her pelisse only sharpening that representation. Tiswell had thought her gone already and was less than delighted to know he was mistaken in that assumption. He would have to be more careful next time before taking his tea and tart, for Lady Trecastle did not abide relaxation from her servants, clinging to the belief that she—and not Lady Augusta—held the ruling hand over the household. Luckily she was often off pursuing her own interests, leaving them all free to enjoy the occasional blissful moment.

"Tiswell," the marchioness repeated, her voice still marked by its usual amplification, "as you can see, I am on my way out. I do not plan to return until the supper hour. Please inform Lady Augusta that I have arranged for Mr. Liviston to come to wrap her hair for the Lumley ball. He will be coming at two o'clock on Tuesday. Tell her she is not to keep him waiting."

"But my lady Augusta does not normally—"

"I don't care what time she pulls herself out of that bed every other day of the week, Tiswell. Tell her that I said she will find some way to take herself off the night before the ball at a decent hour for once, instead of staying out till all hours of the night and morning. She will not miss that appointment. A wrapping with Mr. Liviston is very hard to come by. Two o'clock tell her, Tiswell. Sharp."

"Yes, my lady." Tiswell nodded obediently, a gesture in complete disagreement with his thoughts at that precise moment. He watched as the marchioness turned to leave. Poor Lady Augusta, he thought. This news would not please her at all. He wondered if he would come to regret having advised her to attend the ball. The price of her having entered into her agreement with Lady Trecastle was beginning to seem rather dear indeed.

The butler waited until he was certain the marchioness had gone, surging back through the household toward the rear entrance where her carriage awaited, before he moved for the front door once again. "I beg your pardon for the delay, sir. I—"

Outside, the front stoop was curiously vacant, no sign of its previous occupant anywhere in sight. Taking a quick peek at either side of the front walkway, Tiswell puzzled for a moment and then promptly closed the door to make his way back to the parlor and his waiting teacup and lemon tart.

Outside, Noah slipped around the street corner and whistled for his waiting hackney. He entered quickly and gave the driver his direction before settling back on the squabs to consider what he'd heard while standing at the doorway of the Trecastle town house.

He had gone there thinking to request an audience with Lady Augusta, simply to ask her to return the brooch Tony had given her. At least that had been his intention, until he'd overheard the conversation between Lady Trecastle and the butler inside, a conversation that among other things had revealed Lady Augusta would in fact be attending the Lumley ball.

In a crowded ballroom, she would be unable to prepare

herself for their meeting, for surely once she learned his name, she would know what he had come for, would have her defenses at hand. *The element of surprise,* Noah had once heard the great Duke of Wellington say, *was a truly valuable asset in war.*

And indeed he felt quite as if he were preparing to do battle with this lady.

One thing was for certain. If he hadn't been convinced before that Lady Augusta was the woman who had written the letter to Tony, he could most assuredly be now. The words he'd just overheard at the front door of the Trecastle town house had only added further refinement to the mental image he'd effected in his mind. And if he had somehow still held to any lingering doubts about her authorship of the letter, having been left to stare at the heavy brass door knocker while the butler had been engaged with his mistress inside had completely convinced him.

The design above the knocker cast in gleaming polished brass was the exact duplicate of the seal on Tony's letter.

Chapter Eight

The Lumley ball was an unparalleled event of every Season, officially marking its midpoint amid a profusion of purple and golden crepe and cut-crystal bowls filled with oversweet punch laced with too-sour wine. The event was held on Grosvenor Square, at the grand weathered brick mansion of the Duke and Duchess of Challingford, two of society's most prominent figures, he a staunch Tory and she "The Hostess-*extraordinaire*." Revered by London society, they stood above the gay crowd with all the regalia of a king and queen before their worshipping court, graciously greeting each arriving guest as they were announced by the twin liveried footmen standing either side of the front door.

Inside the brilliantly lit and crowded ballroom, dancing couples stepped and skipped in time to the merry strains being played by an orchestra that was adroitly hidden behind a wall of false shrubbery at the far end of the room. Away from the clamor at the opposite side of the house, the green-baize tables in the Gaming Salon were already seeing the exchange of enormous sums, while men more inclined to discussion than dancing partook of the duke's fine port in the mahogany-paneled Gentlemen's Parlor nearby.

It was indeed a diverse crowd. A bevy of young ladies fresh from grand country houses bedecked in pale muslins had arrived to take the place of their sisters the year before. Their one objective for the evening—and every evening thereafter—would be that of securing themselves the best possible potential husband they could lay their eyes and flutter their fans upon. Meanwhile these same young bucks were out to secure their own fortunes in the form of an heiress, preferably pretty, who would hopefully supply them with numerous children, preferably male. Elderly gentlemen, infirm with gout, settled about the periphery in their Bath chairs, elbowing each other as they ogled the young girls with thoughts of what had once been. On the fringes of it all stood the matrons, aging dowagers and grandams alike, whose sole duty it was to keep a close eye on everyone else and make certain nothing untoward dared occur on their "watch."

Amid this diversion, Augusta had hoped to pass the evening in relative obscurity. Yet despite their agreement, the marchioness still seemed inclined to pointing out several "possibilities" whom she felt qualified to relieve Augusta of her "wretched condition," Charlotte's latest sobriquet for Augusta's unmarried state. She should have known Charlotte wouldn't have given up the quest entirely. She was, however, markedly less insistent in her suggestions. Augusta, on the other hand, found her redress in pointing out to her stepmother the very reasons why she could never consider any of them.

That one standing near the potted palm? Why, hadn't she just seen him spit out the remains of his pickled herring into their hostess's drapery? Yes, well, perhaps the burnished gold brocade Charlotte was so very fond of at their own house would serve to hide the stain better.

It wasn't a quarter hour after their arrival when Charlotte finally gave up the objective, leaving Augusta to stand by her side, smiling at the marchioness's numerous acquaintances and responding politely to their inane questions.

What a lovely shawl, dear, did you stitch the design yourself?

I heard the Regent would make an appearance this evening, poor dear Duchess, she would never recover if he doesn't.

Augusta merely nodded to each one while trying not to openly yawn. If her present company were any indication, the evening would likely prove a lengthy one. Still, in a crowd the size of this, there had to be someone with whom she could converse intelligently, someone who would offer colloquy more lively than stitchery and hair wrapping. Of course, she would likely never see them with her spectacles ensconced away in her reticule as they were.

Augusta's forehead wrinkled in a frown. Charlotte had been adamant that she not wear her spectacles that evening, which had left her vision somewhat blurred; fortunately, though, Charlotte hadn't realized this when Augusta had been making her remarks about the noble young herring-spitter.

Augusta glanced now to where Charlotte stood beside her involved in a conversation of the latest muslin patterns just arrived at Harding Howell & Company—serious stuff, to be sure. Stepping back a bit, she took her spectacles from her reticule and quickly slipped them on to survey the crowd in search of moderately more stimulating company.

Colorful silks and glittering jewels came into immediate focus, a brilliant array in sharp contrast to her own costume, which was not quite pale gray, but not quite beige. The gown was simple, yes, the silk unadorned but for the plain wide satin ribbon that circled just beneath her breasts. It was the most formal gown she owned, still it didn't quite harmonize with the elaborate hairstyle Mr. Liviston had spent hours creating, one which had twisted and pulled her dark locks into a tight mass of tiny ringlets that frothed precariously at the very crown of her head. Charlotte had proclaimed the coiffure "a masterpiece," and "Augusta's only saving grace for the evening." Augusta had wondered that she might topple over from the sheer weight of it. Even now she felt the beginnings of a headache from it.

Augusta had nearly given up hope of finding anyone of interest in the milling crowd when, suddenly, she spotted the earl standing across the room near the balcony doors.

She smiled to herself. She had hoped he would come; in fact the possibility of seeing him was one of the main reasons she had agreed to accompany Charlotte at all. Normally she had to plan their meetings covertly and even then was left to worry that someone might discover them. But here, in a social setting, they could spend some time together without the threat of any speculation.

All she needed was to find some way to slip quietly off while Charlotte was still involved in her conversation.

It was but a moment later when opportunity presented itself in the form of a rather large matron in green satin bearing a path straight through the crowd. Adeptly Augusta slipped behind her, following in her wake as she made her way across the ballroom toward where he awaited.

Noah alighted from the carriage and turned to offer his aunt an assisting hand. They had to step carefully as they approached the front stairs for already the drive in front of Challingford House was littered with muck from the horses who had come through before them.

He'd wanted to be there early, so that he might better watch the door and listen for the footman announcing Lady Augusta's arrival. Though he had formed a clear mental image of her, he could not be certain of her identity. Unfortunately, though, he and Amelia had been detained. Halfway to the ball Amelia had ordered the coach turned around so that she might retrieve her quizzing glass which she had left at home.

"Absolutely not," she had informed Noah at his suggestion that she simply forgo the item for the evening, "for how could I ever successfully pass the night at cards unable to see my own hand? Why, Lady Talfrey would make a mincemeat of me at the tables to be sure!"

Thus they arrived at Grosvenor an hour later than he'd planned, only to be made to wait nearly another hour in the procession of carriages that stretched down Upper Brook Street nearly to Hyde Park.

Now inside Challingford House, Noah walked with Amelia along the long reception line, exchanging polite greetings with their hostess and her prettily made-up daughter, the latest of her brood whose marriage was the prime objective of this whole affair. Challingford had sired six daughters before his wife had finally given him his heir and Noah had often heard it remarked that the Lumley ball, named after the duke's father who had died fighting for his country in the Colonies, had come about not merely as a social event, but as a clever means to marry each of them off.

But Noah needn't worry, for the duchess's smile, although courteous, would extend only far enough to give him the necessarily civil welcome entitled to him by his family's rank. Though he sprang from ducal stock, after the events of the previous Season, no marriage-minded mama would dare come near him with a mind for a match; after all, he had broken the cardinal rule in the game of marriage making. Lord Noah Edenhall had ended a betrothal, a thing no true gentleman ever did.

"My goodness," Amelia said, surveying the crowd that awaited them inside the ballroom, "the duchess has quite outdone herself this year. This turnout far exceeds any from prior years. It looks as if everyone in Town is in attendance this evening."

And thus it would make it that much more difficult for him to find Lady Augusta Brierley amid the milling throng.

Noah frowned, peering around the vast room, scrutinizing every younger female face he found, hoping that somehow, the moment he set eyes upon her, he would know who she was.

They slowly began to circumnavigate the room, their progress slowed because of Amelia's acquaintance with most everyone they encountered, necessitating a greeting and subsequent polite conversation with each. While his aunt chattered away, Noah continued to survey the fringes of the room where most of the guests had begun to congregate in preparation for the dancing. Despite the crowd, it wasn't long before his scrutinizing eye caught sight of a particularly fetching blond who quite aptly suited his assessment of Lady Augusta Brierley.

She was beautiful, indeed, standing like a graceful swan amid an assemblage of admiring bucks who were falling over one another in their attempts to move closer to her. She waved her lace fan before her with practiced skill, cocking her head to the side while smiling in a way that showed her even white teeth to advantage.

Noah stood by, watching her as an actress on the stage, his assiduous eye catching the manner in which she would press her lilac-silk-covered breasts forward ever so subtly. She was indeed well-practiced, playing the role of the coquette as if born to it; he knew this well, for he'd been charmed—and betrayed—by the true virtuoso of titillation.

"Noah, dear?"

Amelia's voice pulled Noah from his study. "Yes, Aunt?"

"Lady Basil was asking how Robert and dear Catriona are faring. I was telling her how you had just returned from a visit to them in Scotland."

Obliged to respond, Noah forced his eyes away from his object of study long enough to apprise the elderly dowager of his brother's well-being in as few words as tact would allow. No, they hadn't planned on coming to London for the Season. Yes, Catriona's absence would indeed be a great loss to every hostess this Season.

When he finally managed to return his sights to the blond coquette, she had vanished, and with her her throng of admirers.

Damn!

Nodding his head in a parting gesture to Lady Basil, Noah began moving through the crowd with Amelia again, all the while searching for sight of Lady Augusta in the crowd. It was nearly a quarter of an hour later when he spotted her again, this time near the refreshments table. Her circle of admiring swains had grown now to where she was nearly eclipsed by them.

He was just readying to ask Amelia for a confirmation of the lady's identity when she said, "Now I see why you offered to escort me to the ball this evening. You came because you are still seeking an introduction to Lady Augusta Brierley."

Noah gave in to a slight grin. His instincts had been right. The blond with all the admirers; she was Lady Augusta. He had known it, felt it from the moment his eyes had first found her.

"Yes, Aunt, and since you are already acquainted with the lady, perhaps you might make the introduction?"

Amelia nodded. "Of course, dear."

But when Noah started toward Lady Augusta and her flock of admirers, he felt his aunt tugging at his sleeve.

"Noah, dear, where are you going off to? I thought you said you wished an introduction to Lady Augusta Brierley."

"And I do." He turned then to see Amelia motioning toward the opposite side of the ballroom.

"But she is there."

Noah followed her direction to where another young lady

stood among her own company of admirers, a smaller group, but nonetheless a gathering.

However, the woman Amelia pointed to was everything in contradiction to the one he had been watching.

This was an angel?

She had hair that was utterly black—there was no other way to describe it—and it was arranged in a froth of curls that was circled by a simple ribbon fillet. The style, however elegant, somehow didn't quite suit her. She was not tall and statuesque like her contemporary across the room, nor did she carry a hint of grace or flirtation about her. Instead she was small, her figure petite and covered from chin to toe by a gown that was plain, colorless, and rather strict in cut. No fresh-faced ingenue she, for her face held a maturity of at least five-and-twenty, perhaps more.

Noah then noticed one other distinct difference between the two ladies. The men surrounding this creature were not young bucks like those fawning around the blond across the room. No, these all were gentlemen, men he knew as having been associated with his father, perhaps even his grandfather—all of them wealthy, if not wealthier than Croesus, and all of them well past their fiftieth year.

Noah narrowed his eyes on the lady. So this was her game? She had decided against wedding Tony, a man more in keeping with her own age, one who might live to see another half century, and had settled her sights on one who couldn't hope to pass another decade. Not only was she ruthless, she was a woman without principle, without morals, without conscience. But then, after reading her letter to Tony, he'd already known that about her, hadn't he? Still Noah found himself glaring at her severely.

"Come, dear, I thought you sought an introduction to her."

Noah didn't move. "No, Aunt, I think I have decided against it."

Amelia nodded. "Ah, so you see now why I said it could not have been Lady Augusta who had written that letter to Tony?"

Noah turned to look at his aunt, his mouth set in an unrelenting frown. "No, actually, Aunt, I see more why she very likely did write the letter. Is it not obvious she is setting her sights on marriage to an older man—one who will provide her with a subsequent widowhood that will leave her both independent and wealthy?"

If the ballroom hadn't been so noisy, he would have sworn he heard Amelia "harumph." "My dear, if you only knew how ridiculous your words were. Those men are more likely than not interested in conversing with Lady Augusta about her father more than anything else. Why is it anytime a lady pays any attention to a man, any man, others immediately think there is some sort of romantic connection to it? Heavens, if that were the case, I'd have been coupled with most every man in London myself!"

Noah stared at his aunt, unable to mask his incredulity. He reminded himself she was unmarried and thus had no notion of the way of such things. In Lady Augusta, she likely saw a younger version of herself, nothing more. But he saw Lady Augusta Brierley in a very clear light, even brighter than the light from the dozen or so chandeliers hanging above them. And his image of her was even more loathsome than before.

Noah watched on as Lady Augusta removed herself, or rather was removed, from her aging company by a woman who looked as if she could be an older sister, if not for the fact that they resembled each other nearly as closely as a rock does a tree. Perhaps even less.

"Charlotte, Lady Trecastle," Amelia stated, having

watched him as he was watching her. "She has been Lady Augusta's stepmother these past ten months or more. I had never seen her before tonight. It is said the marquess wed her in a private ceremony within the space of two months after his return from the East. Hardly knew her."

Noah said nothing, simply watched as the marchioness drew Lady Augusta away from the circle of gentlemen who had surrounded her, her expression one of true displeasure. It would seem her stepmother didn't approve of Lady Augusta's conduct either. And hadn't Tony said as much that last evening?

Noah wondered at how a lady, any lady, could trip merrily about a ballroom after so recently bringing about the death of a man, how she could seem so unaffected when because of her actions, life had been forever changed for both himself and Sarah. Even now he could hear the occasional whisper nearby, for wherever he went, the subject of Tony's death seemed to follow.

The event of that horrible night had provided society with a topic of conversation at a time when, unfortunately, not much else was stirring to take its place. Napoleon was exiled, this time permanently to St. Helena, and for the first time in as long as most could remember, the country wasn't at war. Princess Charlotte had married for love, of all things, and was awaiting the birth of the future heir to the throne. National emotions had calmed, and the future of England seemed secure, so the unexpected death of a nobleman had given the *ton* a much longed-for diversion.

The physician who had come to Keighley House the night Tony had died had held to his original judgment, the coroner ruling the death accidental and thus an inquest was thankfully avoided. Still, the fact the Noah had been there, had discovered Tony's body, wasn't long unknown. Soon it seemed everyone knew. And everyone wondered. And Noah became the font for society's queries.

How had it happened?

It was said the pistol had discharged in Lord Keighley's face. Was he left at all recognizable?

What of the rumors that his hand had been completely shot off? That he had lived several hours afterward in horrendous pain until finally expiring?

The public's morbid curiosity was rife with indiscretion and served only to refresh the memory of that night for Noah each time someone else approached him seeking what should have been sacred details. What good was there to be had in their knowing the extent of his injuries; what purpose could it possibly serve? Still, there seemed no bounds to the questions they would ask, no thought of respect for Tony's passing. Noah could only hope Sarah wasn't undergoing the same inquisition. He prayed that she would be left to mourn her brother in peace.

What was most troubling to Noah was the fact that through it all, first the funeral and now the lingering *on-dits,* Tony's relationship with Lady Augusta had never come to mention. By now Lady Augusta would have learned of Tony's death, should have concluded that he had died soon after receiving her letter. Did she suspect he had taken his own life? Did she feel any amount of responsibility, remorse for her cruel dismissal of him? More than that, did she hold no fear of their relationship somehow being discovered? The very fact that she had come to the ball tonight, obviously in search of male company and but a mere fortnight after Tony's death, painted her far worse than Noah had at first imagined her. He'd first thought her a trifler, a capricious tease. He now saw she had not a shred of a conscience either. She, the very one whose words had spurred Tony's actions, had been left free to move about unmolested throughout every ballroom and garden walk of society.

Until tonight.

"Will you please excuse me a moment, Aunt?"

Amelia nodded and Noah made his way through the milling crowd, across the ballroom to where Lady Augusta had been standing. Yes, he would confront her, but first he had questions to ask and he knew just where to start with them. By the time he had wound his way across the room, but three—and the most prominent three—of her admirers remained.

"Edenhall!" one of the gentlemen exclaimed upon noticing his approach. "My boy, it is good to see you!"

Hiram Singleton, the Earl of Everton, extended his hand in a warm and eager greeting. Everton had been a friend of his godfather's years before and Noah had known him since he'd been a child. Standing beside Everton, the other two men present, the Marquesses Mundrum and Yarlett respectively, extended their hands toward him.

"Say, I thought I'd heard you were going to make an offer on the Grey filly a few months back?" asked Everton. He chuckled then. "Grey filly, rather humorous, what?"

Noah frowned, unable to share his mirth. "I had considered a match with Lady Julia, but decided against it."

Yarlett clapped Noah hard on the back. "Turned you down, eh, boy?"

"You sod," interjected Mundrum. "The boy's lucky nothing came of it. All milk and water, that girl. Head full of fustian and heart empty of a love for anything other than her father."

"Or her father's money," added Everton. He turned grinning eyes on Noah. "But then Edenhall here had already figured that out, hadn't you, boy? Always knew you were a smart lot."

Noah wisely refrained from attacking Julia's character, saying simply, "Quite."

Mundrum surveyed the crowd. "Well, there's a new crop come in this Season that our boy here can wander through, and there's several a fair sight better than that one." He narrowed his rheumy eyes. "Hmm, let's see. Who can we ferret out for him?"

"What about Nisbet's girl?" suggested Yarlett, scratching his brandy-reddened nose.

"You dolt. She's got false teeth and is naught but sixteen. But Tennington's eldest, now there's a sweet piece of—"

"To be sure, and I hear that is a fact confirmed by at least three young gents already," said Everton, effectively removing her from the running. "But Wilberham's daughter, Perdita, now there's a possibility for the boy."

"Uh, actually," Noah broke in just in the nick of time, "I was wondering about the young lady you had been speaking with just a few moments ago."

All three of the gentlemen turned to stare at him, lapsing into a collective silence uncharacteristic for any of them, even more so when they were grouped together.

"You don't mean Trecastle's girl?" Everton finally—bravely—asked.

"Yes, I believe I do."

"Lady Augusta Brierley?" Mundrum added, obviously feeling the distinction necessary.

"Yes, I believe that is what my aunt Amelia said her name was."

Yarlett grinned, elbowing Mundrum beside him. "Amelia Edenhall. Now there's a woman worth her salt."

"Too smart for any of us," Everton agreed. "Tell us, my boy, is she here tonight?"

"No doubt she's already relieved several dowagers of

their quarterlies," said Yarlett. "There's none better at the cards than your aunt Amelia."

Noah broke into their plaudits for his aunt. "Yes, but, about Lady Augusta . . ."

"What? Oh, yes, Lady Augusta Brierley."

Mundrum shot his contemporaries a look then that quickly brought Noah to asking, "What is it, gentlemen? Is there something wrong with Lady Augusta?"

"Not in the least," the earl quickly denied. "Augusta is a fine girl. Just not what I would have thought a young buck like yourself would be interested in. Not many of your age would give her the consideration."

"Is she a simpleton?" Noah asked, curious as to their reaction.

"On the contrary," voiced Yarlett. "She's quite a blue-stocking. Speaks several languages I'm told, Latin among them."

"Has she some physical deficiency then? A clubbed foot? Or perhaps crossed eyes?"

Everton chuckled. "Her step is quite sure and she will stare you straight every time. Some, however, would say she is rather advanced in years to be considered marketable for marriage to a young man like yourself."

Marriage to Lady Augusta Brierley was the furthest thing from his mind, still Noah found himself growing more and more intrigued. "And just what is her age—precisely?"

"Eight-and-twenty, I believe," Yarlett said.

"A bit past her prime, perhaps, but hardly long in the tooth, gentlemen," Noah responded, even as he wondered why he was defending her when he had every reason to despise her.

The three ancients had lapsed back into their particular silences.

"What is it then?" Noah persisted. "You all act as if she carries the plague."

The trio looked at one another, exchanging confidential glances.

"Perhaps you should discover Lady Augusta's true nature yourself, Edenhall," Everton suggested then. "And judge for yourself whether she catches your fancy or not."

Noah's patience was wearing thin. "I have every intention of it, my lord."

"Well, you might as well seize the chance while you have it," Mundrum said, motioning across the room. "She is just going outside on the balcony. I daresay you'll not find a better opportunity."

Noah stared at the door where, indeed, Lady Augusta was presently leaving. She had somehow slipped away from her stepmother again. What the devil was she up to?

He turned, nodding his head to the three. "Thank you for the suggestion, gentlemen. I believe I will."

As he started for the balcony doors, Noah could have sworn he heard them snickering behind him.

Chapter Nine

Noah closed the door to the balcony quietly behind him, walking onto the secluded terrace where he had seen Lady Augusta go moments before him. It was a cool night, dampened by a slight mist which had kept most of the guests inside where it was warm and where their flawless coiffures and delicate silks wouldn't suffer the consequences of the night.

Most, excepting Lady Augusta Brierley.

The terrace landing was deserted, quiet, peaceful, and Noah paused for a moment to rest his hands at the stone railing, welcoming the chill and the quiet sense of tranquility it offered.

A soft breeze slipped through the tangled ivy that crept along the red brick walls at the back of Challingford House as Noah circled around toward the far side of the terrace. The wind whispered through the dark glossy leaves, filling the air with the mingling scents of the gillyflower and sweet violet from the duchess's celebrated gardens. Behind him, candle-light glowed through the tall ballroom windows, the moon above a hazy beacon behind the silver veil of the clouds.

Lady Augusta was nowhere in sight.

Noah followed the stone railing to a set of small stairs that led down to the back gardens. Greek and Roman statuary watched on from the shadows as he moved silently along the secluded walkway. It was dark, but the moon provided enough light for him to see his direction. Still he did not see her.

Then, somewhere ahead of him, he thought he heard the sound of footsteps on the garden pathway, too soft for boot-steps. But a lady's slippers?

As Noah started after them, he didn't know what he would say when he found her. He didn't even know why he felt this compulsion to see her, face her, look into her faith-less eyes just once and have her know she had not gotten off completely scot-free. Was she out here to meet a lover, for what other reason would a lady have for sneaking off from a ballroom alone? Was it the man she had betrayed Tony with? Or her next chosen fool?

Noah came around a turn fringed by a covey of day lilies then and spotted her, and with her a gentleman, standing a short distance away. They were poised at the end of the narrow pathway, cloistered near the overhanging branches of a graceful elm. The moonlight was shining down through the rifting clouds, glimmering like pale blue ice on her dark hair as she stood behind the man a space, facing the back of him while he, in turn, looked to be engaged in a study of the stars over the high garden wall.

Noah lingered behind them, feeling a bit foolish, yet un-able to turn and leave as he knew he should. Anything he saw would only make him angrier and Tony's death that much more senseless. Still, unwittingly, he found himself circling to where he would be better concealed by the shad-ows and the duchess's ornate topiary.

Lady Augusta had chosen well this time, raising her measure from Tony's mere viscountcy to an earldom—and that the very distinguished, very wealthy Tobias Millford, Earl of Belgrace. Even though he was a man old enough to have been her father, the earl had never married, thus he had no children who might stand in the way. He was of medium stature and wore his clothing well, with a head of his own hair that was a peppery gray. A well-respected Tory, his health had never been what one would call robust for he was plagued by a difficulty in breathing that made him somewhat reluctant of society. Even now, standing but a short distance away, Noah could hear a slight wheezing from him as if he'd just finished a run.

"My lord?" Noah heard Lady Augusta call softly from behind the earl. Her voice was soft, not at all unpleasant-sounding. Noah drew slightly, silently closer.

Belgrace turned from his study of the stars. "It is you, Lady Augusta."

So they were already acquainted.

"My lord." She came nearer to the earl, further closing the space between them. "I was hoping for a private moment with you. I have wanted for some time to tell you something of grave importance."

"Is it Cyrus? Has something happened to him?"

"No, my lord, it is nothing at all like that. My father is very well. Indeed I received a letter from him just last week."

Oh, the lady was truly bold to seek to beguile a colleague of her own father.

The conversation halted then as another couple came onto the garden path behind them. Noah recognized the lady of the pair as a countess who had been an acquaintance of his mother before her death. He did not know the man who accompanied her, who was whispering intimately into her ear—he was not, however, her husband. The two walked in the opposite direction, stopping but a short distance away as they murmured softly in the moonlight, oblivious of anyone or anything but each other.

Even a distance away it seemed Lady Augusta couldn't risk their hearing what she had to say, for she took another step closer to the earl.

Noah skirted a flowering hedge, drawing near just as she said, "I wish to speak with you on a private matter to do with"—she glanced around uneasily—"myself."

The countess and her companion circled back toward the pathway. Lady Augusta stepped yet closer to Lord Belgrace, to where her skirts were now brushing against his breeches. Belgrace looked a bit bewildered by her advance and likely would have stepped away to a more acceptable distance had he not essentially been backed against the garden wall.

Lady Augusta's voice was intimately low now, silken, seductive. It was the sort of voice that made a man instantly think of a bedroom and very low candlelight.

"What I wish to tell you, my lord, it is of a rather personal nature. It is something I have never shared with anyone before." Noah inched closer. "You see, I have for some time now shared an affinity for—"

The sound of laughter, impassioned and not so very distant, sounded from the ardent couple in the shadows. Belgrace looked quickly toward the terrace and the ballroom beyond. "Perhaps we should discuss this in a more appropriate venue, Lady Augusta, at another time when others might not happen upon us at any given moment."

He slipped past her and made for the terrace stairs, his shoes grinding over the graveled pathway with his haste.

Lady Augusta started after him. "My lord—"

Belgrace halted and turned, holding up a cautioning hand. "Not here, my lady. You place your character at great risk."

She frowned. "You needn't worry over my character, my lord."

Belgrace wouldn't be swayed. "I would be doing your father no service were I to behave otherwise. Another day, my lady."

"But, my lord—"

Her persistence seemed only to make him that much more

uneasy. "I really must go. It is growing late and I am to ride in the park early on the morrow. I am sorry, my lady."

And with that final word, Belgrace turned, leaving the garden.

Lady Augusta stopped short of pursuing him into the ballroom, realizing at last the impropriety, she, a lady who obviously preferred to keep her improprieties hidden away from the public's notice. She stood alone now, bathed in the moonlight, and frowning at her failure before she turned to contemplate the constellations through the scattered clouds overhead.

From his vantage in the shadows, Noah had a clear study of her. What he saw, however, was not at all what he'd expected. When Tony had first described this lady as an angel, Noah had envisioned someone flawlessly beautiful, elegant, tall, poised, with golden hair arranged like a shining halo upon her graceful head.

Instead Lady Augusta stood perhaps an inch or two taller than his own shoulders and her figure, while petite, told more of agitation than grace. She wasn't a classic beauty, true, but there was an uncommonness to her even in the soft dark curls which trailed along the nape of her neck, brushing over her temple against skin that was ivory pale and smooth. Dark brows arched contemplatively over expressive eyes, eyes whose color he could not quite determine. Her mouth, even though she was frowning, drew the eye of the observer, making a man wonder what it might be like to kiss it, taste it. . . .

Noah hadn't realized he'd drawn closer in an effort to better see her until he had knocked a small potted flower from a stone pedestal onto the garden path. Lady Augusta turned abruptly at the sound. She stared directly at him. "Is someone there?"

Noah stilled, realizing she could not see him in the shadows, and then watched as she fished inside her reticule for something. She removed a pair of silver-rimmed spectacles which she then placed over her eyes, eyes which now looked on him clearly as they narrowed in irritation behind her lenses. Her mouth pinched. "What do you want, sir?"

Noah came deliberately onto the path in response, drawing nearer to face her. He said nothing. Her eyes, he saw in the muted moonlight, were a dusky gray, but they were touched with green and they tilted slightly—provocatively—upward at the corners. Around her neck she wore a curious-looking pendant on a chain, a small golden star and moon that glimmered almost silver in the moonlight. Set with a single peculiar milky blue stone at its center, it appeared almost to glow.

Lady Augusta said nothing as he studied her, just stared at him in turn, assessing him far more critically, far more openly than he had her. She didn't appear pleased with what she saw. She was measuring him upon her mental scale, all while she wondered how long he'd been lurking there in the shadows, whether he had overheard her thoroughly inappropriate conversation with Lord Belgrace. Any gentleman would feign ignorance to spare a lady's modesty, politely excusing himself to save them both the awkwardness of the situation. But then, everybody knew Noah was hardly a gentleman any longer.

"Perhaps I'm mistaken, but I'd always heard it is considered improper for a young lady to approach a gentleman alone and unchaperoned, much less make advances toward him."

It was an ill-mannered thing to say, yet instead of being ashamed at having her actions toward Belgrace thrown at her so publicly, Lady Augusta's frown deepened and she glared back at him every bit as bluntly as he had her. Impertinent was the word that immediately came to Noah's mind.

"Nor did I think gentlemen were supposed to eavesdrop

on what is quite obviously a private conversation. So much for what is proper or not."

Pert was another word he would definitely use to describe her. He watched then as she started to walk past him, dismissing him with a saucy lift of her chin as if to say he had wasted enough of her time. Before he could contemplate his actions, Noah found himself stepping directly in her flight path. In fact she nearly collided with him.

Lady Augusta glared at him. "Kindly allow me to pass, sir. I am in no mood for your childish games."

Her voice, sharpened by disdain, brought a strange sense of satisfaction to him. It reminded Noah of someone else who had done much the same thing to him not so long ago. Julia. He found himself leering at a lady for the first time in his life. "You know his lordship may not have been interested in what you were offering, but I might be persuaded to it."

Noah had been raised to respect women, cherish them. Even now he could imagine the spirit of his mother the duchess standing behind him, watching and shaking her head in utter dismay.

Lady Augusta blinked at him. It took her several moments to realize what had actually been hidden behind his thinly veiled comment. She gaped at him then, her mouth falling open in a manner that would have been unattractive on any other woman. On her, it was oddly enticing. He felt a tensing inside and forced his eyes away from her mouth, focusing instead on her narrowed eyes.

"I beg your pardon, sir."

Noah couldn't help himself. He reached forward and before she could react, he pulled her firmly against the full length of him, crushing his mouth against hers.

He felt her stiffen immediately and struggle to free herself, but she was slight and he had her well and good. Her mouth was warm and soft, as was her body but for the firm-

ness of her breasts that were pressed against him. He took
the opportunity to pull her closer by cupping his hand beneath her bottom in a gesture that only caused her to struggle more. Finally she did manage to free her mouth. It
would prove her worst mistake, for as she prepared no
doubt to condemn his actions, she also afforded Noah the
opportunity to deepen the kiss. And this he did, covering
her mouth again and sliding his tongue against hers in a
most intimate assault.

She tasted of sweet wine, the scent of her was exotic,
spicy, floral. But instead of the loathing he'd expected to
feel at her, Noah's body was responding with a passion he
hadn't felt in weeks, months even. Swift. Hot. Wild. It took
hold of him and sent his senses to reeling.

Stunned by his own reaction, Noah released her, setting
her back on unsteady feet. The abruptness of his actions had
set her spectacles slightly askew. He took in a deep breath.
He shook his head. What in bloody hell was he doing? And
with her? This woman was the very image of everything he
loathed in the female sex, a witch in every sense of the
word. How could he have responded to her in that way?
How could he have been so stupid? He focused his attention
on the look of outrage she wore as she fixed her spectacles
more firmly on her face, seeking satisfaction—and distraction—in knowing he'd put that anger there.

"It would appear it is I who must beg your pardon now,
madam."

It took Augusta only another moment to respond, with a
slap, openhanded and hard against his left cheek. She then
dashed down the path toward the terrace and the doors to
the ballroom beyond.

At that moment, Augusta would have gone anywhere,
hell and back, to be away from him.

By the time she reached the inside of the ballroom, Augusta was so furious she was actually panting. Who did that man think he was? And where on earth had he been raised? In a gutter? This, she said to herself as she charged through the crowd searching for the face of her father's wife, *this* was precisely why she never attended society functions. Even now she could feel his hands upon her, touching her in a way no one ever had before. And his mouth—she would never have imagined such intimacy possible. The men on board the ships she had traveled throughout her childhood had never dared attempt such liberties. And this man tonight was considered a gentleman among society?

By the time Augusta located Charlotte, chattering happily amid a circle of married ladies beside the punch bowl, she was to the point of muttering to herself most every coarse word she'd ever heard on board ship—until she noticed a refined-looking woman with several ostrich feathers in her hair staring at her in shock. Augusta smiled politely to her, tugging insistently at the fan dangling from Charlotte's gloved wrist.

"Charlotte, a moment, please."

The marchioness turned from her company. "Augusta, what is the matter? You are positively flushed, dear."

"I should like to leave." She stared at her, adding with a frown, "immediately."

Charlotte must have sensed Augusta's seriousness for she checked any objection even though it was just past ten o'clock and the festivities had only started to get under way. The Regent had yet to put in an appearance.

"All right, Augusta. But we'll need to fetch our cloaks and call for the carriage."

"I'll see to it."

Augusta hurried off, wanting to do nothing more than remove herself from this house and these people who played at politeness when in truth they were no more civilized than a pack of animals. All she wanted now was to return to the quiet of her solitary life where she could pursue her own interests in relative peace and never, *ever* return.

But then she would indeed have to return. Her agreement with Charlotte ensured it. Oh, why had she ever agreed to this wretched bargain? And how would she ever manage to see it through now?

She had just made it across the ballroom and was waiting to make her way up the stairs behind the cluster of other guests in front of her when something caught her attention. She glanced to the side and saw it was him, the man from the garden, standing several yards away. He was staring directly at her. Openly. Shamelessly. And he was smiling.

Inside now, among the elegance of their surroundings, he'd lost all his sinister qualities from the shadowed garden, taking on the countenance of a gentleman, a veritable wolf in sheep's fleece. His hair was dark and neatly styled, his face clean-shaven. He was civilized in his appearance, handsome even, his refined clothing and impeccable grooming giving no hint to his true lascivious nature. He watched her through eyes that were hazel and that knew how to disarm with their gaze while that same smug smile played across his mouth, the mouth which had touched hers so intimately. His smile widened slightly and he made a very elegant, very mocking bow toward her.

Augusta felt her face instantly color, the heat of it reaching to the tops of her ears. She felt certain everyone around them had taken notice of his gesture, that they all somehow knew of what had taken place in the garden outside. The unmannered cur. Had she a glass of punch in her hand, she would surely have tossed its contents in his face. Instead she turned away and twisted a path through the doorway to leave, hoping she might never set eyes upon the likes of him again even as she wondered who he might be.

Chapter Ten

It was nearing dawn, the first traces of daylight just breaking on the eastern horizon as Augusta stood at the open window, peering out at the burgeoning sky. It had rained intermittently through the night, stopping only an hour or more before, leaving the air to carry with it a damp, breathfogging chill.

Below and in the distance, London stretched limitlessly before her view, bathed in the pale blue glow of the twilight and veiled by the drifting morning mists, the city's imperfections not yet visible to the observer's eye. Nearby, in the fashionable West End, most had by now returned from their evening of social frolic, tucked away in their beds until the sun would rise on yet another day—and yet another opportunity for them to find new and inventive ways to outdo one another.

But it was here, in her private belevedere atop the Brierley town house, where Augusta felt a world apart from that side of life. Here was her retreat, her sanctuary, a place where but one staircase led to, and where not even Charlotte had ever been admitted. It was here all her dreams came true.

Augusta checked the position of the moon one last time before retreating back inside the spacious windowed chamber. She stopped at the worktable to record her observations in her notebook. The single candle standing on the table beside her had burned to a guttering stub during the night, but it provided her enough light yet to study the other notations she'd scribbled there earlier.

What she saw did not altogether please her. Everything was in readiness, yes, but the time she had left to her to complete her task was fast running out. She glanced at her wall chart and the scribble of figures she'd drawn there. Frowning, she looked to the small calendar she'd drawn up that hung crookedly on the wall. The time was indeed ripe, all her preparations complete, except for one final element, the last ingredient which would fulfill her plan.

A soft mewing came from beside her and Augusta turned as the figure of her cat, Circe, leapt upon the writing table to join her. Sleek and silent, Circe was midnight black with the exception of the one white toe on her left front paw. Her eyes, a mesmerizing golden green, shimmered curiously in the candlelight as she greeted her mistress. Augusta had first found her as a kitten several years earlier, cornered by two streetwise toms in an alleyway nearby to a dock where their ship had come in for provisions. Augusta had saved the kitten's life, and the two of them had been inseparable since.

"Good morning, my sweet," Augusta said, stroking the cat's thick inky fur. Circe responded with a contented purr, rubbing her whiskered face eagerly against Augusta's soothing fingertips.

Augusta scratched her behind her ears, a favorite spot. "We are close, Circe, so very close. I have everything else prepared now. All that remains is a bit more time and the Earl of Belgrace, and we might have had him last night, if not for the interference of that cad, whatever his name is."

Circe mewed in feline agreement.

Cad. Much as she would hate to admit it, that cad, and just who he might be, had been the solitary thought which had diverted Augusta's attentions since returning from the ball the night before. All through the remainder of the night and into the morning while she'd worked, she'd replayed the scene from the garden in her mind, his sudden appearance, his bold mockery of her, the slap she'd delivered him in response. If not for the fact that she had tasted him on her lips afterward, she might try to deny that he'd kissed her at all.

What troubled her more was the fact that she wasn't really repulsed that he had taken such liberties with her. She should be, she knew, but instead she remembered not with displeasure the feel of him, a solid wall against her as his arms had closed about her.

Circe meowed loudly then in protest, as if to tell her mistress her head was full of fustian.

Augusta looked at her. She couldn't agree more. "It was nothing, Circe."

Circe, however, wasn't persuaded by the statement.

"I wouldn't even call it a preoccupation. It is only because he kissed me. I've never been kissed by a man before, you know. And especially never like that. Such a thing is bound to give rise to some afterthought."

Another meow, this one decisively derisive.

Augusta frowned. "You are right, of course. It is ridiculous. Really. It was just one of those inexplicable things that happens once in a lifetime—for which there is no explanation, no reason. It will never happen again, so it would be best to just forget about it. Pretend it never even occurred." She glanced at the cat then and for a moment, she would have sworn she saw the creature roll its eyes heavenward.

"I simply need to focus my attention on the task at hand—that of finding a way to meet alone with the earl."

She let go a frustrated breath. "But how will I ever accomplish that?"

Augusta set her chin in her hand and leaned against the tabletop, waiting for inspiration to strike.

It did but a few moments later, in the form of a voice which had spoken to her the night before.

I really must go. It is growing late and I am to ride in the park early in the morning. I am sorry, my lady.

The park. Lord Belgrace had said that he would be riding, and at an early hour, he would very likely be alone. There would be no one else nearby to interrupt, to overhear, to interfere. It would be the perfect opportunity. She would go to the park and she would wait for the earl there, and then once she found him, he would understand. For hadn't she already taken the steps necessary to ensure just that?

Taking up her notebook, Augusta started for her bedchamber, not to retire as she normally did at dawn each day, but to change into her riding habit before heading off for a ride in the park.

The morning was cloaked in a dank and sunless haze for it had rained again late the night before and a faint mist persisted even now, making the street cobbles slick, and the air heavy and still as Noah's horse picked its way slowly toward Hyde Park Corner.

The hour was early, but not too early for Noah knew Belgrace to be a creature of the dawn. He had caught sight of him out on rides a few times previously, always long before the fashionable hour and always alone. Because of his breathing condition, he was a solitary man, somewhat of a recluse even. Although he belonged to the best of clubs, he rarely if ever frequented them. He cared little for appearances, his clothing more serviceable than fine, and he neither drank nor gamed, traits which had allowed him to double his worth since inheriting the earldom from his father nearly twenty years before.

Noah's intentions that morning were simple. He would seek out Lord Belgrace and he would warn him against Lady Augusta's character. He saw this as a service. The man had had no experience with women, thus he could have no notion of the power this lady could wield over him.

But Noah knew very well what she was capable of, how she could muddle a man's senses, even a man as determined as he. Consider how she had nearly brought about his own undoing when he'd kissed her the night before. He'd intended to shock her, perhaps even frighten her a bit before confronting her about Tony and the brooch. Instead she had somehow turned the confrontation about to where he had been the one left befuddled. Only the sharp slap from her hand had managed to break him from his stupor, long enough for him to watch her flee. A man like Belgrace, while fortunate to have never fallen under the wiles of an unconscionable woman before, would be clay in the hands of the potter Lady Augusta Brierley.

Noah spotted a movement then to the left of him, a figure which began to materialize through a break in the trees. Belgrace? A horse appeared, a yellow dun with white socks and a blaze slashed down its face, approaching slowly through the swirling morning mist. It was a small mount, perhaps fourteen hands, and its rider was dressed entirely in black, from the full skirts which draped gently over the horse's hindquarters to the veiled beaver riding hat cocked upon her head. Only the froth of white lace spilling at her neck gave any trace of lightness to the ensemble, a small allusion to redemption against the darkness that surrounded her.

Lady Augusta. Of course she would have come for hadn't Belgrace told her the night before that he'd be riding this morning? She had come seeking the earl again, riding to meet him alone in the park, something no proper young lady would ever dare do.

Noah waited, watching from a place obscured by a heavy overgrowth of shrubbery, one that afforded him a good view of the clearing near the stream. She walked her horse on a bit farther before stopping beneath the sagging branches of an ancient willow. There she dismounted, dropping the reins to allow her horse to graze on the lush grass while she walked slowly toward the placid waters of a nearby pond.

Once at the water's edge, she pushed back the veil covering her face, tucking it upon the hat's curving brim before then removing the hat entirely. Her hair, just as sinfully black as the hat, was caught up in a neat knot at her nape. She looked outward over the dale while she swept a gloved hand back over her forehead to pat an errant tress. She walked a bit, flexing her arms, and then extended one leg forward, lifting the skirts upward over her ankle, as if a pebble might have gotten lodged inside her half boot.

Noah sat slightly taller in the saddle, staring at her leg, the length of white silk stocking revealed beneath her dark skirts. He found himself wondering if her skin was as pale by morning as it had been in the moonlight the previous evening, wondering if she would smell as sweet. . . .

He shook his head once, then twice to clear his thoughts. What sort of witchery did this lady perform? Did she know somehow that he was there, watching her? Was this her method of seduction, this affected unknowing, like an actress before a hidden congregation? It was no wonder Belgrace had seemed so bewitched by her the night before. Everything about this woman was steeped in mystery. She was the image of an enchantress, dressed entirely in black and with that something cryptic about her that unwittingly drew the spectator's eye, until without even realizing, one is totally captivated.

Then, just as suddenly as she had ensnared him, she turned, and the spell was instantly broken.

She had heard something out over the dale. Noah looked, spotting another rider slowly approaching. He recognized Belgrace, his figure tall in the saddle atop his bay stallion. Noah watched as Lady Augusta quickly donned her hat, pulling the veil down to shield her face before returning to her horse.

By the time she had arranged herself in the saddle again, the earl had shifted course. He was heading in the other direction. Had Belgrace seen her? Was he hoping to avoid meeting with her? Did he already know who she was, what she was about?

Noah waited while Lady Augusta set her heels to her horse, trotting after the retreating Belgrace, never realizing that Noah trailed covertly in her wake.

They had reached a field now and Belgrace urged his steed on into a canter, his hardy mount easily clearing a fallen tree that lay in his path. There was no other direction around the tree, and by the way in which it was situated on the pathway, it appeared too formidable an obstacle for a horse as small as hers to clear with any safety.

Lady Augusta rode sidesaddle, precarious even over less treacherous an obstacle. Noah slowed his horse. She would need to find another way through to the clearing, and by the time she accomplished that, Belgrace would fortunately be gone.

But Lady Augusta did not appear to be slowing. Instead she urged her horse on faster, lowering her face against its neck. Noah watched on in disbelief. The little fool was going to try to make the jump, and the fact that she could easily break her neck seemed to hold no concern for her.

She was nearly upon the tree, her black skirts whipping about wildly and—

"Pull back!"

The shout issued from him before he could check it. Noah took in a breath, watching as, at the last moment, she faltered. And in her brief moment of hesitation, her horse abruptly halted inches from the fallen tree, nearly unseating her. Her hat tumbled carelessly to the ground nearby to where she likely would have fallen. As she struggled to aright herself, the horse sidestepped, burying its hoof to its fetlock in the crown of her hat.

"That was my best riding hat, you—" She started to look toward him, peering at him from behind her spectacles. And then recognition dawned on her. In an instant, her surprise turned to outright fury.

"*You!*" Her breath fogged from the cold of the morning. "You are the one, the ill-bred boor from the ball last evening."

Noah didn't think it necessary to confirm that particular distinction. Instead he dismounted and started walking toward her, the tall grass rustling against his boottops. He took up her hat and made an attempt at brushing it off. The black veil was torn and the small jaunty feather that had once decorated its brim was now broken in half, not to mention that the crown was irreparably disfigured. She should be grateful it was only her hat that had suffered the damage. It could very easily have been her head instead.

Noah made to hand the hat to her, asking, "Do you at all realize how foolish it was to attempt that jump?"

Lady Augusta seized the hat from him, giving it a shake that only served to disorder it all the more. "No more foolish than shouting at someone on the verge of taking a jump, catching them unawares, and nearly causing them to lose their seat."

"You could have been killed," he said, not at all surprised at her ingratitude. He had, after all, prevented her from catching up with Belgrace—much to his satisfaction and her obvious chagrin.

"I knew perfectly well what I was doing, Mr.—"

"Lord," Noah broke in. "Lord Noah Edenhall of Devonbrook, at your service, my lady."

He doffed his own hat and bowed gallantly, expecting to look up to an expression of recognition, even appreciation, both due to his lineage and his relationship with Tony. But the face which greeted his pronouncement was genuinely unaffected. The lady had no earthly idea who he was. Surely Tony had mentioned him to her. But then, Tony had said he'd only known Lady Augusta a month, and Tony hadn't been himself for any of those thirty unfortunate days.

Noah cleared his throat. "If you do not care to think of your own safety, at least think of the safety of your mount. She could have broken a leg attempting to clear that hazardous an obstacle."

"Allow me to inform you, *Lord* Noah Edenhall of Devonbrook, that my horse is perfectly capable of clearing that tree, and one even higher. Although she appears small, she was bred specifically for such an endeavor."

The horse pawed the ground in complete agreement with her mistress.

Noah looked at the horse and had to admit that upon closer inspection, she was a hardier specimen than she had at first appeared. Her coat was a shade of dun he'd never before seen, golden yellow and with a curious, almost metallic-like sheen to it. She carried an odd conformation, unconventional, with a long, thin neck set upon sloping shoulders and an overlong back. Her expression was reminiscent of a Barb, a fine head with large eyes set wide apart. Mysterious. Foreign. The horse flared her nostrils then, snorting as if to express her resentment of his critical study.

"Were I you, I wouldn't come much closer," Lady Augusta warned. "I'm afraid Atalanta is not the most gentle in temperament toward those with whom she is not acquainted. She has been known to bite, especially someone who dares to question her agility."

"Atalanta," Noah said. "The famed huntress who refused to wed unless a prospective suitor could best her in a race. Fitting name for a horse."

Lady Augusta sat up straighter in the saddle, but didn't offer any remark to his observation.

Noah grinned. "You should hope she doesn't acquire a fondness for golden apples, like her namesake. If memory serves, wasn't it the apple which led to the goddess Atalanta's eventual downfall and subsequent marriage?"

Lady Augusta frowned. "Atalanta does not eat apples, golden or otherwise."

"Well, then she's not at all like English horses."

Lady Augusta sniffed. "No, she certainly is not. Atalanta is from Russia and she is the finest of horses. Her line comes from the Akhal-Teke, one of the oldest breeds in the world."

Atalanta twitched her tail, both at Noah and his own horse, Humphrey, a liver-colored hunter of dubious birth, who, it seemed by the way in which he was inching closer to her, was more than just a little impressed by his present regal company. Noah gave a tug on the reins, throwing Humphrey a stern look.

"Well, if you haven't any plans to insult my horse or ruin the other articles of my attire, I will be on my way. Thank you, my lord, for yet another unpleasant encounter."

Lady Augusta directed Atalanta around then and proceeded to trot off in the opposite direction, tossing over her shoulder as she went, "Should we have the unfortunate coincidence of ever meeting again, perhaps you might restrain yourself from assaulting my person a third time."

Noah watched her vanish around a grouping of trees. He swung himself up onto Humphrey's back, readying to leave and wondering why the devil he should feel discontented, especially when he had, after all, succeeded in hindering her from meeting with Belgrace. He looked up when he heard the sound of thundering hoofbeats to see Lady Augusta bearing straight for him.

Good God, she was mad!

Noah pulled Humphrey back and out of her path as she galloped straight toward him, racing past and then soaring cleanly over the fallen tree without the slightest trouble in keeping her seat. He watched, stunned, as she turned for a final glance at him over her shoulder—and a final swishing of Atalanta's tail before disappearing from sight around the trees.

Chapter Eleven

The rattle of the knocker on the front door pulled Lady Trecastle's concentration from her watercolor palette. She stood elegant as a Grecian statue, brush poised in hand, waiting for Tiswell's expected arrival in the salon with the card of her visitor, after which she would decide whether to accept or decline the call. *Ah, the Season!*

Several moments passed. The sound of the butler's shuffling footsteps did not sound from the hallway or from anywhere else for that matter. The knocking, however, came again, this time slightly louder.

"Tiswell," the marchioness called in her softest, most pleasant voice, the one reserved for those she wished to impress most. "I believe there is someone at the door."

A moment. Two. No response. She glanced to the door, saying louder but no less politely this time, "Tiswell, are you there?"

Again there came no response to her plea, only several silent moments and then another set of knocks at the door.

"Tiswell! The door!"

Silence. Again. Her ire rose. When she heard the fourth set of knocks coming from the hall, the marchioness abandoned her pretty pose, tossing the paintbrush into the small crystal cup of water on the table beside her easel. Grumbling to herself, she marched furiously to the salon door, yanking it open. "Tiswell!"

The hall stood empty, not even a parlor maid in sight to do the job. What on earth were they paying all these servants for anyway, especially since one could never find one of them when needed?

The marchioness looked then to the front door, warring with herself. She frowned. Ladies did not answer doors. It simple wasn't done, especially when there very likely could be nothing more than a footman on the street side attempting to deliver an invite to some affair that likely would not even warrant her attention.

Or, she considered further, it could be an invite to a distinguished affair, one she would certainly not wish to miss.

Perhaps it might even be an invitation to dine at Carlton House.

Or perhaps it wasn't a footman at all, but one of London's finest ladies out on her round of afternoon calls seeking to pay an unexpected visit.

The knocking sounded again. Surely whoever was there would leave if there came no answer this time, even though they had likely heard her calling to Tiswell. What if it were Lady Marsten or Lady Trussington? She was so hoping to secure a match for Lettie with one of their very eligible and much sought-after sons. She had been cultivating associations with them both over the past weeks aimed at just that goal, doting on them, paying them compliments on their gowns when in fact she thought them hideously lacking in flounces. If she ignored their knocking, all hope would be lost. They would forget Lettie. Worse, they would see her name cut from all the best lists, securing her a refusal into Almack's next Season. Instead that cow-faced Lady Prudence would snare one of the eligible bucks, leaving her beautiful Lettie abandoned and humiliated like last year's ballgown.

The marchioness stared at the door. She simply could not risk it. Not when it was Lettie's future at stake.

Tossing propriety to the wind, she checked the placement of her turban in the hall glass before proceeding to the door, a welcoming smile pasted upon her face.

She opened the door. She immediately lost a considerable degree of her smile, while her face took on a considerable degree of redness. It wasn't a lady at all on the other side, but a young man bearing a package of some sorts.

He doffed his hat. "Good afternoon, my lady."

The marchioness glowered at him. The very idea of answering the door to a mere delivery servant brought her upper lip to curling. "Deliveries are to be made at the *rear* of the house," she measured out, already grasping the door handle so that she might close the door before any passersby saw her standing there conversing with a servant.

As dismissals went, it was really quite good. However, the man was not retreating as she had expected him to do. Instead he was taking a step closer to the door—and to her.

"I beg your pardon, my lady. Apparently there is some confusion. I was not making a delivery. I have come to make a call."

Charlotte suddenly wished she had benefit of her lorgnettes, which she kept hidden away unless, of course, she was alone and safely locked behind a closed door. Instead she squinted slightly in order to better see, this time taking in the superior cut of the man's gray cutaway coat, the richness of his striped waistcoat, the resplendent shine to his Hessians. If she'd had her own spectacles, she surely would have realized immediately upon opening the door that the man was a gentleman—a gentlemen caller—but of course, she didn't have her lenses for it wasn't the fashionable thing to do.

She narrowed her eyes further, attempting to focus on his face. He was a handsome man, thirty perhaps. His hair, a rich dark sable brown, was cut just below the line of his high standing neckcloth. His eyes were brown. No, hazel. His mouth was turned in a slight smile, but a smile that was nonetheless confident. An expensive-looking package took up one hand, the other rested on the golden knob atop his fine walking stick, the brim of his beaver hat hooked under his thumb.

The marchioness's eyes went wide. Good heavens, he had the look of a nobleman. Could he be a suitor already come for Lettie? Perhaps he had seen her at one of the few smaller soirees which Charlotte had permitted her to attend in the weeks before her departure to the country and had become instantly besotted. Good Lord, the girl had yet to make her debut and already prospects were calling at the door. If this were any indication, her Season would be the success of all successes.

"And you have come for . . . ?" she began.

He bowed his head gallantly, presenting her his card. "Lord Noah Edenhall to see Lady Augusta Brierley."

Charlotte snatched the card like a morsel from a near-empty plate. She quickly read its script. *Edenhall.* Wasn't that the family name for . . . ? Good Lord, he was related to the Devonbrook line, no less than one of the wealthiest families in England and now Scotland since the present duke had married that Scottish upstart. The marchioness pasted on a smile to rival the midday sunshine that was beaming down through the poplar trees lining the quaint square she lived on. "My lord, I am so sorry, but my daughter has been gone from the city for some days. I'm afraid she will not likely be coming back to the city until next Season, especially since she hasn't yet come out—officially, I mean. I—"

"But did I not see her on Tuesday last? At the Lumley ball? With you?"

The Lumley ball? The marchioness hesitated then, recalling the rest of the gentleman's words at his introduction, words she had utterly discarded after hearing the name of "Edenhall." What was it he had said? He had come to—?

And then she remembered. But, no, surely she was mistaken. Surely he did not mean to say he wished . . .

. . . to see Lady Augusta Brierley.

"Is Lady Augusta available to callers?" he asked then, thereby removing any lingering doubts she might have had as to the purpose of his visit.

"You wish to call upon Augusta?" she asked, unable to keep the obvious incredulity from her voice.

"Yes, my lady." And when she didn't readily respond, he added, "She does reside here, does she not?"

The marchioness drew in a long even breath in an effort to calm herself. This very thing, it had been a goal she had been working toward for over ten months. Yet even so, she found she had difficulty accepting the notion of it, despite the very tangible proof that stood staring at her from her own doorstep.

Augusta had a caller. A male caller. A Devonbrook male caller bearing some sort of geegaw. She had attended but one ball, the Lumley ball, yes, but still just one ball. And they had even left the event early, before the Regent had arrived. Still, a gentleman caller. For Augusta. She shook her head slightly. It defied all reason.

"Yes, my lord," the marchioness finally managed, despite her sudden shortness of breath. "Lady Augusta does reside here. But I am afraid she will be unable to accept your call at this time. She has not—I mean to say she is yet—ah, Lady Augusta is at the moment indisposed."

Lord Noah Edenhall of Devonbrook considered this a

moment. "Very well. Could I trouble you to see that she receives this package?"

It was all Charlotte could do to keep herself from snatching the thing up from him and tearing its binding open herself. What on earth could this gentleman—this Devonbrook relation—be bringing to Augusta? "Yes, of course, my lord. I will see that she receives it the moment she awakens—ah, I mean to say the moment she becomes available."

As the marchioness stepped forward to take the package from him, something dark slipped past her skirts and onto the front stoop.

"Just a moment, my friend," the gentleman said, reaching down to retrieve what turned out to be Augusta's nasty little cat. He scratched the furry creature between the ears, eliciting her annoying meow.

"Thank you, my lord," the marchioness said, feigning concern. "That is Lady Augusta's cat, Sissy or Cecily—or something like that. A wicked creature from some myth, I believe."

His mouth worked in a smile. "Do you mean to say Circe, the witch-nymph?"

"Yes, that is it. I never thought it a very appropriate name for a cat."

He bent again to usher the beast back indoors. "She is black," he said, standing.

Charlotte stared at him queerly, wondering to herself why the cat's color had warranted mention. "Yes, she is."

"Somehow, I am not surprised." He donned his hat with a parting bow. "Thank you, my lady, for conveying my package to Lady Augusta."

Charlotte stood at the door, heedless now to who might see her there, as the gentleman, Lord Noah Edenhall of Devonbrook, took the steps to the walk where his carriage awaited him.

And what a carriage! A gleaming barouche no less, and pulled by a pair of matched grays the exact shade of his coat. His coachman, decked out in rich shades of gold and blue, snapped the reins after he'd settled himself back against the seat. She remained frozen where she stood until he had vanished around the corner and she could no longer hear the sound of the coach wheels on the cobbles before she closed the door.

Once inside, Charlotte inspected the package, frowning when she realized that it was bound in such a manner as to prevent her from opening it without detection, paper tapes holding its lid closed. A mewling came near to her feet. She glanced to the stairwell, frowning at the cat. Augusta must have awakened for her cat never left her chambers when she was yet abed, instead curling beside her head on the pillow in a manner that both irritated and revolted Charlotte. Why the beast probably carried fleas!

She heard a door open on the upper floor then. Minutes later, Augusta descended. She was still dressed in her nightdress and wrapper, her dark hair ruffled around her shoulders in a frazzled and sad example of a plait. Those ridiculous spectacles were perched on the end of her nose and she was studying a sheet of her nonsensical "formulas," completely oblivious of Charlotte or anybody else who might cross her path. Thank heavens the gentleman had already gone. Had he seen her thusly he'd have surely snatched his package back and fled.

"The maids are supposed to bring your tea up to your room, Augusta. We have a bellboard to summon them for just such a purpose so you are not made to come down in such an unacceptable state. It is, after all, what we pay them for."

Augusta didn't so much as glance up from her paper. "They never know when I'm going to awaken. I see no need to pull them from their other duties when I can just as easily come down."

Charlotte sniffed. They had had this discussion many times, never to any result.

"Who was that pounding at the door like that?" Augusta asked. She had paused long enough to thumb through the morning letters waiting atop the salver on the hall table. "Someone making a delivery?"

Charlotte stared at her. "It was a delivery, yes, but it was brought by a caller."

Augusta yawned behind her hand, disinterested as she abandoned the letters and returned her attention to her foolscap. She shuffled toward the kitchen at the back of the house. "A persistent caller it would seem. Their knocking woke me."

"The caller was for you, Augusta."

Augusta stopped, turning toward the marchioness, her eyes suddenly alert behind her lenses. Her attentions, at long last, were caught. "Surely you are mistaken. I do not receive callers."

"Oh, I am not mistaken. You did indeed have a caller this morning."

"Who in heaven's name would want to call on me?"

"The name on the card he left reads *Lord Noah Edenhall of Devonbrook.*"

Augusta frowned. Obviously this bit of news did not please her. "What did he want?"

So she knew of him. Charlotte's curiosity mounted. "He had come to bring you something. This package."

Augusta took the parcel, regarding it as if it contained a disease of some sort that she feared setting loose on the world. She stared at it for some time before she then placed it on the side table. She turned back and started toward the kitchen once again.

"Aren't you going to open it?" Charlotte asked, stunned at Augusta's reaction, or rather the lack thereof. What lady could ever resist opening a parcel, especially one from a gentleman?

"I must consider it over my morning tea. I may simply return it unopened."

"Augusta!" Charlotte stared at her, astounded. "Never mind your tea. Have you run mad? You must open it—immediately—and see what it is before considering whether or not you should return it. How will you know if it isn't a totally appropriate gift? An expression of this gentleman's esteem for you?"

Augusta let go a breath of impatience before taking up the package once again. "Oh, very well . . ."

She carelessly broke the elegant paper ribbons that bound it and lifted the lid. Inside she pushed through layers of tissue to reveal what would have been a most exquisite riding hat, had it been any other color than the stark and dismal black it was.

She watched as Augusta removed the hat. A delicate veil—equally black—draped around the smartly curled brim. Its black plume fluttered softly as Augusta held the piece up for inspection, giving it no more than a negligible glance before retrieving the small note tucked beneath it inside the box. She read it and the frown on her mouth deepened as she reached inside the hatbox for something else, something round and wrapped in its own bit of tissue. She peeled away the covering to reveal a single golden apple.

"What an odd gesture," Charlotte said. "I mean, the hat is certainly very fine, although you could never consider keeping it as it is a totally inappropriate thing for a gentleman to give a lady he hardly knows. But I fail to understand why he would give you an apple."

"I have every intention of keeping the hat," Augusta said. "And the apple is not for me. It is for my horse."

And with that she took a very big, very loud bite from the side of that same apple before turning for the kitchen once again.

Chapter Twelve

Noah's carriage turned from St. James's Square, slowing to a halt at the corner of Charles Street. He alighted and turned to see an open landau waiting at the front of his house a distance down the lane. He instructed his coachman to return the coach and horses to the stables on the mews that ran behind the row of grand Georgian town houses and then started onward.

He had nearly reached the waiting landau when he recognized Catriona, his brother Robert's wife, inside the coach. While Robert stood at the front door conversing with Westman, she was doing her level best to convince their toddler son, James, that he should not climb upon the coach's collapsible hood while using his father's fine kidskin gloves to chew upon. The nursery maid who'd accompanied them looked as if Bedlam might be a preferable locale to the carriage at that moment. At the front of the carriage sat the coachman, eyes tucked safely behind the rim of his hat, looking as if he might actually be napping, a feat in and of itself considering the commotion taking place behind him.

"James, sweetling, please do sit still for just a moment. I know it is past your naptime, but if you—" Before he nearly toppled over the back of the coach, she took the squirming boy around the waist of his nankeen breeches and lifted him up to face her. "Now what do you have to say for yourself, Master James?" she asked with a grin.

"Mama—down," he mumbled in response before he grabbed on to the rim of her beribboned bonnet and gave a good yank.

The boy giggled while his mother squealed. As the nursery maid came to Catriona's rescue, Noah couldn't help letting go a chuckle at the sight of the stylish hat suddenly drooping lopsidedly over her one eye.

"Dear sister, your own da, Angus, had it right when he said 'that laddie is becomin' a wee bit of a *wud-scud*,'" Noah said, mimicking the Scotsman's heavy burr. "Our own father always told Robert that he would one day have a son who would be just as much a handful as he was. I see he was right."

Catriona pushed the once elegant straw confection back from her head, releasing her coppery brown hair from its neat coiffure to fall about her shoulders in a disarray. Catriona hardly noticed. "Noah! There you are! We were beginning to think you might have vanished off the face of the earth."

Noah came to the side of the landau and took Catriona's gloved hand, placing a greeting kiss upon it. "And I thought you were going to stay in Scotland this year to forgo the rigors of the Season. Or did the rigors of the Rosmorigh nursery prove more exhausting?"

"Actually," Robert said, coming down the steps to join them, "Catriona had a change of heart after you left to return to Town. She decided a good dose of London society was just what she needed, didn't you, my dear?"

Despite his brother's words, two things told Noah that it had not at all been Catriona's decision to come to Town, but instead Robert's: the look exchanged between the two and the fact that Noah knew full well Catriona *hated* the London Season and all its hypocritical glories. "Is that so?"

"Oh, yes, Noah," Catriona said, determined to play her part in the ruse. "I have just received this wonderful new

gown from my sister Mairead in Paris that I am truly dying
to show off and—"

"Catriona."

She looked at him innocently. "Yes?"

"You don't lie well. Not at all."

"It's true, my dear," Robert agreed. "It is one of the
many reasons why I fell in love with you."

Catriona gave it up to failure then. "Oh, very well,
Robert decided we should come, but it was somewhat my
doing. I have been worried about you since you left us. You
seemed unsettled, and I told Robert so."

Robert added, "And now that we have heard the news of
Keighley's accident, I am especially glad we made the journey. We stopped by Aunt Amelia's when we first arrived
this morning. She told us about Tony, and that you were
with him when he died. I am sorry, Noah."

Noah nodded solemnly.

"And Sarah?" Catriona asked. "How is she managing
it?"

Noah was ashamed to realize then he hadn't really
thought of Sarah and how she must be getting on, not since
running across her outside Hatchard's nearly a week before. But his pursuit of Lady Augusta, he reasoned, was for
Sarah truly, for at the very least he would see the Keighley
brooch returned to her. "Sarah is getting on with her life as
best she can," he said, while making a mental note to call
on her first thing the following morning. "She has come to
London now, and is staying at Knighton's."

"Oh, that is good," Catriona said. "Eleanor will see to
her very well. And Eleanor's brother, Christian, has he
come to Town for the Season as well?"

Noah nodded. "Like you, regardless of his disinclination
for it, apparently he is here. And likely he will be hounded
wherever he goes by husband-hunting mamas parading

their young daughters before him. Such is the fate of the only living heir to the Duke of Westover."

Catriona reached out then and took Noah's hand, squeezing it softly. "You are certain you are well?"

Noah nodded, smiling at her.

"There is a marked change to you, though," Robert added, giving Noah's person—on which he wore his finest suit of clothes—an obvious study. "Quite a turnout you've made there, brother. All this time you've made me believe you eschew the rules of fashion, and here you are, the very pink of the *ton*. Even your neckcloth has an impeccable tie to it. What has happened? Did you finally decide to dismiss that hapless valet of yours?"

Noah shrugged. "He left the position himself. Found himself in a bit of a romp"—he glanced at Catriona—"uh, a young lady and decided to wed her. They're settling in Weymouth, I believe, where her family lives. His replacement, Chiveley, did bring some level of experience with him."

"Chively? Wasn't he in service to Brummel before he ran to the Continent? Good God, half the bucks in London must have been frothing at the bit to engage him. How'd you manage it?" Robert hesitated but a moment before answering himself. "Of course. He was Tony's valet, wasn't he? Aunt Amelia had said you'd taken on a number of his servants and I recognized Westman at the door."

Noah nodded. "I initially hadn't planned on staying on in the city and so had made no arrangements for staff. After Tony's death, they were in need of positions. Matters just sort of worked out that way."

"The cane. The fine clothes." Robert raised a brow. "Can there be a lady who has managed to tempt you into staying on in the city?"

Noah immediately thought of Lady Augusta, her triumph at clearing the fallen tree in the park shining at him from behind the lenses of her spectacles when last he'd seen her. Temptation? He shook his head against even the remotest possibility of it. "I learned my lesson just how harshly temptation can burn once already, Robert. You can rest assured it is not a thing I will be foolish enough to do twice."

"Augusta, stop squinting. It makes your face look pinched." A momentary pause, and then, "And fix your hair. There's a bit of it coming loose from the pin on top."

Augusta ignored Charlotte's scolding and went on with her study of the crowded assembly room. How she would have preferred staying home tonight. She really didn't want to be here and had only come because of her stepmother's assurances that Almack's was the place everyone in society flocked to each Wednesday evening. She'd thought perhaps she might find the opportunity to speak with the Earl of Belgrace. But they'd already been there an hour and she had yet to recognize the earl among the silk- and satin-trimmed figures struggling for a position of distinction among the rest of the crowd. She glanced to the clock on the wall beside her. There remained only another half of an hour before the doors would close at eleven, after which, Charlotte had advised her, no one—not even the Regent himself—would be allowed inside.

As Augusta stood among the crowd sipping her too-tart lemonade she couldn't help but wonder why acceptance to this place was considered the truest indication of a person's place in society. What made being given the nod to pass through two doors so important? She just couldn't fathom it. All through the previous weekend, Charlotte had been on veritable pins and needles, waiting for Monday to see if she would gain her yearned-for invitation to this exalted domain. She'd had the support of the Ladies Trussington and Finsminster, yes, and she was the wife of a very respected marquess, but that was no guarantee that she would be given the celebrated voucher that would allow her inside.

The Lady Patronesses whose word held sway over these rooms were very strict in their choice of who to allow in, Augusta had been told. No one, it seemed, was immune to being blackballed. One very celebrated duchess had been refused because she had once disagreed with a patroness's opinion of a painting. Thus, after making her application the previous week, by Monday afternoon, Charlotte had worked her nerves to a frazzle, nearly accosting the young boy who had come delivering the anticipated decree informing her of her acceptance. She'd opened it, read it with shaking hands, and then promptly burst into a torrent of tears before ordering a carriage so she could run off to tell everyone the news of her boon.

And now, here they were, in the celebrated Almack's Assembly Rooms. Charlotte was at her most resplendent in the Brierley diamonds and her gown of pale blue silk flounced and shot through with silver threads. It far outshone Augusta's own midnight blue sarcenet, but then Charlotte had spared no modesty for this evening. She had struggled over her ensemble for two days, passing a full four hours that afternoon and early evening in her chamber with Mr. Liviston, leaving Augusta in the hands of her abigail, who, while excellent in her duties to Augusta thus far, didn't quite match Mr. Liviston's skill for the coiffure.

Charlotte had, of course, criticized the end result, but Augusta found she preferred the elegant plaited coronet Mina had arranged atop her head to Mr. Liviston's more elaborately curled styles. And rather than the pearls or other gems Charlotte had attempted to press upon her for the evening, Augusta had chosen instead her own necklace with the star-and-moon pendant her father had given her when she'd been a child. White gloves extended up past her elbows. On her wrist she wore her best beaded reticule, inside which lay hidden the information she hoped to impart to the Earl of Belgrace. If only she could find him . . .

"Augusta," Charlotte called from the small circle of acquaintances she'd accumulated since their arrival, "would you be a dear and fetch me another glass of lemonade from the refreshment table? I find I am somewhat parched."

Augusta looked across the room to where the refreshments were set up just outside the gaming room, the same gaming room where most of the men in attendance could be found to congregate away from this chattering circle of women. An idea struck her. "I'd be happy to get it for you, Charlotte."

Augusta cut her way through the milling crowd, clutching her reticule, all the while searching for the earl. She paused at the refreshment table, taking up a glass of lemonade from it, and peered nonchalantly into the gaming room. The distinct murmur of male conversation could be heard coming from inside. She glanced over to Charlotte who was totally absorbed within her circle. She wondered if Charlotte had even noticed her leave to fetch the lemonade. It didn't appear as if she had and thus she likely wouldn't notice if Augusta slipped into the gaming room for a quick turn about the room . . .

Noah looked up from his cards, somehow knowing even before he saw her that Augusta was there. Still he wasn't prepared for what he saw. It was Lady Augusta, yes, but she looked nothing at all as she had on the previous two occasions he'd seen her. No, tonight, her hair shimmered beneath the light of the candle branches, pulled atop her head in a style that should have been severe, but that only seemed to set off her face and the slender line of her neck to advantage. Small wisps of the black stuff caressed her nape and the pale, pale skin of her shoulders bare above the deep neckline of her dark blue gown.

She didn't wear her spectacles tonight and he watched her eyes, brows slanted, as she glanced about the room, squinting slightly. No doubt she was searching for Belgrace, but with the darkness and her poor eyesight, she would have to be nearly upon him for her to notice him, if he was present at all; Noah hadn't noticed him since arriving.

As he continued to play his hand, Noah kept one eye on Augusta's progress through the room. She spoke to no one, merely watched all that went on around her. And when she had come full circle, she hesitated at the threshold, peering back one last time before exiting through the door.

Noah made to rise from his chair.

"Giving up already, Edenhall?" Christian Wycliffe, Marquess of Knighton and the future Duke of Westover asked.

Christian was what the more romantically inclined young ladies would call "a dashing buck," with his dark hair and silver blue eyes. He was also the heir to the wealthiest man in England, a lethal combination. Christian was a close family friend to both the Devonbrooks and Keighleys, and it was at his town house Sarah was staying while she remained in London, Christian's sister, Eleanor, acting as her companion. After leaving university, Christian's one ambition had been to be a soldier, and he would have made a fine one had his grandfather, the current duke, not seen him refused a commission for the fear that he might not return. Such was the lot of many an heir.

Noah's eyes were still fixed upon the doorway where Augusta had just departed. "I think I've given you enough of my coin for one night, Knighton. It is best to call 'quits' when one still has the shirt on one's back."

As Christian chuckled behind him, Noah stood and made for the door, thinking he would just see what Lady Augusta was up to. He found her standing with her stepmother among a group of society's most prominent ladies, but while the rest of the assembly were engaged in animated conversation, laughing and chattering on, Lady Augusta looked bored to her toes as she stood with them, however at the same time apart from them.

She might appear to be looking on while the dancing and conversation took place around her, but Noah knew she was only interested in one thing. *Belgrace.* He could see her now, scanning the room, searching every face for the earl's. And it was while she was engaged in this study that she spotted Noah. Her eyes locked with his. He smiled and bowed his head to her. Her mouth promptly turned in a frown and she looked away, this time concentrating her attention on the opposite side of the room from where he stood.

Noah did the only thing he could think of; he started toward her.

"Good evening, Lady Augusta," he said, making his leg, bowing before her with a flourish.

He had intended his greeting to be noticed and in this he wasn't disappointed. The conversation of her stepmother and associates immediately silenced. All eyes turned toward the two of them.

Augusta glared at him in irritation, looking sidewise at the others. Why did he seem to turn up wherever she went? "Good evening to you, sir." And then she added smartly, but with a bored yawn, "I'm sorry, but I'm afraid I'm at a loss. Have we met?"

Noah grinned slightly. "Why, yes, my lady, indeed we have, although you might not readily recall it. It was at the Lumley ball on the—"

"Oh, yes," she cut in before he could truly humiliate her,

"you do look somewhat familiar." Her lips pressed firmly together. "It is a pleasure seeing you again."

"In any case," he said, determined to continue their conversation, "we have never been formally introduced." He took her gloved hand, executing a deep bow. "Lord Noah Edenhall at your service."

Augusta wished she could cosh him on the head. Instead she extracted her hand from his as quickly as she could without drawing attention. "Thank you, Lord Noah. It is a pleasure to make your *formal* acquaintance, sir."

She turned to dismiss him. She glanced back once out of the corner of her eye in what would prove a most foolish move.

"Lady Augusta, I was hoping I might beg the honor of the next dance from you? I believe the musicians are just readying for it."

"Thank you, but—"

Suddenly, it was as if a royal fanfare had just sounded for at that moment, the entire room was seized by an anticipatory standstill. Everyone nearby to them snapped to attention. No one moved or made a sound. Some perhaps feared to so much as breathe.

What in heaven's name could be the matter? Augusta wondered, peering to see if someone had perhaps dared attempt to gain entrance after the forbidden eleven o'clock hour. But instead a lady came forward through the crowd. Regal, with the look of haughty disdain she'd perfected, no doubt, since birth, she nodded to a privileged few as she passed. Her gown was a rather peculiar shade, not quite yellow, but then not quite green, and Augusta felt certain she had never seen so many diamonds upon a single person in her life. They circled her neck, drooped from her ears, and even garnished the neckline of her gown. Augusta found it a wonder she could lift her hand at all for the number of bracelets that circled her gloved wrists.

Still she managed, and as she came forward, Noah took her extended hand, bowing his head just as gallantly as he had to Augusta moments before. "Lady Castlereagh, you are looking exceptionally well this evening."

Castlereagh. Augusta recognized the name immediately as that of one of the Lady Patronesses of Almack's who had granted Charlotte the entrance she'd so desperately wanted. She tried to think back on what Charlotte had told her and remembered Lady Castlereagh was not one of the ladies known for her kindness. She could, in fact, in a moment's time have anyone cut from admittance to the assembly rooms with a mere nod of her diamond-studded head.

Augusta glanced over at Charlotte, who was staring at Lady Castlereagh with a mixture of abject fear and veneration. She chanced a glance at Augusta, who because of her proximity to Noah, stood nearer to Lady Castlereagh than anyone else. Charlotte begged Augusta with her eyes not to do anything untoward.

"Lady Castlereagh, allow me to present to you Lady Augusta Brierley," Noah said.

Augusta could have killed him for bringing this supreme woman's notice to her, but now that he had, there was little else she could do other than bow her head and lower into a curtsy. "It is an honor to meet you, Lady Castlereagh."

The lady puffed up her chest, staring at Augusta closely. Augusta felt certain she was about to give the order to have her tossed to the street, for if anyone didn't belong in this exalted sanctum, it was surely she.

But her dismissal did not come. Instead, Lady Castlereagh said, "You are Cyrus Brierley's daughter, are you not?"

Augusta inclined her head. "Yes, my lady, I am Lady

Augusta Brierley. My father, Lord Trecastle, is presently abroad."

"Your mother was Marianne."

Augusta lifted her eyes at the unexpected mention of her mother's name. "Yes, my lady, she was. Did you know her?"

The Lady Patroness's mouth turned in a slight smile, something Augusta would guess she rarely if ever did. "Yes, I knew Marianne. Knew her very well. She was a true lady in every sense of the word."

"I'm afraid I did not know her very long. She died when I was but a child."

Lady Castlereagh nodded. "You look very much like her." She grasped Augusta's wrist with one hand then, and Lord Noah's with the other. "Come. I believe this fine young gentleman was begging the honor of a dance with you. I have detained you too long."

And thus there was no choice left for Augusta other than to dance—with him.

"I believe they were just readying for a quadrille," Lady Castlereagh said, and even if the musicians hadn't been, they certainly were now. "Let us just hope we can keep Lord Tilbury from attempting another entrechat and repeating his disastrous display from Wednesday last."

The quadrille. Augusta stopped dead even before she reached the dancing area. It was a newer dance and she had heard it described as one of the more difficult to execute. It had first been introduced at these very rooms, making it the dance of choice from that moment on. And Augusta had no earthly idea how to make a single step of it.

Prepare yourself, Charlotte. You are about to lose your precious subscription.

"My lady, I must beg you—"

"Lady Castlereagh," Noah said before Augusta could finish voicing her humiliation, "Lady Augusta was telling me she had hoped instead to dance a waltz. She has only just learned and has not yet had the opportunity to try her steps away from her tutor's eye."

Lady Castlereagh gave Noah a curious look. "Indeed." She hesitated a moment and then turned back toward the dancing area. "Then a waltz it shall be," she said loud enough to give the musicians in the balcony above her head the cue to change their sheet music once again. And then she turned and added, more quietly this time, "You certainly have a penchant for setting tongues to wagging, my boy. You are just fortunate I am so very fond of your brother's wife."

Noah grinned. "And Catriona returns your regard twofold, my lady."

Lady Castlereagh broke into another rare smile and left them, standing alone, in the middle of the vast dancing area.

Noah looked at Augusta. "Are you ready, my lady?"

She quickly looped her train over her arm in the way Charlotte had instructed her. "I don't know whether to thank you or scorn you. I'm afraid I am as unfamiliar with the waltz as I am with the quadrille."

Noah set his arm lightly around her waist, taking her hand with his other. "Just follow my steps and you will do fine."

Augusta glanced around his shoulder at the empty dance floor. "Why is no one else preparing to dance?"

"They will, after we have begun and taken several turns. Unfortunately Lady Castlereagh's invitation for us to dance is an exclusive one. It is ordained that we must open the floor alone."

The musicians began and Augusta immediately dropped her head to study Noah's feet.

"Therein lies the path to certain disaster," Noah said to

her, squeezing her hand so that she would look up at him again. "Now keep your eyes on my eyes and allow me to do the rest."

"I am doomed," Augusta said as she made her first turn and felt the toe of Noah's boot under her slipper. She wondered if the Lady Patronesses held the power to exclude someone from the entire city of London as well. One thing was for certain; Charlotte would never forgive her this.

But into the second turn of the dance, Augusta had completely forgotten about the vacant dance floor, her stepmother, and, for that matter, Lady Castlereagh as well. In fact she barely even heard the music as she moved across the room in step with Noah. Somehow, by looking into his hazel-colored eyes she had discovered the ability to dance, to move with him in perfect time with the music, something she had rarely ever attempted for she'd never thought to need it.

All while they danced, Noah never took his eyes from hers and the power she recognized there held her spellbound. It was the same power she had felt that night in the garden. Through each movement of the waltz, they swayed and turned about the floor as if borne on the wind, just the two of them.

Who was this man? she couldn't help but think. *And why did he seem to want to seek her out?* She would never consider that anyone could have an interest in her, at least not in the ways a man was interested in a woman. And certainly not this man in particular, a man who really was incredibly handsome and likely could have half the female population of London at his disposal. And yet ever since the Lumley ball, whenever she turned around, he seemed to be there. Almost as if he were watching her every move. Almost as if he suspected her secret . . .

The music came to a finish and with it their dance. The spell that had given her feet grace had been broken. Augusta glanced around them and saw there were still no other dancers on the floor, and those looking on from the fringes of the room suddenly began to applaud. Augusta felt her face color at having the scrutiny of every pair of eyes in the room upon her as she stood before this man, wondering who he was, wondering more how much he knew about her.

What if he knew the truth? What if . . . ? Augusta was suddenly seized by the need to get away—from him and from everyone else in this room.

"Thank you, Lord Noah. That was most enjoyable, but I am afraid I am a bit winded and would like to take a rest now."

"Can I fetch you a glass of lemonade? While tasteless, it might at least serve to refresh you."

"Yes, thank you. That would be nice."

Only I will not be here when you return with it, Augusta thought, turning for Charlotte, who stood waiting for her at the side of the dance floor.

"Augusta, you shock me. I never knew you could dance like that. And how you impressed Lady Castlereagh, but perhaps next time you might find the opportunity to introduce me to—"

"I must leave, Charlotte."

"Leave? Whyever for? They have only just closed the doors. The evening has just begun . . ."

Augusta searched and spotted Lord Noah at the drinks table, readying to return to her with the lemonade. "I am sorry, but I cannot stay. I do not wish to spoil your special evening; I know how much this means to you, so please you must remain and enjoy the benefits of your subscription. I will have the doorman call a hackney to take me home. It isn't a far drive. I will be very safe."

She turned before Charlotte could make any protest and cut through the crowd toward the door—and escape.

Noah took up two glasses of lemonade from the drinks table and made to return to Augusta. But when he looked to where he had left her, she had gone. Vanished. He skirted around the edge of the drinks table and nearly collided with Eleanor Wycliffe, Christian's sister. Standing beside her was Sarah. Both women were staring at him.

"Eleanor. Sarah. I wasn't aware you were going to be coming to the assembly rooms this evening."

Eleanor looked confused. "Do you mean to say Christian didn't tell you?"

"No, he did not." As a matter of fact, Noah thought to himself, Christian had not made a mention of it through the several hands of whist they'd played.

"Well, I thought it might do Sarah some good to get back out among society. Isolation can be recuperative, but too much of it can also prove unhealthy."

"Very true," Noah said, handing the glasses of lemonade to Eleanor so that he could take Sarah's hand. He kissed it lightly. "You are looking better each time I see you," he said.

Sarah colored above the modest neckline of her black bombazine gown from his praise. "Thank you, Noah. I was hoping you would still be here tonight. I know I'm not supposed to dance while I am in mourning for Tony, but I so hoped we might have a chance to visit a bit. I haven't seen you very much of late . . ."

A stab of guilt went through Noah at both her words and the look of loneliness that shone in her delicate blue eyes. He had been so involved with discovering Augusta's identity, and then trying to figure her out, he had been neglecting Sarah. He would have to make it a point to pay a regular visit to Sarah each week so that she didn't feel so abandoned and alone in her new world. Eleanor was right. Sarah had spent far too much time indoors, isolated from the rest of the world.

"How would you two ladies feel about a drive along Rotten Row with me tomorrow?" he asked, ready to say anything to take the shadowed darkness from her eyes.

Sarah's face immediately lit. "I would love to." She hesitated. "But would it be considered proper?"

"Of course it would," Eleanor broke in. "I'll even convince Christian to come along and we can make a picnic of it. I'll ask the cook to pack us a basket. What a splendid idea!"

Chapter Thirteen

If it were possible for one to actually die of boredom, Augusta was surely as near as she now could be to the hereafter.

She was seated in the morning parlor at the sunny eastern side of Lady Finsminster's town house on Cavendish Square in a chair that had surely been intended as a torture device. In this chair, she had spent the past hour studying the intricate pattern decorating the rim of her feldspar porcelain teacup and saucer. The hour prior to that she had memorized the sequence of the cherubs frolicking across the carved wood *boiserie,* convinced they were laughing at her, although it could be that the overpoweringly sweet scent coming from the countess's silver pastille burner was somehow making her giddy.

In any case, with no other amusement left to her, she turned her contemplation to the placement of the tea leaves at the bottom of her cup, wondering what it might spell for her future. Across the room, Charlotte and her associates were busy chattering endlessly about dress patterns and fabrics and coiffures and every other subject of feminine interest—subjects in which Augusta had no interest at all.

In attendance this fine morning were the Countess Finsminster, of course, and her daughter, Lady Viviana Finsminster—or "Bibi" as her mother persisted in calling her, a name which curiously made one somehow take full notice of the girl's carroty orange hair and freckle-dotted face. Dressed in lime green sarcenet gowns which were exact copies of one another, the two comprised the lower end of the rounded Turkish ottoman sofa that filled the center of the room. Seated to their right were the Countess Trussington, in pale lilac muslin, and Charlotte, in her newly acquired cherry-and-rose silk, while the Viscountess Gunther sat in yellow, with daughter Prudence in sky blue, completing the color spectrum at the opposite side.

Augusta, whose addition to the gathering had presented the countess with her six-seat couch with somewhat of a dilemma, had taken the single parlor chair nearest to the windows, across from the others and far enough away to have spared her any real involvement in their conversation.

But that hadn't stopped them.

Immediately upon their arrival, the congregation had ritually taken turns complimenting one another on their respective ensembles—their hair, even their gloves.

Until they'd gotten to Augusta, of course.

Her simple gown of beige and cream had been the lightest one she owned, but it was a pale bit of reedy grass when compared to the colorful pastel arrangement of the other blossoms in the parlor garden. Still, they had managed approval of her hair, calling the simple style Mina had arranged it in "quaint" and "well-suited to the shape of her eyes."

And then the prattle had begun, into which they had attempted to introduce Augusta by occasionally asking such things as "Wouldn't you agree, Lady Augusta?" or "Haven't you found it to be so?" Augusta would always nod her head even though she rarely knew what it was she was agreeing with, and instead occupied herself with thoughts of computing precisely how many more minutes it would take before they might exhaust every topic of conversation left available to them. They'd already covered the various patterns of stitchery and had effectively settled the debate of whether a shawl was deemed a proper article of evening attire or not. What else could they possibly have left to discuss?"

"Lady Augusta," Lady Finsminster said then, catching Augusta in midyawn. "I was quite surprised to see you dancing with young Edenhall the other evening at Almack's."

She paused. The other ladies peered covertly over their teacups at her. "I hadn't realized he'd returned to Town after the events of last year, nor had I realized that you had been introduced to one another."

"Yes, my lady," was her response, a polite one that offered absolutely nothing to perpetuate the conversation. She peered at the toe of her slipper resting on the Kidderminster carpet.

Lady Finsminster, however, wasn't discouraged.

"Fine family, Edenhall. I knew the duchess"—she cleared her throat meaningfully—"the previous duchess, of course. Knew her very well indeed; she was the mother of the present duke and your Lord Noah."

Augusta opened her mouth, readying to inform the countess that he wasn't "her Lord Noah" at all, but the farthest thing from it. She never succeeded, though, in getting the words out before Lady Gunther broke in with a comment of her own.

"Yes, I was acquainted with the duchess as well. Strove always to keep her family free from any trouble, she did, even though her husband, the old duke, was a bit of an odd sort. Still, despite even recent events, the Devonbrooks do seem able to rise above any touch of scandal."

Charlotte wasted no time in snatching onto that tidbit, or one of the fresh lemon biscuits just placed before her by the countess's serving maid. "Recent events? Scandal?" she in-quired, taking a quick nibble.

The assembly of ladies turned collectively toward her, to which Charlotte replied with a modest smile flecked by bis-cuit crumbs, "As you know Augusta had been abroad for some time before taking up residence in London and so would know nothing of these events you speak of. Given their, a, 'acquaintanceship,' she should be apprised."

"Certainly she should," Lady Trussington said, stepping in. She quickly adjusted her skirts. "And thus it is our duty to counsel her."

Counsel? Augusta furrowed her brow. Surely not.

The others quickly murmured in agreement.

Augusta attempted to dissuade them. "You are all much too kind, but it really isn't necessary—"

"Well, of course, first there was the fire."

That was all it took. The conversation headed off, most everyone having completely forgotten Augusta as they clustered together on the Turkish sofa.

"Fire?"

"Oh, yes, dear. Utterly destroyed the family's hereditary seat in Lancashire, and under very mysterious circum-stances. Of course the house is being rebuilt now and with no expense spared by the present duke, I might add. Oddly enough, it was the present duke who was at first suspected of having set the fire, in order to assume the title that would have naturally gone to his elder brother, who along with their father perished in the fire. It was indeed a tragedy."

Charlotte was leaning so far forward, pitched at the very edge of her seat, that Augusta feared she might actually topple. Her eyes were fixed with fascination. "How truly terrible."

"Yes, well it would have been," Lady Trussington went on, "had he not been cleared of the suspicion when it was discovered that the fire had actually been set by a careless valet."

"So the duke's reputation was restored?"

"Yes, but then there was his marriage," Lady Finsminster broke in with a knowing nod. Beside her, her daughter Bibi matched the gesture to perfection.

"The valet was married?" Augusta tossed in, unable to resist.

The countess never caught on. "Oh, no, dear, I am speaking instead of the marriage of the present duke. You see, after the fire, His Grace vanished from all good society, removing himself to the remotest part of Scotland, no one knew where. It was while he was away there that he met the present duchess, Catriona."

Somehow Augusta knew there must be more. There just had to be, and she wasn't left long waiting.

"Raised as a crofter, the duchess was."

Charlotte was aghast. "A crofter?"

"Yes, and another tragedy it was for she was truly an heiress!"

Charlotte somehow managed to lean yet a bit further forward. "An heiress? Are you certain?"

"Oh, yes, and a lovely girl she is," Lady Trussington added, no doubt fearing retribution should it be learned she had besmirched the name of a duchess. "They now have a son—the Devonbrook heir—and are quite the picture of happiness. Oh, how he dotes on his duchess, the duke does."

The others responded with a collective "Ahh."

"Of course it was the more recent scandal that was nearly the undoing of the Devonbrooks," Lady Gunther injected.

The others nodded. Charlotte looked as if she might surely burst from anticipation. Augusta, on the other hand, had very little interest in discussing the misfortunes of others. She returned her attentions to the tea leaves as the viscountess went on.

"And it was this scandal that involved Lord Noah—and a duel."

"A duel!" Charlotte exclaimed. "Do tell!"

"Well, it is truly a tragic tale. You see, Lord Noah had contracted a marriage with Lady Julia Grey, daughter of the Earl of Delbridge. A brilliant match, advantageous to both, and they made a most handsome couple. It was to be the wedding of this past Season—until the duel, that is. The events surrounding it all are as yet uncertain, but what is known is that Lord Noah met Sir Spencer Atherton at dawn over pistols to satisfy an affront to the honor of Lady Julia. When all was said and done, Atherton was left horribly scarred and Lord Noah walked away from both society and his betrothal."

Charlotte's mouth fell open in shock. "Unthinkable! No gentleman can break an engagement!"

"Whyever not?"

All heads turned toward Augusta, six pairs of eyes staring at her in openmouthed disbelief. She hadn't wanted to take part in the conversation at all, and even now wondered what had induced her speak.

Charlotte shook her head pitifully. "Augusta dear, it simply isn't done. Once a betrothal announcement is made, only the lady of the two may declare it broken. Never the gentleman."

"Surely you are mistaken."

"Oh, no, dear," Lady Finsminster said, "I assure you it is quite true. The honor of any gentleman who sought to break an engagement would surely be called to question. And Lord Noah was no exception to this rule, but then he is a Devonbrook, and Devonbrooks have a way of resurrecting themselves from scandal. Even a scandal as shocking as this one eventually turned out to be."

"What happened next?" Charlotte asked.

Lady Finsminster started to answer, then glanced over at her daughter. "Bibi dear, why don't you take Prudence out to the conservatory to see the primroses? They are in bloom now and truly lovely."

"But, Mama . . ."

"Bibi." The countess's tone was markedly sterner this time. "The primroses."

What she was preparing to say was obviously not something someone of Bibi, or Prudence's sensibilities should hear. Her concern, unfortunately, did not extend to Augusta, who thought even primroses preferable to this conversation.

Bibi stood from her seat, carroty curls bouncing, hesitating long enough for a pout to form on her lower lip before motioning for Prudence to follow her toward the garden door. When they were safely out of earshot, Lady Finsminster resumed her conversation, her voice lowered to a discreet whisper now. "It was rumored that Lady Julia was with child."

Charlotte gasped, pressing a hand to her breast, hardly able to contain herself. "Lord Noah walked out on the marriage and his child! The blackguard!"

"One might have thought as much," Lady Trussington said, "but not so. I have heard it reported that the child was born not four months ago quite fair-haired and very markedly in possession of the trademark Atherton blue-green eyes."

This final statement sent everyone else to gasping. Charlotte collapsed back in her seat as if she'd just climbed three flights of stairs at a dead run. In the time since Augusta had known her, she had never seen her stepmother at a loss for words. Until now.

Finally, Charlotte managed to find her tongue. "Lady Julie had played Lord Noah false with Atherton."

"Indeed. Lady Julia is of course completely ruined. A favorable opinion of her character is unrecoverable after something like this. She can never be received among good society again. I have heard that her father is attempting to wed her off to an Italian *comte* even now, increasing her dowry to monumental proportions in hopes of better convincing the prospective bridegroom to agreement. The child has been left to be raised *incognito* by poorer relations in the country. And Atherton, well, he is no better off, of course, with his dishonor indelibly marked across his face by Lord Noah's pistol shot. No principled parent would so much as consider allowing their daughter to wed him."

A momentary silence followed while the ladies all digested the substantial conversation. Having been force-fed her fill, Augusta readied to stand, to signal to Charlotte that she had exceeded her obligation to their agreement and it was past time they left. Lady Trussington, however, spoke out then, stopping her cold.

"Lord Noah, on the other hand, has seen his honor restored, at least to most. A gentleman who survived the treachery and betrayal of a faithless lady, he will emerge a truly romantic figure. Every eligible young miss in Town will be seeking to mend his broken heart. And with all that Devonbrook wealth, every regardful mother will, too. Securing him would be quite an accomplishment. In fact, I believe I will invite him to the assembly we are hosting. So you see, you couldn't ask for a better connection than to the Devonbrook title, Lady Augusta."

Augusta stood then, placing her teacup gently on the table beside her. "Well, I would certainly thank you, my

lady, if that were my true ambition. However, I am not looking for a connection to the Devonbrook title. I am not looking
for a connection to any title." She paused, making certain all
attentions were focused on her, before adding, "I have come
to the decision that I shall never marry."

And at that, the room fell silent for the first time that
morning.

The party set out for the park at midday, Sarah and
Eleanor Wycliffe seated opposite each other in the
Knighton barouche, while Christian and Noah rode on
horseback alongside as they tooled their way along the
sandy track running through Hyde Park known to most as
"Rotten Row."

It was a fine day, after several dampened by rain, and so
already this early before the fashionable five o'clock hour,
the park was bustling with carriages and riders. Ladies rode
in the two-seated vis-à-vis accompanied by liveried footmen or some instead on horseback, always sidesaddle. Gentlemen turned out in their finest striped waistcoats, strutting
proudly about on their high-stepping mounts, while their
children, dressed equally as finely, pranced behind on spir-
ited ponies. It was the grandest parade to be had in London.

As he came under a cherry tree, Noah reached up and
plucked a small spray of the snow white blossoms, trotting
over to the carriage to bestow them gallantly on Sarah who,
in turn, beamed under his attentions. She looked better than
he had seen her look since that horrible morning when he'd
had to deliver her the news of Tony's death. Her color had
improved and a light had returned to her eyes that he hoped
never to see gone again.

They settled on a peaceful spot away from the rest of the
populace beneath an ancient-looking willow near a small
pond littered with lily pads. While Eleanor directed the ser-

vants where to spread out the blanket, Sarah began removing the various wrapped foods from the baskets they'd brought along. Christian and Noah took a moment to walk together to the edge of the pond.

"She loves you, you know," Christian said, looking back to Sarah, who waved cheerfully to them. He turned, taking up a flat stone and skimmed it easily across the still surface of the water, sending small ripples drifting to the pond's edge.

"I know." Noah replied, staring at the ground and frowning in his admission.

Christian stared at him. "Listen, if you want me to keep out of this, just say so."

"No, that isn't it, Christian. I have nothing to hide, especially from you. Sarah's a sweet girl. I've known her nearly all my life and there isn't a day that I don't hear Tony's voice in my mind telling me to marry her, but . . ." He hesitated, struggling to put his feelings to the words that would best explain.

"But you don't love her," Christian finished for him.

Noah looked up, frowning. "No, I don't. I've tried, but I can't get beyond friendship to anything even close to love. And then I find myself asking just how many marriages actually are based upon love."

"Your brother's marriage is the only one I know of." Christian shook his head. "And I'm certainly not the one to ask on that score, my friend. With my position, my family, I'll be fortunate if I so much as see a likeness of my future wife before the contracts are signed. My grandfather would wed me to a horse if he thought it advantageous."

Noah regarded his friend. Christian Wycliffe was the sole heir to a ducal fortune, a fortune currently controlled by the present duke of Westover, his grandfather. Most everyone knew of the power the old man held over Christian's future. It was a fact Christian had been forced to accept, like a bitter swallow, even though he hated it. Every decision in his upbringing, his friends, the skills he'd pursued, even the subjects he'd studied at university, everything had been decided for him by the old duke. And it was a fact of his life Christian could never change for his hands were unequivocally tied, both financially by his grandfather who controlled the future of his inheritance and emotionally as well, by the memory of his dead father. It had been his father's last wish to his son that he carry on in his place, that he make the Westover title what he himself had not been given the chance to in his short lifetime before his illness had taken him from his family. It was an obligation that Christian had no choice but to fulfill.

So while many might envy Christian his birthright—the wealth, the prestige—few others knew the terrible price that came along with it. And that was the price of Christian's freedom.

Noah kicked at a blade of grass with the polished toe of his Hessian. "Before last year, before I met Julia, I'd have sworn never to wed unless I truly loved the woman who would be my wife. And then I did just that. I fell in love passionately and completely and it ended in sheer disaster. I swore just a handful of months ago that I would never marry. And then Tony died and now I find myself torn. Sarah has nothing. I am all she has left. I'm fond of Sarah and we get on well enough."

"And there are a number of marriages who cannot hope to claim that."

Noah nodded. "Yes, but then another part of me cannot overlook the fact that she should spend her life with someone who will worship her and love her fervently, not someone who simply regards her amicably."

Christian tossed another stone, evicting a frog from his lily-pad perch. "Then why don't you find Sarah a husband?"

Noah looked at his friend, smiling. "Are you applying for the post?"

"If it weren't beyond my capabilities, I might. Sarah is a sweet girl and it would be a match on a better scale than I might one day find myself in. However, we both know the fact of that matter is my grandfather would never stand for it. You see I am destined to wed a girl of fortune, whose family can trace back no less then ten generations. A connection to Henry VIII would help, for Grandfather has a special regard for Old Hank. But consider this: other than the other night at Almack's, Sarah has never been taken out among society. She's been hidden away at Keighley Cross all these years, dreaming of only one possible mate—you. Now, while you are certainly a fine choice, she can have no idea of what else might await her. She's a lovely girl and accomplished in all the best feminine arts. She's certain to inspire someone to poetry, even someone who'll be willing to overlook her lack of a dowry. And perhaps, once she is out among other young bucks, she'll lose her girlhood infatuation for you. Between the two of us, we can drop enough hints among certain circles to encourage an interest in her. Word of mouth is a powerful tool. Sarah's own looks and personality will do the rest."

Noah weighed Christian's words. It wasn't an idea totally without merit. In fact, when one got right down to considering it, it could be the solution to all his problems. If he could see Sarah safely and happily wed, he could then rest assured knowing he had done everything for her that he could. His own private obligation he felt to Tony's memory would be fulfilled. Except for one final matter . . .

. . . the Keighley brooch.

But if he had anything to do with it, Sarah would have that as well.

"Sarah must never know of it," he said.

"Of course not. She would be crushed and worse, she would resent you for attempting to bring it about. She is too young, too naive to understand."

Settled in their plan, the two men returned to the ladies and the waiting picnic luncheon, eating and chatting pleasantly through the next three-quarters of an hour. The sun had risen high, filtering down softly through the leaves of the willow above them. Song thrushes chirped happily from the branches, filling the air with their avian merriment. Christian and Eleanor were seeing the baskets returned to the carriage and Sarah had gone off to the pond to toss some leftover crusts to the ducks. Noah took a moment to lean back against the willow's trunk, closing his eyes as he mentally tallied a list of eligible suitors for Sarah. He didn't even hear Sarah approach until she spoke.

"Isn't that the lady you were dancing with at Almack's the other evening?"

Noah opened his eyes, shielding them against the sunlight as he looked in the direction she pointed. It was indeed Lady Augusta, for although he couldn't see her face beneath the veiled hat she wore, he recognized her curiously colored horse as she trotted across the adjacent field.

"Lady? I do not recall anyone in particular."

Still he stood, watching as Lady Augusta disappeared through a break in the trees. Somehow he knew she was going to meet Belgrace.

"How would you like an ice, Sarah?"

"Oh, that isn't necessary. Really, Noah."

"Nonsense. It is a warm day and I think an ice would be the perfect ending to our picnic. I know of a place where a vendor always sets up to sell them near the park's entrance. It will only take me a moment or two to fetch them."

Sarah watched him as he made for Humphrey, who stood happily munching a tuft of grass nearby. "If you insist."

He had already swung himself into the saddle and was heading off toward the break in the trees where Lady Augusta had vanished moments earlier—in the opposite direction from the park entrance. So intent was he in his pursuit, he never noticed Sarah's frown.

As he came through the trees, Noah searched the isolated glade for Augusta. She couldn't have gone far; there really was nowhere else for her to go to, other than a small secluded embankment that lay beside the pond beyond the tree line.

And that is precisely where he spotted her as he drew nearer. She was standing at the water's edge, contemplating the pattern of the lily pads, completely unaware of his approach behind her.

Finally she looked up from her study when he was nearly upon her. He noticed then she wore the hat he'd sent her, its dark veil pulled down to shield her face. Thus he could not see her expression when she noticed him; it mattered naught for he soon heard well enough her reaction.

"Please go away, sir."

Noah ignored her plea and dropped down from the saddle, walking to her. "And miss the chance to admire the hat I sent to you? I had begun to wonder if you had received it at all."

Lady Augusta lifted the veil to reveal underneath a very cross expression, her brows narrowed behind her spectacles. "Well, as you can see I did indeed receive it. I thank you for replacing the one you in fact ruined. It was very courteous of you to do so."

Noah smiled, but didn't abandon his approach. "You vanished the other night without saying good night."

"Really? I thought I had." When she saw he was making no appearance of leaving, she said, "Well then, I apologize for the oversight." She inclined her head. "Good night, Lord Noah. And good-bye."

Noah didn't budge. "For someone who didn't know the steps of the waltz, you danced very well."

She wouldn't look at him. "I think you must have consumed one too many glasses of punch, my lord. I was about as graceful as a cob horse."

Noah didn't rise to her retort. Instead he just stared at her.

Sensing his scrutiny, Augusta measured a quick glance toward him, and then looked to the break in the trees. Why would he not leave? She had sent a note to the earl very early that morning beseeching him one more time to meet with her here in private. She had purposely misled him, too, giving indication that what she had to speak with him about had something to do with her father. Augusta didn't much like deceiving Lord Belgrace, but she knew of no other way to induce him to the park. She had to speak with him and very soon, before the time she had left to her ran out. She knew he would come. What she hadn't counted on was the interference once again of Lord Noah Edenhall. She was beginning to wonder if the man wasn't following her. She needed to get rid of him quickly and before the earl arrived.

"Pray forgive me for speaking bluntly, Lord Noah, but I must ask that you return to wherever it was you were before you came here. I wish to be alone. I've some thinking to do and that is never a very productive enterprise when one is accompanied."

He wasn't dissuaded. "On my honor as a gentleman I could not possibly leave you now, my lady, and especially at this part of the park. These woods are very often the haunt for footpads and the like. You could easily be set upon by bandits. My conscience could never willingly allow any lady to come to harm when I might do anything to prevent it."

Augusta sucked in an impatient breath before pressing on. "I assure you I am quite safe, sir. There are nothing except the songbirds and pond fish anywhere in the vicinity."

He wasn't moving. "Perhaps now it is so, but one can never know when a footpad might happen upon a poor helpless lady."

Helpless? She frowned. "I prefer to take my chances—alone, sir."

Noah nodded. "Certainly, my lady. If solitude is what you wish then I shall willingly remove myself to that tree stump over there, far enough away to afford you privacy for your contemplation, but near enough that I might still spring to action should the need arise."

And before Augusta could respond, he tromped across the embankment to the very stump he'd pointed out that stood just inside the entrance where the trees broke. He made quite an effort of lifting his coattails before lowering himself to sit, crossing his booted legs at the ankles before him. Augusta just stared at him. He gave a little wave. She frowned and crossed her arms over her chest, wishing for a sizeable rock to hurl at his head.

Moments later she heard the sound of another rider approaching, a rider dressed all in black, his face obscured behind the wide brim of his hat. He halted just inside the break in the trees when he spotted her there—and with her Lord Noah still occupying his place on the stump. It was Lord Belgrace and he promptly turned about, heading off in the opposite direction. He was gone just as quickly as he had appeared.

Augusta was so angry, she wanted to scream. Instead she watched, furious inside, as Noah stood from his stump and retraced his steps to her. "That was indeed fortunate for if ever a figure appeared nefarious, it was he."

Augusta didn't offer a response. Instead she spun about and walked over to where Atalanta stood waiting for her. Perhaps, if she hurried, she might catch up with the earl before he left the park. It would be difficult for she had no idea in which direction he'd gone. Still she must try. She mounted quickly, using the stump Noah had been sitting on as a mounting block, and then trotted off, holding in check the profound desire to run down the irksome Lord Noah Edenhall as she passed.

Chapter Fourteen

By the time the next sunrise peeked over the tranquil tree-tops of Bryanstone Square, the world as Augusta had known it ceased to exist.

In its place had emerged absolute bedlam.

The first indication of it was the appearance of Charlotte at Augusta's bedchamber door. Augusta had just awoken and was in the process of arranging her hair into its more practical knot when she caught a glimpse of her step-mother's figure lingering in the doorway. She took a second glance to make certain it was, indeed, Charlotte, for something was curiously different about her. The marchioness was still. She was silent. She wasn't storming in to bemoan the miserable state of her existence. Instead Charlotte was grinning ear to ear quite like Circe whenever she caught one of the garden mice, only the moment she noticed Augusta looking at her in the reflection of the mirror, Charlotte burst all at once into a chaos of words, racing forward to take Augusta by the hand.

"Augusta! Oh! Thank heaven you are awake. I have been completely overset all day. You will not believe it. It is just too inconceivable to be believed! I would not be believing it if I hadn't seen it for my own eyes!"

Augusta froze in her chair. "What is it? Has something happened? Something with Papa? Has he returned from abroad?"

Charlotte fluttered her hand, laughing gaily. "Oh, good heavens, no, my dear." She reached forward to adjust the lapel on Augusta's straw-colored poplin day jacket, a motherly sort of gesture entirely out of character for her. It brought Augusta to wondering if she had perhaps been tippling too much of the Madeira. As if to credit the thought even more, Charlotte reached down, scooping Circe from the carpet, and began *willingly* to scratch the cat behind her ears. Augusta simply stared. Had someone taken off her stepmother, only to leave behind this thoroughly agreeable model in her place?

She turned to face the marchioness, her face set soberly. "Something has happened, Charlotte, and I insist that you tell me, no matter what it might be, bad or good."

Charlotte even then continued stroking her fingers through the cat's thick black fur. "Yes, something has indeed happened." She looked over to Augusta and smiled. "It is you, Augusta dear. *You* have happened. I am happy to say that your secret has finally been discovered."

Augusta felt a rush of pure ice run along her spine. Her secret? Discovered? Good God, she prayed she'd heard Charlotte wrongly. "I—"—she cleared her throat of the lump that had formed in it—"I beg your pardon?"

"It is as I said, Augusta. You are *it. The thing.* You have become a sensation and you have done it virtually overnight. Since your dance with Lord Noah Edenhall, and acceptance by Lady Castlereagh at Almack's, everybody now knows who you are. What is more they have come to worship at your feet. The knocker has not stopped all morning. Letters, invitations, packages, even callers have come, all for you. It is not to be believed."

Augusta shook her head, struggling to follow through all of Charlotte's babble. "I have received a caller?"

"Depend upon it, my dear. Several. One gentleman in particular awaits in the parlor."

A gentleman caller? For her? Who on earth could it—?

Belgrace. Of course, it had to be him. After their failed attempts at meeting elsewhere, he had decided to come directly to her, a thing allowable for a gentleman, but unthinkable for a lady. The frustration which had followed her home from the park after their last failed meeting and which had kept her from her work the night before instantly vanished as Augusta turned from her bedchamber, heading for the parlor and the waiting earl.

Finally, she thought as she skimmed the steps to the lower floor, finally the waiting would be over. He was here and she would now have what she had waited for so long. . . .

"I hope you haven't been kept waiting too long, my lord. I—"

Only it wasn't the Earl of Belgrace whom she found waiting for her in the parlor. It was someone else entirely, indeed a gentleman who stood and smiled warmly to her.

Augusta stared silently at her visitor. He was an older man, not overly so, perhaps forty. Dressed in a very distinguished suit of clothes, he stood tall and slender. His eyes had a certain kindness about them and he smiled as he came forward to bow over her hand in greeting.

"My dear Lady Augusta, thank you so much for receiving me on this fine day."

At first she didn't recognize him, but then she vaguely recalled having been introduced to him before—where had it been? And then she remembered—it had been at the Lumley ball the previous week when she'd been in the company of Lords Mundrum, Yarlett, and Everton. "It is Lord Peversley, isn't it?"

He seemed flattered that she'd remembered him, nodding. "I hope my visit hasn't disturbed you."

Instead of responding, Augusta narrowed her eyes curiously. Why was this man, a marquess, calling upon her? They had only just met in passing that evening and hadn't seen each other since. But hadn't Lord Yarlett said something about the marquess being a close acquaintance of the Earl of Belgrace? Augusta smiled. Of course. Now it made perfect sense. Belgrace had sent Peversley in his stead to avoid any hint of calumny. Perfect sense, indeed.

"Oh, no, my lord, you have not disturbed me at all. Your visit is a most pleasant and unexpected surprise." She noticed Charlotte standing in the doorway, listening to the exchange. "Can my stepmother offer you tea?"

Lord Peversley smiled and winked at her before peering at Charlotte. "Oh, no, my thanks for the offer, but I really cannot stay. I had come in the hopes that I might persuade you to take a turn with me in my landau in the park tomorrow at midday." He glanced at Charlotte once again. "Your lovely stepmother, of course, would accompany us."

"We would be delighted, my lord," Charlotte crowed in, even before Augusta could respond. Augusta shot her a glance.

The marquess took Augusta's hand then, pressing a kiss to it before departing. He whispered to her, "I believe I have something to tell you that you could find most beneficial."

She stared at him. She had assumed right. Lord Belgrace had sent him here, for what else could be the man's meaning? And how very clever of the earl to take the matter of their meeting into his own hands, arranging it so that Lord Peversley might occupy Charlotte while he and Augusta met in private. What an ingenious plan!

Augusta smiled to the marquess, inclining her head in silent accord. "Tomorrow then, my lord."

"I shall count the moments until we meet again," Lord Peversley said before taking his leave with a gallant bow.

Charlotte saw the marquess to the door and then rushed back to Augusta in the parlor. "To think, you—we are going out driving with a marquess. And not just any marquess, but Peversley." She fanned herself. "I would that he had arranged the drive closer to five o'clock, when the park will be teeming, but what's done is done and all that. Oh, a marquess. The Marquess of Peversley. He would be quite a conquest, Augusta."

But Augusta was too involved with taking in the room around her, the number of packages placed upon the side tables, the flowers which abounded from every available bowl and vase, to have even registered Charlotte's enthusiasm.

"What has happened here?"

"Oh, isn't is simply marvelous? It is as I told you, Augusta. These are all for you, my dear. Tokens from your many admirers."

Admirers? Augusta slipped on her spectacles to get a better view. What she saw was most peculiar. Roses, daisies, hothouse blooms, nearly everywhere she looked there were flowers, and where there weren't, there were packages, some brightly decorated, some wrapped in delivery paper. She'd never seen anything like it in her life. "Surely you are mistaken."

"Not at all, my dear. Nor can I be mistaken about these." Charlotte held out a stack of correspondence, invitations, and letters inches thick, placing them before Augusta on the calamander wood sofa table. An ornamented silver bowl filled with numerous calling cards, many with corners ticked, already was there. "It would seem you made quite an impression on society at Almack's the other evening."

Augusta thumbed through the letters, scanning the numerous invitations to events being held for weeks to come as well as the more personal solicitations offering a ride in any number of carriages, visits to the theater, museums, most every diversion London could offer, every one of them geared to turn a young lady's fancy. But instead of naming Charlotte as the addressee, as was usual, each of these begged acceptance from *Lady Augusta Brierley.*

Convinced that this was all some terrible misunderstanding, Augusta looked up at Charlotte, who was standing there watching her and beaming. Tears had even formed at the corner of her eyes.

She clapped her hands. "You are a success, Augusta. I know it is difficult to believe, but just look around yourself at the number of gifts already arrived from your admirers. I knew it all along. All you needed to do was apply yourself like I have told you. Oh, your father will be so proud."

Augusta ignored her and went over to the side table, where a good number of the packages had been stacked. She removed the lid on the first beribboned box to reveal a small, elegantly carved silver trinket box. When she lifted the lid she found tucked away inside a litter of pale pink rose petals that instantly filled her senses with sweet perfume. Beneath the petals lay a small note which read, "With my undying esteem." It was signed by a man whose name she had never before heard. Undying esteem? And she didn't even know who he was?

Other packages revealed similar tokens; fine stationery, ornamented bottles of scent, delicate fans hand-painted and stretched upon carved ivory sticks. Some had been sent anonymously, or with silly chimerical names like "Amorato" or "Devotine." Of those which were signed,

Augusta had no idea who the gentlemen were much less how they seemed to have acquired such fond affections for her. How could they? They knew nothing of her. It was all too much to be believed. And how could this all have come about simply because of her visit to Almack's? She had scarcely spoken with Lady Castlereagh, had danced but one dance, and hadn't even done that all too well. It made absolutely no sense and she said as much to Charlotte.

"This makes no sense at all."

"Oh, it makes perfect sense, my dear," Charlotte said. "You have captured the fancy of Town society, Augusta. By falling under the attentions of the notorious Lord Noah Edenhall and then by gaining the patronage of Lady Castlereagh, you have all but secured your future. I daresay your calendar will be filled until after the close of the Season, and I would not at all be surprised if you were to receive any number of marriage proposals because of it."

Marriage proposals? *Oh, no.*

Augusta set the stack of correspondence aside with a grim frown, shaking her head once again. "There is some oversight in all this. I have been mistaken for someone else. That is it. These gifts are not mine. They were meant for another and so as soon as we can arrange it, they must all be returned. The anonymous ones will simply have to be given away to charity."

Just then the knocker sounded from the hallway. Augusta stood and made immediately for the door. It was time to put a stop to this once and for all.

She heard Charlotte call behind her, "Augusta, do have Tiswell answer it. A lady does not open her own door. It isn't fitting."

Propriety be damned! She yanked the front door wide, but there was no delivery awaiting on the other side. Instead it was Lady Finsminster and her daughter, Viviana, standing on the front stoop. Both were smiling at her as if she alone held the secret to something very valuable.

"Lady Augusta," the countess said, "May I call you Augusta? Oh, Bibi and I have come bearing the most interesting news. We simply must tell you." She peered past her to the hall. "Is Lady Trecastle at home?"

Without waiting for a reply or even an invitation, the countess issued past and headed straight for the parlor, where indeed she found Charlotte. The chatter began at once.

"Charlotte, dear, you simply must hear the news. Bibi and I were to Grafton House this morning."

"Grafton House?"

"Oh, to be sure. We are in search of a yellow sprigged muslin for an afternoon dress for my Bibi."

"Oh, yellow will be fetching on her."

"Indeed. Well, we arrived later than usual, a quarter hour before noon because Bibi was wont to leave her bed before ten this morning after having been out last evening until very late. Well, by the time we arrived, the counter there was thronged and we were made to wait nearly a half hour before we were attended to."

Charlotte's expression looked stricken. "A half hour? How dreadful for you."

"Yes, dear, I suppose it could have been, however, on this occasion it wasn't without its advantages, for it was while we were waiting that we heard the news." The countess took a deep breath for which Augusta was very grateful since the woman had scarcely drawn another since appearing at the doorstep.

The countess shook her head. "It is not to be believed. I fear I may not be able to repeat it, it is so very shocking."

Charlotte patted her hand. "Do try, dear."

Standing at the doorway, Augusta rolled her eyes.

The countess nodded, making a great show of summoning up all her energies so that she might impart this incredible bit of news. "Prepare yourself dear . . . I am shocked to tell you . . . Prudence is ruined!"

Bibi squealed.

Charlotte gasped.

Augusta was confused. "Prudence, Lady Gunther's daughter?"

Lady Finsminster nodded, her mouth turned in a frightful grimace that was not at all attractive on her. "Yes. Even now Lord and Lady Gunther have removed the knocker from their door and are packed to leave immediately for the country. And, oh, it is the most terrible of circumstances."

"What has she done?" Augusta asked, wondering why she should even care. Still, she had to admit that the shock and dismay shown by Lady Finsminster had sufficiently aroused her curiosity.

The countess glanced a moment at her daughter. "Bibi, I will allow you to hear of this only so that I may protect you from plunging into the depths of the same situation." She looked at Charlotte. "Sometimes I fear keeping the true nature of the world from young girls is what can lead to their ruination."

Charlotte nodded. "Too true. Too true."

The countess began slowly. "Well, it would seem Prudence was found in an indelicate position last evening with the younger son of the Earl of Natfield." She added, "A most indelicate position."

Charlotte's face turned positively white. "Oh, dear, poor Lady Gunther. Prudence had such excellent prospects."

Lady Finsminster nodded. "It seems the two have been secretly carrying on for weeks behind closed doors. Remember at the Lumley ball when she disappeared for over an hour only to return saying she'd gotten lost on the way to the supper parlor? Seems she lost more than her way that evening for she was actually engaged in the upper chambers with Natfield's boy."

Charlotte shook her head dolefully. "It is a truly tragic ending for young Prudence."

"Indeed so," echoed Lady Finsminster.

They lapsed into a doleful silence.

"Why?" Augusta finally asked. "Will not the young man wed Prudence?"

"Of course he will, dear," Lady Finsminster said. "He has little choice in the matter. From what I understand, Lord Gunther has already paid a visit to Lord Natfield to work out the details."

"Then I fail to see what the tragedy is. These two people obviously have an affection for one another. Lord and Lady Gunther should be pleased to know their daughter has found happiness."

All three ladies turned to regard Augusta with varying looks of disbelief and condolence registered in their expressions.

"Augusta, dear," Charlotte said, "it is a tragedy because Natfield's son is a *detrimental*—a younger son. His chances for elevating to a title are very, very slim."

"But were you not all singing the praises of Lord Noah Edenhall, who is also, I believe, a younger son?"

"Yes, but only because Lord Noah is a man of his own fortune, past his thirtieth year, and independent. Even if scandal should touch him, he emerges unsullied. The Devonbrook name is esteemed. Natfield's son is all of seventeen and has yet to finish his studies at university. Worse, he is the youngest of several male children whose father is a known gamester and reprobate and who has as many illegitimate children as he does legitimate ones. The differences between the two are quite like day and night."

"And so because of his father, the younger Natfield should be eschewed?"

Lady Finsminster took over the task of explanations then. "Dear Augusta, while this young man might be all charm and handsome looks, his chances for a decent inheritance are very slim indeed. Prudence is the only daughter and sole financial heir to Viscount Gunther. She should have at the very least wed an heir to a viscountcy, although Lady Gunther had aspirations to as high as a marquessate for her daughter."

Charlotte shook her head. "Now all hope is dashed. However, it would be far worse if she weren't to wed the young man. To be found in such a position is the very example of ruination. No one in good society would have anything to do with Prudence again. Her dance cards would be immediately bereft of any entry and all doors would be closed to her. At least by agreeing to the marriage, even though it is a terrible coming down, Prudence might return next Season without very much notice."

The other three ladies shook their heads in shared commiseration. Augusta, however, still failed to see the terrible tragedy.

Tiswell came into the room then, carrying yet another package, causing Lady Finsminster to suddenly take notice of the room and its newly arrived additions.

"But it certainly looks as if you, my dear Augusta, will be the one to benefit most from Prudence's indiscretion. From the looks of things here, you have already assumed her position as the Belle of the Season."

Augusta frowned. "Surely you exaggerate."

"Not at all. You have every qualification now to be a rousing success. You are the daughter to a marquess. You attend social events without any regularity, so no one knows when you will appear and when you will not. Pray look around you at the flowers, gifts, and invitations already delivered. Every hostess will be begging for your attendance at her event and every buck will aspire for the honor of a single dance in your company. I daresay you shan't have an unoccupied moment through the rest of the Season. It is a true triumph for you."

Augusta frowned. They were much the same words Charlotte had spoken earlier. Still Augusta told herself they were wrong. Terribly wrong. This sudden interest in her was naught but folly, a coincidence come about by her very public dance with Lord Noah and the ill-timed change in Prudence's situation. The furor would die down and this ridiculous delusion would pass just as quickly as it had come. By tomorrow, all will have returned to normal. They would see. This was all a misunderstanding. Nothing more.

Nothing more at all.

Chapter Fifteen

Charlotte awoke early the next morning so that she might thoroughly prepare for their ride in the park with the Marquess of Peversley. Augusta awoke at a quarter hour before eleven after passing the night before working till the dawn. The marquess arrived promptly at half past eleven. Standing at the top of the stairs, Augusta found Charlotte awaiting her in the entrance hall below, watching the marquess at his carriage on the square outside through the front window.

Charlotte was turned out well in a pin-striped blue-and-green walking dress with a matching parasol and bonnet, every color, every accessory about her in harmony. When she heard Augusta's descent on the stairs behind her she turned. She took in the unadorned ash gray cambric walking gown and simple straw bonnet Augusta had opted to wear and frowned her disapproval.

"Plainer gowns are fine, Augusta, if they are dressed up with embellishments or trimmings, but how will you ever be noticed when you eschew any possibility of color in your costume? Now that you are recognized in society, we will have to make arrangements for your wardrobe to be brought more up-to-date." She narrowed a critical eye. "Yellows and turquoises I think shall do well with your coloring. I shall schedule a round of fittings with my own modiste immediately. Until then, we will simply have to make do." She patted Augusta's hand. "I know it is not your fault, dear. You do not know the way of these things yet, but you will learn. And it is most fortunate that you have me to help guide you."

The marquess's landau was actually very fine and the ride was smooth and even as they tooled along the narrow lanes to the west toward Hyde Park. The sun was out and Augusta turned her face full into its light, drinking in its warmth until Charlotte moved her parasol overhead to shield her, whispering a reminder to her of Mr. Bell's philosophy that young ladies should take great pains to avoid a *browned* complexion. Augusta turned then to watch the passing scenery instead.

One thing Augusta did notice as they rolled along was that most every gentleman they passed took the time to tip his hat while muttering a "Good day, Lady Augusta," or "You are looking most fetching this morning, Lady Augusta." And even the ladies who had previously ignored her as being hardly worth their time now nodded their heads in friendly greeting. She frowned to herself. Things hadn't returned to normal as she'd thought. Not at all. Suddenly the anonymity which had protected her all her life had gone, leaving her every move now open to view and speculation. Augusta hated it.

They had taken several turns around the park and were coming around to the Serpentine when the marquess asked his driver to pull off the path near the park entrance so that he might fetch a bouquet of flowers from a vendor there. He excused himself and went off, leaving Augusta to look about the vicinity, wondering when Lord Belgrace might make his appearance. She had thought the earl would arrange it for them to cross paths at some time, hence the purpose for Lord Peversley having taken so many turns around the park. But there had been no sign of Lord Belgrace at all. And now they were at a more public area of the park, carriages and riders abounding. Perhaps the earl might be hidden away among them?

As Augusta scrutinized the crowd, Charlotte leaned closer to her beneath the cover of her parasol. "His lordship has been most attentive and gentlemanly this morning, has he not?"

Augusta regarded a gentleman who she considered might be Lord Belgrace, only to be disappointed when he turned about to face her. Without benefit of her spectacles, he would be difficult to pick out. "Yes, Charlotte, the marquess has been very polite."

She frowned when a rather stout sort of buggy blocked her view.

"And do you not think he looks most distinguished for a man of his age?"

Augusta glanced over to where the marquess stood with the flower vendor, browsing the blossoms for sale. Even though she could not see him all too clearly, she said, "I suppose he has a certain air of distinction about him. For an older man."

Charlotte was quiet a moment, peering about at the other park goers. She snapped to attention suddenly. "Oh, goodness, there is Lady Trussington over beneath that strand of trees. I simply must speak to her a moment. Come along, Augusta."

Augusta really didn't care to be the subject of that lady's scrutiny again, nor did she care to hear yet another lamenting of poor Prudence's ruination. It had been the sole topic of conversation everywhere they'd gone since the previous morning. "You go along, Charlotte. I will await you here."

Charlotte looked toward Lord Peversley, who was still, it seemed, caught in his decision of which flowers to purchase. "All right. Nothing improper can happen in so public a place. I shall only be a moment and I will be right over there should you have need of me."

Augusta nodded, thinking Charlotte far too resolute in her duties as chaperon. "I'm sure I will manage until you return. But if the need should arise, I will fan myself to signal that I am in need of you."

"Very clever, Augusta. I shan't be long."

Augusta watched her stepmother depart at a steady pace toward the imposing figure of Lady Trussington. It wasn't long before others came to join them. Augusta turned a bit in her seat, reaching down to adjust the lacing of her half boot. And it was in that moment that the marquess returned from the vendors.

She smiled to him. At last they would have a moment to themselves so that he might impart Lord Belgrace's message to her, to tell her where they might meet.

"Lady Trecastle has gone?" Peversley said. He handed Augusta the pretty beribboned posy of daisies and seashell pink roses.

"Yes, she wished to speak with Lady Trussington a moment. I told her we would await her here."

Peversley glanced around them. "It is growing a bit warm, Lady Augusta. Would you care to walk a bit beneath the shade from the trees?"

"Certainly," Augusta said, taking his outstretched hand so that she might climb down from the carriage. Lord Belgrace must be waiting for them nearby.

The marquess directed them beneath the sheltering branches of a nearby oak. From where they stood, they were somewhat secluded from open view, yet still visible enough for propriety's sake. It was a perfect situation.

"Lady Augusta, there is something I must say to you."

She smiled, eager for news for the earl. "Yes, I know, my lord."

Peversley looked startled at her response. "You do?"

"Yes, my lord. In fact I am quite anxious for it."

"You are?"

"Yes. I could hardly sleep last night for the waiting and all morning I was hoping we might manage a moment alone."

"I am very glad to hear it, Lady Augusta." The marquess took in a deep breath that puffed up his chest while a smile turned his mouth. "I had wondered how you might receive my message."

Augusta glanced over to where her stepmother still stood chatting with Lady Trussington. They looked to be in the throes of some serious chatter, no doubt about Prudence. Her privacy with Lord Peversley would be secure.

But when she looked back she found the earl suddenly down on one knee before her, taking her hand in a gesture that was horribly unmistakable. "Lady Augusta, I would beg—"

Oh good God, he was proposing! "No! Sir! Please do not!"

Lord Peversley looked confused. "But, my lady, I thought—"

Augusta glanced around them and saw that some of the other park goers had begun to take notice of the two of them, and especially of Lord Peversley who was still down on his knee before her. She quickly opened her fan to signal to Charlotte that she needed to return—post haste. "Please, my lord, make haste. Rise to your feet."

"But, Lady Augusta, I had thought you understood me. I should like to make a proposal of—"

She fluttered the fan faster before her. "I know very well what you are proposing, sir. Please, my lord, for your sake and my own, do not do it!"

In a move that could only make matters worse, he grasped her free hand and kissed it earnestly. "Surely you must realize I adore you!"

Augusta yanked away, the fan moving furiously now. "Release me, sir. Lower your voice! I fear the exposure to the sun has affected you! Please, I beg you to come to your senses!"

But Lord Peversley clutched at her arm. "I cannot when I am so much in love with you! Fate has brought us together today. Say you will be my wife and make me the happiest man alive!"

A crowd was fast forming and Lord Peversley was making no move to rise to his feet and stop this madness. If anything he was growing but louder in proclaiming his regard for her. Augusta tried to step away, still fruitlessly fanning herself in hopes of drawing Charlotte's attention, the only one in the park, it seemed, who wasn't presently focused on them. When the marquess reached frantically for her hand again, Augusta did the only thing she could think of to break the man out of his mania. She slapped the side of his face with the sticks of her fan. "Control yourself, sir!"

By now a crowd surrounded them, through which Charlotte was just emerging to see what was about. At the sight of Lord Peversley, still unhappily down on his knee, his face flaming scarlet from his embarrassment, her eyes went as wide as her best porcelain saucers. No explanations were needed for her to figure out what had just happened.

"Augusta!" Charlotte's voice was aghast. "What in heaven's name have you done?"

Lord Peversley stood then, straightening out the tails of his coat. He bowed his head. His voice was noticeably quieter now. "I am sorry to have offended you, Lady Augusta. I was led to believe that you would welcome my proposal of marriage."

Augusta crossed her arms sullenly before her, looking

away from him, from the crowd, from Charlotte. "It was a false impression, sir," she murmured.

"Yes, I see that now." He motioned toward his waiting carriage. "Allow me to escort you and your stepmother home then."

Augusta did not move. She focused her sights on the gnarled root of the tree breaking through the dirt at her feet. "Thank you, no, sir. Under the circumstances, I believe it would be best if we were to find ourselves a hackney."

She looked out of the corner of her eye as Lord Peversley bowed his head once again in as civil a manner as he could manage before turning to take his leave. The crowd parted to allow him access to his coach. In minutes he was gone, back stiff, staring straight ahead, as his coach rolled swiftly through the park gates.

The silence that followed was deafening, but soon, with the spectacle now at an end, the onlookers began to disperse, glancing back perhaps over their shoulders as they latched on to yet another conversational morsel.

Only this wasn't just a morsel. Augusta feared instead it would prove a feast. And her suspicions were confirmed the moment her stepmother spoke.

"That was very badly done, Augusta."

Augusta looked at Charlotte with a frown. Of course she would find fault with her actions, but what of the marquess's? "Whatever you may think, this wasn't my fault, Charlotte. The man proposed marriage to me—publicly! He refused to assume any hint of discretion, even when I begged him to. He was nonsensical. What else did you expect me to do?"

"He is a very wealthy and distinguished man, Augusta. You could have at least considered his offer and spared him the utter humiliation of this public spectacle."

"Considered his proposal? The man is older than my own father!"

"That never bothered you before when you were leading him on, spending all that time with him and his associates whenever we were out socially."

"I had met Lord Peversley once, at the Lumley ball. And conversing with a man on subjects of common interest does not necessarily mean I would want to spend the rest of my life with him!"

"In this society it certainly gives the impression of it. Augusta, you must come to the realization that you are no longer on board some ship where you can do as you please without repercussion. You cannot continue to pursue the past occupations you have. You are the daughter of a marquess. You have drawn society's notice so others are watching you closely now. This little exhibition will no doubt be talked about for weeks to come. Whether you like it or not, you have become a social icon. It is time you started behaving as one. Now let us be off to home so that I may begin making the necessary inroads to turn this whole debacle to your advantage."

Augusta glanced at the neat pile of invitations she found waiting for her on her desktop and frowned. The note sitting beside it, in Charlotte's flowery script, read, "*Augusta, dear, I have arranged these in order or importance with the most beneficial events topmost. Those marked with a check are mandatory. Please adjust your calendar accordingly.*"

Augusta set Charlotte's note aside. She could not continue on like this. Since Lord Peversley's proposal the situation had declined to where it was worse now than it had ever been. Charlotte's notion of averting the disaster of the park was to fill every spare moment of Augusta's social calendar and for the past week, she'd done precisely that. In public, she said, Augusta must show that the Peversley proposal had not affected her badly, and in order to do that, she must be seen everywhere and by everyone. Her future, the futures of her father, Lettie, and Charlotte as well depended upon it.

To make matters worse, Charlotte had enlisted the aid of her contemporaries, Ladies Trussington and Finsminster, so instead of contending against one, Augusta faced three formidable ladies very determined to see her reach the heights of the success she'd tasted. The only thing they didn't particularly care to hear was that the taste of success was both bitter and undesirable to Augusta.

For three days and three nights they had traipsed Augusta about on an endless round of teas, dinners, routs, and balls until Augusta felt as if she might truly drop from exhaustion. Her dancing card was always filled, sometimes with a partner listed in reserve should an opening arise, the faces, the names were all naught but a blur to her bewildered mind. The only thing Augusta was certain of was that this madness could not be allowed to continue. Her work was paying the worst penalty of it.

But how? How to stop the tidal wave against which she floundered now that it had begun?

Charlotte was obsessed. Even if Augusta refused to step foot out-of-doors again, she knew her stepmother would then set her sights on making Augusta's life as miserable as possible. Hadn't she said as much by casually reminding Augusta just that morning of the requirement of both their signatures on any financial transactions? If need be, Charlotte would keep Augusta from any pursuit of her own by stifling her finances.

Oh, Father, why did you leave me in such a position? Augusta asked herself, even as she knew he could have done no differently. To have left Augusta exclusively in charge would have been a slight on his wife, but to leave Charlotte solely responsible would have been an absolute disaster. So he'd invented this method of checks and balances, leaving the duty of balance to Augusta.

But there had to be a way around this ridiculous situation, some way in which she could extinguish her brightly glowing social flame.

And then it occurred to her in a single word.

Ruination.

Augusta took up the stack of invitations and began thumbing through them in search of the one that would provide the best backdrop to her plan. She wasn't made to search any further than the topmost card.

"Their Graces, the Duke and Duchess of Devonbrook request the honor of your presence for an evening of music and conversation Thursday, the twenty-third beginning at 8 o'clock."

Lord Noah's brother and his wife. All of London would be there, to see and be seen. It was perfect.

As she began mentally sketching her plans for the evening, Augusta suddenly realized why she hadn't shared Charlotte's dismay at the end result of Prudence's liaison with her young lover. It had given the girl the luxury of no longer having to fret over the placement of every flounce, the impression of every word she spoke. What is more it had given Prudence *freedom*, the only difference being that Prudence's actions had taken her to marriage, her suitor forced to do the only fitting thing by making her his wife.

With Augusta's present predicament, she might have any number of young men willing to aid her in that sort of a ruination for they, too, would then insist on the same end result as poor Prudence. And the last thing Augusta needed now was a marriage. No, instead, what Augusta needed was a gentleman who really was no gentleman at all, a man who would do something as unthinkable as walking out on his own betrothed.

And there was only one man she could think of who would do something like that.

Lord Noah Edenhall of Devonbrook.

Chapter Sixteen

"Color can be a lady's finest asset, setting her apart among others in a crowd. For without the flower, the garden is naught but soil and weed, without the rainbow, the shower but dim and gray..."

Augusta closed the copy of *La Belle Assemblée* she'd asked Mina to fetch for her, but one of the wealth of pocket books Charlotte kept stashed away in her bedchamber bureau. With Mr. Bell's prophetic words ringing in her memory, she stood from her chair and crossed the room to her standing rosewood wardrobe. She peered inside, furrowing her brow at the array of grays, browns, and beiges which met her scrutinizing eye.

Weeds. Much as she hated to admit it, these would not do, not for an occasion such as this. Tonight she must dress differently. Tonight she must *be* different. She must not blend into the woodwork as she normally preferred to do. She must dress to be noticed, to, as Mr. Bell had put it, "set herself apart among others in the crowd." She must try to be a flower. Quite simply, Augusta would have to assume the role she'd spent nearly the entirety of her life avoiding.

To prepare herself for this imperative impersonation, Augusta had spent the entire morning poring through numerous copies of pocket books, studying each and every fashion engraving while committing the venerable dictum to memory. It was a task she undertook as she would any other, through the reading of every article she could find and a thorough study of the evidence around her. She'd scrutinized the details of any lady she'd come across in the past days, from debutante to aging dowager. She analyzed what was deemed a success and what wasn't, mentally cataloging the results for comparison. She'd even abandoned her ancient texts for the reading of more popular fiction— Mrs. Radcliffe and Maria Edgeworth among them.

And because of it, she now understood why Charlotte had always looked at her so queerly when she'd done something so seemingly insignificant as wearing her comfortable half boots to go walking. "Unless riding, a lady," according to Mr. Bell, "wore slippers befitting her dainty feet." But Mr. Bell hadn't indicated what a lady whose feet were slightly more than "dainty" should wear, much less a lady who'd spent her childhood climbing rigging and mastheads.

Still, Augusta did now have at least a fundamental knowledge of the female role, enough necessary at least for the task she had before her that evening. And since she was prepared, she could now commence with the construction of her new self for the evening, but how was she to put her knowledge to work when the resources she had available to her were so very limited?

Quite obviously she would need help.

"My lady?"

Augusta looked to the doorway to see Charlotte's personal maid suddenly standing there. She'd been so lost to her thoughts, she hadn't heard her come in. "Yes, Lizette?"

"My Lady Trecastle wished me to *ask* you *if* she has arranged for the carriage to be ready at eight."

Augusta smiled. The maid was young, pretty, and above all else, French. Fresh from Paris, Lizette had come to the Trecastle household soon after Charlotte had become marchioness. Her abilities to dress hair and sew a perfect stitch were incomparable. Her ability to master the English language was, however, somewhat less encouraging. "Thank you, Lizette. Please tell the marchioness that I will be ready."

The maid bobbed her capped head and turned to leave.

"Lizette," Augusta called before she'd vanished down the hall.

"*Oui*, my lady?"

"What did you do with Lady Trecastle's new gown?"

Lizette returned a confused sort of look. "Gown, my lady? What gown do you mean?"

"The gown that was delivered to her yesterday afternoon from her modiste. The one she was so unhappy with. I believe she asked you to destroy it. Did you?"

Lizette bit her lip, caught with indecision as to whether she should lie to Augusta and risk her discovering the truth, or tell Augusta that she had kept the gown for herself instead of discarding it as she so obviously had. Augusta spared her the decision.

"Lizette, if you still have the gown, I should like to propose an arrangement with you."

"Arrangement, my lady?"

Augusta tried the French equivalent instead. "*Oui, un arrangement.*"

Lizette nodded. "*Oui, un arrangement, Qu'est-ce que c'est que ça?*"

"I should like to wear Lady Trecastle's gown this evening—but only for this evening and then you would have it back. I know Lady Trecastle told you to destroy the gown, but I cannot believe she really meant you should ruin such a fine garment. But if she had, she could not be upset if I were to tell her I decided I'd wanted it. Then, after I wear it tonight, I will tell Lady Trecastle that I gave it to you after I decided I no longer liked it either. That way she will not be angry with you for having kept it. Do you see?"

Lizette listened carefully to Augusta and her eyes grew wide with understanding. "*Oui*, my lady, I do see. You are right. I believe I do still keep the gown. I go and bring it for you."

Lizette returned minutes later, the gown draped elegantly over her arms. "Here it is, my lady. I promise you I have not worn it."

Augusta took the gown, holding it up against her. The rich deep ruby silk felt whisper-soft against her fingertips, the matching satin ribbon which decorated it shimmering in the afternoon sunlight beaming in from the windows. It had been too plain a design for Charlotte, not nearly enough flounces to satisfy her more sophisticated tastes. But with a few modest adjustments it would suit Augusta's needs for that evening very well.

Augusta looked to Lizette. "Will you help me try it on so I might see if it will fit me?"

"*Oui*, my lady."

Lizette helped Augusta out of her dove gray striped muslin, slipping the red gown over her head and letting it glide against her in a cascade of rich silk. The maid quickly fastened the long line of buttons at its back, stepping away as Augusta moved for the pier glass to study her reflection with a critic's eye.

Since she and Charlotte were similar in size, the gown very nearly fit her. A tightening of the banding beneath the bodice and a shortening with the removal of the ruffled hem was all that would be needed to make the garment suitable. Yes, it would do very nicely.

When she turned back toward Lizette, she found the maid staring at her oddly. She looked down at the gown to see what was amiss. "What is it, Lizette? Is something wrong?"

"Oh, no, my lady, it is right, the gown. *C'est très joli* on you. The *couleur,* it is *parfait* on you. I want you should keep the gown."

"No, Lizette, I really shan't need it after tonight. You will have it. But before I can wear it, it will need a few adjustments—and then, I, too, will need a few adjustments, too. Do you think you can help me?"

The Duke and Duchess of Devonbrook's Grosvenor town house had been transformed for the evening from its usual quiet and tree-shaded elegance into a bustling, hustling hive of society activity. The staff had been doubled so that every need might be met, every detail seen to; each would be appointed a designation of the guests to ensure it.

The Italianate marble floor, which the servants had likely spent the entire morning polishing, was hardly seen now through the crush of company. Musicians, a flutist and strings, added a refined backdrop, although they were barely heard against the steady buzzing of conversation and rustling of sumptuous silk as ladies tried gracefully to dodge both the occasional dollop of hot wax dripping from the numerous chandeliers overhead and the more frequent groping hands of one of the codgers seated about the periphery.

At the top of the stairs overlooking the assembly, the host and hostess stood greeting each arrival from the steady legion of advancing guests. This was to be a marvelous event for the popular Duchess Catriona rarely entertained, thus when she did, it was always certain to be a crush. In fact nary an invitation had been declined even though her decision to host this evening's informal entertainment had come but a week prior—unacceptable for most anyone else—causing those who had arranged other affairs months in advance but on that same evening to reschedule at the last minute for the fear of a dwindling guest list.

Standing just outside the midst of the crowd, Noah sipped a glass of port while exchanging pleasantries with a longtime family acquaintance. From where he stood, he had a clear view of the assembly room as well as the adjoining supper parlor. He'd chosen the spot precisely for its locale, so he would be assured of noticing when Lady Augusta arrived.

He hadn't seen her since the morning he'd been riding along Rotten Row with Christian, Eleanor, and Sarah, when he'd managed to foil yet another of her attempts to meet privately with Lord Belgrace. But he hadn't forgotten her or his quest to uncover the truth of her involvement with Tony and recover the Keighley brooch. In fact, he'd spent the past several days making inquiries in an attempt to finally confirm the connection between them and eliminate the niggling doubts which seemed to plague him more and more.

He'd checked first with Tony's former steward to study his calendar in the weeks before his suicide. From there, he'd acquired copies of the guest lists from the various social events Tony had attended. Most every one of them had included the *Marquess of Trecastle and family* among those listed, however, none of the hostesses could recall ever having noticed Lady Augusta in attendance with her stepmother.

Noah had then questioned Tony's former servants, both those he himself had later employed as well as the others. He hadn't, however, found much luck in that endeavor either. But what he did learn was that Tony had been extremely secretive in the last month before he died, neglecting to allow Westman or even his valet to know what it was he was about. He'd sometimes disappeared for hours on end without notice and many times, when he had gone off in the evening, Tony had chosen to hire a hack instead of taking his own carriage.

Every turn Noah took seemed to lead only to an impasse, causing him to consider that he might never learn the full truth of Tony and his connection with Augusta. It wasn't until just the previous day, when Noah had paid a visit to Tony's solicitor to request that he forward all debt notices to him directly for payment rather than Sarah, that he'd found the hint of real evidence.

It came in the form of a jeweler's note, the same note Sarah had received when Tony had had the heirloom Keighley brooch reset. More curious than suspect, Noah had decided to pay a visit to the jeweler's shop to see if he might recall the piece.

"Oh, indeed, my lord, I do remember that item. It was quite extraordinary," the jeweler had said. *"One doesn't see many like that in a lifetime."*

"It is valuable?" he'd asked.

"Invaluable is a more apt description of it for it was made up of the Queen's blue diamond."

"The queen? Queen Charlotte?"

"Oh, no, my lord, not our present queen. Queen Elizabeth, the Virgin Queen. I noticed her marking on it when I had removed the stone from its original setting. I did a bit of research and found that it was one of numerous pieces given her by Sir Francis Drake upon his return from his travels around the world. The stone is Spanish in origin and dates from the early 1500s. It came to Lord Keighley through an ancestor who'd been an advisor to the queen."

"Did you inform Lord Keighley of the stone's origin?"

"Indeed, sir. And I also told him I knew of one gentleman in particular who would pay a princely fortune to ac-

quire it, but Lord Keighley wouldn't hear of it. He said he'd intended the brooch as a gift for a lady, and a special lady she must be to receive such a priceless piece . . . "

"Lord Noah?"

Noah suddenly realized that all the while he'd been standing there thinking on his visit to the jeweler, the elder viscount beside him had been carrying on at length with him, a conversation which had just ended with the man asking Noah his opinion of whatever it was he'd been speaking of. Uncertain as to what the topic of interest might have even been, Noah uttered an "I couldn't agree with you more," and quickly excused himself, telling the man he was needed by their hosts as he motioned to where Robert and Catriona stood with his aunt Amelia across the room.

As he approached, Noah noticed immediately Catriona's strained but polite expression while she conversed with the two women standing before her. He couldn't recognize either of them for their backs were to him, but whoever they were, they no doubt were busy bending Catriona's ear with some precious tidbit of gossip, one which Catriona quite obviously cared little to hear for she was not one given to calumny.

"Lady Finsminster," Catriona said, her expression turning to one of relief as he approached, "have you been introduced by my dear brother, Lord Noah Edenhall? Noah, allow me to introduce to you Lady Finsminster and her lovely daughter, Lady Viviana."

The countess turned. "Oh, yes, Your Grace, I do know of Lord Noah. We have never been formally introduced, although I did see him several nights ago dancing at Almack's."

"You were dancing? At Almack's?" Robert asked with a distinct air of disbelief.

Noah shot his brother a glance. "Yes, I was there." He

turned to Catriona. "In fact, dearest sister, Lady Castle-reagh sends her regards."

"And a fine dancer you are, Lord Noah," the countess said, refusing to drop the subject. "All of us in attendance that evening were saying so." She took a quick breath. "In fact the young lady who Lord Noah partnered that evening is the very one I was just telling you about, Your Grace— Lady Augusta Brierley. They cut quite a dashing figure together, although after her actions in the park the other day, I rather doubt we'll have the opportunity to see her dancing with Lord Noah again."

Good God, Noah thought to himself, *what had Augusta done now?*

"Of course," Catriona broke in, "it wasn't very well done of the gentleman either to make his proposal to her in so public a place as Hyde Park. I would never wish for any lady to feel pressured into accepting an offer she didn't want just because she wanted to avoid public embarrassment."

What's this? Noah thought, Augusta had managed somehow to eke a proposal out of Belgrace, but then had refused him? And after all her efforts to see him alone? But if she hadn't been pursuing him for an offer of marriage, what the devil was she about?

"To be sure," the countess readily agreed. "However, Lady Augusta isn't getting any younger. She should have perhaps given the proposal a bit more consideration. It's not like she's as young as my Bibi here."

"Mama," Viviana broke in then, in an obvious attempt to stem her mother's rattling tongue, "it is possible Lady Augusta was taken unawares by the marquess's proposal."

"Marquess?" Noah said, voicing his confusion. "The gentleman she refused was a marquess?"

Everyone turned to look at him, no doubt wondering at

his sudden interest in the story of Lady Augusta's refusal. Robert was grinning.

"Yes, Noah dear," Amelia said. "It was Lord Peversley." She shook her head dolefully. "I don't know what the poor fool could have been thinking of to have botched it so badly. He and Lady Augusta would never suit, not at all." She paused a moment, staring across the room and into the crowd, lost to momentary thought. It wasn't but a few seconds later that a subtle grin tugged at her mouth. "However, I wouldn't wager on the prediction that Lady Augusta will be cast out of good society for her refusal of him. From the looks of it, she's even more highly regarded than she was before."

Noah turned toward where Amelia was looking, to where all heads in the room, it seemed, were suddenly looking, as well. He stared. He blinked. And then he wondered what trick his eyes were playing on him. Standing in the doorway flanked by the Devonbrook footmen were Lady Augusta and her stepmother, the marchioness. But this wasn't the Augusta he was accustomed to seeing, with a frown on her face and her spectacles perched upon her nose. Not at all. Instead she had been magically recreated into a different—incredibly beautiful version of herself.

Gone was the prosaic dark gown lacking any hint of fashion, the simple serviceable styling of her hair. Instead her face was framed by soft dark tendrils set off by a gown of rich shimmering burgundy silk that fell in a graceful line from bodice to toe. Tiny capped sleeves, white gloves extending past her elbows, the heart-shaped neckline of the gown was cut dramatically over her breasts—breasts Noah found himself staring at, gawking at. Somehow, before, he'd failed to truly notice that part of her anatomy, which was ridiculous for now he couldn't seem to take his eyes away. Just looking at them promised the truest bliss and he found himself wondering how they would feel beneath his hands, how they would taste to his mouth. The longer he stared, the warmer and more uncomfortable his body grew, still he wouldn't look away. He couldn't. She was absolutely radiant.

She had just made her entrance, at least she had attempted to before she had become mobbed by several overeager young bucks who, it appeared, were all vying for the honor of her company. Some bowed before her, others brought glasses of champagne. Augusta, however, didn't look particularly pleased by the attention. In fact, she looked annoyed by it.

With her appearance, the whispers weren't long in following. By now everyone had heard of Augusta's refusal to Lord Peversley's proposal. Peversley had left town for the country, it was said, gone into seclusion, humiliated beyond bearing. Those who didn't know Augusta wondered out loud who she was; those who did proclaimed it proudly. The fact that she had been away from England throughout her childhood only added to the aura of mystery surrounding her. Predictions were made on the size of her dowry. Speculation was rife, but no one seemed to know for certain much of anything about her.

Noah watched as she and the marchioness made their way through the crowd to where Catriona and Robert had come forward to greet them. Augusta stood, exchanging pleasantries for a few moments, and then broke away to walk with her stepmother toward the refreshments table. She took up a glass of ratafia and was just sipping it when she noticed Noah watching her from across the room. And then she did the oddest thing. She smiled at him and nodded her head pleasantly in greeting.

After their last meeting, when he had refused to leave her in the park, Noah had expected at least the usual frown, perhaps even a scowl from her. But instead she was smiling and it was the most seductive smile he'd ever before seen, reaching to those captivating green eyes and turning her mouth enticingly. Even now he could feel his pulse leaping in response, his entire body tightening as if he were some randy schoolboy staring for the first time at the naked female form. Good God, was he losing his mind?

The Marchioness Trecastle must have noticed the exchange and must also have clearly read Noah's thoughts because she promptly moved between them, urging Augusta to walk with her toward a small circle of her acquaintances at the other side of the room. Confused, bemused, and worse, utterly aroused, Noah turned and headed straight for the door.

He needed to get away before he truly embarrassed himself. And a very cold bath might be a better option.

Noah made his way through the house past servant and guest to the silence and solitude of his brother's private study. The room was situated on the eastern side of the residence, accessible only by a narrow cloistered door perfect for his current purposes. Inside the richly paneled room, a fire burned low in the hearth. The papers scattered across the desktop gave the indication that Robert had been there tending to ducal business earlier that evening, and would no doubt be returning later. Perhaps Noah would just await him here, safely away from the others.

Crossing to the sideboard, Noah quickly poured himself two fingers of brandy, swilling it down with one thorough swallow. As he felt the soothing potion start to ease his all-too natural tension, he poured himself another glass, sipping at it leisurely this time.

Noah took a seat in one of the two armchairs set near the windows where he could see the fire and watch the street outside through the narrow opening in the drapery. The coachmen had grouped on the footpath outside, exchanging jests over hot cider while standing about the brazier Robert had set out for them to keep warm while they awaited their masters inside. Propping his booted feet against the floor, Noah turned his attention to the flames as they danced slowly in the hearth beside him.

There was one thing of which he could now be certain; after seeing Augusta tonight, the change in her, he no longer wondered how she had affected Tony as she had. It was, in fact, quite obvious to him now. Just look what seeing her had done to him, a man who, of any man, had no possible interest in her. Just glancing at her once had utterly muddled his senses. It was no wonder that Tony had been completely intoxicated after having fallen under her spell for the space of an entire month. No woman should be allowed to look so desirable, so alluring. She was a most dangerous sort of female; a witch, indeed.

Noah closed his eyes, resting his head against the soft velvet at the back of the chair. The question which remained now was what to do about her?

At the whispering sound of silk coming from the direction of the doorway, he found his response.

It was Augusta and she came to a standstill not three feet from him. She said nothing, just stared at him, those lovely breasts gently rising and falling with her breathing above the dark red silk of her gown. A single twisting tendril of black hair rested against the column of her neck, beckoning him to touch it. He stared at that tendril wordlessly and wondered if somehow he'd conjured her up in his thoughts.

Finally he spoke. "This is a private area of the house, my lady."

"Yes, I am aware of that, my lord."

Her voice wrapped around him like a silken cloak, warming him to his very toes. She took a step forward, touching her gloved fingertips to the desktop. "Your brother and his wife are very personable."

What game did she play at? Noah wondered, watching as she peered up at the portrait of Robert, Catriona, and baby James that hung above the hearth.

"Yes, they are," he said.

"They seem very happy."

"They are fortunate to have found one another."

Augusta looked at him again, nodding, and then glanced at his glass which sat, still half filled, on the table beside him. "Is that brandy?"

"Yes." Noah watched her still. Why was she here? What did she want? "Would you care for a glass?"

Augusta nodded, smiling politely as if he'd just greeted her in the street. Noah rose and walked over to the drinks table, pouring a small splash of brandy into a glass. He turned and handed it to her, watching as she took a small sip, her murky green eyes fixed on his over the rim of the glass. He still couldn't get over the change in her. How had she hidden so many things about herself? And more importantly why had she?

When she pulled the glass away from her mouth, her lips were moist in the firelight. Noah was seized by an immediate and irresistible urge to pull her against him and taste the brandy on her. He forced his eyes away as the room began to grow noticeably warmer. He turned as if to tidy the drinks table, when in reality he was only trying to quell the pounding of the blood through his veins. "Was there something you wanted, my lady?"

"Yes," she said behind him. He heard her move, her skirts rustling again. He froze when he felt her hand against his arm. "I want you."

He had to be dreaming. He accepted that now and in the next moment, whatever command he might have had over his senses completely vanished. Noah turned and pulled Augusta swiftly into his embrace, taking her mouth in a kiss of pure hunger and passion and need. Unlike the first time when he'd kissed her in the gardens beneath the moonlight and she'd been stiff and fighting against him, this time she was soft, pliant, leaning into him as her hands moved slowly over him, her body pressed intimately against the increasing hardness of him. He tasted the brandy on her, yes, and more, so much more. And she intoxicated him. When he deepened the kiss, stroking her tongue with his, she returned the kiss with an equal passion, running her hands upward to circle around his neck, drawing him closer still.

The need to have her ran like wildfire through his veins. Noah's fingers worked feverishly at the buttons along the back of her gown, loosening the bodice until it was sagging loosely in front of her. He kissed a line along the column of her neck, that tendril of hair, her throat, delving deeper until he reached the rise of her breasts. A sigh escaped her mouth as he leaned her back, supporting her with one arm. He fought against the layers of fabric until finally he freed her. He felt her body jerk when he rubbed his thumb against her nipple and caught her tightly against him. He covered her then with his mouth, drawing, suckling, until he thought he'd surely lose his mind.

This woman was truly an enchantress, but he no longer cared. Nothing mattered except the need he felt to have her, to know her, to take her completely and utterly.

And nothing—not even the fire of hell—was going to stop him from doing that very thing.

Chapter Seventeen

Augusta felt a whisper of cool air brush against her skin as Noah pulled his mouth from hers. She gazed through lowered lashes, through eyes that were barely open, and saw he was looking at her as if she were the most beautiful, most desirable woman on earth. His eyes held a fire of pure sexuality behind them. He wanted her. Badly. She could barely breathe.

"We shouldn't be doing this," he said then as he kissed her ear, his breath hot against her. "This isn't the proper place or time . . . but God help me, Augusta, I just can't seem to stop myself."

His fingers were stroking circles over her skin, light, seductive caresses sending small tingles rushing outward throughout her body. It was unlike anything she'd ever felt before and she never wanted it to end. She could feel her gown loose around her, the hardness of him pressing intimately against her, and she was seized by the need to feel his bare skin beneath her hands.

Noah slipped behind her then, pressing hot, moist kisses along her bare shoulders, her neck, her back. "Perhaps we should remove ourselves to my carriage and—"

Leave? "No, we cannot . . . not yet . . ."

Noah stilled. "What do you mean 'not yet'?"

Augusta pulled away, holding the front of her gown over her breasts to shield herself, a ridiculous gesture she knew given the fact that moments before he'd had his mouth, his hands, his fingers there; still she felt the need for it somehow.

How had things progressed so far so quickly? She'd only meant to have them found together alone—compromising enough in itself, but certainly not like this. But from the moment Noah had first taken her into his arms, she'd completely forgotten about her purpose in coming here. She'd only meant to make it look as if she'd been ruined; she'd never intended to actually ruin herself in the process. She hadn't been prepared for how being with him would make her feel, how it would lead to more than just a few chaste touches. How it would make her want more. If this was ruination, it was no wonder to her now why Prudence had fallen into the temptation.

Standing across from her, Noah was watching her with a look of curious confusion. He glanced at the door, to where she had left it slightly ajar, enough for anyone passing by to have a clear view inside. She watched as he crossed the room to it, opening it further, leaving the room only to return a moment later holding her handkerchief, the one she'd left lying in the hallway. He closed the door and turned the lock. Then he turned to face her. The look on his face was a far cry from what it had been moments earlier. Instead of hunger, it was made up now of anger and suspicion.

"What game do you play at?"

Augusta feigned innocence, even as she knew she was a terrible actress. "What do you mean, sir?"

Noah strode to her, shoving her handkerchief under her nose. "I think we both know we've come far beyond the need for the use of the word *sir*, Augusta. Or were you someplace else when I had my mouth on your breasts?"

Augusta felt her face color at his acrimonious words. She

tried to look away, but Noah took her chin between his thumb and forefinger, forcing her to face him. "You wanted us to be found here alone together, like this, didn't you? Damnation, you even arranged for it!"

She wrenched away from him, seizing her handkerchief. "Why should it be of any matter to you? I was to be the one ruined by it!"

"Ruined? Why, Augusta? Why would you do it? What did you hope to gain? Did you think you could trap me into marrying you? Has that been your scheme all this time since that first night in the garden at the Lumley ball? Is that why you refused Peversley's proposal in the park the other day?"

"Well, of course there must be some explanation for a lady not to agree to wed any gentleman who asks her." Augusta turned to him now, anger and no longer humiliation coloring her face. "Allow me to remind you, *Noah,* that it was *you* who pursued *me* at the Lumley ball! I didn't even know who you were, and then it was you again who followed me to Hyde Park the following day! And if it hadn't been for you asking me to dance at Almack's that night, I wouldn't have been trying to ruin myself in the first place!"

Noah cocked his head, narrowing his eyes on her quizzically. "Let me understand this—you are trying to ruin yourself? And it is because of me, because of my actions, my attention to you? Pray tell me, madam, how one dance necessitates this ridiculous stage show!"

Augusta gritted her teeth, so furious she hardly knew what she was saying. "If you wouldn't have danced with me that night, charming Lady Castlereagh into all but falling at your feet, I wouldn't have these silly men knocking at my door day and night, praising me to my eyebrows and then asking—expecting me to marry them. Before you came along, I was perfectly happy. I went about my business and I was bothered by no one. Now I cannot find a moment's peace! The only way I could see to stop this madness, to return my life to what it was, was to ruin myself. But I needed to find someone who wouldn't insist on marrying me to save my name."

Noah's face had darkened. "And obviously I was the best candidate?"

"Yes. You had been seen with me in public and you have already walked out on one betro—"

She caught herself too late.

"Betrothal," Noah finished coolly. He nodded. "So, of course, since I'd already done the dishonorable thing by walking out on one marriage, you decided I would surely refuse to marry you when we were discovered here together *flagrante delicto* tonight. Then you would be happily ruined and all your faithful suitors would find another prize to seek. And of course I would benefit most of all from your clever little contrivance, madam, for you see, I would be deemed even more of a blackguard than I already am."

Augusta shivered against the unmistakable chill she heard so clearly in his voice. Why did her actions suddenly sound so despicable when he voiced them out loud?

"Well, my lady, since you've gone to so much trouble to stage this drama of yours, at least allow me to spare you the humiliation of being found by the best of London society with your gown hanging to your waist. I certainly wouldn't think that had been part of your plan."

He came behind her. With no other option left to her, Augusta could but stand stiff as a stick as he fastened the buttons at the back of her gown. The touch of his fingers against her skin no longer gave her a delicious tingle. Now it only made her shiver uneasily.

Noah remained standing behind her when he was finished. Neither moved or said a word for several moments.

"Was it worth it, Augusta?"

His voice was quiet now, injured. She looked at the floor, the burgundy satin toe of her slipper peeking from beneath the hem of her gown. She didn't respond, but bit her lip instead.

"Was it worth allowing me to undress you, touch you, to do all those things I did to you? Surely just having us discovered here alone would have been sufficient enough for your ruination. When you realized it had begun to go beyond that, why didn't you stop me from further violation?"

Because it hadn't been a violation, she wanted to say, but her answer never came. Instead the voice of the marchioness, Augusta's stepmother, suddenly sounded from the other side of the study door.

"Augusta, are you there, dear? The footman said you had come this way to rest, that you had grown faint inside the Assembly Room. Are you all right, dear?"

Augusta turned around to look at Noah. He was staring at her with a dark look, his voice acrid with sarcasm as he said low so that only she might hear, "You certainly thought of everything, didn't you? Even going so far as to tell a servant where you were just in case your handkerchief was never found?"

Tears of regret were springing unbidden to her eyes. Augusta dashed them away with an angry swipe of her hand. Why should she feel this way, why should she feel as if she'd wronged him somehow after all he'd done to ruin her peace the past days?

The handle on the door rattled as the marchioness tried to open it. "Augusta, are you there? Are you well? Can you hear me?"

Staring at Noah, Augusta lifted her chin the slightest bit as she said clearly, "Yes, Charlotte. I will be there in a moment."

Noah didn't flinch. "Well, my lady, you may think you'd thought of everything for this little plain of yours. But I assure you, you haven't considered one thing. I will not be a willing participant in your ruination."

And with that he walked to the far side of the room, pushing on a corner bookcase to reveal a false door hidden behind it. He vanished without saying another word to her, without giving her another look.

"Augusta?" Charlotte knocked at the door again.

Augusta turned. She wiped her eyes, sniffed, and smoothed a hand over her gown. Then she crossed the room to the door, turning the key. The door came immediately open. Charlotte, the Duke and Duchess of Devonbrook, and several other guests stood hovering in the hallway.

"What were you doing in here?" Charlotte asked, issuing past her to inspect the room.

Augusta spoke quickly, hoping she wouldn't notice the two brandy glasses. Suddenly her ruination held very little appeal. "I am sorry to have worried you. I wasn't feeling well, so I thought I would remove myself to someplace quiet for a few moments to rest."

"You've been gone quite some time," Charlotte said, returning to her. She hadn't, it seemed, noticed the glasses.

"I don't know what could have happened. I must have dozed off in the chair."

Just then, a tendril of her hair came loose from its pin, falling suggestively over her forehead. Charlotte looked at her with ill-concealed suspicion. Brandy glasses or not, she didn't for a moment believe what Augusta was saying.

"Are you all right, Lady Augusta?" the duke asked then. "Should I call for a physician?"

She shook her head, smiling politely. "Oh no, Your

Grace, I am feeling much better now. I'm sorry to have intruded on your study."

Augusta glanced back to see Charlotte still staring inside the study as if waiting for something to appear.

Or someone. She watched on in silent terror as Charlotte crossed the room, taking up one of the two glasses. "Please, do not worry yourself over it," the Duchess Catriona said. She stepped forward to take Augusta's arm, hooking it with her own as she began to lead her back toward the Assembly Room. "If you should feel as if you'd like to lie down, I would be happy to show you to my own chamber upstairs. My bed is vastly more comfortable than those chairs. And as you can see my husband's study is in need of tidying."

Augusta smiled at her in gratitude for having diverted attention away from the scene of her failed attempt at ruination. "I am fine now. Really. Thank you for your concern. I truly never wanted to prompt all this trouble."

When they were back inside the Assembly Room, the others returned to their conversation while the musicians began a lively sonata. Augusta took the glass of lemonade offered her by the duchess and excused herself, wandering to the far side of the room where it wasn't as crowded and noisy. She lowered herself onto an elegant carved bench against the wall and quietly sipped, trying to get the image of Noah—the anger, the hurt, the accusation—out of her mind's eye, while she tried also to get the feeling of regret out of her heart.

"Good evening, Lady Augusta."

Augusta looked to see a petite blonde suddenly standing before her. The girl looked all of nineteen, thin, but pretty with large blue eyes and pale skin. But her most noticeable feature was the mourning black she wore from chin to toe. "Good evening—I'm sorry, have we been introduced?"

"No, not as yet. I am Miss Sarah Prescott. I had the pleasure of seeing you dance at Almack's last week."

Augusta nodded, thinking surely everyone in London had seen her that night. "It is a pleasure to make your acquaintance, Miss Prescott."

"Would you mind terribly if I sat with you? I have so wanted to meet you."

Although she wasn't much in the mood for conversation, Augusta nodded cordially, motioning to the space beside her. "Of course."

Sarah lowered herself onto the bench, folding her gloved hands modestly in her lap. They both were looking out toward the assembly, Augusta sipping her lemonade, Sarah lightly tapping the toe of her slipper to the floor. There were a few quiet moments before Sarah spoke again. "Your gown is very beautiful."

Augusta looked down, suddenly hating the garment and everything it represented. "Thank you, but I cannot take credit for it. My stepmother chose it."

"The color is quite lovely against your skin." She picked at the edging of her own gown. "Black is such an ugly color. I wish I no longer had to wear it."

Augusta looked at her. "Oh, I do not think black is an unfavorable color. In fact, I am very partial to it."

Another quiet moment and then, "Everyone ignores you when you are in mourning." Sarah sighed. "They don't know what to say, how to react, so they just smile politely and leave you alone to your thoughts, as if you carry some horrible disease they fear catching."

Augusta watched her, curious. "I am so sorry. You lost your—?"

"My brother, Lord Anthony Prescott, Viscount Keighley."

"How tragic for you. I do not have a brother, but I have a

stepsister and I know how terrible it would be for me if I were to lose her."

Sarah nodded. "Noah has been truly wonderful since Tony died."

Augusta tried to ignore the immediate sense of warmth she felt rise to her face at his name. "Noah? You mean the duke's brother?"

"Yes. You danced with him at Almack's that night, didn't you?"

"Yes. I'm afraid I wasn't very good. I—"

"We are to marry as soon as I am out of mourning."

Marry? Augusta stared at her, wondering if she'd heard her right, hoping she hadn't. "You and Lord Noah are betrothed?"

"Yes, we are. Well, not officially. Not yet. It wouldn't be fitting to announce our engagement so soon after Tony's death. We are waiting until next year. Then we will marry. It will be a *grand affaire*. We've known each other since we were children." She nodded once, playing with the handkerchief she held. "Noah gave this to me. It is his."

And, indeed, Augusta could see his initials stitched in silver thread upon it.

"We are very much in love," Sarah finished with a satisfied smile.

Augusta felt a sickness begin to swell in her stomach as she thought of how, only minutes earlier, she had been writhing against him, how he had touched her more intimately than she'd ever thought possible. If she hadn't stopped it, she might very well right now be lying together somewhere with a man who was already promised to this sweet girl.

"I—I wish you every happiness." Augusta stood, her feet slightly unsteady beneath her. "If you will excuse me, I think I'm beginning to feel unwell again. I believe I should probably retire for the evening."

Sarah nodded. "Of course. It was a pleasure to make your acquaintance, Lady Augusta. I hope we shall have a chance to chat again soon."

Augusta nodded and started off in search for Charlotte, knowing if she didn't get out of this place soon, she would most certainly be ill.

Augusta closed the door to her bedchamber with a little more force than was necessary, the sound of it echoing out through the empty hallways of the silent and sleeping house.

She tossed her reticule on the bed and kicked her slippers off her feet. She struggled to unfasten the buttons of her gown herself and succeeded in loosening it enough to push it over her hips. She let the scarlet garment drop to the floor before she picked it up, swiftly relegating it to exile in the corner of the room.

Clad in her chemise and stockings, she crossed the room to the windows and threw the drapery and then the windows open wide. She drew in a deep breath of the cold night air, wrapping her arms around herself as she stared at the stars glittering far above the lights of the city. She thought to how many times she'd stood before this same window, staring at those same stars. She chewed her lower lip and wondered how she had come to be the person she now was.

Tonight she had purposely seduced a man who was promised to another, and she had very nearly—willingly ruined herself at the same time. What had happened to her? Not a month earlier, she had been content in her life, in her work, in her future. She'd never given time to frivolous things such as gowns and hair ribands; in fact, she'd disdained the very thought of them. She'd attended that first ball with Charlotte, even then with the purpose of it still focused on her work—until she'd turned beneath the moonlight of the garden to see Lord Noah Edenhall standing before her.

And nothing in her life had been the same since.

Everything that had happened in the past weeks could be attributed to one person. While she accepted responsibility for what had taken place earlier that night in the duke's study, she couldn't help but allow herself the disapproval that Noah had been such a willing participant, knowing as she did now that he was betrothed to Miss Prescott, that he had been betrothed to her even when he'd come upon her in the garden, when he'd followed her to Hyde Park, when he'd danced with her at Almack's. He was dangerous, a blackguard in the truest sense and she pitied Miss Prescott for having fallen prey to his good looks and persuasive airs, all while thanking the stars above her that she had so slimly avoided being taken advantage of herself.

It was not an opportunity she had any intention of allowing Lord Noah again. She would expunge him from her life, wouldn't so much as acknowledge him should she cross his path in public again. She would return to the one thing she knew would never fail her, the one thing that had been hers and hers alone all along. Her work. It was all that mattered and completing the task of it was all she would focus on now. In order to do that she needed to find a way to get to the Earl of Belgrace.

And she had an idea of how she might just accomplish that.

The coach slowed to a halt two doors down from Numbers 37 and 38 St. James Street, just as Augusta had instructed the driver to do. She parted the small curtain on the window only slightly, peeking through to the night and the lamp-lit street outside.

So this was White's famed gentlemen's club. It was an ordinary-enough-looking sort of establishment, she thought, similar in style to those on either side of it, but with the distinction of its celebrated bow window made famous by Brummel years earlier. Candlelight glowed from behind the drapery, silhouettes moving about inside, and Augusta watched as two gentlemen alighted from a stopping coach, proceeding up the stairs to the front door. Even before they entered, the door opened to reveal a porter whose duties no doubt were to discern if anyone wishing entrance were indeed a member and not simply someone who didn't belong there.

Someone like her.

The idea of this being an establishment which catered only to a male clientele didn't bother Augusta at all, not as it did Charlotte, who seemed to ever bemoan the existence of the St. James clubs and their part in "taking away all the good ones from Almack's." Now that she had begun accompanying Charlotte out among the *ton,* Augusta completely understood how any gentleman might seek an escape from it. Each time she suffered through an evening with Charlotte and her acquaintances, Augusta found herself longing more and more for the end to this Season and her agreement with Charlotte, an agreement which she realized now she'd never truly considered the consequences of.

Augusta studied the facade of the club, looking for any indication of how she might gain entrance to it. Certainly there must be food and drink offered at this sort of an establishment, and if so, then there must also be a kitchen, likely situated somewhere at the rear of the building. This was undoubtedly the busiest time of the night for the club. The kitchen would therefore be bustling. Stewards and porters, kitchen boys, footmen, all would be rushing to and fro to see to the patrons' needs. Perhaps, amid such confusion, she might just slip in through the kitchen entrance unnoticed. . . .

Augusta flipped the coach's half-window open, calling to the driver perched upon the seat outside. "Davison."

The coach pitched and swayed. Moments later a face appeared in the window, a face that was full and round and which bore an uncanny resemblance to the illustration of a rather madcap sort of king which had decorated her favorite storybook as a child. The only difference was that because of either the cold or the small flagon of spirits she knew he kept secreted in the compartment under his seat, Davison's nose was noticeably redder.

"My lady?"

"I should like you to drive around to the stable yard at the back of this row of houses, please."

Davison's mouth puckered in a frown. "Oh, my lady, I'm not thinking that a thing you should be doing. Lady Trecastle will dismiss me for sure if she learns I brought y'out like this at night let alone that I let you go traipsing off in these dark alleyways."

"Nonsense, Davison. Everything will be perfectly all right. Lady Trecastle has nothing to do with the running of the household. That is my duty and I would never think of dismissing you for doing something I myself asked you to do. So you see, there is nothing to fear. I have the situation well in hand."

Well, not exactly, Augusta added to herself, but Davison need not know that.

The coachman raised his bushy brows and took in a breath which spoke of his frustration before turning from the window. Another pitch and a sway and he was back in the coachman's seat, clucking softly to the horses to "Get on now."

Augusta watched their progress through the window

opening. Access to the stable yard was through a narrow passageway, shrouded in darkness and imbued with the heavy smells of damp, refuse, and manure. As they rolled along, Augusta kept a count of the chimney stacks in the moonlight. Hoping she had figured correctly, she tapped on the ceiling when they had reached the one she sought. A pitch and a sway and Davison was at the door again. For a moment, Augusta thought he might perhaps try to prevent her from exiting, for he did not immediately open the door as she had expected. But then he did finally step back and pulled the door open, letting down the steps for her, but not without one more attempt to dissuade her.

"My lady, this is most dangerous, your being out here at this place alone and at this time o'night. Surely I can take yer message to the door and ask the porter to see it delivered to the gentleman you seek."

"Thank you, Davison, but I must deliver this particular message in person." Augusta smiled and patted his arm. "There's nothing at all to worry over. I will only be a quarter hour or so. Once I find my way inside, I will locate the person I came to see and I will be gone before anyone else is the wiser. You just wait here for me to return. All will be well. You'll see."

She smiled reassuringly to him, pulling her hood over her head as she padded across the rutted mud track to the gate at the back of the property.

She saw no one inside the small shadowed yard and slipped through the gate without any trouble. But as she moved around to the front of the stables, she heard the sound of voices approaching. She hesitated, searching for a place to hide. She darted through a small door into a storage closet of sorts at the side of the stable. It was the only haven she'd seen. Pressing her back against the door, she listened as the voices came closer, praying they did not mean to enter. In the moonlight that shone through the small cobweb-strung window, she spotted some clothes then, breeches, and a coat, hanging on a peg set in the wall.

An idea struck her. Surely a woman trying to gain entrance into a men's establishment would warrant notice, but what if that woman were dressed as a boy?

In minutes Augusta had removed her gown and was pulling on the breeches, which fit a bit loosely, but with her chemise tucked into the waist, they certainly would suffice. Her own white stockings and black slipper shoes would pass for proper footwear. But what of her hair? Quickly she removed the pins, pushing her fingers back through the length of it. She bound it at the back of her neck with a bit of leather stripping that had been looped through the handle of a nearby pitchfork. She then stuffed the tail of her hair underneath the high collar of the coat, a smart-looking piece that was likely intended for use by a tiger or groomsman.

Slipping out from the closet, Augusta made slowly for the house. The kitchens were indeed bustling, and no one paid her any mind as she moved on through and into the central entrance hallway. The rooms on either side of her were quiet, but as she came around the bottom of the stairs, she heard footsteps begin to descend above her. She ducked into the space beneath the stairs. Here, in the light of a wall sconce, above her head, she saw numerous pegs sticking out from the wall and cloaks hanging from a good many of them. Over each peg was an engraved plate bearing the name of one of the members of the club. She scanned the plates until she found the one bearing "Tobias Millford, Earl of Belgrace."

A dark cloak and hat rested on the peg. He had come.

"Tell that sloth Will to get Lord Davenport his supper before I take a stick to his backside," said a voice near the foot of the stairs. "I've got to fetch Lord Cantwell's cloak."

Good heavens! Augusta had but a second to slip behind the nearest hanging cloak, quickly arranging the woolen folds to conceal herself while praying that the name on the plate above her head did not read CANTWELL.

Blessedly it did not, but one nearby to it did and Augusta found herself holding her breath as she listened to the shuffling sounds of the steward on the other side as he retrieved Lord Cantwell's belongings. She didn't release her breath until several moments after she was certain he'd gone.

Augusta edged her way out from behind the cloak and hastened toward the stairs, skimming them silently to the upper floor. Just as she reached the topmost step, she spotted two gentlemen coming from one of the nearby rooms. Quickly, she turned to the wall, making as if she were adjusting a candle in a sconce burning there. They were behind her, walking, conversing, then nearly past. They hadn't noticed her. Augusta stepped off in the opposite direction and—

"You there, boy."

She froze. She didn't turn. Indeed, she daren't even breathe.

"Lord Wolfton here left behind his gloves in the Card Room. Go fetch them—there's a shilling in it for you if you make a quick business of it."

Augusta glanced at the door the men had just come through. The muffled murmur of male conversation sounded from the other side. She considered her options: she could run and pray she made it out of the house before anyone caught her, but then the entire venture would have been for nothing. Or she could fetch Lord Wolfton's gloves and see if Lord Belgrace was among those in the Card Room.

"Boy, do you hear? Fetch us Lord Wolfton's gloves!"

Augusta lowered her voice, mumbling a "Yes, my lord," and then tucked her chin to her chest as she headed for the Card Room door.

Chapter Eighteen

Christian Wycliffe, Marquess Knighton and future Duke of Westover, threw his head back as far as his fashionably high cravat would allow and laughed out loud. "You should have partnered me, Devonbrook, instead of that improvident brother of yours. That's the third rubber now he's lost for you. Care to make it four? I'm certain Tolley here and I can find new and inventive ways of spending the Devonbrook fortune."

Bartholomew "Tolley" Archer, Viscount Sheldrake, chuckled in agreement over a sip of his port. Handsome, fashionable, in his younger days Tolley had been known among the *ton* as a bit of an eccentric, always speaking whatever thought might come to mind, and most often thoughts which fringed on the outrageous. For the past several months, though, he'd been away from England, traveling abroad on a whirlwind honeymoon trip. Having returned from Paris with his new bride on his arm, Tolley had taken on a subtle maturity that had given him an air of ease and distinction. Marriage to his young wife, Elise, certainly agreed with him.

Across the table, Noah's brother Robert hadn't joined in on the playful banter. Instead he watched his brother closely, realizing what the others hadn't, that Noah's ill fortune at the cards was more than just coincidence. He rarely lost at cards, and never this badly; Aunt Amelia had taught them both better than that. And it wasn't only the cards. Noah hadn't been acting himself much at all lately, especially when he'd simply vanished without explanation the night of their assembly at Devonbrook House. Although Noah had refused to divulge anything about it when questioned later, Robert somehow couldn't get the suspicion out of his mind that it had something to do with Lady Augusta Brierley.

"Perhaps we should dispense with the whist play for the evening," Robert said. "My brother's attention seems to be a bit preoccupied this evening."

Noah frowned, ignoring Robert's stare as he took up the next hand of cards. "No, let us at least finish with this set. Surely my luck must turn about some time."

And at that the table fell silent as the four men began to study their respective hands. Robert watched Noah a second longer, then shook his head, thinking his brother a stubborn fool as he turned his attention to his own hand. Once the play began, so again did the conversation.

"Sarah had a visitor yesterday," Christian said. "A young pup named Tidney."

"Good lad, Tidney," Tolley piped in. "Heir to a baron in Wales, I believe. Always seems to present himself well. Admirable polish to his boots."

Noah looked over the tops of his cards to Christian. "Did she receive him?"

"No." He shrugged. "Even Eleanor couldn't convince her to it. Said she wasn't up to any visitors and certainly couldn't receive a male caller who wasn't a friend of the family while she was still in mourning for Tony."

Noah frowned. "Sarah cannot continue to hide herself away from society as she has been. It isn't good for her."

"I didn't think she looked particularly well at our musicale the other night," Robert said. "Even Catriona remarked upon it. In fact, she thinks Sarah looks to have worsened since we've come to town. She's grown quite pale and her eyes have such an emptiness about them."

"Eleanor says the maids report that Sarah hasn't been eating either," Christian said. "Nor does she sleep. They say she can be heard up each night pacing the floor in her bedchamber, weeping sometimes. Whenever Eleanor tries to comfort her, Sarah only tells her she has nothing to live for, no hope for a future. All those years, she filled her days with running Keighley Cross and taking care of Tony's responsibilities. It is all lost to her now."

Due to the sudden arrival from the Continent of their distant Keighley uncle, a man whom they'd always known existed but whom they had never actually known. No sooner had he set foot on English soil than the new Viscount Keighley had made his claim to the title—and with it the estate at Keighley Cross. His solicitor had sent a letter simply thanking Sarah for having kept the estate so well during her time there and bestowing on her the small quarterly allowance she was to be allowed by the estate. Although she hadn't disclosed the amount, Noah knew it couldn't be much. Even though he had assumed all of Tony's outstanding debts, with the Keighley town house yet unsold, Sarah had been left virtually dependent upon the charity of others. It was a fate similar to many young women.

"She has nothing to occupy herself," Tolley said. "No husband. No children to see to. It would be good for her to marry. Marriage does wonders for the humors of a lady."

The table fell silent. When Noah next looked up from his cards, he saw the others were staring at him, their thoughts easily readable. They expected he should wed Sarah, to remedy her troubles with an exchange of the vows. Even he himself had found himself considering the possibility of it, and in fact when he'd paid a visit to her earlier that week, it had been with that sole thought consuming his mind.

Noah tried to return his attentions to his cards, but the thoughts came unbidden. Yes, a marriage to Sarah could be the perfect solution. It would ease Sarah's burdens both financially and otherwise, and it would resolve him of his own personal duty to Tony at the same time, that he would always take care of Sarah. But try as he might to think on Sarah as a man would a wife, whenever he'd taken her hand, kissing it cordially, Noah had felt nothing more than the affection and brotherly regard he'd always known for her. He just couldn't get the image of her out of his mind, seven years old, having a tea party with her dolls on the south terrace of Keighley Cross. She'd always looked on him as her hero of sorts. The difference was when she would look at him now, her face, her eyes were always filled with that same adoration, and something else—naked and obvious hope.

What a paradox his life had become. Not two years before, a marriage without love, without passion would have been incomprehensible to him. He had rebuked his own brother Robert when he had arranged a marriage with a woman he freely admitted held no love. Thankfully that marriage had never come to pass and when Robert then found love with Catriona, it had only strengthened Noah's resolve never to marry without that same feeling. It had been soon after when Noah had first met Lady Julia Grey and he'd believed his bachelor days at a happy end.

Julia had been everything he'd ever envisioned for himself in a wife, a lover, and a mother of his children. Blond, classically beautiful, from the moment she'd turned those china blue eyes his way, he'd been consumed with having her, his sole aim the previous Season to make Julia his wife. But at nearly the eleventh hour, Noah had learned the terrible truth about Julia, a truth that eventually brought him to a dueling field one early late summer dawn. All of his hopes for the future, his future and that of his children, had gone up in the blackened puff of powder and smoke that had followed the firing from his pistol.

So why not undertake a marriage with Sarah? He'd tried a pairing of passion and had only found despair. Why not a pairing of companionship instead? He certainly knew Sarah better than he knew any other woman, he knew her gentleness, her innate goodness. With Sarah he need never question her faith, need never fear what had occurred with Julia. But could he truly spend the rest of his life with a woman he felt no sexual desire for? Simply the thought of bedding Sarah seemed unnatural to him. And in realizing this, he knew that no matter how he might consider it, no matter how it might resolve his troubled thoughts, he could never actually see through to an actual marriage. He refused to confine Sarah to a future such as that, not when she deserved so much more. Sarah deserved happiness. She deserved to be worshipped, adored, cherished. She deserved more than he could ever offer her. And she would have more, a love more cherished, more wonderful than that which she believed she felt for him. Noah was determined that she would.

But not by hiding herself away as she was.

"Well, that finishes off the set," Robert suddenly said, pulling Noah from his thoughts and back to his cards. "And I believe my brother could benefit from a brandy. That is if I can still afford one. Let me see if I can find a steward . . . or perhaps that boy over there can see to it."

Noah glanced negligibly toward the figure that was threading its way across the shadows at the far side of the room. As the boy passed, he swore he caught a glimpse of something, something familiar, a wisp of midnight black hair against skin as pale as moonlight, very like . . .

Good God, was he losing his mind?

Robert stared to rise from his chair. "If you'll excuse me, gentlemen."

"No," Noah said, snaking out a hand to stop him. "I'll go."

Ignoring Robert's curious look, he stood and made across the room. Noah spotted Lord Belgrace sitting in the corner with a colleague conversing over port. He tried to discount what he already suspected, that Augusta had pursued the earl here to White's of all places. He tried to convince himself he was mistaken even as he headed for the figure of the boy. The jacket was oversized, the breeches baggy, yes, but surely he would know if they concealed a female form, wouldn't he?

By the time he had come upon the boy, Noah had convinced himself it couldn't possibly be her.

Until he saw the slim, shapely calves and small slippered feet.

Good God! Augusta had stolen her way into White's, the very sanctum of the male population of London, one of few places where those of the female population were expressly forbidden. Did her boldness know no bounds?

Noah stopped directly behind her. The familiar scent of her, spicy and floral, reached to him then, finally confirming that it was indeed her. He tried not to acknowledge how damned alluring she looked in a pair of breeches as he said, "Some brandy for myself and my companions, boy, and be quick about it."

He saw her start and then immediately she grew still, obviously trying to figure what she could do now. He had lowered his voice purposely so she wouldn't realize that it was him behind her. Without turning, she nodded her head and tried skirting around to the far side of the table.

Noah pursued her, cutting her off in mid-flight. "And some bread and cheese."

She responded with another nod, head down, trying to move off the other way. He stepped in her path once again, adding, "And one golden apple."

She was cornered. He knew it. She knew it. And she knew who stood behind her. With the way in which they were situated, Augusta stood in the shadows, hidden from sight of the other patrons by him. She slowly lifted her chin. With no other choice left open to her, she simply glared at him.

"Are you quite finished?" she whispered, peering around behind him. She did not wear her spectacles and he watched as she squinted against the darkness, studying the patrons seated behind him. Noah waited until he was certain she had spotted Belgrace, the look on her face confirming for him that it had indeed been the earl she'd come there seeking.

"It isn't every day one finds a lady dressed as a boy inside a club held strictly for men. Surely you can't fault a gentleman for having a little fun."

She frowned. "I wouldn't, if there were a gentleman present."

Noah smiled at her sarcastic wit. "You wound me. Especially when I have been nothing but the most honorable of gentlemen with you."

"Ah, yes, the Honorable Lord Noah, from the very moment you came upon me on the terrace at the Lumley ball. As I recall you were quite the gentleman that night."

"I did replace your hat."

"To be sure, after you had destroyed my other one."

"And did your horse enjoy the apple?"

"No. It carried a worm."

Noah's smile deepened. No other lady of society would stand before him, dressed in a boy's breeches and coat, in the midst of an exclusively male club like White's, finding fault with a gift he'd given her horse. No other lady except Augusta.

"Tell me, my lady, do you have any idea how foolish it was to—"

"There he is!"

At the gruff voice coming from behind Noah, Augusta shrunk further into the shadows.

"What the devil are you doing, boy? I told you to fetch Lord Wolfton's gloves! I've half a mind to call Raggett up here and have you tossed to the—"

"I don't think that will be necessary," Noah said coolly, cutting the intruder off. He turned, and in doing so, shielded Augusta from the two figures advancing behind them.

The men were no strangers to Noah. The first, Lord Archibald Wolfton, immediately paled at the sight of him. The second man, Sir Spencer Atherton, returned a look of pure and unveiled hatred.

"Edenhall." Instinctively he reached up to touch the slash-shaped scar that crossed his left cheek, ending at the place where the lobe of his ear had once been, but was no more.

Noah kept his face expressionless as he stared silently at the man who had nearly destroyed him the year before. Sir Spencer once had been the darling of the *ton,* a close friend of Brummell, a man who seemed to endear himself more to society every time he broke one of its sacred rules. Sandy blond hair topped a flawless face that looked carved from fine marble. Lazy blue eyes that knew every way to seduce even the most reluctant of maidens. A mouth that seemed ever curved in its peremptory smile. They had called him Adonis, Sir Spencer Perfection, and his looks had gained him a status among society which his lack of fortune might otherwise have prevented.

It had been nearly nine months since Noah had last seen him that early morn twenty paces apart across the foggy field on the outskirts of London. Atherton's own shot had fired wide, missing Noah to bury itself in the fat trunk of the oak that stood a yard beside him. Noah hadn't yet fired and was just readying to discharge his pistol into the ground, to call the affair settled, when Atherton had delivered him a blow even more injurious than if he'd shot him through.

She carries my child, he had said with a sneer as Noah had stood frozen by the words.

Without thought Noah had raised his arm again, his pistol aiming straight for his adversary's chest. Robert, acting as his second, had called for him to stop. But the gesture of a pistol aimed straight at him hadn't frightened Atherton. It had only incited him on.

Did you think she wanted you in her bed when she already had me? She read me your letters, your foolish drivel, and she laughed at how she'd deluded you. She never wanted you. It was the money, the famous Devonbrook fortune . . .

Trembling with his outrage, Noah's finger had pulled on the trigger reflexively, the shot slicing across Atherton's cheek, taking his ear with it, and forever marking the man whose visage had been likened to a god.

"You have no business with this," Atherton said to him now, his face grown as rigid as the scar which crossed it. He tried to reach around Noah to grab Augusta. "I gave the boy an order and he failed to follow it. Raggett will deal with him."

Noah stepped forward, deflecting Atherton. Fortunately no one had yet noticed the two of them standing together. Everyone's attentions seemed focused on one of the tables where no doubt a fast fortune was about to be passed. But the history between the two men was well known. It would only be a matter of time before someone saw them together. Then all eyes would be on them, and on the "boy" who crouched behind Noah.

Noah knew he had to get Augusta out of here.

He shrugged. "Then summon Raggett. It matters naught to me."

"You will regret having interfered with this, Edenhall."

Atherton turned then, hieing off to call for the club's owner. Wolfton, his ever present shadow, followed. When they were gone, Noah grabbed Augusta by the arm, leading her through a narrow side door.

"Where are you taking me?"

"Just come with me and be quiet."

He took her to another door that opened onto a small stairwell at the back of the building, a servant's stairwell that gave off into the kitchens. They proceeded through without drawing notice and quickly slipped out into the yard.

Once a safe distance away from the house, Noah turned to face her, still clutching her arm. "Now, you have precisely five seconds to start explaining."

But Augusta had other ideas. Before Noah realized what had happened, she slipped away, leaving him standing alone, holding the sleeves of her coat as she dashed for the stables. All he caught was a flash of white skin and dark hair before she was gone.

"Wait, you little—" Noah gave chase, running for the stables in pursuit. There was no light inside, not even moonlight to guide him. He halted, listening for her in the darkness. He could only hear the sounds of the horses moving restlessly in their stalls. And then the stable door closed, and he heard the sound of the latch being slid into place. Moments later, coach wheels sounded on the mews behind the stable.

Noah knew then the next time he saw Lady Augusta Brierley, he would have no choice but to kill her.

A horse whinnied at him in the darkness, a sound not at all unlike a laugh. Noah would have sworn it was his own horse, Humphrey.

A quarter of an hour later, Noah heard the latch slide back on the stable door. It opened to reveal a boy, the same one who had taken his horse at his arrival earlier that night. Silhouetted by the moonlight, he spotted Noah immediately where he sat on a hay-strewn trunk. "My lord?"

Noah stood and dusted off his breeches. "Yes, Harry. It's me." Then taking up the coat Augusta had been wearing, he started for the door. "My horse, Harry, if you please."

Augusta closed the door to her bedchamber quietly, hesitating a moment to make certain no one was coming after. Thankfully she had not come across Charlotte when she'd returned to the house, for if her stepmother had seen her as she was, dressed only in her chemise and a pair of dirty boy's breeches, her hair down and wild about her shoulders, she would surely fall apoplectic.

A failure! The night's excursion had been a terrible defeat and the fault of it all rested solely on the shoulders of that abominable Lord Noah Edenhall. Why, if he hadn't interfered—again—she would have been successful. She would have gone into the Card Room, would have gained the attention of the earl, and would have implored him to meet with her privately outside. And she would have been able to give him the—

Augusta sat bolt upright on the bed, her hand coming up to cover her open mouth. Oh, good Lord no. The coat. The inside pocket. In her haste to get away from Noah, she'd completely forgotten what she'd put there. She'd slipped out of the coat, leaving him holding it.

And now Noah had it. He had the coat.

And with it, he had her secret as well.

Noah sat in the study at his house on Charles Street, a glass of brandy set on the side table beside him. The fire burned low at his feet and though he couldn't see the clock across the room, he knew the hour was well past midnight. He'd been home for some time, having left Robert, Christian, and Tolley at White's soon after being sprung from the stables by Harry. Upon his return indoors, only Robert had commented on his absence, saying he had thought it due to the appearance of Atherton, who apparently had made quite a scene upon returning to the Card Room with the club's owner Raggett to find both Noah and "the boy" gone.

Noah had done nothing to convince Robert that his disappearance had been for entirely different reasons. No one ever realized that there had been a woman amidst their misogynist club. And no one had noticed the small bundle of clothing Noah had left with, a dark woolen cloak in which was wrapped the lady's gown, both of which he'd found hanging on a peg in the stable's storage closet when he'd gone to return the coat Augusta had worn.

But it wasn't the gown, or even the cloak Noah studied now. Instead it was the folded sheet of foolscap he'd found hidden away inside the pocket of the coat she'd worn to disguise herself. It was a curious sheet, covered on both front and back with strange-looking symbols and numbers, a system of codes that was incomprehensible to him. It must have been written by Augusta though, for the text was small, neat, and decidedly feminine. What it was, however, and why she had carried it in the pocket of the coat she'd disguised herself with in her pursuit of Belgrace was what left him wondering.

It only added credence to suspicions that had been niggling on the fringes of his mind from the very first moment he'd seen her, nay even earlier than that.

In the beginning, Noah had tried to tell himself that his notion about Augusta's involvement in the practice of some sort of witchcraft was only his imagination running wild. He had only begun the postulation as a lark, as some sort of farfetched explanation for Tony's obsession with her and his subsequent death. But now, faced time and again with the odd coincidences that only seemed to support that theory, he found he could not bring himself to accept that Augusta could actually be the witch he'd imagined her.

It wasn't that he totally discounted the existence of those individuals who might secretly practice the dark arts. He'd studied enough of history to know that witchcraft in its various forms had been around for centuries. It had, in fact, been less than a century earlier that those suspected of it had been burned at the stake. But in his mind, whenever he considered the subject, Noah could only summon the image of some haggard-looking crone stirring a cauldron away in a cave somewhere in the far reaches of the country. Whatever else he might imagine, he certainly could not envision a witch posing as a lady of society in the middle of civilized London.

The curious star and moon amulet Augusta wore around her neck, her propensity for dark clothing, the fact that she slept during the day and was awake through the night, even her cat colored black, all of it could easily be written off as coincidence. But what of Tony's death? Had Augusta truly had a hand in it? The more Noah saw of her, the less he found himself willing to believe it. This petite, albeit secretive creature a murderess? It somehow didn't seem likely, still he could not abandon the thought all together, for it had been Tony's death which had brought him to encountering Augusta in the first place. First there had been her strange actions to consider, and now he'd found this peculiar sheet of figures in her coat. Symbols, stars, numeric designations. What could it possibly mean? Was Augusta truly a witch? Could these figures be some sort of a spell she'd planned to exercise upon an unsuspecting Belgrace? Perhaps the same sort of spell she'd exercised upon Tony already?

Good God, Noah thought, shaking his head against the seeming ridiculousness of the idea. He really had lost all sense. A witch? Was he seriously now considering it? If anyone else should discover what he was thinking, they'd think him mad.

Still the fact remained that whatever this sheet of figures and images was, it had definitely been the incentive for Augusta having gone to White's in search of Lord Belgrace. And she had taken great risk in doing so. So if she were willing to go to such lengths to bring this sheet of foolscap into an exclusive men's club, how far would she go to get it back?

It would take some preparation, and careful planning. But, if he played his hand rightly, this scrap of paper might just help him answer his questions once and for all.

The gaming salon held a half dozen or so tables, each bathed in its own incandescent aura of light from the four tall candlesticks set in holders at every corner. The air was filled with the scent of fragrant beeswax and conversation was subdued, a sharp contrast to the clamor of the adjoining ballroom and supper parlor. Here every sort of game could be had—whist, piquet, faro, even hazard for the more riskily inclined, stakes rising easily into the tens of thousands.

Among those already deep in play were Euphemia, Lady Talfrey, a society matron formidable in both situation and size and Amelia's biggest rival in card play. Across from her sat the eminent Idonea, Duchess DeWinton, a consummate gambler whose skill at the cards, unfortunately for her, hadn't managed to improve through her years of perpetual practice. It was rumored that Her Grace's debts would often rise in excess of ninety thousand pounds, a dilemma she had been known in her younger days as a celebrated beauty to have used her sexual favors to satisfy. The fact that three of her ten children bore none of the trademark DeWinton features but instead those of other prominent noble lines and were known privately as "The DeWinton Debtlings" certainly seemed to support this belief.

Noah saw his Aunt Amelia to her companions, watching through half of the first round before making his way across the room to another table, one set off in the far corner and currently occupied by Lord Everton and his usual two companions, Lords Yarlett and Mundrum. The three were, it seemed as Noah approached, engaged in play at the outdated game of ombre.

Mundrum was grumbling over his cards. "Come on with you, Yarlett. Name the trump already. I feel my arse taking root in the lumps of the cushion on this chair from the waiting."

"Well, perhaps if your mouth could stop running long enough for me to study my cards in peace, I might manage to do the job."

Shaking his head at the other two, Lord Everton lay his hand facedown with a slap upon the tabletop. "If the both of you would stop wagging your chins like a couple of gibbering noddies, we might actually finish a round by the dawn."

He looked upward in exasperation and it was then he noticed Noah standing there. "Ah, Edenhall, my boy. Take pity on an old man and rescue me from this blethering hell."

Noah grinned. "Actually, I was wondering if I might join the game?"

All three of the men looked at Noah as if he'd just announced his intentions to join a band of Gypsies. "You say you want to play cards? With us?"

"No offense, gentlemen," Noah said, his eyes never leaving Everton's, "but I was of a mind to play a two-handed game. Would his lordship indulge me?"

Everton watched him, a subtle smile of understanding creeping upon his mouth. "I'm certain my friends here wouldn't mind leaving us for a time, would you?"

Yarlett and Mundrum quickly took their leave, departing for the more crowded side of the room.

Everton motioned across from him. "Here, my boy, take your ease. What'll you have, sir? Port? Brandy? Yes, you look more the brandy sort than the port sort."

He chuckled at his own wit and waved quickly toward one of the attendants hovering in the shadows. "You there, fetch Lord Noah a brandy, will you? The best you have and be quick about it!"

He started shuffling the cards. "What's your game, Edenhall? Piquet? Comet? You call the method and I'll join you in the madness."

Noah was beginning to wonder if he shouldn't just excuse himself, turn about, and leave. Why did he seek to involve himself any further in this? Why could he not simply forget Lady Augusta, leave her to her game—whatever it was—and let Lord Belgrace find his own way out of her snare? What was it about this lady in particular that plagued him so thoroughly?

Even while he thought this, he found himself suggesting a *partie* of piquet with Everton.

The earl dealt out each hand, placing the remaining cards between them on the table. Noah replaced three of his cards, Everton four before turning what remained in the talon faceup.

Noah studied the cards before him. "Point of seven," he said, announcing his opening play as he began to work out what he would say to the earl. First he would ally himself to the man with card play.

"Making?" Everton asked.

"Sixty-four."

"Good."

After proceeding through the next categories, Noah quickly took the first hand. They were into the last hand of the *partie* when Everton spoke out. "So, my boy, you don't expect me to believe you really only came here to play a hand or two at cards with a shopworn old buzzard like me. Surely there must be something more to it than that. Out with it now."

Noah looked at the earl. "Actually, my lord, you are right. I did have another reason in seeking you out tonight. It has to do with something I chanced upon last night while I was at White's."

Everton raised a brow. "White's, you say? Hmm, I haven't been to the club in a week or more and I haven't found anything missing, so whatever it is, it likely isn't mine."

"Curiously, I had been led to believe you might be familiar with it." Noah reached inside his coat. "If it isn't yours, perhaps you might be able to ascertain the true ownership of the item."

He unfolded the sheet of figures he'd found in the coat Augusta wore and placed it upon the table in front of Everton. The earl glanced at it, but if he did recognize it, he certainly was adept at hiding any reaction to it from Noah. His eyes didn't so much as blink as he turned his attention back to his cards. "Interesting bit of work there, Edenhall, but I can't say I've ever seen it before. You say you found it at White's? Odd sort of thing to come across there. Indeed. Sorry I couldn't have been more of a help to you, my boy."

Somehow Noah didn't believe Everton totally ignorant of the sheet or its cryptic figures. Even though he had managed to shield his reaction, the earl knew something. Noah decided to press on.

"I was going to toss the thing into the fire, but I found myself growing more and more curious as to its meaning. In trying to ascertain the nature of the sheet, I was studying the figures drawn upon it. Peculiar sort of design. Somewhat mystical even, don't you think?"

"Mystical?"

"Yes." Noah grinned. "At first I even thought I'd perhaps happened upon a witch's spell of some sort, but then I thought certainly no such creature could be found in this day and age and especially in a civilized town like London."

Everton laughed, but his humor now had a somewhat strained tone to it. "A witch? Here in London? A jocular sort of notion, wouldn't you say." He glanced at Noah to see if he was sharing in the mirth. He cleared his throat, adding, "Most jocular, indeed."

The earl managed to restrain himself but a few moments longer before he said, "You know, Edenhall, I have quite an extensive library. I could take this sheet and see if I might be able to use my resources to decipher it for you."

And when he said that, the earl's voice broke, only slightly but it was all the confirmation Noah needed. "My thanks to you, my lord, but I think I will continue in my efforts to figure it out myself, you know, what glory is there in the hunt if one does not do the riding oneself? I'll be sure, though, to let you know if I am successful in deciphering its meaning." He laid his cards upon the table. "It looks as if our card play has come to an end as well. The congratulations go to you, my lord, for you have trounced me soundly."

And with that he took up the sheet, bowed his head, and turned to leave the room.

Chapter Nineteen

The package arrived early the following morning and was waiting for Augusta in the parlor when she awoke that afternoon. Inside were her gown and cloak, the clothing she'd worn to White's the previous evening, carefully folded. One golden apple lay wrapped in soft tissue atop them. The note she found buried with the items inside was not, however, her sheet of formulas, but one which read instead:

> My lady, I chanced upon the enclosed items when I endeavored to return the coat you had borrowed from the stable closet. I thought you might appreciate their return. Also, please accept this apple in place of the other. It is guaranteed free of vermin.
> Your Servant, Edenhall
> P.S. The grooms at White's certainly have unusual tastes in reading material.

Augusta glared down at his script. What game did he play at now? He had her sheet of figures. It was obvious from the postscript. Any gentleman would have returned them with the other items. Why had he kept them, unless . . .

. . . he knew what they signified.

And if that were the case, heaven help her.

A chill of realization at having her worst fear come true settled over Augusta. She dropped back into the chair behind her, staring down at the Kidderminster carpet in disbelief. All her years of work, all this time she'd managed to keep anyone else from knowing the truth of what she did. Only her father knew of her secret, of how she occupied the nighttime hours in her rooftop belvedere, and he had sworn to tell no one, not even Charlotte.

And now through her own carelessness, she might have lost it all—but only if Lord Noah knew the true significance of what he had found. What if he did not? What if she were jumping to conclusions? There was always that hope.

And thus there was only one thing she could do. She had to get her figures back, no matter the risk it entailed. She was so very close to attaining her goal, a goal that would see her life changed forever after. She had worked so hard, she could not allow anyone to ruin her objective now—she looked down at the apple—most especially not Lord Noah Edenhall.

Settled in her decision, Augusta took a bite of the apple and started off for the kitchen and her morning tea, wondering fleetingly to herself if a sentence in prison awaited her at the end of her journey. A knocking on the door, however, delayed her departure.

Tiswell presented himself at the parlor door. "My lady, this message just arrived for you."

"Please put it with the others on the hall table, Tiswell. I'll see to it later."

She started to walk past him.

"My lady, the messenger said it was an urgent missive and requested your immediate reply."

"Urgent? Who is it from?"

"I do not know, my lady. The messenger only said you would know."

She would know? Augusta looked at Tiswell incredulously. She took the letter and quickly opened it.

My lady, our very mission is in peril. We must meet and discuss a course of action before it is too late. I beseech you to come tonight, at the customary time and place.

Augusta folded the letter and placed it in the pocket of her daygown.

"My lady?" Tiswell asked. "Shall I instruct the messenger to wait until you pen your response?"

"No, Tiswell," she said on a grim frown. "That will not be necessary. Just tell the messenger to relay to the sender that the message was indeed received."

The streets of London were remarkably quiet at three o'clock in the morning. But an hour earlier there had still been elegant coaches delivering their late-night frolicking lords and ladies home, and but an hour hence there would be street vendors and market hawkers emerging to set up their wares in the market squares.

But for now, for this one hour, the city slept.

Once the coach turned down Piccadilly, heading south, they passed no one save a lone charley who sat, chin to chest, truncheon in hand, dozing in his sentry box. The waters of the reservoir at Green Park shimmered beneath the muted moonlight. They soon arrived at Number 25 St. James Place. The house was dark, as was usual whenever she came here, but a single small candle burned in the entrance hall window.

Augusta entered quietly through the unlocked front door and took the candle, silently climbing the second, and then third flights of stairs before coming to the door she sought.

Without knocking, she turned the handle softly and stepped through into a place unlike any other on earth.

The room was modest, originally intended for the housing of servants, one of four identical to it on each upper corner of the stately town house. The main feature of the chamber were the two tall windows standing adjacent from one another on either side of the far corner. Taking up nearly the entirety of each wall, no drapery or even a simple swag adorned them. They had replaced the smaller, ox-eye openings which had once gazed onto the outside.

All around the crowded room were various instruments of science; altazimuth and repeating circles, telescopes, quadrants, and sextants. Each wall and table were covered by numerous charts and graphs and unattended sheets of paper littered the floor here and there. Among this endless clutter, with his back to her as he studied the view outside one of the tall observing windows, stood the Earl of Everton.

Gone were the elegant silks, the starchy white cravats he normally wore when he went out among the *ton*. Now he wore his usual attire for this chamber, a loose banyan-like coat over trousers, his peppered hair slightly tousled from his habit of ruffling it when deep in thought. He hadn't heard her come in and likely wouldn't have noticed had she dropped one of his thick reference volumes on the floor for he tended to be rather oblivious when immersed in his work.

Augusta stood behind him a moment, waiting, watching, observing, wondering if the day might come when she would be so brilliant, wishing that the earl's brilliance weren't hidden away from the rest of the world as it was.

Everton pulled his attentions away from his work for a moment to take a sip of tea, no doubt long cold. As he turned to replace the cup on its tray, he spotted her standing there.

"I was beginning to wonder that you might not come," he said with his usual brevity. He turned back to the window.

But Augusta wasn't distressed by his reception, for she knew his brusque manner was but a façade to hide the true gentle man inside. She'd first met the earl not long after she had returned to London ten months ago. She'd been to Hatchard's where she had happened to take a seat across from him in the reading lounge. She couldn't recall what she'd been reading that day, for it wasn't long before she was peeking over the pages of her own book, her attentions having strayed from her reading material to his. She remembered how he'd stepped away, only to return moments later to find her secretly perusing his copy of The Royal Society's *Philosophical Transactions* he'd left on the table between them. From that day forward, they had been kindred spirits, their meeting seeming destined by fate.

"Charlotte was late retiring. I had to be certain she wouldn't hear me leaving."

Everton gave a single nod, turning for the tea tray again. "Tea?" he asked, picking up the pot and lifting the lid to peer inside. The look on his face was less than enthusiastic. "On second thought, perhaps claret would be better." He poured her a glass from the crystal decanter set near the tray. As he handed it to her, he said, "You are wondering why I summoned you here so urgently."

"Your note was intriguing."

"I thought you might be interested in the chat I had with a certain individual yesterday."

"Indeed," she said, taking a small sip of the claret. It was sweet and very smooth, warming her inside.

"Yes, indeed. Perhaps you know him—Lord Noah Edenhall."

Augusta immediately frowned as if the wine had gone sour. Somehow she knew she wasn't going to like what the earl was about to say.

"He came to show me something, to ask my opinion of it, actually. It was a scrap of paper he says he found at White's of all places."

He waited a moment, watching for Augusta's reaction.

She hid it behind another sip of claret.

"Augusta? You went to White's?"

She glanced at him, setting her glass casually on the table. "I could think of no other way to approach Lord Belgrace. Our attempts to meet in the park have failed at every turn. Time is running out. I certainly cannot go marching to his front door, especially now with every pair of society's eyes upon me."

"Well, you weren't successful going to White's either since Edenhall now obviously has your notes in his possession. I won't even ask how you managed to get inside the place."

She frowned again. "I will retrieve the notes from him."

"And how do you propose to do that?" The earl was scowling.

Augusta scowled back. "I do not yet know. I am contriving a way to—"

"Before he figures out what it is that is written on that sheet?"

Augusta blanched. "How could he know? It is written in my own code. No one knows it but me. Not even you."

"Were it Yarlett or Mundrum, I wouldn't worry, but I would put nothing past a man like Edenhall. He's smart and he's shrewd just like his brother. Give him enough time and he'll figure it out." Everton paused then, but only a moment. "We are, for the moment however, safe. His initial theory about your notes is quite contrary to the truth."

"What do you mean?"

Everton chuckled. "I don't really know how to tell you this, except to simply say it. I am afraid, my dear Augusta, that Edenhall suspects you are a witch."

Augusta stared at him. "A witch?"

"Yes, my dear, in the truest sense of the word, you know, cauldrons and broomsticks and pointy hats. At least the idea has crossed his mind, even as the more sensible side of him tries to deny it. Now were I you, I would do everything in my power to support that notion and keep him from learning the truth of what you're really up to. You might even consider fashioning a wart for the end of your nose. Otherwise everything you've worked for all these months will be lost for even if he cannot decipher your notations himself, consider that all he need do is take them to Belgrace himself . . ."

"And what harm would that do? We wanted Lord Belgrace to have the notes. Lord Noah would be doing us a service if he were to show the notes to Belgrace."

"Have you learned nothing from me?" Everton burst out. "This is a matter which must be handled delicately. What if Belgrace should take those notes straight to the Society? They'll listen to him, yes, but your discovery would become yet another entry in the history books with the credit for it going straight to one of them. Is that what you want?"

Augusta frowned. "Of course not, but how can you be so certain that the Society would claim my discovery for their own?"

"Because I know those men all too well. Need I remind you I was once one of them? Believe me well, girl, when I say nothing is more important to them than their blasted male ambition. Nothing! They have succeeded nearly two

centuries in excluding women from fellowship, women
who might contribute greatly to the scientific community,
all for the sake of their misogynist pride. But you stand at
the precipice of something they cannot discount. You could
be the first of your sex to make a difference, to demand
recognition, unless they learn of it in time to stop you. Listen to me, well, Augusta. Trust no one."

And with that, Lord Everton turned from her, striding
away to the opposite window to stare sullenly outward. Augusta remained where she stood, chastising herself for having
ever questioned his judgment on the matter. How could she
have doubted him like that? He, of all people? The earl had
taken her when she'd been naught but a novice, when she'd
known scarcely a thing of the stars and midnight sky. He had
tutored her, encouraging her despite the fact that she was a
woman. It was not a thing many men of his status in life
would do, thinking women too empty-headed, too simple-
minded to take any significant place among the scientific
community. The earl had shown her the way, leading her with
his gentle guidance to the very brink of discovery.

And it was her discovery, that tiny, unaccounted-for
spark in the night sky, for no one else had ever recorded its
movement, the prominence that made it something much
more than just a star. For years she had gazed upon it with
wonder, for months she had been following it, measuring it,
carefully recording its progress through most every night,
her own little midnight jewel. She'd checked every calcula-
tion thrice until, when she had been confident in her findings, she'd gone to her friend, her mentor, the most notable
Earl of Everton.

His observations had concurred with hers; there was indeed something there out of the ordinary. But the recording
of its existence, especially by an unknown, an amateur, *a
woman,* would require delicacy with the esteemed and

tightly knit Royal Society, who looked on any outsider with suspicion, women especially so. Everton had been a fellow at one time and thus could guide her to eventual due accreditation, but the patronage of a current fellow of standing would assure her recognition.

After careful consideration, he'd finally suggested that she approach his friend, the Earl of Belgrace, whom he thought honest and whom he believed wouldn't try to eschew Augusta because of her gender. And they had been so very close to that final stage of their plan, but she'd bungled it all by losing the very proof she had of her waiting discovery.

The earl was right. She had to get those notes back from Noah, no matter the cost.

No matter the risk.

No matter the consequence.

Noah removed his gloves and laid them with his tall beaver hat on the side table. He had just returned home from a drive about town with Eleanor, Christian, and Sarah. They had gone to visit Amelia seemingly for tea and cakes, but Noah's secret hope had been that his aunt's naturally cheery disposition would help to brighten the dolor that seemed forever shadowing Sarah's blue eyes.

And after three hours, countless sweet cakes, and several pots of Amelia's flowery lemon tea, he had to admit Sarah's demeanor had improved. Amelia had delighted everyone with anecdotes of her most memorable card-playing triumphs—even stoic Finch hadn't been able to suppress a smile at some of them—and afterward, Amelia had even divulged one of her secret strategies to them, swearing them all, of course, to sacred silence.

By the time they'd left, traces of the Sarah he'd known and grown up with had resurfaced, leaving Noah hopeful that she would soon be on her way to healing her grief and moving on with the rest of her life.

A small stack of letters lay waiting for him in the salver on the side table, along with a couple calling cards from acquaintances. Noah took up the letters and started sifting through them as he made his way to his study, categorizing them in his mind as to importance. There was a message from his solicitor informing him that the last of Tony's debtors had been paid the week before and Sarah would now no longer have to worry. Another letter had come from the steward at his country estate, Eden Court, in York, a family holding bequeathed to him by his father and one which had seen a great deal of history, Cavaliers and Roundheads having waged battle on her verdant turf two centuries before.

Noah set these two most important of the letters atop his desk and was just preparing to lay the others aside until later when one in particular caught his attention. It wasn't so much the letter, but the handwriting on it that made him give it a second glance for it was a script that was neither distinctively male nor female, but unnatural, as if someone had taken great care with the shape of every letter. Noah took up the letter, noticing that it was sealed with a plain black wafer on its underside. He quickly opened it and read the message inside.

> You think yourself clever
> But I am cleverer still
> You play at a game of danger
> That win, you never will

There was no signature, no indication of who might have sent it, no explanation of the author's meaning. Only those four short ominous lines.

Noah read the message again, his gaze settled on one particular word. *Danger.*

His most immediate consideration was Atherton. The hatred between them was bone-deep and Atherton had recently returned to town, making his first appearances since the duel the previous Season. If their confrontation at White's the other night had been any indication, Atherton had not acquired a rational thought by any means. A man who would stoop to impregnating another man's betrothed certainly would not show himself above sending threatening letters. But to what purpose? Atherton would have to know he would be the likeliest suspect. Could he be that nonsensical?

Noah considered Lord Everton then. Although he'd tried to disguise it, when Noah had shown the earl the sheet of notations he'd found in Augusta's coat, Everton had become noticeably uncomfortable. Was this a warning from the earl aimed at frightening Noah into returning the sheet of figures? And if so, then who was to say this message had not come from Augusta herself? He hadn't seen or heard from her since the night at White's, as if she'd gone into seclusion, giving up altogether on her pursuit of Lord Belgrace. If this note did have something to do with her, then what could be so important about the odd figures drawn on that paper?

A knocking on the door drew Noah from his thoughts. He looked to see Westman standing patiently in the doorway.

"My lord, this message was just delivered for you."

Another? Noah took the letter and glanced at the direction. This was a decidedly feminine script, yet bold. He turned it over and noticed the design imprinted into the wax seal. It was identical to the one which had adorned Tony's letter the night he'd died. The Brierley seal. A message for him from Augusta? Noah's curiosity mounted.

My Lord, you are no doubt aware that there is something you have in your possession which I desire returned to me. Should you like to explore this issue further tonight at the ball being held at the Earl and Countess of Danby's, I shall be in the garden at 11 o'clock.

Anticipating the promise of your company, A Lady

Noah walked behind his desk and sat down. Across the desktop he placed first the letter he'd just received so obviously from Augusta, second the anonymous bit of menacing poetry, and then opening the top drawer of his desk, he retrieved both the letter Tony had received the night he'd died and the sheet of figures he'd found in Augusta's coat, placing them third and fourth before him. He studied each letter separately and then compared them collectively.

Of the first three, none of the handwriting matched, not even a slight resemblance among them, yet they all could be attributed to Lady Augusta in some way. The sheet with the figures was difficult to decide since it contained mostly drawings and symbols instead of words. It did seem to have some similarity to the writing on the letter he'd just received, but that still left the other two unaccounted for. Even if she hadn't written the note of warning, at least two of the correspondences were signed by her—Tony's letter and the note he'd just received—both sealed with the Brierley imprint.

What game did the lady play?

Noah quickly glanced at the ormolu clock beside him. He hadn't planned on attending the Danby ball that evening, in fact had told Sarah and Eleanor he couldn't escort them because he'd planned to stay home all evening. Secretly he had wanted to make further attempts to decipher the figures on the sheet he'd found in Augusta's coat. But this latest letter from her had definitely intrigued him. Perhaps the time for trifling between them was over. Perhaps it was time he simply confronted Augusta with all of it—the sheet of figures, the note of warning, Tony's suicide, and her presumed possession of the Keighley brooch.

It was a perfect night for lawlessness.

The moon was hidden behind the cover of the dusking clouds, the cobbles damp and slick from the past hours of a slow and steady rain. A midnight mist clung to the gas lamps lighting Charles Street, casting a murky halo of pale light through the thickening fog. Yes, indeed, a perfect night.

Augusta asked the hackney driver to stop at the street corner. She hadn't asked Davison to drive her because he had a family to support and should she be discovered tonight, she didn't want anyone else implicated in her plan.

She was, after all, about to break the law.

"Are ye sure ye're wantin' to be dropped 'ere, milady?" the driver said, eyeing the area suspiciously as he accepted her coin.

"Yes, sir. Thank you for your concern, but my sister's house is right there." She pointed to the nearest dwelling, where not a candle burned behind the darkened windows. "She is staying with me this evening and forgot to bring with her a few things she really must have. You know how we ladies fret if we don't have our favorite bottle of scent or best hair ribands." She smiled confidently in the light of his small lantern. "Likely the house is dark because the staff has already retired for the evening."

The driver didn't look convinced. "It isn't a busy night,

what with the weather and all. I could just pull over to the side of the street there and wait for ye to fetch yer sister's things, then see ye safely home."

"Oh, no," Augusta said, alarmed. She patted his gloved hand. "Thank you, kind sir, but that really will not be necessary. I've some other things to see to for her that will likely take me some time. Household business and all." Although, Augusta thought, she would certainly need a way to return home once she had retrieved her sheet of figures from Noah's house. "But perhaps you might just return in a couple of hours? I should be finished with seeing to my sister's business by then."

This seemed to appease the man's conscience for he nodded. "Two hours it be then."

Augusta smiled and thanked the man before pulling on her hood in the pretense of shielding herself from the rain. In fact, she wanted to shield herself from anyone who might be watching as well.

She walked slowly toward the house she'd led the driver to think she had come to. He began to pull away slowly, watching her. She waved and made as if she were fishing in her reticule for a key, then even rattled the door handle a bit. The rattling, however, roused someone inside for moment's later, candlelight could be seen in one of the upper windows. Fortunately, though, the light also appeased the coachman's concern for her and he clicked to his horses and moved on his way.

As soon as the coachman had turned the corner, Augusta slipped away from the door and into a small alcove nearby where she waited as a butler opened the door, poked out his balding head and scratching it in confusion before retreating back indoors to the warmth and comfort of his bed. Augusta waited a few moments more, making certain no one else was about, before heading for Number 20 Charles Street, the home of Lord Noah Edenhall of Devonbrook.

Every window was dark as she approached. It mattered naught. She'd been coming to this place the past three nights and had studied it well. As chance would have it, Charlotte had been stung on her nose by a bee in the rose garden and so hadn't attended any social engagements, keeping herself and her very swollen, red nose behind the closed door of her bedchamber. Augusta had been free to steal away, to watch the house and the nighttime habits of those who lived there.

She stood on the footpath outside a moment, staring up at the window on the first-floor western side, where she knew she'd find his study. It was the room where Noah spent most of his time when he was at home, sometimes until the very early hours of morning. Since he was a nocturnal creature like herself, Augusta knew she could only come on a night he would certainly be away.

And thus, she had had to provide some sort of inducement for him this night.

She had to allow herself a small grin as she tried to imagine how Lord Noah Edenhall must be feeling at that same moment. The note she sent him hadn't been signed for the express purpose that he should think she had sent it. However, it wouldn't be she he would find *anticipating his company* at the Danby ball this evening as he'd no doubt been led to believe, but instead Lady Viviana—"Bibi" Finsminster, who wore the fact that she adored the man in her eyes whenever she saw him. With any luck, by the time he managed to extract himself from her, Augusta would have retrieved her notes and have gone on her way.

Augusta slipped down the small set of steps which led to the area below street level in front of the basement entrance where most deliveries were made. The door was locked, as she had expected, but the window, she had noticed on one of her earlier visits, didn't quite close right, leaving a small corner of it on the right aslant, and thus unable to be locked. With a little bit of patience and some delicate urging, the window yielded enough to allow her to reach inside and free the lock on the other side of the door.

The fire was yet burning in the basement kitchen, allowing her to see her way through to the small flight of steps that would lead her up to the first floor and the study. Circe couldn't have slipped so silently through the house had she tried. Once inside the study, Augusta had to rely on the light from the gas lamp on the street corner outside to find her way across the room to the desk. She pulled the drapery closed and then removed the sealed tube holding the phosphorous taper she'd brought along from her pocket.

She broke the tube and the taper immediately ignited.

Augusta took a moment to peer about the room around her, indulging her curiosity. She was a little surprised to see such a vast number of books, and even more so by the rare editions she found among them. The artwork, however, she had expected for she had heard of the Devonbrook collection, and she wasn't disappointed. Antiquities, paintings, statuary, Lord Noah's taste was superb, the pieces in perfect placement about the richly paneled room.

She moved behind the neatly arranged desk, seating herself in the large leather-covered chair, and tried to figure out where he might have put her formulas. Thinking the desk too obvious, she moved across the room to a chair set near the fire. A book lay open, facedown on a table beside it.

Intrigued, Augusta picked it up.

It was a study of witchcraft through the ages and as she skimmed the page, she remembered the Earl of Everton's words, of how Noah had suspicions of her being a witch. She focused on a line written in the text.

". . . and should a man choose to couple with a witch, he himself would then become a servant of the Devil and a child the Devil's spawn . . ."

Augusta turned the page and was immediately assaulted by gruesome images, engravings depicting vicious women in various stages of devouring men while clutching evil horned infants to their breasts.

This was what he believed her to be?

She set the book aside and took up another, this one written by a man named Dr. Richard Picklington, noted physician and authority on those afflicted with the "condition" called witchcraft. In his book, Dr. Picklington related tales of his many experiences with witches, even listing common traits among them so that the unaware might better protect themselves. And in reading through them, she had to admit, there were quite a few that might actually be attributed to her.

There was the wearing of dark clothing, which in and of itself wasn't a true characteristic of witchery, but compounded with such things as nocturnal habits, secrecy, and the presence of a medium, a creature to act as a channel to the otherworld most often found in the form of a cat—a black cat—and a century or so earlier, she might have found herself facing a tribunal.

She turned the page and read on, how witches were known to wear strange symbols depicting their black art. Augusta reached up and unfastened her necklace with the star and moon pendant, holding it up before her. The oval-shaped moonstone glowed ethereally in the light of her taper.

"Well, it certainly isn't every day a man can come home to find a female thief sitting in his armchair."

Augusta gasped and turned to see Noah, who was suddenly standing in the doorway. She glanced to the clock. It was nearly midnight. Oh, why had she started reading that ridiculous book?

Noah came into the room, halting only when he stood before her, dangerously close to her. She knew he expected her to step away, but she stood still, refusing to be daunted, even though she had been caught red-handed.

The question was now that he had her, what did he intend to do with her?

Chapter Twenty

"Funny," Noah said, staring down at Augusta, looking suddenly taller than she had remembered, "I felt certain your note had instructed me to meet you in the garden at the Danby ball, not here, in my study of all places. But then I should have realized something was wrong for when I went there to the garden, I found someone else entirely expecting to see me."

Augusta remained silent, watching him. He was dressed impeccably in a suit of black with a crisp white cravat circling his neck. His dark hair glistened and the rigid line of his jaw was defined in the candlelight, the pleasingly slight scent of bergamot clinging to him. His hair fell ruffled a bit over his forehead, giving Augusta the urge to reach up and touch it. Why, oh, why did he have to look so damned handsome?

Noah leaned one hand against the wall behind her. He was so near, she could feel his breath against her temple when he said, his voice growing softer now, "That wasn't a very polite thing you did to me, my lady. A moment or two more alone in the gardens and I might have found myself forced to wed the sweet Viviana."

Augusta lifted her chin, trying to ignore the nearness of him, a senseless notion entirely. "Well, that surely must have been awkward for you, my lord, given the fact that you are already betrothed to another."

Noah stared at her, puzzled. "I beg your pardon?"

She frowned.

He smiled. "Pray, tell me, madam, what the devil you are talking about?"

"I believe she said her name was Miss Sarah Prescott."

"Sarah? What has she to do with any of this?"

His confusion was so genuine Augusta faltered. "She seemed to believe you were to wed."

Noah shook his head. "Well, she is wrong. I have never proposed to her, and I have no plans to."

That he was telling the truth was obvious. Augusta wondered at the feeling of relief she felt at the news. But she must not forget her purpose in coming there. She had to retrieve her notes and leave before she forgot herself again, as she had that night in his brother's study. "That is, of course, your business, my lord. Now, if you'll simply return my rightful property, I'll be on my way."

But he made no move to fetch the notes for her. Instead he stepped away, heading for the sideboard. "At least allow me to offer you a glass of claret before you take your leave. Surely housebreaking must be thirsty work."

Augusta could do nothing other than stand while he walked to the sideboard and poured. He returned with two glasses, one filled with claret, the other brandy. He offered her the claret, but she reached for his other hand and took the brandy instead, an action which elicited a slight smile from him. She tipped the glass to her lips and took a small sip, trying to ignore the strong sensation of it as it slid down her insides to her belly. She remained still as he reached for the glass. But he didn't take it from her. Instead he covered her fingers with his and tipped the glass to his lips to take a drink himself. A strange sort of thrill went through her at the intimacy of the gesture. When he was finished, he didn't take his hand from hers. His eyes never left hers.

"Aren't you at all frightened of drinking from the same glass as a witch?" she asked, her voice teasingly sarcastic. She tried to quell the strange feelings she was experiencing at the nearness of him, but her awareness of him was nearly overpowering.

"I don't know," he said. "Perhaps I should try taking another drink. I do prefer to live dangerously."

Noah took another swallow and then took the glass and set it on the table beside him. He came forward slowly and touched her chin between his thumb and forefinger, caressing her skin softly. Her pulse surged, her breath hitched, and she stood stone-still as he lowered his mouth slowly over hers.

His lips, his mouth, tasted of the brandy, and of the purest need. And from the moment he touched her, Augusta was helpless to do anything except surrender to the fire of his touch. The feelings she'd first experienced that night alone with him in his brother's study instantly returned, and no matter that she might try to tell herself she should stop, run away as fast as her legs could carry her, she knew she could no more do that than sprout wings and fly. She wanted to be with this man, needed to know him somehow. No other man had ever made her feel this way, so desirable, so wanted, so totally woman. From the moment she'd turned to see him in the garden at the Lumley ball when he'd taken her into his arms and had kissed her for the first time as a man kisses a woman, he had awakened something new within her, touching her with feelings she had never dreamed possible.

And now she wanted no one else to fulfil those needs but him.

Augusta raised her hands to his shoulders, uncertain of

what a woman would do, and slid her fingers along his neck until they were threaded in his hair, pulling him nearer to her. She drew him close, instinctively pressing herself against him. She felt him groan against her mouth. She had done something to please him. She wanted to please him more, to explore his needs even as she explored her own. Slowly she ran her fingertips along the column of his throat. She felt his pulse drumming there a rapid staccato. She trailed her fingers downward over his chest to his waist.

She could feel his erection as she moved her hand lower, stroking the length of him through the fabric of his breeches. Noah's body lurched in response and in one swift moment, he swept her against him and lowered them both to the carpet, where he began a frenetic campaign to loosen the fastenings of her gown. While he worked the tiny buttons, she quickly unbuttoned the front of his shirt, loosening his cravat and drawing the length of it slowly from his neck. Moments later they had both succeeded.

Noah sat back a moment and started to loosen the tie that bound the top of her chemise, whispering to her, "I would that we retire to my bed, my sweet witch, but I fear if I should move, if I should even breathe, you might vanish before me in a cloud of brimstone."

"Then you should not risk breaking the spell, my lord."

He yanked at the ribbon and in his haste, it pulled apart. He slid the chemise upward over her head, tossing it aside, leaving her sitting before him totally uncovered. He took her lips in another kiss and at the same time, removed the pins that bound her hair, loosening the dark rich waves around her shoulders. He sat back on his heels and stared at her. "My God, but you are a beautiful creature."

No one had ever spoken those words to her before and hearing them now filled Augusta with a feeling unlike any other. She reached for him, pulling him to her, reveling in the feel of his skin against her breasts, the dark hair covering his chest teasing her nipples to hardness. He kissed her hungrily now, running his hand from the side of her face down her neck to her breast, cupping the weight of it in his hand as he brushed his thumb against its taut peak.

Augusta gasped at the rioting sensation he evoked in her and Noah began kissing a trail down her neck to where his hand massaged her, taking her as she leaned, arching her back against his suckling mouth. And while he teased her, driving her to distraction, his hand continued ever downward, parting her legs, sliding against her. She felt his finger nudge against her, against the wetness of her, and then retreat to stroke over her swollen folds, knowing just where to touch her until she felt certain she would die from this sweet agony. She felt him draw away then and she sagged back onto the carpet, whispering out his name.

A breath later he had replaced his hand with his mouth, sending pleasurable sensations rocking throughout her body. *My God,* she thought, *this is heaven,* and it was nearly too much for her, but she daren't stop him because the feelings were building, tightening, swelling. She closed her eyes, lost on the surge and ripple of her coming release, and when that release finally came, she cried out, her body shuddering as each wave of pleasure took her beyond all reality, beyond anything she could have ever imagined, to the very heights of pleasure.

Through the haze of her consciousness, she saw Noah rise up on his arms over her, stretching his body over the length of her as he moved between her parted legs.

Looking down at her, Noah watched Augusta's eyes as he started slowly to enter her. She was still lost to her release, eyelids lowered, fluttering helplessly. He hesitated when he encountered her maidenhead, thinking he shouldn't continue. Somehow he hadn't even considered the possibility of her virginity and he wondered if she realized the finality of what he was on the very verge of doing to her. "Augusta, I—"

She reached for him with one hand, touching him softly on the side of his face as she whispered, "Please show me what it is to be a woman. I want only you to show me."

It was all the reassurance he needed. Noah gathered her to him and with one thrust, rent her innocence and buried himself within her. She did not cry. She did not push him away. She only clung to him more, pressing light kisses against his neck and shoulders.

"Thank you," she murmured against him and instinctively she tightened her legs around him as he started to withdraw. He moved slowly with her, fearing she might hurt, until he felt his own tenuous hold loosening and his thrusts grew deeper and she dug her fingers into his arms, taking him into her so completely, touching him so remarkably as she offered him the most precious gift she had—herself.

Noah squeezed his eyes closed, trying not to lose what little he had left of his restraint as he came to his own exquisite climax. It overtook him as he buried himself one last time, deeply, spilling his seed and he cried out his release against her neck. "Oh, God, Augusta."

She held him close against her, lightly stroking her fingers through his hair, across his temple, over his back as he lay his head against her breast and closed his eyes.

Contentedly, she did the same.

When next she stirred, it was as Noah was kneeling beside her, covering her in the thick, soft folds of a quilted blanket. She didn't know how much time had passed, wrapped as they had been in the wondrous aftermath of their lovemaking. She watched in silence as he stood to stoke the hearth, magnificently naked, every turn of his body defined. As the fire caught, his skin glowed in its growing amber light, smooth as marble. Without thinking, Augusta stood and came behind him, running the palms of her hands upward over the muscles of his back, stretching them beneath his arms to encircle him as she pressed the length of her body against the welcoming heat of his, scattering light kisses over his shoulder as her fingers caressed the skin of his chest, stroking downward over his belly.

Noah turned to face her. "Madam, I'll not be responsible for my actions should you contin—"

He drew in a sharp breath as she closed her fingers over his hardness. She kissed his ear, his Adam's apple, pressing her breasts against him. She felt his body stiffen as she moved her fingers lightly over him. She kissed his shoulder and noticed his one hand was gripping the mantlepiece, knuckles white. She exulted in knowing she could affect him so.

"I am sorry, my lord. Perhaps I should take my leave and—"

She never finished the thought, for Noah took her up, lifting her against him and kissing her fully as he lay her upon the blanket before the fire, resuming his magical courtship of her. He worshipped her with his hands, with his mouth, until she was oblivious, delirious, and when he finally took her this second time, his need for her was no less fierce, no less desperate.

Later Augusta rested her cheek against Noah's chest, listening to the slowing tempo of his heartbeat. They lay watching the flames flutter down in the hearth, wrapped together limb to limb in the warmth of the blanket and each other.

"I think you must be a witch, my lady, for you have certainly enchanted me."

She smiled. "Does this mean you think me as the images in your book?"

He moved so that she lay on her back, facing him. He kissed her. "Definitely not. I simply tried to find a common explanation for the puzzle of you. But there is nothing common about you."

"And that pleases you?"

"More than you can ever know."

She smiled. "I think I shall have to consider a serious pursuit in housebreaking. The consequences are rather pleasing."

"As long as the only house you break into is this one."

They could have lain that way for hours, wrapped together, sharing the words of lovers, but those blissful moments were soon interrupted by a high-pitched mewing. Augusta turned to see a fuzzy, purring black face beside them. She reached for it, taking the tiny creature into her two hands.

"You have a cat," she said, scratching it behind its tiny ears.

"Yes, he is a recently acquired addition to the household," Noah said. He watched silently as Augusta cuddled the kitten close to her. She gave a girlish giggle as he rubbed his face against her cheek, purring loudly.

"I found him on my doorstep actually, abandoned."

"Oh, no—someone just left him there?"

Noah nodded. "It would seem so. He was pathetically thin and looked as if he'd nearly been drowned." He laughed when the kitten batted his paw at a tress of Augusta's hair that hung down over her shoulder. "As you can see he's made a complete recovery. He's already stretched his claws in most every chair and sofa in the house."

"My own cat Circe would love him," she said.

"I thought he looked rather like her when I first saw him."

Augusta looked up at him. "You've seen Circe?"

"Yes, when I came to deliver the hat I'd gotten to replace your damaged one. She'd nearly slipped through the door while I was standing there. Your stepmother told me she was your cat."

"I'm rather surprised Charlotte didn't let her go. She's not very fond of Circe."

"I gathered that when she called her 'flea-ridden.'"

Augusta set the kitten down, watching as he rolled on his back and grabbed at his tail between his legs. "What's his name?"

"I haven't yet come up with one that I thought suitable. I'd considered Henry, to go along with Humphrey, my horse . . ."

He hesitated when he saw Augusta wrinkle her nose. "You don't care for Henry?"

"Why do you give your animals such terrible names? Don't you like them?"

Noah grinned. "And what would my lady suggest?"

Augusta thought a moment, staring at the cat, cocking her head to the side as she rested her chin in her hand in a gesture that was far too enticing on one so naked. It took everything in his power not to lay her back and make love to her again.

"Were he mine, I think I should call him Pan. He will likely stay quite small even when grown, and he is a most impish fellow." She stroked him between his pointed ears. "And his mew sounds about as frightening as a blast from Pan's fabled conch shell."

It astounded Noah how much thought she put in to such a thing as an animal's name, even more so her knowledge of mythology, one of his favorite subjects. "Then Pan he shall be," he said. "I'd wager our little friend would like a dish of milk, and I'm a bit famished myself. Would you care to come with me to the kitchens to see what we might scare up?"

Augusta nodded. She rose to her feet and quickly slipped on her chemise while Noah stepped into his breeches. She pulled on her stockings and then slid her gown over her head, standing still as Noah worked the buttons for her. When she lifted her dark hair, now hopelessly tangled about her shoulders, he couldn't resist the urge to kiss her on her neck. She skittered away, smiling. "To the kitchens, my lord."

Together the two of them walked toward the back of the house, taking the stairs to the kitchen below where Augusta had come in earlier. Noah lit a couple of candles and headed for the pantry while Augusta poured Pan a dish of milk. She was stroking Pan's back as he eagerly lapped at the milk when Noah returned with a loaf of bread, a brick of cheese, and an apple—a golden one.

She thought back to the day when she'd gone riding in Hyde Park in the hope of meeting with the Earl of Belgrace. She remembered that it had been early in the morning and that the night before she hadn't slept a wink because thoughts of a mysterious man who'd approached her on a midnight garden path, kissing her more thoroughly than she'd ever thought possible, had invaded her dreams. When she'd heard his shout that morning and turned to see him sitting there astride his horse, berating her for attempting to make the jump over the fallen tree, she'd thought she'd conjured him up somehow, just as she had the night before. She remembered his remarks about her horse, his tongue-in-cheek comment about the legend of her goddess namesake having been trapped into marriage when she had lost a footrace by stopping to pick up three golden apples.

He'd given her one apple with the hat he'd sent her, a second when he'd returned her gown from White's stables. Now he offered her a third golden apple, just like in the legend.

Augusta looked up at Noah, but if he meant the apple to be significant, he said nothing. Instead he set about slicing the bread and cutting the cheese into small, bite-sized wedges. She watched him work and wondered at the small scar she noticed on his hand. She mused about the way his hair would fall slightly into his eyes, and how it gave him a sort of boyish quality. She stared at his mouth and any thoughts of boyishness disappeared. Lord Noah Edenhall was a man, a man unlike any other. But dare she trust him?

He placed a small china plate before them and she took a small apple slice, chewing it quietly. They sat at the huge center table in the kitchen and watched Pan as he licked the last remnants of milk from the bottom of his dish. Neither spoke of what had happened between them, as if fearing the words might cause the wonder of it to vanish, might forever take away the beauty their coming together had created. Augusta could only think that should her world end tomorrow, she would know she had been touched my magic.

"My lady?"

Augusta turned toward him. "I really think that, under the circumstances, you could certainly use my given name."

"Augusta, will you excuse me a moment? There is something I need to do."

"Of course."

He disappeared up the stairs. Right after he'd gone, Augusta heard the sound of a coach outside. She walked toward the basement entrance where she'd come in and where the door was still slightly ajar, and took the stairs toward street level. The hackney coach she'd taken earlier that evening had returned and was waiting for her just outside. Like the fabled Cinderella, the clock had struck and her once-in-a-lifetime fairy tale had come to a close.

She turned back for the kitchen.

Noah had returned, and was holding something, a sheet of paper in his hand. He held it out to her. "I believe this is yours."

Augusta took her sheet of figures and placed it quietly in her reticule. "Thank you."

He hesitated a moment. Finally he asked what she had known he would ask, but had hoped he wouldn't.

"What is it, Augusta? What do those figures mean?"

Augusta looked at him. After what he had just given her, a woman's most precious gift, she wanted nothing more than to share with him everything about her. She wanted to tell him of her childhood, wanted to know about his. He hadn't shown her figures to anyone, but had kept them secret for her. He hadn't taken them to Lord Belgrace as she had feared. Surely she could trust him, couldn't she?

But even as she thought this, she could hear the Earl of Everton's reproving voice in her head.

You could be the first, Augusta . . . unless they learn of it . . . trust no one . . .

"I cannot tell you. I'm sorry."

Noah frowned, disappointment darkening his features. "Did what we just shared together mean nothing to you?"

"Of course it meant something to me. It means a great deal. But what we shared does not entitle you to be privy to every aspect of my life."

Noah was staring at her, his disappointment having turned to anger. "That is all well and good, madam, but pray tell me, what will you do if a child results from what we shared tonight?"

This thought stopped Augusta short. She hadn't even considered the possibility of a child.

"I will not have my son or my daughter labeled a bastard, Augusta."

"Nor would I, sir."

"At least in that you're speaking sensibly. When did you last have your monthly?"

Augusta started at the frankness of discussing such a subject with him, something never mentioned in the Brierley household despite that it was occupied chiefly by women. "I will inform you, my lord, should you have any reason for concern when the time comes. Now I should like to leave. There is a coach waiting for me outside."

Noah took her arm and turned her abruptly to face him. His eyes were cold, unforgiving. "I had every reason not to trust you, Augusta. I hope whatever it is you seek to hide from me is worth what is lost because of it."

Augusta pulled away from him and turned on her heel, leaving before he could see the tears of regret that were rimming her eyes.

Chapter Twenty-one

A pounding on the door awoke Noah after what seemed like only a couple of hours sleep, and indeed, if the blurred image of the clock beside him were accurate, it had only been a couple of hours since the last time he'd checked it. He had retired at dawn after spending the remainder of the night after Augusta had gone sitting in his study, in the same chair where he'd found her when he'd first returned home. Only instead of reading as she had been then, he'd spent the time staring at the carpet, the rumpled blanket where they had made love, where she'd given him her virginity.

He'd thought of her reaction to his question about the sheet of figures. Why did she refuse to trust him? What was it she was hiding? Throughout the night and into the morning, the answers to this and many other questions hadn't come and he'd finally fallen asleep in that same chair, leaning to one side as the fire had slowly died in the hearth.

Now the fire had been stoked once again, likely by Westman, a good flame licking at the fresh coals in the grate. On the sideboard stood a kettle on its stand over a spirit lamp, ready to provide fresh coffee for Noah upon awakening; thank the heavens for Westman.

Noah was just rising from his chair, running a hand back through his hair to neaten it when the door suddenly opened across the room. He turned to see Sarah standing there. Westman looked agitatedly on from behind.

"Noah, dear, would you please tell Westman it is all right for me to be here? I know it is early but we are friends, after all. Friends should never stand on ceremony."

Noah glanced at Westman, who faced quite a predicament for Sarah was the sister of his former employer and thus his refusal to admit her would be a slight, yet he owed his loyalty to his current employer. Noah stepped in to spare him. "Actually, Sarah, I believe Westman's reluctance was more aimed at protecting your name than my privacy. You have been raised in the country and are accustomed to country ways. Here in town, it isn't considered fitting for a lady, an unmarried lady to pay a visit to an unmarried man's home. Should anyone have seen you coming in, the potential for disaster is high." He glanced out the door to the hall. "You did not bring Eleanor along with you?"

Sarah pouted, something Noah had once found endearing when she'd been a child of seven and he and Tony had refused to allow her to join them on a journey to the fishing pond. It was not, however, something she wore well now.

"No," she said. "Eleanor had to go off on an errand this morning, and Christian left early as well. The maids were all off seeing to their duties. I was growing very lonesome, so I asked the coachman to bring me here for a visit." Tears had begun rimming her eyes. "I'm sorry. You must think me utterly without fashion, but I never considered that it would be thought of as improper to visit someone I've known all my life."

"It is all right," Noah said, frowning. "There is a house full of servants here, so it should be safe—this time." He continued on across the room to the sideboard, truly in need now of that cup of coffee. "Would you care for any coffee, Sarah?"

She shook her head, sniffing. "I do not care for it."

"Tea?"

She glanced at Westman. "That would be lovely."

The butler took his cue, muttering that he would return shortly. He left the door open fully, in easy view of the hall and the servants who were seeing to their daily duties throughout the house.

Noah took his cup and returned to his chair, motioning for Sarah to take a seat in the opposite one while she waited for Westman to bring her tea. He took a deep swallow from his cup, savoring the strong flavorful blend and the instant warmth it brought to his belly. He ran a hand over his beard-roughened chin. "My apologies for my appearance this morning. I was working over some papers until late into the night and fell asleep here in this chair. I haven't yet had the opportunity to shave or change my clothing."

Sarah shook her head. "It is all right, Noah. It is not as if we are strangers, you know." She glanced around the room then, taking in the furnishings and decor. "I understand from Lady Danby that you were at the ball last night after all."

So that is what prompted this early morning visit, Noah thought. He had, after all, declined the invitation to accompany her there. "Yes, as a matter of fact, I did go, but only briefly."

"I'd thought you had said you weren't able to attend."

Noah took in a breath to ease his growing impatience. "Yes, I had, but as fate would have it, immediately after I told you that, I learned that someone I needed to conduct business with would be there. I didn't think to tell you of the change in situation since I only planned to put in a brief appearance and then take my leave."

Sarah peered at him through her lashes. "And were you able to conduct your business?"

The slightly bitter tone in her voice was not lost on him. She was angry. He thought of what Augusta had told him the night before, of Sarah's statement to her that they were betrothed. She was acting far too wifely already. "Not exactly. Seems I was misinformed. The person I was to meet wasn't there after all."

"Oh." She seemed to brighten. "That is unfortunate."

Westman came in with the tea tray then and neither Noah nor Sarah spoke as he prepared a cup for Sarah, tucking one of the cook's currant scones alongside on the saucer. Pan had come darting in after the butler, no doubt looking for a treat. When he didn't find one, he occupied himself with swatting at the hem of Sarah's gown.

Noticing him, Sarah hissed, "Stop that!" and pulled her feet toward the other side of the chair as she swiped a hand at him.

Noah took up the kitten. "He's just a curious kitten. He really meant no harm."

"Your servants shouldn't allow their animals to run freely through your house. He should remain in the kitchen to catch the mice as is his purpose."

Noah looked at her. "Pan is my kitten, Sarah."

"Oh." She furrowed her brow at that. "I was just afraid he might snag the hem. This is my best gown."

"I'll just have Westman take him away."

"No, it is all right."

"He'd probably like a dish of cream, which the cook can give him in the kitchen."

The butler took Pan and headed for the door, leaving them with a bow once again.

"So you were able to complete your work last night after all?" she said, putting an end to the awkward silence which had followed the butler's departure.

"Somewhat." He furrowed his brow, thinking of Augusta's abrupt departure. "There are still some details I need to reason out."

"You must be very tired after having stayed up all night to work. What is . . . ?"

Sarah's words dropped off and Noah noticed she was staring at the carpet, at something she'd spotted there. She reached down to retrieve it and when she returned to her chair, she held in her hand a chain, suspended from which was a glittering star and moon pendant. Augusta's pendant.

"Why is this on your floor, Noah?" The outrage sparking her voice told that she indeed knew who the owner of the necklace was.

Noah reached for it. *Damnation!* Why had she, of all people, found it? "Sarah, I—"

"She was here, wasn't she? Last night. That is why you wouldn't take me to the Danby ball, because you wanted to be with her. You went to the ball, yes, but you went looking for her, and then the two of you came here. And you preach to me about propriety! No wonder you were agitated when I arrived. Was she still here, hiding behind the drapery? Did your whore have to sneak out the back door so no one would see her leaving your house unchaperoned?"

Noah narrowed his eyes at the ugliness he heard in her words. "Sarah, that is enough. You overstep your bounds."

She didn't hear him. "I knew you were carrying on a tryst with her. Anyone could see it that first night at Almack's when you danced with her. And then the night at your brother's musicale. You had been with her then, too, in the study, hadn't you? She tried to pretend she'd locked herself in and everyone believed her. Everyone, but me. I saw the two glasses and knew, but who would suspect someone like her of impropriety? And now this, even after I told her about us."

"Yes, Sarah," Noah said calmly. "And what you told her was a lie. We are not betrothed."

The minute the words passed his lips, Noah knew he shouldn't have spoken them, for in them was an acknowledgment of everything Sarah had just accused him of.

Tears were now streaming down Sarah's face, her cheeks mottled as she sobbed into her hands.

Noah came before Sarah, kneeling before her and taking her hands, forcing her to look at him. "Sarah, you must listen to me. I am very sorry. I know you wish us to be married, and were I able to do so with a conscience, I would. I care for you deeply. I do not want to see you hurt. But I do not feel for you as a man feels for a woman who will share his bed. I know you do not believe this, but were we to wed, you would eventually grow to hate me. You would be bound to a passionless marriage with a man who cares for you as a sister, not as a wife or a lover. You deserve more, Sarah. Much more. And you will have more, Sarah, if you would only allow yourself to see what awaits you. There is nothing to hinder you."

She stared at him and for a moment he thought she might be listening to him, listening to reason. He soon learned he was wrong in that hope. "That is why you took care of Tony's debts, isn't it? So there would be nothing to ward off suitors. That is why those men have come calling. Have you arranged a sizeable dowry for me, too? Bait to catch me a husband? What did you do, Noah, publish an announcement in your club that Miss Sarah Prescott could be had for a generous sum?"

"Sarah, please, calm yourself."

She pushed him away, standing, moving for the mantel. She turned her back on him. "Why, Noah? Why do you want her? Why do you not want me? Tony wanted you to marry me. He told me so, told me he would make certain you knew . . . "

She burst into another fit of tears and Noah could think

of nothing else to do but to put his arms around her. She fell into his embrace and sobbed into his shoulder for several minutes before she began to quiet. Finally she lifted her head, sniffing loudly. Noah gave her his handkerchief.

"Sarah, I only wanted what was best for you. I want you to marry a man who will worship you, adore you, long for the sight of you. Tony might have wanted us to wed, but when he found out the truth, he would have agreed with me that you deserve far more than I can ever offer you. I care for you as if you were my own sister and it pains me to see you hurting. I can only hope that someday you will realize I did what was best for you."

She dabbed at her eyes with his handkerchief and made to return it to him.

"Keep it, Sarah."

She tightened her gloved fingers around it and looked up at him. Her eyes had grown empty, her mouth a rigid line. "I should like to leave now."

"Allow me to escort you home."

She shook her head. "No, my lord, that is not possible for you know quite well that would not be at all fitting. I will manage on my own. If you will please excuse me?"

"Of course."

Sarah started for the door, her mourning skirts brushing his legs as she turned. She hesitated at the threshold and looked back at him. Her voice had grown ice-cold. "I am sorry for any inconvenience I have caused you. I will not trouble you again."

Noah felt a twinge of guilt at the stricken and lost look that filled her eyes. "You could never inconvenience me, Sarah. No matter that you may think otherwise, I am here for you. I hope you will know that and remember that I am, and will always be, your friend."

She made no response as she moved through the door to leave. And after she was gone, her coach moving away from the front of the house, Noah heard a voice, Tony's voice, in his head.

I always knew you'd be there to take care of Sarah . . . You are the only one I would ever trust . . .

Chapter Twenty-two

The Earl of Countess of Finsminster were pleased to announce the betrothal of their only daughter, Lady Viviana
Finsminster, to the heir of the wealthy and distinguished
Marquess of Fairmonte, a young man of four-and-twenty
considered by most to be one of The Catches of the Season.
Lord and Lady Finsminster were so pleased, in fact, they
decided to host a grand fete in celebration of the upcoming
event, a masquerade ball to be exact, costumes most certainly required.

The invitations were issued but a sparse five days before
the ball, which, especially for a masquerade, was most un-
heard-of, five weeks being a more acceptable period of
time for guests to prepare. Still no one dared decline what
was sure to be the most talked-about event of the Season. It
was said no expense would be spared by the Finsminsters
for this, their only daughter, their beloved "Bibi." Thus
fashionable London soon became Pandemonium as the *ton*
besieged every dressmaker and tailor in Town with requests
for the most elaborate, most original costumes to be had.

Charlotte was pleased as ineffable punch by the news
and had already set to work on preparing her costume—
something elaborate, no doubt. A simple domino would
never do for such a distinguished event. Augusta, however,
failed to understand the significance and instead spent her
morning polishing the lens of her telescope, wondering

how she might decline the invitation politely. She even thought she'd come up with a serviceable excuse until Lady Finsminster and Viviana came to call that same morning.

They were in the parlor having tea with Charlotte when Augusta came down from her chamber in search of a clean polishing cloth. She had heard their voices when on the stairs and tried quietly to slip by the room without anyone inside taking notice of her. She had nearly made it past when Charlotte summoned her back.

"Augusta, dear, come join us. I have wonderful news."

Her hopes dashed, Augusta took a deep breath and turned for the parlor, pasting on a polite smile.

She greeted the countess and then Viviana, congratulating the latter on her impending marriage before turning toward the marchioness. "Yes, Charlotte? You said you had news to tell?"

Charlotte set her teacup aside. "Indeed. Lady Finsminster and Lady Viviana have come to tell us something grand, very grand indeed." She smiled, raising her eyebrows and fidgeting about on her seat. "Guess who is to be Lady Viviana's bridesmaid?"

Augusta shrugged. "The Queen?"

"Of course not, you ninny," Charlotte said, laughing lightly. "You will, of course."

Augusta stared at her. "Me?"

All three nodded in unison.

"Oh, please say you will," Lady Finsminster burst out. "Bibi is so very fond of you. You are the model she seeks to follow. She would be so disappointed if you weren't there with her. You have become her dearest friend this Season, you know."

"I have?" She looked to Viviana, who nodded assuredly.

Augusta remained doubtful, for even though they'd been thrown together much in the past weeks, she could not recall a single meaningful conversation between them. The only thing she did seem to know about "Bibi" was that the lady liked to dress very similarly to her mother. It was the differences between herself and Viviana that Augusta noticed more. They were a good deal contrary in age, certainly even more contrary in their interests and pursuits. What other than gender could they possibly have in common between them?

"Will you?" Viviana asked. "Will you please stand beside me?"

Still, Augusta could find no immediate reason to decline. "I suppose—"

"You see!" Charlotte cut in. "I knew she would do it. And I know just the gown for her to wear. It is the palest yellow with tiny little . . ."

Any attempt to qualify her response would do her little good, so instead Augusta quietly excused herself and turned to leave the room, doubting they would even notice her departure. But as she reached the door, Augusta chanced to hear the countess say, "I am determined that this will be the most talked-about wedding of the Season, and it will be, especially now that we have the notable Lady Augusta Brierley for a bridesmaid."

And, suddenly, everything came very clear. Their reason for asking her to attend on Bibi as a bridesmaid had nothing to do with friendship, or even compatibility. Instead it had been prompted by but one thing—notoriety. In essence, they wanted Lady Augusta Brierley, The Conversation Piece, not Lady Augusta Brierley, The Person.

Well, she thought as she started back down the hallway, if they wanted a sensation, then by all means they should certainly have one . . . and she had a good idea of just what to do to provide it. She had turned for the stairs and was making for her bedchamber when she heard a summons from Tiswell below.

"My lady . . ."

"Yes, Tiswell, please tell Cook I have decided to take tea in my chamber this morning. I've some things to see to."

"Yes, my lady." He paused, and then, "A letter came for you this morning."

She didn't stop. "You can put it with the others in the hall, Tiswell. Lady Trecastle will attend to it."

"But, my lady, I found this letter sitting on the doorstep this morning. It reads 'Confidential' beneath your name."

Augusta turned. Her first thought was of Noah. It had been a week since her departure from his house that night. Undoubtedly he was writing to ask whether there existed the probability of a child, although it was yet too soon to tell. Even so, she had found herself considering the possibility of it often in the past days, wondering how a woman knew when she carried a life within her, other than the obvious. She had overheard Charlotte once talking with her companions of how she'd been ill for four months straight when she'd been carrying Lettie. But certainly there must be other things a woman would feel when she had another being growing inside of her, certainly a feeling of motherly intuition would come about, something other than this unknowing, this fear, this wonder . . . this expectation.

She retraced her steps, taking the letter to inspect it. It wasn't franked so it had been personally delivered. Why wouldn't they have left it with Tiswell instead of just abandoning it on the doorstep?

"Thank you, Tiswell," she said as she started back up the stairs, opening the letter as she went. She paused when she saw that the words written within were not an inquiry from Noah after all, but instead:

Heed me now, lady, else you will see
Danger lies in wait for thee.
Abandon the path which you now tread
Else you will soon find yourself . . .

The last word of the sinister poem had been purposely omitted, but the message came through quite distinctly.

Abandon the path which you now tread . . .

Someone had uncovered the truth of her discovery. Lord Burbage had been right in his suspicion. Somehow she'd been found out, and the only way in which that might have happened was through her notes.

And that involved only one person other than herself or Lord Everton.

Noah.

She thought of the last words he'd spoken to her that night, his question of trust. Had he betrayed her? She would need to speak to Everton, to decide their next course of action. She immediately started up the stairs to pen him a message.

The invitations indicated that the Finsminster ball would begin at nine, and by a quarter hour after the street in front of the Finsminster town house was thronged with countless coaches and conveyances. Even those who customarily made the late appearance forsook the fashion this time so as not to miss a thing at this much-anticipated event.

The groom's family, the Fairmontes, were there, distinguished and no doubt quite pleased, for the rumor at White's had the reason for the haste in this match due to the younger Fairmonte's apparent curiosity in one of the family's maids, a girl all of thirteen and apparently well on her way to bearing the duke his first illegitimate grandchild.

On the other hand, the Finsminsters had done well, too, seizing while opportunity was ripe and elevating their stature by marrying their daughter into the Fairmonte marquessate. This without a moment to spare, some whispered, for it had been noticed that Lady Viviana had disappeared from the Danby ball weeks earlier at nearly the same time as Lord Noah Edenhall, each heading in the direction of the gardens. Had they been found together, it would have spelled certain disaster for Lady Viviana, and while a crisis had been averted on that particular occasion—Lord Noah having vanished, leaving Viviana alone when her parents had come looking for her—the earl and countess weren't taking any further chances. Bibi would be wed by month's end, the preservation of her virtue well worth the cost for the special license.

Such was one of the drawbacks to being costumed, Noah thought as he dodged the rotund shepherdess and her gossipy fairy-winged companion who he had heard speaking of him. At a masquerade one could no longer be assured that they wouldn't overhear when the whispers were about themselves. But he hadn't come to the ball tonight to hear anecdotes about the young bride-to-be and her groom. He'd come with a much different reason in mind.

He'd come to find out who the bastard was who was sending him those damnable letters.

The second one had come the week before and had been just as cryptic as the first, giving words without much meaning. But the third he had received only that morning and this time the threat within it had been abundantly clear.

> You persist on your path of deception
> The truth you seek to hide.
> It is time for the unmasking
> At a place I'll hence provide.
> A garden bathed in moonlight
> But I warn you, have a care.

> This time there can be but one victor,
> Come, if you still should dare.

Across the bottom of the page had been written the words "Finsminster" and "Eleven o'clock."

Noah now had little doubt that the person who had written the threatening notes was Sir Spencer Atherton. Augusta had received her notes from him, thus she and Everton would have no reason for it. Atherton, on the other hand, was finding himself an unwelcome addition to society this Season, few willing to put aside his part in the scandal with Julia the year before. Noah hadn't found that same rejection, so surely Atherton would turn his thoughts of revenge on him. But if Atherton sought another duel, he was going to be sadly disappointed for that was one experience in his life Noah had no intention of ever repeating.

He skirted the edge of the ballroom, and spotted Robert and Catriona standing with others near the doorway. They were costumed as Tristan and Iseult, the fabled Irish lovers, Catriona's coppery hair done in a classic goddesslike style, circled by a golden band that suited her beautifully. Robert wore a richly brocaded tunic, the perfect complement to her ethereal silken gown.

As he headed for them, he noticed the clock standing in the corner behind them. It was ten o'clock.

"Well, that menacing figure can be none other than my brother," Robert said, noticing his approach from behind his half-mask.

"Noah," Catriona added, "you look positively frightful. Like the highwayman Jonathon Wild."

He did admittedly look sinister for he'd dressed himself completely in black, covering the upper half of his face with a black silk mask that tied around the back of his head, an outdated tricorn slanted over his brow. He took Catriona's hand, so white against the black kid of his glove, kissing it. "And you make the loveliest Iseult I've ever seen."

She curtsied. "Thank you, kind sir."

"Unhand her, knave!" A dashing cavalier cut toward them through the crowd, sporting a penciled-in mustache and flashing a smile that revealed him as Christian beneath his red half-mask. "Good evening, my lords and my lady," he said, taking off his wide-brimmed plumed hat as he swept into a gallant bow.

"Beware, my love," Catriona said to Robert as Christian took her hand to kiss it most gallantly. "I have always had a weakness for a cavalier."

"Uh, Christian," Robert said when Christian didn't release his hold—or his lips for that matter—from Catriona's hand, "you can cease with the theatrics now."

"Theatrics?" Christian said, raising his chin. He assumed an accented voice. "I know not of what you speak, my lord. And who is this Christian? You must have me confused with someone else. I am not Christian, but DeClerq, finest swordsman in His Majesty's army!"

"Well, I suggest you unhand my wife, DeClerq, else you'll be putting your skill at the sword to the test."

Christian wasn't yet ready to relinquish his fun. "Wife? But, sir, she assured me she was not married." He cocked his head aslant and lifted one dark brow. "Or was it only that she had never met a man to compare with me?"

Catriona played along. "But, oh! Husband, my lord and master, I knew not what I was doing for he plied me with music and much wine."

Laughter and applause erupted from those standing nearby who had been watching the impromptu performance. Christian, normally quite staid and reserved, took Catriona's hand and bowed to the crowd while she lowered into an elegant curtsy. It was indeed astounding how the donning of a mask could bring people to do things they might otherwise have never attempted.

"Did Eleanor come tonight?" Catriona asked Christian after the interest of the crowd had moved elsewhere.

"Yes, she and Sarah made for the ladies' retiring room to repair a slight tear in Eleanor's costume brought on by the spurs of a passing knight-errant. We convinced Sarah to abandon her mourning behind a mask for the night."

Noah turned then and spotted the unmistakable form of Augusta's stepmother, Lady Trecastle, as she stood atop the stairs leading down to the ballroom. She was dressed as an angel, complete with a golden looped halo perched over her head, her gown consisting of layer upon layer of filmy white flounces. None of the others standing with her looked as if they could be Augusta, all either too ample of body or advanced in years for even a slight resemblance.

"Ah, here are our fine ladies!" Christian said, drawing Noah's attention to Sarah and Eleanor, who had joined them.

They had come as Terpsichore and Clio, two of the mythical Muses, dressed in flowing chitons, their hair arranged and wound in a Grecian style. Noah hadn't seen Sarah since the morning she'd come to his house and found Augusta's necklace and he wondered if there might be an awkwardness now between them.

"You two are lovely enough to inspire even a lame man to dance," Robert said. "And I hope the enchanting Terpsichore would deign to bestow one dance upon a mere mortal such as I."

"Only after she has danced with me," Noah stepped in, hoping to put aside the chill from the previous week.

Sarah looked at first uneasy, but then smiled and said, "Of course."

The dancing was scheduled to begin at ten-thirty and while they waited for the musicians to ready their instruments, Noah told the others about the threatening messages he'd received from Atherton.

"Just don't let him provoke you into another dawn meeting," Robert said. "He's far more irrational now. He even cuffed a fellow bare-fisted the other night whom he perceived an affront from. Poor buck was only trying to catch the eye of the lady standing behind Atherton. And when explanations were made, Atherton refused to apologize. In his current frame of mind, there is no telling what he might do."

"I have no intention of dueling with him, which is precisely what I plan to tell him when I meet him in the garden tonight."

"Are you certain it's safe to go alone?" Catriona said. "Perhaps Robert and Christian should stay close by."

Noah shook his head. "This is my problem and I will handle it myself, and a far sight better than I did the last time."

The musicians were then ready and Noah took Sarah's hand to lead her out onto the dance floor.

He showed her to her place along the female line of dancers and then took his position across in the male line. He bowed. She curtsied. And thus the dancing began. They headed into the first turn, circling back near to where the others stood before they came to a portion of the dance where Noah joined hands with Sarah as he led her down the line of the other dancers. He took the opportunity to try to smooth over the discord between them.

"I'm glad you decided to accompany Eleanor this evening. It has been too long since you have danced."

She nodded. "It is a pleasant diversion."

She moved away and then back.

"Sarah, I hope—"

"Don't, Noah. I know what you are going to say. Please don't worry. I had no right to burst in on you like that, especially after all you have done for me since Tony died. I decided to take your advice and look to the future."

They became separated then by the steps of the dance. They circled again, and joined hands through another series of steps.

"I feared we might lose our friendship," he said.

Sarah shook her head. "That can never be. We have known each other too long and too well for that. I only hope you can forgive the ridiculous ravings of a silly girl."

"Of course."

They reached the end of the line and the dance came to a close. Noah bowed, then promenaded Sarah halfway around the floor before returning with her to the others. The clock now showed five minutes to eleven. It was time to meet Atherton in the garden.

Noah bowed to the others. "If you'll excuse me."

He started to turn.

"Noah."

He looked back at his brother.

Robert was frowning with worry. "Be careful."

Noah nodded once and headed off for the gardens.

Augusta surveyed the crowd through her mask, trying to spot Charlotte without the use of her spectacles. She had just arrived, having purposefully taken time in getting ready, knowing that with Charlotte's eagerness for this event, she would certainly accept Augusta's offer to leave before her. She hadn't wanted Charlotte to see her costume, for she knew, if she had, eagerness or not, the marchioness would never have allowed her to leave the house.

Augusta gave in to a slight smile as she thought of the utter mortification that would greet her the moment Lady

Finsminster recognized her. Charlotte would be furious, of course, but it would serve her right for trapping her as she had into agreeing to be Viviana's bridesmaid when she knew perfectly well it was only so Lady Finsminster could feed her self-importance.

Augusta had purposely worn a smallish mask so that people might chance to recognize her more easily. And notice her they already were as she started across the ballroom in search of Charlotte.

It didn't take her long to find the angel marchioness, clustered as usual near the refreshments table. She watched as Charlotte gave her approach a glance then looked away, only to glance again and stare in abject horror.

"Augusta!" she said, her voice hoarse with disbelief. "What have you done to yourself?" And then, "Oh, dear God, we are ruined!"

Augusta came to stand before her, looking down at her ensemble. "You do not like my costume?"

"Of course I do not. You—you can see your legs!"

Augusta looked down at her white-stocking-clad legs. "Well, I do have them, legs I mean. Why should I pretend not to?"

Charlotte looked as if she actually might faint, her eyes fluttering momentarily before she managed to take hold of herself.

Augusta, however, failed to share her agitation. Had she been a man, no one would think to question her choice of costume. Her hair was arranged in a simple style, tied back with a single black bow at her nape, the weight of it hanging in loose curls to her waist. Admittedly, the breeches didn't quite fit right, being a little too tight in places, but the Brierley footman was a rather slender sort of man so a certain disproportion was to be expected. The coat, however, fit very well, the cuff of it brushing her gloved hands, and she'd done nicely with the cravat too, she thought, especially considering she hadn't arranged men's neckwear since she'd been a little girl and had begged her father to show her how. Nor was the color displeasing. In fact she'd always thought the Brierley livery splendid with its royal blue trimmed with gold, the polished buttons glittering beneath the chandeliers above.

All in all she thought it a fine costume, certainly one befitting a *notorious* personage like Lady Augusta Brierley.

Unruffled, Augusta walked to the refreshments table to fetch Charlotte a glass of much-needed wine. When she returned, Lady Finsminster and Bibi had joined Charlotte's assembly of friends and already the whispers abounded. Conversation, however, stopped the moment Charlotte noticed her returning.

"Good evening, Lady Finsminster, Lady Viviana," Augusta said. "Lovely gathering." She handed Charlotte her wine. "Here, Charlotte, you look as if you could use this. I'll be in the Gaming Salon should you need me."

And with that she walked back the way she'd come minutes earlier, heading not for the Gaming Salon, but for the garden, where she'd asked Burbage to meet her, satisfied that she'd now at least done something worthy of meriting her much-esteemed *notoriety*.

Noah stood just off the garden path, obscured behind the midnight shadows and sheltering boughs of a willow. From his vantage, he had a clear view of the walkway that extended from the stairs of a terrace that was modest enough in size that he would see anyone who came out of the ballroom onto it. He tried to determine how long he'd been waiting there and figured that it had been perhaps a quarter hour. He'd nearly given up, thinking this some inane jest on

Atherton's part, when he noticed a figure emerging onto the terrace.

It was a slender figure dressed in coat and breeches, looking about as if searching for something—or someone. He walked about the terrace a bit, waiting. When that same figure started down the stairs toward the garden, Noah drew further into the shrubbery, watching Atherton's approach along the shadowed pathway. When he stood nearly in front of him, Noah stepped onto the path, blocking Atherton's way back to the house. "I was beginning to think perhaps you'd come to your senses, Atherton."

But it wasn't Atherton who turned to face him in the moonlight as he'd expected. Instead it was Augusta, and she was wearing a man's clothes.

Chapter Twenty-three

"Augusta?"

Augusta turned about on the garden path, expecting to see Lord Everton. Who she met was someone else entirely.

It was Noah and he stepped phantom-like from the shadows, coming to face her. Her pulse quickened at the sight of him, even more so due to the ominous costume he wore.

He scowled down at her. "What are you doing here?"

Her fascination at the sight of him abruptly ended. Why was he angry with her? She should be the one angry, for it was he who had placed her discovery in danger. Hadn't the note she received said as much? "I might say the same for you," she replied. "Why are you following me?"

"I believe I was here before you, my lady."

"Well, I am meeting someone here, so please go back inside."

Noah smirked. "I'm afraid I cannot do that, madam, because I, too, am meeting someone here."

She frowned.

He frowned. He said, "It would appear we are faced with a bit of an imbroglio."

She said, "Indeed."

There was a silent moment while they each tried to decide what to do about the other and the situation they now found themselves in.

It was clear to Noah that Augusta had no intention of leaving, at least not until Belgrace, whom she no doubt had finally managed to arrange a meeting with, arrived. But if Atherton should come first, he would likely turn and leave before Noah had the opportunity to confront him about his threatening letters.

"May I make a suggestion?" he said finally.

"Something is better than nothing at all, I suppose."

Noah allowed himself a grin at her sullenness. "There is a small stone bench sheltered there beneath the branches of that willow. Perhaps we might both withdraw there and await our individual parties. Whichever of the two makes an appearance first decides who shall stay and who shall leave."

He looked at her in the moonlight. She had listened to him and by the thoughtfulness of her expression, she was actually considering his suggestion. While he waited for her response, he took in her costume, appreciating the way the breeches hugged her hips and bottom. He never would have thought a woman could look so damned desirable in a pair of breeches. She had proved him wrong in that notion twice now.

Finally she looked at him and said simply, "Agreed."

Noah motioned toward the bench, bowing to allow her to precede him, which she did.

They sat in silence at first, Augusta staring at the toes of her slippers, the narrow leaves of the tree beside her, everywhere, it seemed, other than at him. She made no mention of the night she'd come to his study, of what had taken place. She made no mention of anything at all.

"Do you plan to avoid ever speaking of it, Augusta?"

She kept her eyes forward. "There is nothing to discuss."

"Is there nothing? For certain?"

She looked at him, saying nothing, and he saw uncertainty, and perhaps even fear, in her eyes.

"Augusta, do you carry my child?"

"I—" She hesitated. "I do not know."

"You have not bled?"

She shook her head quietly.

"And when did you last have your monthly flow?"

"Why should that be of any concern to you?"

"Augusta, I'm not totally ignorant of women. Has it been longer than a month?"

She shook her head.

"You will tell me if you carry my child."

She didn't answer.

"Augusta, do you think I would abandon my responsibility to you, to our child? Is that the sort of man you believe me to be?"

She turned to him then, her mouth set in a dour frown. "It has nothing to do with you. It is me. I do not wish to marry."

"Is it just me you're reluctant about, or the very idea of a marriage itself?"

"I do not wish to wed anyone. There are things I must do"—she hesitated—"things I want to do."

She was talking. That was good. Perhaps she had rethought her decision not to trust him. Noah pressed on. "You are talking about whatever it is that is signified by your notes."

She stared at him in the moonlight, obviously at war with herself. Finally she nodded.

"And marriage would prevent you from doing these things?"

She frowned, turning to stare ahead again. "There are few husbands who would support it."

Was she truly involved in some sort of witchcraft? Noah just couldn't believe it. There was something more. "Augusta, people are not always what they seem. You do not trust me; at least you are uncertain as to whether you can. But have I given you any reason not to trust me? Have I done anything to make you think I would ever betray you?"

"No—" She faltered. "Yes—I do not know." She stared at him closely as if trying to see clear to his soul, to decide if she should, if she could . . . she reached inside the pocket of her coat and removed a scrap of paper.

"Did you send this to me?" she asked. She watched for his reaction closely, he could see, hoping to find something in his expression that would reveal if he had had anything to do with the letter.

Noah took the sheet and read it.

He was silent as he folded the letter and returned it to her. He then reached inside his coat and removed another sheet of paper, handing it to her.

"Read this. I received it just this morning."

Augusta took the page and quickly read it. The words, so similar to those on the letter she had received. She looked up at him. "I do not understand. Who would send us each a message like this? And why?"

Noah's answer never came. Just as he was ready to speak, there came a sudden loud crack from somewhere in front of them. In the next second, Noah had grabbed her and was taking her to the ground with him, pulling her further back into the heavy growth along the garden wall.

Augusta felt a pain in her arm and branches scratching at her on her legs and face. "What was—?"

"Shh," he whispered as he crept carefully through the darkness. The only sound was their movement through the trees, the rustling of leaves, the soft crunch of their feet on the ground. She could not tell if they were pursued. She could barely hear above the pounding of her own heart.

After what seemed an eternity, Augusta heard a rattling

sound, like a latch on a gate. A moment later, they had emerged onto the dark and shadowed mews behind the Finsminster town house.

"What happened?" she asked. Her arm still ached where she had fallen.

Noah took her hand and kept walking, skirting the edge of the stables with the ease of a cat. "I believe someone shot at us. They could be following us. We need to leave."

He came to where the mews opened onto the adjacent street and paused to look about. A moment later, he led her around the corner and hailed a hackney that was stationed there.

Augusta fell back in the seat as they started off. "Why would someone be shooting at us in the Finsminster garden?"

"I can only assume the author of those letters decided to make good on his threats. Augusta, who were you meeting in the garden tonight?"

"Noah, why is it growing darker?"

She saw Noah turn to her in the thickening of the shadows. "Augusta?"

She thought she heard him rap on the roof of the coach. They stopped, she knew that because she heard the door open. Noah had gotten a lamp somehow and was staring at her, but the light from the lamp was dimming curiously, growing more and more shadowed until she could barely see it at all. She heard his voice, speaking to her, but it sounded as if it were coming from afar. She tried to speak, but couldn't seem to get the words past her tongue, which had suddenly grown heavy in her mouth.

It was just before the darkness overtook her that she heard Noah's voice one last time.

"Good God, Augusta, you have been shot!"

*   *   *

Augusta opened her eyes very slowly, wondering why they felt so very heavy on her.

It was dark in her room, but she could see a finger of light across the room creeping through the narrow slit in the drapery. She felt the pillow beside her, frowning when she didn't find Circe curled up at her usual spot. She didn't know what it was, but somehow, something didn't seem right.

That thought was confirmed the moment she tried to sit up. A sharp, fierce pain shot down along her arm to the very tips of her fingers. She must have cried out at it for she realized then that someone else was there with her, in her room, someone who was moving to the drapery and pulling them open to allow in the sunlight.

She squinted against the sudden light, against the figure standing before her. Her vision began to clear then and she saw it was Noah. She also realized that she wasn't in her room at all. This room looked nothing like hers with its dark and antiquated walnut bed, the posters carved from top to bottom and nearly as thick as a tree trunk. She had no earthly idea how she'd gotten here.

She stared at him. "Where am I?"

"You are at my town house, on Charles Street."

"Why am I here?"

Noah sat in a chair beside the bed. "You don't remember any of it?"

She thought, but remembered nothing after meeting him in the garden. She shook her head.

"You are here because last night, at the Finsminster masquerade, while you were out in the garden with me, someone fired on us and your arm was hit."

She looked down at herself, then, and saw that there was indeed a length of white bandage tied about her upper arm. She tried to speak, but her throat had gone very dry.

Noah took a glass of water from the bedside table and touched it to her lips. It tasted like nectar from the gods. She closed her eyes and swallowed slowly, fully, until he tilted the glass away. Then she looked at him. "Why don't I remember anything?"

"Because you fainted."

Augusta made to rise from the bed. "I never faint."

And with that, the darkness promptly closed in again.

When next she woke, it was as a vinaigrette was being passed under her nose. She coughed against the strength of its foul vapor, coming to. She peered up at Noah. She had fainted.

"Lie still while I summon the physician."

The physician seemed there the next moment. He smiled kindly at her and introduced himself as Dr. Merrimore, and asked her if she were in any pain. She nodded slowly. He asked her to lie back while he checked her arm and re-dressed the wound. Afterward, he peered deeply into her eyes, looking at first one then the other.

"What is it?" she asked.

The physician looked at Noah. "I do not advise moving her for at least three days."

Augusta frowned. "Is there some reason why you cannot tell *her* that directly?"

The physician looked at Noah again. "Perhaps four days."

Four days? Alone in a man's home? In his bed? Well, if she'd truly wanted to ruin herself, she'd certainly made a success of it this time.

"What of the child?" Noah asked the physician, having obviously already informed the man of her possible condition.

The doctor shook his head. "It is too soon to confirm if she is, in fact, with child. If she is, it would be an explanation for her continued faintness. But so then could the wound. A good physician must consider all the factors for his patients. Thus until we can know for certain, I would advise she keep to bed, get a goodly amount of sleep, and avoid any activity that might be overtaxing."

Noah nodded. "Thank you, sir. I will see to it."

Augusta scowled and waited until after he'd gone. Then she tried rising from the bed again.

Noah was there in an instant. "What are you doing? Did you not hear what the physician said?"

"How could I when he refused to direct any of it to me?"

Noah eased her back. "Augusta, you heard what he said. You must stay in bed."

"Impossible! Charlotte would be apoplectic."

"I'm afraid she already has."

Augusta looked at him. *Dear God.* "Charlotte knows I'm here? In your bed?"

"I had to inform her of what had happened and why you had disappeared from the masquerade without giving her notice."

"She likely wasn't alarmed."

"At first she wasn't, until I told her what had happened. She was rather upset when I told her that you had been shot."

Augusta sagged back against the pillows, pulling the coverlet to her waist. "She was probably more upset to learn I was here in your house with you."

Noah frowned. "Augusta, she is genuinely worried about you. She even sent your maid, Mina, here to stay while you convalesce." He hesitated then. "She has also consented to our marriage, on your father's behalf."

Augusta turned sharply toward him. "She cannot do that. I am old enough to decide for myself who, when, or if I shall ever marry. You heard the physician. We do not even know if there is the possibility of a child yet."

"Augusta, it has gone beyond the issue of a child. Your very presence here now has assured that."

Augusta frowned, staring down at her fingers as she played with the edge of the blanket. She scolded herself for her sharp tongue. She had no right to be angry at Charlotte, at Noah, or anyone else. It wasn't they who had gotten her into this mess. She was the one responsible and now she would have to be the one to pay the consequences. And the price of these consequences couldn't have come higher.

"Is it the idea of me as your husband that causes your distress?"

She said to her feet, "First the physician and then Charlotte, everyone is deciding my life for me."

Noah took her hand. "Forget the physician. Forget Charlotte. You make the decision, Augusta. Would you do me the honor of becoming my wife?"

She peered at him and answered in the only way she could, in the only way her heart would allow her. "Yes, Noah, I will."

It was late and Noah was sitting at the desk in his study, working a column of figures in his head when he heard the quiet sound of the door handle turning across the room. He looked up to see Augusta standing in the open doorway.

"Augusta, what are you doing out of bed?"

She came in on bare feet, her toes peeking out from beneath the ruffled hem of one of the nightgowns Charlotte had sent for her, a most modest piece that covered her from ankle to chin. The full sleeve of her right arm had been rolled to nearly the shoulder to allow the physician access to her wound. Her arm was now positioned before her in the sling he had fashioned to keep it immobile while it healed. Around her neck hung her star and moon necklace, which he had kept with him since the morning he'd found it in his study. In her other hand she held a single candlestick. Her dark hair was loose and curling down her back. She wore her spectacles and she looked adorable.

"I was . . . I mean . . ." she hesitated, "I was wondering if I might ask for your help."

"Of course." Noah stood and came before her. "What is wrong? Are you in pain? Would you like something to eat or drink?"

She shook her head. "No, it is nothing like that. I would—" She hesitated. "Will you come with me?"

Intrigued, he nodded and followed her as she turned from the room.

Augusta led him toward the back of the house, past closed doors and through the darkened, deserted hallways. It was late, past midnight, and the staff was abed, so the house was silent and still. She took the stairs, but didn't turn down the hall that led to the chamber she'd been using. Instead she continued, climbing the next flight of stairs, and then another until they came to the small doorway that led off to the roof.

Like many of the houses in London, there was a flat roof surrounded by a decorative stone railing. Noah had sometimes come here to reflect and to look out over the city. Set near to the eastern side, he noticed something standing and as they neared it he realized it was a telescope, about three feet in length. He watched, curious, as Augusta walked over to it, then turned to face him. Her expression was wary, even frightened. He noticed she took a deep breath that fogged from the midnight chill before speaking, as if summoning up her courage with it.

"I remembered something about that night in the garden when I was shot. I remembered you asked me if you had ever given me reason to think I could not trust you. You were right; you have not. And I hope you will remember that when I show you what I must show you now for I have only shared this with but one other person."

She motioned toward the telescope. Noah glanced at her, curious, and walked slowly toward it. He had to bend his knees a bit to position himself at the eye piece as he peered through it toward the night sky. On the other side, set in the very middle of the scope, was a speck of distant light.

"It is a star," he said, focusing on the tiny white spark he saw. He stepped away from the telescope and looked at her. The nocturnal habits, the figures drawn on her sheet, her necklace. Suddenly things began to make absolute sense. "You are no witch. You are an astronomer."

She nodded, showing a slight smile at the appellation. "I like to think so." She looked up at the sky. "When my mother died, my father told me she had gone to live on a star where she could watch over me every night and keep me safe. At night, when I couldn't sleep, I would go up on the deck of our ship and stare at all the stars, at the one my mother had gone to. I used to look out through the ship's perspective glass, searching for her out there, thinking perhaps I might see her somehow.

"About ten months ago, when I came to live in England, I was looking up at the night sky and the star where my father had told me my mother had gone. It shone brighter and the flicker I seemed to see in its light was like a signal from her. I began observing it whenever the sky was clear enough for me to see it. I obtained a telescope, this telescope, and I charted it, measuring its proximity to the other stars around it. Over a period of time, I noticed that another star near to it, so tiny it could barely be seen, seemed to have moved."

Noah was fascinated. "Then it was not a star?"

Augusta shook her head. "I thought perhaps that it could be a distant comet, but the more I observed, the less that seemed likely. I checked the star catalogues and but one catalogue noted it as a star. Others didn't include it at all."

"So if it wasn't a star, or a comet, then it would have to be . . ."

". . . something else," she replied. And then smiling, she added, "Something much more significant."

"A planet?"

"I do not think it is large enough to be a planet, not given its position in the sky. But I do think it might be a fragmentary one. There have been several such 'asteroids' discovered, the first by a man named Piazzi in 1801. But since 1807, there has been no evidence of another."

"Until now," Noah finished. "Augusta, why haven't you gone to the Royal Society with your discovery?"

"I did. About six months ago, I sent a letter to the Society announcing my findings. It was soon after that the object vanished from the sky. The Society responded that they had determined that what I had found was merely a comet, or a shooting star. They congratulated me and agreed to enter it as such. I didn't concur. I believe that it had moved too close to the sun to be observed. Thus far I have been unable to detect its reappearance. The instruments available to me are limited. The star you see there in the scope is the one that led me to it. Something similar occurred when Piazzi made his discovery and with some mathematical formulations, the position of the object at reappearance could almost be predicted. I believe that if I weren't a woman, the Society would have taken my findings more seriously; women of science are usually considered hobbyists, nothing more. Since I cannot change my sex, or force them to listen to me with an unjaundiced ear, it was suggested to me that perhaps I might do better to gain the patronage of a member of the Society, someone who would be willing to support my efforts."

"Belgrace," Noah said. "He is a member of the Society, very respected. He has even been suggested as its next president. That is why you have been pursuing him, and why you have been so secretive about it."

Augusta nodded. "There are members of the Royal Society who refuse to accept that a woman might have something to contribute to the astronomical, or even the scientific world in general. They have sought to exclude any evidence presented by women in the past, minimizing their efforts as folly. I needed to decide upon a member who wouldn't share that prejudice. It was told to me that Lord Belgrace would be the likeliest member."

"That's twice now you've indicated you have received outside advice." Noah asked. "From whom?"

"Lord Burbage. It was he who suggested Lord Belgrace, who is an associate of my father's."

Noah nodded. "You know there is another to whom you could apply for support, someone who is even more esteemed by the Society than Belgrace."

"Who?"

"Sir William Herschel."

Augusta looked slightly startled at the suggestion. "But Sir William has been ill and has gone into seclusion. It is said he no longer allows visitors to his observatory at Slough."

"Yes, perhaps, but he would certainly receive his godson."

"His godson . . ." Augusta looked at him. "You? You are Sir William Herschel's godson?"

Noah nodded. "When Sir William first came to England, my father was his patron, but at first he was a patron of Sir William's musical talents. It wasn't until later that he learned of Sir William's interest in astronomy, which was his true passion, but which didn't earn him an income. My father supported Sir William financially for a spell and he was also instrumental in convincing the King to grant Sir William a yearly pension so that he might devote his life to observing."

Augusta was stunned. "Sir William has the most powerful telescopes in England. The figures on the sheet of paper you found that night at White's are my closest estimate to the object's position and its movement. I took my observations and charted a path for its orbit based upon its movements and the movements of the other asteroids already discovered. With Sir William's more powerful telescope, I might be able to detect its reappearance and then submit my reapplication to the Society, to convince them that this is not merely the comet or shooting star they have deemed it."

Noah nodded in agreement. "Well, then I can see only one solution, madam. We must pay a visit to Sir William directly."

An hour later, they were on the road to Windsor and Slough, the home and personal observatory of Sir William Herschel. Despite Augusta's obvious eagerness to arrive there quickly, Noah insisted that they travel at a slow pace so that the jostling of the carriage would not aggravate her wound. It was past three in the morning by the time they arrived, a perfectly acceptable hour to pay a visit to an astronomer who worked all night and rested during the day.

The modest red brick house was set back from the road and as they rolled along the length of its drive, coming to a stop at the front door, a figure emerged, a woman who was small and slight and slender.

Noah exited the coach first, handing down Augusta before he turned to greet the waiting woman. "Hello, Miss Caroline." He gave her a warm hug before turning toward the coach. "Come, I want you to meet someone. Lady Augusta Brierley, allow me to introduce Miss Caroline Herschel."

But Augusta needed no introduction for she had modeled her entire life after the woman who now stood before her.

Caroline Herschel was the sister to Sir William and had been his lifelong companion and helpmate in his observatory. In her own right, she had discovered countless comets with her own "sweeper" scope made for her by brother William. Despite her advanced age of nearly seventy, one could see that her eyes were shrewd and missed nothing. The face which peeked out from beneath the frills of her mobcap wore a kindness that extended to those same eyes.

"Miss Herschel, I am honored to make your acquaintance."

She barely stood five feet, still Augusta was awed by her presence. Caroline smiled warmly and took Augusta's hand, squeezing it as she said, "Welcome to Slough, Lady Augusta."

"How does Sir William fare," Noah asked.

Caroline gave a slight shrug. "He has his good days and his bad days. Right now he is doing better. He will be happy to see you." She motioned for them to follow her into the house. "So tell me what brings you to Slough."

"Well, let us meet with Sir William and I will tell you both together."

Caroline looked at him with a curious smile. "You are up to something, aren't you?" She glanced at Augusta. "He always was a sneaky boy."

They had walked clear through the house by way of its central hallway and exited out the back door onto a vast yard area. Beyond that lay several smaller brick buildings; in the midst of the circle they formed stood a large triangular construction. Augusta could but stare. She had seen engravings of it, but had never imagined it so large. This was the famous twenty-foot reflecting telescope with which Sir William had discovered the planet Uranus.

Caroline came to a small door on one of the outbuildings and knocked twice. "William, are you there? Noah has come to see you."

A grizzled voice, accented with German, sounded from inside. "Noah, you say? Well, then, what are you waiting for? Bring the boy in."

Chapter Twenty-four

Sir William Herschel, discoverer of the only planet ever first recorded since the dawn of history, rose from his chair and gave Noah a welcoming embrace. He was not a large man as certainly one would expect with a man of his distinction, but rather stout with a kindness about his face like that of his sister. Augusta watched on as they exchanged greetings and conversation of family, catching up on the time which had separated them. After several minutes, Sir William spied her standing a bit away. He smiled. "And who have we here?"

"Sir William," Noah said, motioning for her to join him, "allow me to introduce to you Lady Augusta Brierley. Augusta, this is Sir William Herschel." The man stepped forward to take her hand and Noah added, "Augusta has consented to be my wife."

Both of the Herschels gave a collective "Ah!" and Sir William exclaimed, "Welcome to Slough, Lady Augusta!"

Caroline gave Noah a nudge. "No wonder you would not tell me your news until we had come to William. But you needn't have brought this sweet girl out at such an unholy hour just to meet us."

"Actually, there is another reason we have come. You see, Augusta is also an astronomer, and she has reason to believe she may have made a discovery."

Sir William's eyes lit up at the first mention of the word

discovery. "Lina, come here. Did you hear? A discovery! Tell us, pray tell us what it is."

Noah nodded his head to Augusta to indicate she should be the one to respond.

"Well, Sir William, Miss Caroline," she began, ". . . it all began when I had been observing a star—"

"Which star?" Sir William asked eagerly.

"William," Caroline scolded, "let the girl talk."

Augusta smiled. "It was number 357 from Flamsteed's catalogue."

"Ah, yes," said Sir William, nodding, "I know it well."

"There was a smaller star nearby to it, much dimmer, that I couldn't find a notation of in Flamsteed's catalogue, and in but one other catalogue as well. About ten months ago I began charting it and noticed that it seemed to move."

"Do you hear this, Lina? She's found something!" He looked at Augusta. "Go on, dear."

Augusta smiled again. "Well, I began to follow its movement, recording it for over months before I then sent my findings into the Society. By then, though, the star had vanished because of its proximity to the sun and the Society deemed it a comet."

Caroline shook her head. "Fools, the lot of them."

Sir William was nodding his head in agreement. "And how long ago was it that the object vanished?"

"It has been nearly six months. But I have continued its charting based upon my initial observations and if my calculations are correct, from what I determined, it should be visible once again. However, my instruments lack the strength for me to locate it again."

"Do you have your charts and figures with you now?" Sir William asked.

Augusta held up the small packet of sheets she'd brought

along which she had asked Tiswell to send to her at Noah's house, her future home. "They are here."

Sir William looked at her, his eagerness shining clearly in his eyes. "Would you mind if I were to take a look at them?"

"Not at all, sir. I would be honored."

Sir William and Caroline turned and went to stand at a long table set near the center of the room. They spread out Augusta's notes and began studying them. Augusta watched on in abject fascination while Sir William started making some additional notes all while he was calling out names of publications and books which Caroline set immediately to retrieving from the bookcases that filled the far wall. They worked with the precision of a machine, perfectly in sync, Caroline alternately bringing books and catalogues, and then taking them away when Sir William was finished; all the while he scribbled furiously. Finally, after nearly a half hour, Sir William stepped back from the table, holding up his own analysis.

"Your observational skills are excellent, Lady Augusta. I just quickly did a recalculation and my results concur with yours. Now, all we need do is see if my twenty-foot reflector can find your little discovery."

The party moved from the house back to the yard. They came to a halt at the bottom of the tall structure. Augusta was in awe. "This is it, sir? The telescope on which you found Uranus?"

Herschel nodded, saying, "Uranus, ridiculous name, do you not think? That just goes to show what a motley lot those at the Society truly are. I wanted to call it 'Georgium Sidus' in honor of His Majesty the King; should be my right as its discoverer, wouldn't you think? But they wouldn't stand by my decision, said they 'couldn't depart from the age-old custom of giving names from Greek and

Roman mythology.' Bah! Same reason why they won't admit women to the Society; they've even refused to acknowledge our Caroline here other than to commend her on her sweeper work. Antiquated the lot of them. So what do they name it, my planet, my Georgian planet? Uranus! I wouldn't name my dog such an appellation. Hmph. To me, it is and always will be 'Georgium Sidus.' Remember that when they try to tell you what you should name your discovery, dear."

Sir William turned then and climbed the ladder to the platform that stood halfway to the top. He made some adjustments, repositioning and then repositioning again, then peered into the eyepiece. He did this several more times, adjusting, focusing, adjusting again, until he finally turned and motioned for Augusta to join him.

"Come, dear, come see what I've found. This is your discovery, after all, not mine."

Since Augusta's arm was injured, she would not be able to climb the ladder on her own, so Noah started up first, then reached back with one hand to help guide her to the platform. Once there, Sir William motioned for her to peer inside the eyepiece.

"If you look very closely," said Sir William beside her, "you can just make out its planetary disk. You were right in your conclusions, Lady Augusta. That is no star, but I believe another of the small bodies we've come to term an asteroid."

Augusta positioned herself at the eyepiece, took a deep breath, and looked through it into another world that both excited and astounded her. Magnifications hundreds of times larger than she had observed with her own instruments awaited her eager, wide-eyed view. The stars were now so brilliant, so beautiful, one could almost reach out and touch them. Thousands of them, like glittering dia-

monds, and nestled at the center of this midnight wonder-
land was indeed the "star" she had discovered, having come
back from its journey around the sun.

"I knew it," she whispered and a feeling of utter satisfaction and accomplishment swelled through her and she
smiled, adding a quiet "hello" as she continued peering
through the eyepiece.

Noah and Augusta returned to Noah's town house just as
the sun was rising on the city. Neither of them had had any
sleep but even then the thought of resting was the furthest
thing from Augusta's mind.

Sir William had offered to present Augusta's findings
himself to the Royal Society at their next meeting, and with
the support of his own observations coupled with her own,
the establishment of the discovery as hers was sure to be
recognized. They would have no other choice.

It was more than Augusta could have ever hoped for. All
of her work, her dreams, had culminated through the tiny
opening of that eyepiece. And she had but one person to
thank for granting her that dream. If not for Noah, she
might never have seen that bright burning circle ever again.
It might have gone on undiscovered, or worse, someone
else might have claimed it as their own. And if not for
Noah, she might never have had the chance to meet her
lifelong idol, Caroline Herschel.

She looked over to Noah as he sat next to her on the
coach seat, watching the scenery through the window. As if
he could sense her looking at him, he turned toward her and
smiled. Her insides went warm. She smiled at him and said
softly, "Thank you."

Noah moved closer to her and drew her gently into his
arms, careful not to disturb her injured arm. Softly, ten-

derly, he touched his lips to hers in a kiss that thrilled her to her toes, a kiss that went on as they drove into the city.

They never even realized that the coach had stopped until the coachman pulled open the door.

"Looks as if there's visitors, my lord," said the coachman, directing their attention toward a pair of coaches standing at the curb in front of Noah's town house.

Augusta immediately recognized the first one. It was the Brierley town coach, the Trecastle crest emblazoned on its gleaming black door in gold. Her first thought was to wonder what Charlotte was doing there at so early an hour. Her second thought was to wonder why she had used the formal town coach when she normally used the smaller and smarter barouche.

Westman was awaiting them at the door.

"My lord, we were beginning to worry . . ."

Noah helped Augusta down from the coach. "We decided to take a late-night drive to the country, Westman."

"Well, there are—"

But it was too late for before the butler could finish his sentence, two people came out on the front stoop to meet them.

"Papa!" Augusta hurried to him. Heedless of her arm, she skipped into his open embrace. "When did you arrive? Why didn't you write to say you would be returning?"

Cyrus Brierley smiled down at his daughter. He shared her dark hair, and despite his lack of height, he was a formidable man in presence alone. One need only see the way he looked at his daughter to know how he felt about her. She meant the world to him. "I came as soon as I received Charlotte's summons."

"Charlotte sent for you?"

He nodded. "She told me you'd been fired upon. I didn't waste a moment." He looked at the bandage she wore, inspecting it. He then looked at Noah standing slightly behind her. "She also wrote me that you had been thoroughly compromised by this young man."

"Papa, I—"

"You are going to marry my daughter, aren't you, sir?"

Noah nodded. "I have every intention of wedding Augusta, Lord Trecastle."

The marquess stared at him. "Do you love her?"

"Papa!"

"It's a reasonable enough sort of question, Augusta Elizabeth. Compromised or not, I won't have my daughter wedding a man who doesn't cherish her as much as I do. I made a promise to your dear mother before she passed and I mean to see that promise kept."

Noah turned to regard Augusta. He grinned as he said, "I would have to say I have found it nigh impossible not to love her, my lord."

Augusta smiled. "It seems to be a shared impossibility."

"Good," said Cyrus, "then I believe if you step into your parlor, Lord Noah, we can see to this business right now. I've already procured a special license and I have the minister awaiting us there. I'm not leaving until I see my daughter married well and good."

An hour later, Lady Augusta Brierley's days of celebrated spinsterhood came to a close. Instead a golden ring resided on her finger, the ring that had been her mother's which her father had brought to give to Noah for her.

They shared an early supper and Augusta told her father about her visit to the Herschels', finally revealing to Charlotte the secret of what she'd spent her nights doing the past ten months. Good cheer surrounded the assembly and plans were made for a wedding breakfast to be held the following week at the Brierley town house so family and friends could come to extend their best wishes to the newly wedded bride and groom. It was nearly nightfall when Cyrus and Charlotte finally bid the new couple farewell.

That evening, Noah had gone into the study to see to some papers while Augusta retired upstairs to her chamber to rest. He spent nearly an hour updating his account records, and penned several quick notes for delivery the next morning to Robert and Catriona, Amelia, and Christian, Eleanor, and Sarah, informing them of his marriage to Augusta and inviting them all to the wedding breakfast.

He had just finished the last of the letters when Augusta came into the room. "I thought you were going to rest," he said, moving to join her.

"Noah, what is this?"

In her hand she held out a folded sheet of paper. Noah immediately recognized it. It was the letter Tony had received the night he'd died, the letter Noah had credited her as writing so long ago.

"I found it when I was putting away some of my things in your standing dresser," she said. "It carries my father's seal and is signed by an *A*, but I did not write it."

Noah took the letter. "I know you didn't write it, Augusta. At least I know now you didn't write it. For a time I thought you had. In fact it is what made me search you out in the beginning at the Lumley ball."

He took her hand and led her to one of the two chairs set before the hearth. He lowered himself into the other, telling Augusta everything, about Tony and his suicide, and of the part he believed the letter—and she—had played in it. As she listened to him, he could see that she was horrified to know that the words written on that page, words clearly attributed to her, had been instrumental in the ending of a man's life.

"Although I suspected, I finally knew you hadn't written the letter the day I received the message from you requesting that I meet with you, or rather Viviana, at the Danby ball. I compared the handwriting from it with the handwriting from this letter and your sheet of formulas, and while the two I knew you had definitely written seemed to match, the writing on this letter was too dissimilar to have been yours."

"You must have thought me truly horrible."

"I did." He looked into her eyes "Until I met you. From that first moment I saw you, no matter how I wanted to believe it had been you who had written the letter, your appearance, your actions, most everything about you was in complete contradiction to it."

Augusta sat, chin in her hands, brow furrowed in thought. "But it had to be someone who had access to the Brierley seal . . ." She reached for the letter, studying it more closely. "And I think I just figured out who."

Noah looked at her, waiting.

"I think it is Charlotte."

"Charlotte? But why would Charlotte write a letter like this to Tony and then sign it with your initial at the bottom?"

Augusta got up. "I cannot say, but Charlotte signed our marriage certificate today as a witness. Let us compare the two to see if they appear to be the same."

Noah retrieved the certificate from his desk drawer. They held the two letters side by side and compared. The handwriting on each of them matched. Charlotte had written the letter to Tony that night.

"Augusta, do you think it could have been Charlotte who had been carrying on a tryst with Tony?"

Augusta shrugged. "I suppose it is possible. My father had been away for some time, but it just doesn't seem likely."

"Well, there is only one way we might find out," said Noah. "We'll just ask her when we go to Bryanstone Square for the wedding breakfast."

*   *   *

Noah and Augusta went to the Brierley town house earlier than they'd been expected the day of their celebration.
Charlotte, Tiswell told them after shaking Noah's hand and
giving Augusta a congratulatory hug, was occupied in the
kitchen with Cook over the morning's menu. Quite beset
she was, he'd said, something about the unthinkable absence of strawberries on the menu.

While they waited to speak to her, they went to the parlor. Augusta's father, the marquess, was there, reading his
morning newspaper. At the sound of Augusta's voice as she
called a greeting to her father, a pretty blond head poked inside the doorway.

"Augusta!"

They turned to see Augusta's stepsister, Lettie, coming
into the room.

"Lettie!" Augusta exclaimed, giving her an affectionate
hug. "I had thought you were staying in the country until
after the Season."

Lettie stood nearly half a head taller than her elder stepsister and looked a great deal more mature than her sixteen
years. What endeared her most to Augusta, though, was her
complete inability to give notice to how truly beautiful she
was. "I was, but when Mother wrote to tell me you had gotten married, I left right away. She wasn't going to stop me
from coming back then. It's not every day my sister becomes a bride." She walked straight to Noah, dropping a
polite curtsy. "How do you do? I am Augusta's sister, Lady
Alethea Brierley."

Augusta and Noah each turned to look at the other at the
same time.

Alethea.

A.

Augusta motioned to Noah to wait a moment. "Lettie, I

need to tidy my hair. Come with me upstairs so we can visit a bit, would you?"

Once they were upstairs, Lettie took a seat on the edge of the bed while Augusta made as if she were checking her hair in the looking glass.

"He's very handsome, your Lord Noah," Lettie said, playing with the pillow edging.

Augusta tried to watch her in the reflection of the looking glass. "It won't be long before you have many handsome men begging you to wed them, too."

Lettie frowned. "Only so long as Mother approves him."

Augusta turned in her chair. "Lettie, I need to ask you something that is very important."

Lettie watched her.

"Why did Charlotte send you away to the country?"

Lettie didn't readily answer, she just stared at the carpeting in silence. Augusta stood and came to sit beside her on the bed. She took her sister's hand.

"It was because of Lord Keighley, wasn't it?"

Lettie looked up sharply at her. "How? How did you know?"

"Well, it was because of Lord Keighley that I came to know Noah."

Augusta took the letter Tony had received that night, the letter they now knew had been written by Charlotte, and handed it to Lettie. She watched as Lettie opened it and read it. When she was finished, she turned to look at Augusta. "Mother wrote this to Tony?"

Augusta nodded. "Lord Keighley was a friend of Noah's. He had thought perhaps I'd written the letter."

Lettie didn't notice that Augusta had referred to Tony in the past tense.

"Mother was so angry when she found out I'd been meeting with Tony. I knew she'd never consent to our marriage; she wanted me to marry Lady Trussington's son. So we decided to run away to Gretna Green. But she must have suspected as much because on the night we were to leave for Scotland, she stayed home from the ball she had planned to attend. She was waiting for me when I tried to leave. She told me to write to him and tell him I had never loved him, but I wouldn't. I love Tony, and I want to be his wife. So instead I told her I would go away from the city. I had only planned to leave until your father returned, and then I was going to speak with him, hoping he might help to persuade Mother to give me her consent." She looked at the letter again. "I didn't know she would do this. I only hope Tony will hear my explanation and—"

"Lettie, I have to tell you something. I don't know how—that night, when you were supposed to run away, after he received this letter, Lord Keighley took his life."

Lettie looked at Augusta. She didn't say a word. Her chest was rising and falling rapidly, but she only closed her eyes as tears began to trickle down her cheeks. She then lay back on the bed, curling up against the pillows as she wept. Augusta set her arm around her and offered her the only comfort she could. "I am so very sorry, Lettie."

"Would you mind if I asked for a few moments alone?" Lettie whispered some time later.

Augusta squeezed Lettie's hand then turned to leave her in privacy.

She met Charlotte in the hall.

"Where is Lettie? The guests have begun to arrive and I would like her to be with me when Lady Trussington arrives."

Augusta frowned at Charlotte. "Lettie won't be coming down for breakfast, Charlotte."

"Nonsense," Charlotte said. "What is she doing?"

Augusta handed her the letter. "She is in her room, crying. Her heart is broken because I just had to tell her that the man she'd fallen in love with, the man you refused to allow her to wed, took his own life."

Charlotte's hand came up to cover her mouth. "I never wanted . . ." Tears were filling her eyes and she made hastily for Lettie's door, knocking softly. "Lettie? Lettie, dear, please let Mother in. I never meant for this to happen. I just wanted what I thought was best for you. Please, my sweet, let Mother in . . ."

Augusta turned and continued down the hall.

Noah stood outside looking out over the back garden as Augusta, Robert, Catriona, and Amelia played at bowls with little James. He heard the door open behind him and turned to see Christian coming down the walkway toward him.

"If you've come to rib me about the surprise of my marriage I—"

Christian pulled something out of his pocket and handed it to Noah. His expression was grave. "I thought you might like to see this."

It was several sheets of paper with what looked like just words scribbled across, until Noah looked a little closer and noticed one of the lines that had been written on it.

"You play a game of danger that win you never will . . ."

Noah looked at Christian.

"Eleanor said she found those in Sarah's room."

Noah closed his eyes. The letters to him and to Augusta had come from her . . . the gunshot that night in the garden . . . "No, not Sarah . . ."

"I also checked my gun case and one of my pistols is missing."

Noah stared at Christian and then asked, "Where is she?"

"She is in the parlor."

Noah found Sarah sitting alone, reading a book in the Brierley parlor. She looked up when he came in and although she smiled, he could see a darkness in her eyes that he had never noticed before. Noah said nothing, just set the scraps of paper down before her on the table.

She looked up at him, but didn't speak.

"Why, Sarah?" he asked. "Why would you do this? Why would you want to hurt me, and hurt Augusta?"

She didn't falter in her response. "It should have been me you married, not her. She is not good enough for you. I know you only married her because you believe she carries your child. But she is a whore and she doesn't deserve you."

"That is enough, Sarah," Noah said sternly.

She quieted.

"I'm afraid I must ask you to leave now. Christian and Eleanor are waiting for you in the carriage outside. I will tell no one else, other than Augusta, of the part you played in this. I hope you will find a way to live with what you have done, what you very nearly did. For your sake, for the sake of Tony's memory, do not attempt to contact me or my wife again."

Sarah said nothing. She simply stood and walked from the room and out of Noah's life forever.

Epilogue

July, 1820
Eden Court, York

Noah stood on top of the roof of the small red brick out-building, checking his measurements against the figures on the plan with a length of rope. The observatory was being built on a rise with a fine view of the house nearby and the surrounding parkland. He had hoped to have it finished in time for Sir William and Caroline's visit so that they could see where Augusta would continue her work with the newly built seven-foot telescope they'd sent her. They would be arriving in a fortnight. It was going to be close.

Noah had dismissed the workers for the evening shortly before, they being inhabitants of the village close by to the estate. He'd made it a habit now to stay on after they had gone, for he found that checking the design and inspecting the work himself gave him a sense of being a part of the building itself, something he found he truly relished. It was a trait he shared with his father-in-law, and when Cyrus and Charlotte had been at Eden Court a fortnight earlier on a visit, both men had spent time together each evening surveying that day's progress.

Theirs had been a happy and unexpected visit, for Augusta had thought her father wouldn't return from his latest ambassadorial assignment until after the babe was born. He had surprised her both with his visit and with the news that the family had taken a property in East Riding but five miles away. It had been during their visit that Cyrus had told Augusta he had decided to resign his position with the government, happily retiring to his upcoming role as grandfather. It had also been during their visit that Augusta had discovered her stepsister, Lettie, had found love again with a dashing young earl who had brought the smile back to her eyes.

"Noah!"

He turned to see Augusta climbing the small slope toward him. Noah stood, watching his wife's slow progress, for she was nearing the ninth month of her pregnancy. Because of her small size and the comparatively large size of the infant, the physician had advised Augusta to keep off her feet as much as possible. But with a woman as determined as Augusta, that wasn't an easy task, and Noah very nearly admonished her for disregarding that advice. Instead he found himself holding his words in check. He just couldn't help it. The sight of her, her belly swollen with his child, made his insides tighten with pride.

Whenever he saw her thus, Noah found himself thanking the heavens and anyone else involved for having seen them through that hellish Season two years before. He tried not to think of what could have happened had the shot that had caught her in the arm gone but inches aside to her chest. The Sarah he'd faced that day in the Brierley parlor, when he'd confronted her with the truth of her actions, had not been the Sarah of his childhood. The tragic events in her life, that of losing her parents, her brother, and the life she had known had changed her into someone he no longer recognized. He hadn't seen her again since she'd walked from the room that day. Sarah had complied with his wishes, he had learned, taking herself far from England, across the ocean to America. Despite all she had done, Noah still felt the hope that she would find some semblance of peace there to see her through the remainder of her days.

Noah's thoughts turned from the past as Augusta came to stand beneath him, shielding her eyes against the summer sun while she looked up to him on the roof. She was a vision of true maternal beauty. She wore a loose, light muslin gown sent to her by Catriona's sister, Mairead, in Paris, which she'd designed especially to keep her comfortable throughout the pregnancy. Her hair fell in soft curls about her shoulders. Her spectacles blinked at him in the sunlight. That feeling of inner pride immediately surged through him again.

She held out a folded paper. "Noah, I just received this letter. It comes from Sir William."

"He is not coming?"

"I do not know. I wanted to wait for you to read it."

Noah climbed down, joining Augusta, and together they read the letter.

My dearest children,

   It is my honor to inform you both that the Royal Society of London has seen fit to grant a petition presented to them by myself and the most esteemed Lady Augusta Edenhall, that the planetary asteroid of her finding shall be known hereafter as the Atalanta asteroid. (You see, my dear, I knew they would never grant your first choice for a name, that of your dear mother, Marianne, but it was worth a try, wasn't it? If not only to ruffle their stodgy feathers, especially since they refuse to consider a full fellowship for you. Stubborn lot they are!)

Augusta and Noah chuckled together, and read on.

   It is also my duty as well as my esteemed honor to inform you that the newly formed Astronomical Society of London, housed at Lincolns Inn Fields, and of which I am co-founder and president, has unanimously voted to confer upon the same Lady Augusta Edenhall their Gold Medal of Honor for her singular contribution to the advancement of astronomical study. All of London is abuzz with the news. Lord Burbage begs me to send to you both his best wishes. But, my dear, since you are unable because of the child to travel to town in person, I, as president, shall present this medal to you upon my arrival in York next month. And I, as your honorary godfather since you married that rascal boy, could not be prouder.

God bless,

Yours . . . Sir William.

Noah hugged his wife as closely as her belly would allow, kissing her softly on the forehead. "Congratulations, Madam Astronomer. It seems I've wed a celebrity."

Augusta smiled, but there remained a stubborn tilt to her chin as she stared down at the letter, rereading the words. Noah knew that look, and knew the trouble that came along with it.

"Augusta, what is it? Is something wrong?"

She looked at him and shook her head. "No, I was just wondering when the men of the Society will ever consider that simply the fact of being a woman should prevent one from a full fellowship among them. I know were it up to Sir William, there would be no question of it, but they did not even allow him to formally name the planet he alone discovered. What makes it most difficult is that I know were I a man, I would easily be admitted for my work."

Noah drew her close, kissing her on the forehead again while trying to soften her mood. "Well, I, for one, am very glad you aren't a man. As is, I'm certain, our child."

She managed a smile, but he knew her vexation on the subject wouldn't pass quite so easily. It was a particular bone of contention for her.

"Let us fight one battle at a time, my dear," he said. "I have no doubt that if anyone will ever change their misogynist minds, it will be you. Come, sit with me a spell now." He helped her to sit on a grassy knoll and poured her a cup of lemonade from the jug he'd brought there. "Now, you know, we've another discovery that will soon be arriving that we have as yet to decide upon a name for."

Augusta laughed. "After what you did to poor Humphrey, and what you nearly did to Pan, I shudder to think of what you might come up with."

He sat beside her, helping her to lean back against him, her head against his shoulder, as they looked out at the sun setting over the distant treetops. "Well, I've been thinking about that, my dear, and I think I've come up with a perfect choice." He paused, smiling into her hair. "What do you think of Aloysius?"

Augusta turned her head to look at him, all traces of good humor vanishing from her face. "You are jesting." She hesitated. "Aren't you?"

Noah persisted in his teasing game, moving a bit to sit more beside her as he stole a sip from her lemonade. "But Aloysius is a fine name, my dear. We can begin a new tradition for the Edenhalls, a name to carry on through each generation to come."

Augusta's eyes widened, and she drew in a heavy breath in preparation for her coming disagreement. And come it did. "If you think, Lord Noah Edenhall, that I will ever consent to name our child such a horri—"

The remainder of her protest died when Noah took his wife's lips in a silencing—and quite passionate—kiss, lowering her as he did to the soft grass beneath them and leaving her—and himself, for that matter—far too breathless to finish her thought.

It wasn't until several moments later that she spoke again, looking up at him through soft green and certainly less combative eyes. She smiled as she said, "I shudder to think what you would wish to call our child should she prove a daughter."

Leaning on his elbow above her, playing with the bit of her hair which curled about her forehead, Noah said, "On that, my dear, I would prove most stubborn, for I would consent to one name and one name alone for so cherished a creature. That the name of her enchanting mother, my love, Augusta."

There came no further protest from her, for Augusta was far too busy pulling her husband closer to her so that she might return with equal passion the kiss he'd given her moments before.

Author's Note

I hope you have enjoyed reading about Noah and Augusta. It was a pleasure to write their story and, with Augusta, delve further into the history of astronomy, which has interested me all my life.

Sir William Herschel and his sister, Caroline, did truly exist during this period of time. Sir William began his life as a musician, and when he traveled to England from Hanover, it was for the purposes of music, not science. Years later, he brought his sister, Caroline, to live with him for further education in music, and together they soon changed the history of astronomy with numerous discoveries, including that of the planet Uranus (a name that indeed Sir William refused to acknowledge, terming his discovery instead "Georgium Sidus" or simply "the Georgian Planet" throughout his life).

Caroline herself was a noted cometary discoverer. However, she thought them nothing compared with the assistance she had given her dear brother throughout his life. And so, when Sir William died in 1822, aged eighty-four, so did life as Caroline had known it until her own passing in 1848. Like Augusta, Caroline was never granted a fellowship in the Royal Society—in truth, it was not until 1945 that women were admitted. But again like Augusta, Caroline was conferred the Gold Medal of the Royal Astronomical Society, a separate society formed apart from the Royal Society in 1820, just before the closing of the story.

The Atalanta asteroid is a creation of my imagination. From 1801 to 1850, only thirteen such asteroids were discovered and were at that time in truth considered small planets. But since 1850, as technology has improved, hundreds more have been found, so many that it has even been suggested that these planetary objects were actually fragments of a larger planet that had somehow exploded, a theory, though, which has never been proven. Needless to say, it soon became difficult to find names for all of them in the traditional sense of using the appellations from mythology, and perhaps had Augusta discovered her asteroid at a later date, she might have succeeded in naming it "Marianne" for her mother. It was in 1850 that one did finally succeed in changing that tradition, naming the twelfth such asteroid "Victoria" for the reigning English monarch at that time.

White Magic is the second book in a trilogy I am writing set during the Regency period, a trilogy that began with Noah's brother Robert and Catriona in *White Heather*. Can you guess whose story will be told in the third story of the series? Consider Noah's friend, Christian Wycliffe, Marquess Knighton and future Duke of Westover. Handsome and carefree, you listened as he told Noah the plain and obvious facts of his marital future. Assuredly, as heir to a vast fortune, his will be an arranged marriage, decided upon not by himself, but by the Wycliffe patriarch, his grandfather, the current duke. And when you met him in this story, he seemed resigned to his fate, didn't he? Without a word of disagreement?

Well, let me just say that appearances can be deceiving, and they can also make for a bumpy and exciting story. I hope you will look for this final story of my trilogy, coming in 1999.

My address is P.O. Box 1771, Chandler, AZ 85244-1771. You can email me at *jacreding@inficad.com,* or visit my web site at *http://www.inficad.com/~jacreding*. And I would love for you to share your thoughts with me about any of my stories. Thank you.